NOW IS THE TIME

ENERGY
THE MOTION OF INFINITY

Jerry Noel Ilé and Jordan Young-Noel

You Spiritually

www.YouSpiritually.com
www.reddit.com/r/youspiritually

Energy – The Motion of Infinity

Published by: You Spiritually
Cover Art by: Quincy Gordon - www.mequincy.com
Interior book design by: Armlegga
ISBN: 978-1-7399116-0-7

Disclaimer
The advice and strategies found within may not be suitable for every situation. This work is sold with the understanding that neither the author nor the publisher are held responsible for the results accrued from the advice in this book.
This book is not intended as a substitute for the medical advice of physicians. The reader should regularly consult a physician in matters relating to his/her health and particularly with respect to any symptoms that may require diagnosis or medical attention.

Dedicated to the loving memory of my Uncle Jim.

You left just before we got to give you a signed copy, so now every single one of them will celebrate your wonderful energy.

Acknowledgements

Special thanks to the wonderful beta readers, Bolanle and Slim, your feedback and encouragement has been truly empowering.

Massive thank you to Quincy Gordon, the Artwork is phenomenal brother, the intricacy and just general overall talent is a beautiful thing to see.

And of course, Mum, Hoa Powa, Lydia and all family and friends that have supported both of us in so many incredible ways, even though you may not fully understand our levels of weird. Thank you!

Available next in the ***'Now Is The Time'*** *series.*

Enlightenment: A Young Awakening. *For those curious to know how a then 20-year-old young man, gained the ability to access the remarkable information you are about to read, this book documents our journey of spiritual evolution over the first 7 months of practice, beginning with Jordan's very first attempt at channelling Source.*

Contents

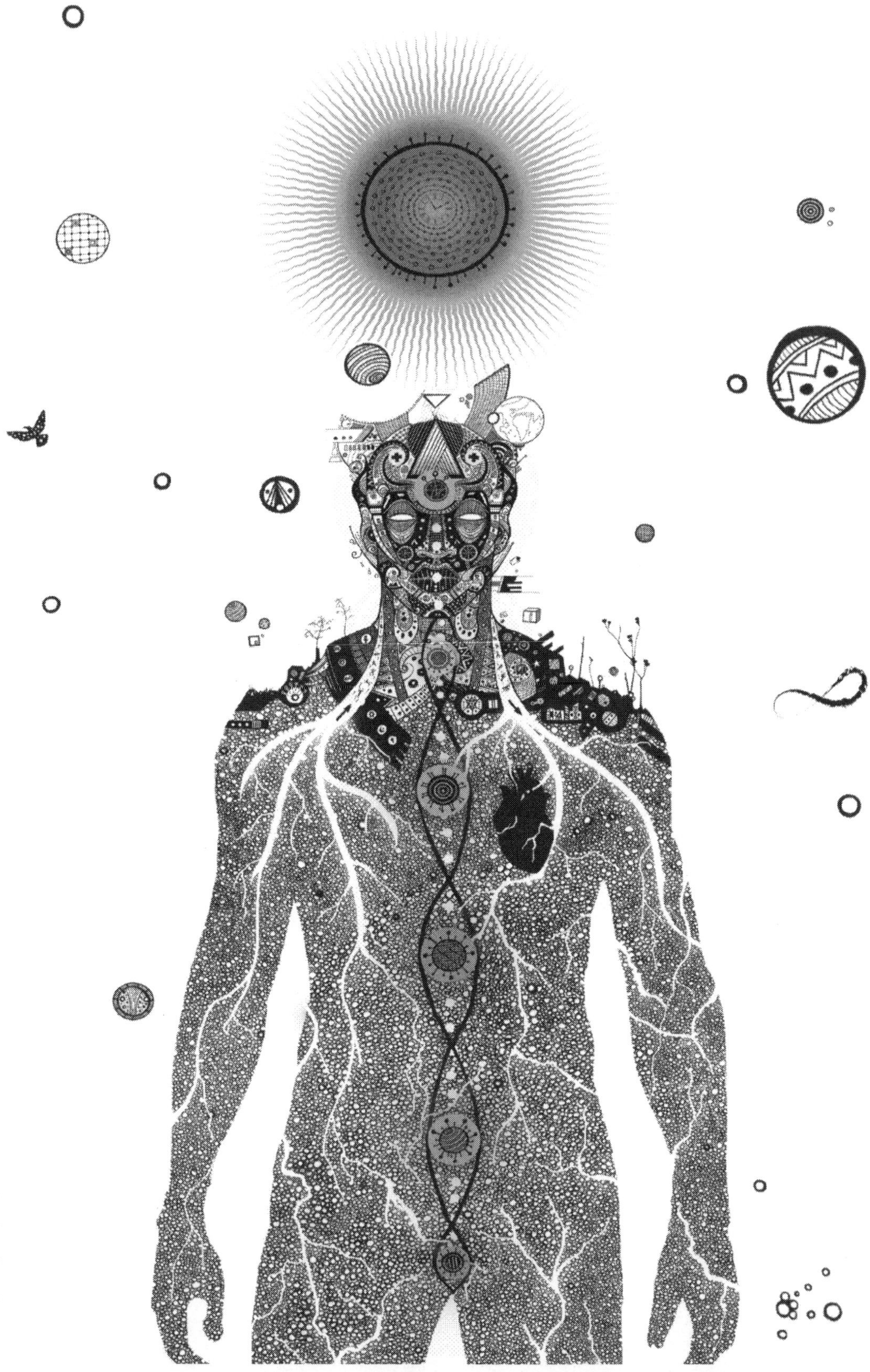

As this is channelled information we feel is of great importance, if needed, a free pdf version can be downloaded at www.YouSpiritually.com/energy-book

Preface

To preface, I do not have any personal claim to this knowledge, I am simply reporting and compiling channelled information that we, being my son Jordan (the channel) and myself Jerry (the conductor), have received through the various questions we have asked on this essential topic. We use various protocols and techniques Jordan, with a highly unusual amount of discipline for his young age, has been intuitively mastering over the years to access more of the natural human potential we all have. We call these communications 'readings' and use them to obtain answers that would not usually be available to the standard conscious processing of the mind via the evaluation of known data.

If you have ever had an 'aha' or 'eureka' moment, where the answer to a puzzling question has just randomly popped into your head with little or no conscious effort on your behalf, then for ease of explanation consider this practice to be akin to having the ability to access that state of eureka at will. Here information is obtained from various Sources, in some cases these intuitions come from our own greater consciousness, the Higher-Self as it might be termed, other times they may come in a more telepathic manner from the various benevolent guiding forces that exist in our multidimensional universe, and sometimes may come from Sources even greater than these.

There is a wealth of new and fascinating information in these pages, provided in the hope that it will be of some aid to your spiritual development, understanding and positive evolution through life. You have no obligation to believe a word that is written here, therefore we would simply ask that you use your discernment, read this new information with an open mind and if it resonates with you then you may just have found the Source you are looking for.

There exist many wonders in this unfathomably large universe, and in its expansiveness, there are multitude forms of intelligent life of which we humans on Earth appear to be just a small part. This information on energy is mainly given by a Social Memory Complex that have transcended names, however we affectionately call them J+ or simply J.

The 'J' being a symbol - the straight part represents discipline, the curved part represents compassion, and the '+' represents unification for this is a grouping of entities, these beings are members of the confederation and operate in service to the One Infinite Creator.

They are our benevolent higher dimensional family upstairs, however let us be clear, these beings are not God, we don't term them as Angels or such like, although I'm 99% sure in less scientific eras, that this is what we would have called benevolent beings from a higher dimension who have evolved beyond a physical body into a lighter one. To our knowledge they are entities just like us, souls that have gone through their own path of evolution on their own planets, learning the deeper realities on a journey of growth back towards the One Infinite Creator, and in their journey of spiritual evolution they offer service to others. This book and the information they provide is a part of that divine service, I will utilise some of their own words from our readings to allow them to further explain.

The confederation as you call it, are beings among the dimensions, typically beyond the 3rd dimension *(4th and above)*, that offer themselves in service to the One Infinite Creator through the giving principle rather than the taking principle. The Confederation of Entities are what you might call Extra-Terrestrials, there seem to be many names in your societies for us, we have played a significant part in many of your religious teachings, as you would call them religious teachings, we have been a major influence on this planet's events on the positive spectrum and equally on the negative spectrum with regard to the innocent learnings of our mistakes so to speak.

The Confederation of Entities would be like a gathering of beings all of which seek greater benevolence and wisdom and unification with the One Infinite Creator God. Here our service is a giving service, a service nonetheless. C001 A4

What we would like to say is wisdom such as ours is easy to come by if one undergoes a rigorous routine. Spirituality in today's Western society has been more so understood as a race and everyone seeks to be efficient in this. You see us as Extra-Terrestrial species, as Aliens perhaps you could call us, or for some people they call us Angels as we appear to people as balls of light but that is only due to our vibration. Western society has confused spirituality to be a race, an expectation, a jog, looking for the most efficient technique to run the course. Wisdom such as ours is accumulated over time and over practice, what is normal for us is abnormal for Western society, the way we use our willpower would be more so to direct our attention to daily meditation, we would prioritise this over any form of entertainment for we did even have entertainment on our planets, not so much such as yours but we had the same sort of things, acting – these sorts of phenomena.

We had to find ourselves practicing a routine where we would dedicate time and effort into this, where we would say, 'No!' to the distractions and we would put ourselves forward in the position that would be idealistic to what you would call spiritual practices or spiritual training.

It would all be based on what we would call discipline. We see the discipline in 'J' as the stick, the line you see of the 'J' itself. This is a part of our philosophy that discipline is a matter of will, compassion is a matter of the feminine characteristic of imagination, for compassion requires imagination and discipline requires will, and so it is we sought to balance these in our practice and we found that if we stuck to discipline and we used compassion to give ourselves the necessary self-love that we would need, we found great wisdom being bestowed unto us by what you would call God, by what we would call Higher-Self, and even by what you would call at your current time, Extra-Terrestrials, Angels, beings, Astral beings, for we see that these have had experiences of this.

There is not much difference you see, from our evolution and what will soon be yours, the messages that we seek to give is that the willpower is powerful, the will can be used to discipline self, one does not simply have to go by the floatiness of feelings, they can say, 'No!' using their will and disciplining themselves, so if it is wisdom you seek, mystical experiences you seek, healing you seek, this all lies within a steady and daily practice of meditation. This is our core belief, this is the belief of the Confederation, the Confederation of Extra-Terrestrial Entities that seek to give what we call the 'Law of One'. J+012 A3

Additional quotes are taken from Source Readings; consider the Confederation, J+ or Mini readings (those with references starting with a C, J+ or M) as an energetic telepathic connection, an exercising of muscles that lay fairly dormant in most of us. The telepathic muscles are, although not the same but interestingly by way of analogy, remarkably similar to the concentrations that become active when we can't get a song out of our head. If you notice, even though you will be thinking and having your normal level of internal dialog, all the while the song will be repetitively playing in a way that feels external as it plays in the background as a separate entity without your influence, one your mind does not seem to be connected with as it is noticeably difficult to interrupt or stop. Although this is not the telepathic muscle in operation, the experience of controlling music in your mind is similar to the experience of being able to control the signals of the brain's telepathic receiver and transmitter.

To distinguish between Confederation and J+ readings, consider Confederation readings to be Narrowband and J+ to be Broadband. The Narrowband connection is highly nuanced, and Jordan has only recently achieved the level of evolution to fully practice this finite form of narrow channelling. We were informed that these J+ readings documented in this book will be among the rare ones performed utilising that level of channelling since Jordan's progression and the J+'s desire to be of greater service means they would almost be doing a disservice to all parties to continue to operate at the Broadband level. You could view it as the difference between talking to the upper management in the normal work environment compared to meeting them in the boardroom, the readings are a lot more personable in the broadband form, whereas in the narrowband format we will in future publications be operating at a much deeper and precise level of communication.

Broadband is a term that may indicate the pristineness of the light that in-pours into the entities mind. Broad is of a general nature, general information in a digestible format for entities upon this plane who are perhaps a little too average to be able to digest something that is seemingly so alien. The narrow connection, a more clear-cut coherent experience of energy, is somewhat of a delicate practice which none-the-less allows for 'J' to 'intelligelise' if such a word could be used.

Let us imagine that 'J' at this moment in broad channelling use perhaps 5-10% of their beingness, and at the narrow channel they would seek to bring that into a higher octave or degree so their truer expression of intelligence can stream through the boy. It will be somewhat of a long road to establish 'J' at the level to which they would like to work through the instrument, but it is to say that 'J' at this time would only channel such a small portion of their intelligence, so much potential is there.

'J' wishing to access this potential on behalf of the entity Jordan's desire to seek the infinite, would then lead to a very precise, almost engineering level degree of communication. Therefore, the communication, at least in the narrowband for them, merely is them using more regions of their brain if you could understand this. S083 A5

Source or Quantum Readings (those references starting with an S or Q) should be considered as a much deeper psychic connection, rather than a telepathic one. With Source Readings there is the setting aside of what you could class as the individual self or ego, and this setting aside allows room for as much of the vibration of the God-Force, in the purest form the body can handle, to come through. You could consider this to be the pure or true form of Jordan, as it would indeed be the true form of anyone capable of accomplishing the practice of Source Reading as the subconscious has a natural unity with all things. During a Source Reading one becomes more interconnected to allow all aspects of God, all sparks to unify, with that connection made, it becomes possible to access and vocalise intelligent information on practically any subject, as long as free will is not compromised. With Quantum readings we connect specifically to the Higher-Self rather than the larger array of universal forces.

If this is all too hard to believe, if your scepticism cannot accept channelling as being real, then simply imagine that my son has the ability to somehow, utilising the power of the mind, accomplish a complete change within the personality, allowing new perceptions and perspectives to be given on subjects that would otherwise be unavailable to the normal conscious state.

Some seem to regard channelled information as a form of divine absolute truth; realistically however, the Source may be infallible but the human instruments singing it, maybe not quite so. With that said, as we evolve and grow towards our goal of completing the evolutionary process of this particular school or prison depending on perspective, we will naturally get closer to the perfection we seek, and the clarity along with the integrity of the information provided will also gain its perfection. We are still learning, therefore as we spiritually evolve, the loving truths that we are taught also appear to evolve.

The 'loving truth' appears to be an important distinction, for instance, the loving truth causes a parent to not destroy a young child's innocent belief in Father Christmas until it is ready for a deeper truth, that truth being that the god like entity it held in such high regard throughout its childhood - one that with some form of omnipresence sees everything we do, then uses that divined knowledge to morally judge good or bad deeds, traversing the world in one single omnipotent night bestowing generous gifts created by magical elves to those that didn't get put on the naughty list - was in fact their biological parent and no different to them, just older, more evolved, and in fact would be them at a later date.

The point being that as one soul may view this Father Christmas story as lying to your child, another will view it as an act of loving your child, however the loving truth does not appear to have the human dualistic distinction of right or wrong, there is no judgement on good or bad, it is just love expressing itself. Negatives do not exist; they appear to simply be catalysts for change.

The loving truth is only interested in correction, and correction leads us away from dualistic concepts and back toward unification. In this Christmas themed analogy, the loving truth knows when you are ready to be put in the driving seat and capable of accepting a new form of reality that may shatter your previous perceptions. The loving truths contained in these readings may well shatter your current perceptions, we predict however that one should be prepared for these to be superseded and expanded by future perception changing truths as we are still neophytes, child souls growing along our journey, and children as all parents know, are attached to their stories.

Italics are my own contributions to further clarify any necessary points. I have done my best to provide word for word transcriptions of the readings, however on some occasion's sentences may be reworded slightly for clearer understanding. Throughout the readings you may find that the sentence structures and, in some cases, words themselves, do not conform to the standard English grammatical rules, personally I find this to be a major part of the charm of these channelled sessions.

As given, the codes at the end of quotes are my reference numbers from the various spiritual readings the data was compiled from.

There are further explanations on these different types of reading protocols explained in detail within another book title within this series called:

'Now is the Time – Enlightenment: A Young Awakening'

This book contains the linear journey of spiritual evolution Jordan experienced over the course of our first 7 months of practice, starting from our 1st attempted Source Reading and the various developments that led to the other forms we now utilise, fortunately I was able to record and journal the entire expansion of consciousness, and the various mind-bending progressions in real time.

Thank you for reading this book.

Introduction

'Everything is energy and that is all there is to it.' **Bashar**

'If you want to find the secrets of the universe, think in terms of energy, frequency and vibration.' **Nikola Tesla**

It is an important working to begin to understand that to which you are made from and made of; we would only seek to preface this book with a simple statement. It follows a little hierarchy:

I Am Infinity
I Am Awareness
I Am Thought
I Am Emotion

Acknowledge life in that very order and you may find some pleasure in feeling a little more at home, and even pleasurable within the creation of the One Infinite Creation.

Imagine for a moment a child who is born and raised in a family which teaches him that creation is evil inherently and that he will go to hell one day. Imagine being raised in a family that teaches the child that creation is merely atoms and then the child goes along thinking that his existence is but a flip of a switch, a click of a button; in one moment it is on and in the other it is off. Imagine dearest one, what it is like for some people who do not have the opportunity to really comprehend what they are, what they are made of, and *how to* begin to enjoy the process of understanding nature itself.

Life is strange in this way for people always choose their incarnative desires and always have opportunities in the life to unconfuse themselves, we enjoy the privilege of being able to give information on these matters. Creation is something that entities should build a relationship with, not something that should be reduced in a reductionist fashion or claimed to be some kind of hellish phenomenon as a religious individual who would be bias towards their religious teachings would understand.

There is no hell, there is only heaven in various forms and formations, thus what you might call Earth is a heaven, but it is hellish, paradoxically. Thus, you would find you live in many heavens, many planes of existence of varying motioning energy constructed by infinity, awareness and thought. J+018 A1

Note: Although this book is written in a linear format, life's path seldom moves in a straight line, therefore please feel free to examine the 'list of contents' and jump directly to any subjects that resonate.

Energy Glossary

Energy, Kundalini, Prana, Chi, Density etc... all the same thing, all energy and all life changing once you begin to gain a deeper insight. Different terms are used throughout this book when referencing energy. The following are the specific use cases based on the way we have directly received the information:

Chi

The basic quantity of life-force that an entity has, that is freely available for manipulation through the body, *between the Root and* the Solar Plexus. Chi is able to travel beyond the Solar Plexus and become a kind of Kundalini energy, as we would be using the term, that is able to transcend from Chi to Prana as you would understand. S081 A4

Prana

Prana would be most appropriately a reference to Chi moving from the lower Chakras, the lower three as you would understand, and coming into the 4th Chakra, moving into the 5th, 6th and passing through the gateway of the 6th to the 7th. Prana you would see as an energy that seeks to depict all Densities and Chakras beyond the first three. S081 A5

Kundalini

Think of the Kundalini as a snake as you would understand, that is currently dancing, the harmony of the dance is determined by your thoughts, depending on the harmony of your thoughts the *snake* will dance at a higher Chakra, causing a higher experience, or it can dance at a lower Chakra causing a lower experience. Kundalini always then being concerned with the quality of one's thought, the quality of one's consciousness. When one's mind is harmonic, this will in essence determine which Chakra the Kundalini is resting at. S081 A6

Density

Density would be a reference to the amount or degree of light that is able to be encompassed within the crystal of your Chakras, it is in essence to understand that there are varying degrees of intensity of light which at any time can shine into the Chakras. If the Chakras are crystal clear the density of light that can shine in, is an infinite density. If your Chakras are not clear crystals then the densities diminish until you find that the only Chakra which can contain any kind of light would be the first Chakra for the other Chakras are akin to black, as you would understand, and do not allow light to pass through freely. Density being a reference to the density of light which is able at any time to shine through the Chakras. S081 A7

Astral

The Astral relates to the non-physical realm, the more heavenly realms, those associated with the 4th Chakra and above. The lower 3 Chakras or energy centres or dimensions, are associated with the physical body and mainly related to survival, interpersonal relationships, and control/power. You may have heard of Astral projection, this is basically the conscious leaving of the physical body, which also occurs during Near-Death Experiences (NDEs), interestingly this also happens during dreams, lucid dreams being the more conscious form of this however in both cases we enter a non-physical state, an Astral state, in which we are strangely still able to feel the 5 sensory abilities of sight, sound, smell, taste and touch, although we are no longer sensing the atomic dimension. Some additional senses also come in to play at the Astral level.

References

The code at the end of each quote pertains to the source of reference. Telepathic readings beginning with C, J+ or M are a communication with our teachers, some would call them guides or angels, but essentially these are a specific group of Extra-Terrestrial dimensional beings communicating from a higher frequency to our lower frequency, that are also on their own path of evolution.

Source and Quantum Readings, those prefixed with S or Q, are a psychic rather than telepathic reading, this is a communication with the logos itself, Intelligent Infinity, Brahman as it is known in the Hindu culture or Universal Consciousness as it may be referred. Your Higher-Self or Over-Self is the gateway to Source.

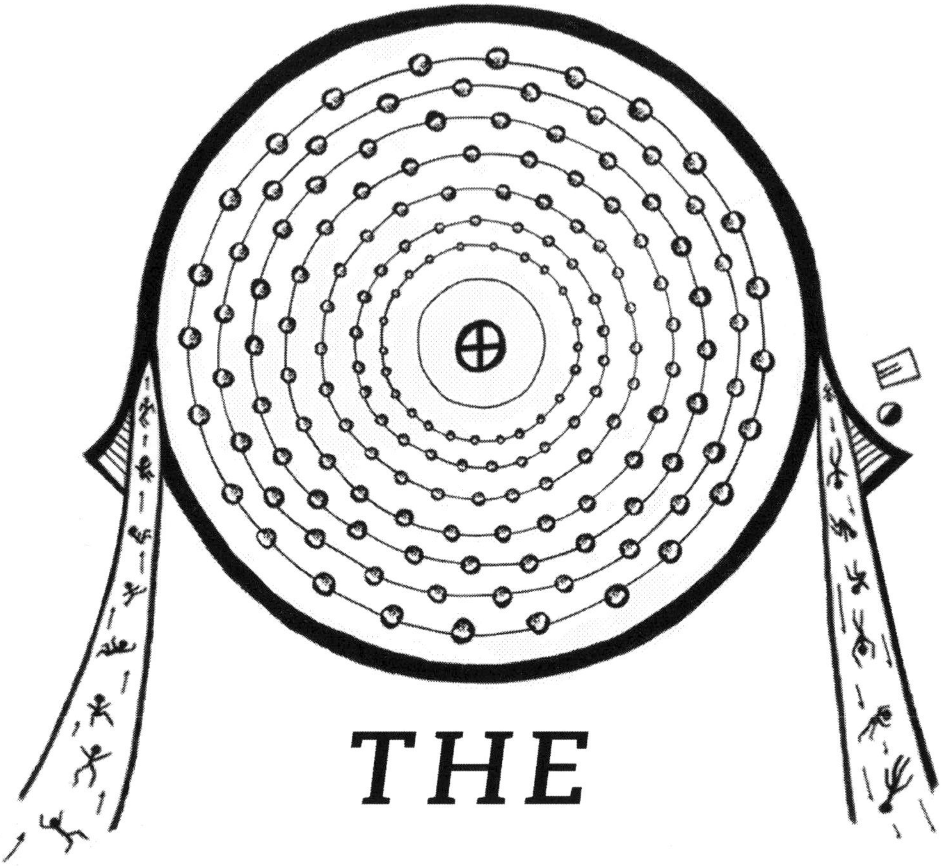

THE PHYSICAL

The Human Body

'Your body is a crystal, and crystals absorb light do they not?'

The physical body is comprised of liquid crystal systems. Cell membranes, intercellular fluids, as well as the larger structures such as fatty tissues, muscular and nervous systems, lymph, blood and so on are all liquid crystal systems.

Before continuing I will reinforce this claim using this extract from New Scientist, 18 May 1991, by Richard Templer and *John Seddon.*

> Without liquid crystals there would be no life. Even the simplest single-celled creature has an outer skin whose fabric is liquid crystalline. It is this skin that forms the membrane separating the inner workings of the cell from its surroundings. More complex life forms, such as human beings, use liquid crystalline membranes for a vast variety of biological processes, for example, transmitting nerve impulses and digesting fats.
>
> You might be surprised to find out that cell membranes are liquid crystals. In fact, the first recorded observations of the liquid crystalline phase were of myelin, the material that coats nerve

fibres. In 1855, a German ophthalmologist called C. Mettenheimer was studying myelin under a polarising microscope, and noted that, although it flowed like a liquid, it was brightly coloured, or 'birefringent' like a crystal when viewed between crossed polarisers (see 'The fourth state of matter', New Scientist, 4 May). It was not, however, until much later that myelin was identified as a liquid crystalline material.

We now know that the liquid crystal structure of myelin consists of regularly stacked layers of membranes, with each membrane consisting of molecules that move around freely within it. In the direction of the stacked membranes it behaves like a crystal, but in the plane of the membrane it behaves like a liquid. Without exception, all biological membranes behave simultaneously like a liquid and a solid, so liquid crystallinity must play an important part in the function of cells.

Read more:

https://www.newscientist.com/article/mg13017695-400-the-world-of-liquid-crystals/#ixzz6nQk3j1kw

With this understood or at least considered, the human bodies potential capabilities quickly become very interesting, and a vast number of metaphysical claims made by guru's and practitioners alike, that have understood energy and/or mastered the human body to some degree, suddenly become very feasible as a greater understanding is outlined.

The physiology, it is a regular structure, a crystal as you would understand from cells to bones, to all things of the nature of the body. What you exist in right now is indeed a liquid crystal or as Jordan has called it in what he calls a write up of his, a soft crystal. J+020 A3

It would be understood that you would have a body and your body is a crystal, and crystals absorb light do they not? J+020 A1

Take for example a quartz crystal, does it not allow light to pass right through it?

Here is an example, a living example of absorbing light from infinity itself. Your Chakras mirror this directly, it is in fact almost a superposition in that your Chakras are crystals absorbing light coming from infinity, in the same way the quartz crystal absorbs light coming from your soul. J+020 A10

The crystalline properties of a human are such that the human truly is a crystal which is always at a constant basis, absorbing light. The degree to which a human is able to absorb light depends on the quality of their consciousness, this would refer to the density of one's consciousness, the density of one's thought, this thus determines the density to which one is absorbing said light. When you understand that all around you are crystals absorbing light and radiations coming from all kinds of dimensions and densities, you would begin to comprehend or rather grasp the thrust of this experience of what you understand as energy. J+020 A2

The degree or quality of light that a crystal can absorb depends on how efficient or functional the crystal is. The human body is a liquid crystal, this liquid crystal when organised in the correct mannerisms by which one's emotional experience of life has become crystalised, begins to absorb what you understand as Astral light which endows the physiology with great powers and great abilities. Astral light therefore is absorbed or begins to be absorbed by entities whom take the time, dedication and discipline to begin to crystalise their physiologies emotional configuration which alters those, let us call them, quantum vibratory oscillations that happen in the small,

small realms of life, which then travel through the body at the atomic level and alter the electrical circuitry of the body.

The one whom has crystalised their experience of emotion and thought, the quality of their consciousness, these entities are thus able to become what you would call endowed with great abilities for they are now absorbing that light you would call Prana or the Astral light that would exist in 4th density. Here we would be referring specifically to 4th density Prana rather than the other Pranas of the lower densities or higher densities. J+020 A1

So, you're a soul that's woke up in some form of a liquid crystal body, provable by the traits of cell membranes... congratulations and welcome to Earth! You are now a soul with a body. ***Special note:*** *I'm not saying you have a soul, I'm saying you are a soul, what you have is a body! And the more crystalline you can make it, the more the soul that you are, can display its real powers!*

Crystalising the Emotional Experience

The human physiology can exist at many levels, the level that you are familiar with at this current time is the chemical and atomic experience of life in which what Jordan most comedically calls 'little marbles' tug and pull on each other to create the atomic vehicle.

Whilst the atomic vehicle is a beauty, the experience that is most influential is that experience of the quantum realm, quantum referring to the extremely small realm of reality in which the atom begins to become energy in the sense that it no longer is a marble, but is more of a, let us call it - a wave, and in this waving experience of life, in this waving energy, in this almost liquid like energy that is extremely fluid in comparison to a liquid like tar which moves awfully, that quantum realm of reality where atoms no longer exist but energy moves in that kind of wave form so easily; when this form of one's energy begins to crystalise, the atomic body begins to respond to the crystalline structure of one's quantum body or of one's super small body, the body composed predominately of energy that is not atoms. Once this quantum portion of one's physiology is crystalised one begins to experience what you call enlightenment. J+020 A3

In somewhat, as they say 'layman terms', the body and its emotional configuration is akin to a body that is composed of easier moving, freer fields of energy. This freer body as is termed usually 'a subtle body', begins to become regular as the emotional state of the being achieves a coherent tone like a pleasant humming noise, similar to the sounds of your binaural beats which have a pleasant, repetitive, varying in intensity frequency, and increasingly pleasant sound.

The typical humans emotional energy field upon your plane is akin to... if the moon suddenly got close to the waters of the Earth and then suddenly moved back - the turbulence and the waves, the crashing and the relative incoherence caused by the gravitational changes, is perhaps an analogy to describe the humans upon this plane and how their emotional energy fields work together. Humans are far too upset and angry with life, and how it has painted itself as the modern society has become more controlled, and as things are seemingly becoming a little questionable on your cyberspace.

Equally humans in their interrelationships find constant stressing factors disturbing the coherence of their emotional energy field causing the energy field to, once again, behave erratically. This does not generate a pure tone, it generates a noise as incoherent as a bad singer and so one feels emotionally incoherent, and any energy that would otherwise be attempting to enter into the body from the ambient environment to which the emotional body exists, for as your physical body exists in a realm of air, the emotional body exists in the realm of energy. Indeed, the ambient energy in the surroundings cannot make its way through the emotional body for it is making its way through something incredibly erratic, being pinged like a tennis player blocking a tennis ball from scoring on the other side, or alternatively a surface that moves in a crazy way, the energy tries to get through but the surface moving in crazy ways inhibits this process.

When the emotional body is coherent and has a pure tone, a gentle wave, it creates energy pathways that are clean and regular, and that Astral Energy that has been spoken about begins to stream in and out in a gentle and coherent fashion. Q013 A4

We would go as far as to say one would have to become, dare we say, peaceful or tranquil. Let us consider for example the monk who spends 1,000s and 1,000s of hours meditating for his entire life. In the earlier stages it may take upwards of 5 years of consistent meditation to achieve any level of emotional tranquillity, for the process of meditation is not so quick, for consistency is key, length is key, and the manner in which the practice is executed is key; but the, let us call it infant, soon finds that after some many years of practice that he sits on the bench and is serene, that an argument bears near but he remains serene, that an entity troubles him or does something that is seemingly unforgiveable yet he remains serene, for the emotional energy body is like a crystal, so coherent and regular, like a beautiful tone emanating from a speaker as your technology would have it. Have you seen the patterns of sound dearest one, expressed on surfaces of water, sand? *(We recommend the reader look up 'cymatics', to see the geometric beauty of sound and vibration)*

Are they not beautiful structures when the sound is a perfect tone?

It's a crystal and herein lies then the nature of what is seeking to be had, thus an entity will become tranquil, at peace, serene, and this is then called balance, for balance could only be when two sides of a coin are operating in harmony with each other, like the piano where you play usually one cord above to make sure the sounds do not clash. A and C, rather than A and B as such, the sounds running with each other are coherent thus they produce something harmonious to the ears - tranquillity, balance. Q013 A5

Crystals are not limited then to what is understood as objects that do not move, crystals can be liquid like, gaseous; gaseous is gridded in the manner into which it vibrates, it has a matrix, a patternated structure usually referred to as geometry. Imagine liquid geometry, gaseous geometry which remains in place because the plasma or the electricity, the energy is structured in the manner to which it sings.

The plasma is the energy, the energy fields themselves. That is electricity as some may call it, for electricity and plasma are the same thing usually used to describe different systems.

Plasma is but the loose electrical fields, loose electricity that finds ease of movement, it moves faster and quicker, and vibrates at a quickened speed, crystals are made, yet the crystals are liquid in nature or we would prefer to say gaseous, as in free in travelling like a bird in the sky. They move swiftly, extremely fast, especially for the perception of a human.

The plasma, this energy, it crystalises in the way it vibrates, in the way it sings, as does sound in the air crystalise, as does the laser* find itself in crystalline structures, it could be described in such a way when it is interfering with itself constructively rather than destructively. Q013 A6

The seeking toward the God-Head is but the altering, changing and coherifying of disorganised energy. For what purpose?

The purpose is this, infinity pours into you but if your, let us call it, capacity to absorb the light of infinity is minimal for your structure is un-crystalline, then you will not be able to lens* let us say, the light coming into you, thus you will feel moody, depressed, suicidal, but dearest one, if it is so that you can crystalise your vibration then you can absorb the light that is outpouring from infinity itself and in this absorption you will be more infinite and you will feel blissed, joyful, happy and the various other terms you may use.

As pertaining to the manipulation of energy itself this is but the playing with awareness for when you play with awareness, you manipulate energy itself. J+020 A8

**Where lens was referred to, the image would be that of a magnifying glass and its ability to use its lens to focus light to the degree that it could start a fire, you could also imagine a bathtub where the plug has been removed and the concentration of the water as it starts flowing in a vortex like motion.*

**Where laser was referred to, lasers are super coherent light beams. Observed with the correct sight they are seen as a beautiful spiral and would appear regular, crystalline. Their incredible coherence is why we are able to use lasers to achieve tasks that require extreme precision.*

Let us take consciousness and let us reflect consciousness within the body and its centres of energy, as the quality of your consciousness in how it manipulates awareness to create energy increases, this alters exactly what Chakras are operating or energy centres as you might call them, such that if the quality of your consciousness is focusing awareness in such and such a way that the awareness is being focused to create a crystal that can harness infinity or infinite light coherently, then you will get activations in the upper Chakras of your physiology.

Thus, it is the quality of one's consciousness which naturally focuses awareness into energy and determines what energy centres operate within the body and thus how one feels within themselves.

Thus, if you alter your consciousness, you will alter your experience of awareness in how it creates energy and when this is done, where your kundalini naturally sits will be appropriate to the quality of your consciousness.

Take for instance the brother Jordan for we are with this instrument thus we are intimately aware of how his energy works. His energy naturally focusses at the 3rd eye or the Indigo Chakra, for 3rd eye is more of a Western term, the correct term for the energy centre is the Indigo energy centre which is an incredibly perfect crystal and thus when one's consciousness is of such a crystalline nature the energy centre vibrates accordingly, so thus forth the entity Jordan absorbs light, or energy if you prefer, into his Indigo energy centre and thus he has experiences of bliss consciousness, and if he would begin to really hone in on perfecting that Chakra, in which he would perfect his consciousness for when you perfect your consciousness you perfect your Chakra, then that Chakra or crystal, for Chakras are crystals, will be able to absorb that energy coming from infinity, or light if you prefer, even more so and he will achieve enlightenment, as can anyone as long as they are willing to crystallise their consciousness. J+020 A9

It may help to view the body as an instrument, the energy centres as the notes that vibrate within the instrument, and the song as your soul. Perhaps in this metaphor the energy coming from infinity could be classed as the conductor.

Stress, drama, anger and all those unorganised forces, make for an unrefined instrument, so bad that some notes aren't even available to be played, they are just too high up the scale, out of reach and out of tune. There's a big difference between a note and a noise, so whilst we may try to play these higher notes anyway, the sounds the notes create will likely be very weak and basically a bit rubbish.

By increasing the quality of your consciousness, the instrument gets tuned, more complex notes become available and the song, that beautiful song we call your soul, can better express in more of its infinite glory.

The Metabolism of Light

The cells and their activity are carried out through the cells receiving their energy from the consumption of basic food and electrolyte compounds. That is, a cell finds its function in the fact that it has the energy to do its work through the food you consume. The food you consume is catalysed, that energy is used by the nerves, the neuron cells as such or the cells in general, then as to the metabolism of what is called light, there are two facts to consider if you will.

One, you are always metabolising light, for the food you hold in your hand is in fact made of light.

And then secondly, that the literal metabolism of light is in that idea, or rather reality, that there are cells of certain levels of existence that find their ability to retain their existence through the consumption of their environment, which happens to be light itself. It is to realise that you do not have one body, there exists many bodies. S087 A2

As there would be this physical body which would be composed of electromagnetic, as it is termed, fields. These electromagnetic fields vibrate at a certain rate making them have the properties they do, but if you could take an electromagnetic field and make it vibrate a little quicker, you would cause that field to proceed into the next occurring density, and so as much as you have a cell in physical reality, in faster vibratory existences are there different kinds of cells, which find that their vibration is so many times faster which allow for a different experience of what could only be described as consciousness. S087 A3

To understand this process, it is well to understand that the body is quite translucent, this is well understood by those that shine a torch underneath their skin and see the redness of their vehicles, in this very sense you would have varying spectrums of light from the radio waves, all the way to the visible and ultra-violet light spectrum and all that in-between. This is being constantly processed as it is absorbed through the body. The quantum processes of the body, which soon will be somewhat of a mysterious discovery by scientists, enjoy abundance of light for the process of metabolising light, as does a cell metabolise carbohydrates and various things as you would understand the same.

For as much as you have a cell for the process of atoms, so do you have a cell for the process of the digestion of light and the reutilisation of the same, and it is to be very well understood that the configuration of the quantum field is the only reason why your body is able to maintain its structure. If the quantum field of your vehicle shifts into a different memory everything will change, if the quantum field that is holding your body together falls apart, thus biodegradation happens with relation of course to the sturdiness of a chemical structure.

Thus the body is able to metabolise photons as much as it is able to metabolise atoms, and at each portion of the vehicle, whether the quanta or the atom, it is all connected as one organism that is constantly absorbing and radiating light and atoms as you breathe in and out, as you are truly a crystal taking in the radiance of the surroundings and turning this into what you would understand as Prana or vital lifeforce.

Then you would find your Chakras are always felt within the vehicle, for as they step down the hierarchy it affects the vehicle directly. The hierarchy starts in those small, small realms you would call the quantum realms, and transitions down into the body yielding differences in neural activity and hormone productions. S082 A12

The Chakras exist in a realm that is timeless, in that the concept of time in its linear sense is an illusion. You were always with God and never left God, thus time cannot exist for it would imply that you could separate from the same, that Chakras could have, as you would term it, a death or a bringing to the life, that Chakras could have polarity. Polarity cannot exist in Chakras thus they are timeless, they are always existing, always have existed and always have been one with the Creator.

The Chakra is the very reason you are able to have a vehicle in the first place. S082 A13

Your atomic body merely exists to process the light atomically that is coming from the non-atomic world, your atomic body is but a shadow or a mirror as you may say, of light coming through your energy centres.

So as your energy centres change your bodies functioning changes, entities who have crystalised their energy centres are entities whom have become so coherent that they are absorbing an infinite amount of light from infinity, these entities are enlightened. Thus, their atomic body responds to this directly, for the atomic body is only a mirror, a reflection, or a shadow as you term it, of the energy centres and the energy centres are only but a mirror or a reflection of the quality of your consciousness.

Further explanation would lead us to the following: The energy centres themselves do have a physical existence, they are tangible at a certain density that extends far beyond your reach and our reach, for the energy centres exist in a timeless dimension.

This may be a rather, as the entity Jordan terms it, psychedelic thought. In this timeless dimension the energy centres are 'this' close to consciousness, in that the only way to the Father is but through me.

You may term the energy centres as the Christos, although the term Christos has become a little confused, here you are learning now metaphysics. Please see your energy centres as the Son of God and your consciousness as God, which alters the energy centres.

The only way to the Father, is but through consciousness improving in quality and changing the energy centres in their ability to absorb infinity itself. J+020 A11

Welcome to a philosophy of life, a way to perceive life, different perhaps to how your scientists perceive life. We hope this philosophy of life brings you great pleasure for if you have the correct lens to perceive life through, life becomes alive and joyful for you perceive creation not in a distorted fashion, but for what it is with the humbleness of knowing that you do not yet know all things, as do we not either. J+020 A8

To briefly summarise, your body is a liquid crystal, the cells do not just process atoms, they are also designed to absorb and process the light hitting us from multiple dimensions, the degree to which you can absorb light depends on your quality of consciousness, the density of your thought. (This will be explained in more detail later in the book)

All beings regardless of how big or small have Chakras. As our experience of emotion and thought moves beyond the lower 3 Chakras, those relating mainly to the physical survival of both species and self, our quality of consciousness increases improving the structure of our Chakras making them more capable of taking in higher forms of light, such as 4th dimensional Astral light or Prana. This improvement affects our body at the quantum level, the super small level where our body is made of waves of energy rather than atoms.

As your ability to absorb light at this level increases, you are able to take in more of the Creator's light and quite wonderful experiences begin to occur. This is all possible because the body's cells are made of a liquid crystal and crystals absorb light, in fact our Chakras mirror this taking in of light directly.

As the Bible says, 'Let there be light'. Pertinent as the key to spiritual growth appears to be just how much of that original light you are able to let pour through your being. The light will pour on you regardless, the issue is really down to the quality of your crystals, the quality of your consciousness, of your thought.

Imagine two crystal clear glasses, one filled with pure still water and one with water muddied in some way, maybe someone poured a decent brandy into it, or better still as I do not wish to give anyone a complex and I've been good friends with brandy over the years, let's swap that for some polluted water from the River Thames since that analogy pops up later in the book. As we hold both glasses up to the light, one allows light to pass through effortlessly, there is a little refraction and reflection but no rejection as there is little to no distortion, and the other, well... hardly any gets through.

Our Chakras work in a remarkably similar way and strangely drugs are a great way of explaining this use of the light from infinity itself, so next we look at psychedelics.

Psychedelics

'Spiritual growth is not about having large Chakras that absorb large volumes of infinite light, spiritual growth is not this you see.'

There should first be the understanding that upon the consumption of these substances there is then the increase in chemical activity within the body at the base of the spine causing the kundalini to be aroused by the spike, then the rising of the same, then the opening of the Chakras - that ability then to become more enlightened then before causing as it were the lack of inhibition, or rather the easing of the ability to do activities that would otherwise be difficult for the being.

There would also be those various other spiritual experiences that come with the opening of the Chakras, and the Chakras being forced open as we would see, is unhealthy for the being or the body.

If then one is considering the use of such substances, only use them in very small amounts. Society and societies before this took them in incredible doses, as it would be understood, and this destroyed the natural systems in the body causing them to become lethargic and reliant on the drugs, be them the weed, the psychedelic substances, and any other drug, for the body would begin to rely on having Chakra openings caused by the chemical components rather than having Chakra openings caused by the God within that is the intelligence, the natural spark of being that comes from the force of God himself, that would be that Christ force that indwells, that allows one to even have *thought* in the first place.

If the Chakras then are forced open and remain open due to the incredible amount of dosage used in this dimension with psychedelics, this then can have such long-term consequences. The negative effects would be that one would not be able to reallocate self to individuality within the 3rd dimension but would be stuck with incessant voices in the head, that forced opening of telepathy can cause one to become very schizophrenic not knowing what voice is theirs and what voice is not, in conjunction with various clairvoyant imagery which can be grotesque due to the insanity of this dimension. S042 A4

If there is ever the curiosity, for curiosity is healthy, then there should be the taking of this in very small amounts so that the beings that these are, can maintain who they are, and can never fall privy to anything that is not what they are ready for, then there will never be any permanent consequences but only instead positives. S042 A5

Yes, this reading did just allow for the use of drugs, but specifically microdosing. We recommend with most drug experiences, if your determined to go there, then stick to just once or twice. Curiosity is completely natural and sometimes being temporarily kicked out of your comfort zone to experience a greater reality is of great benefit. However, please be aware that this is not a shortcut to spiritual growth, yes it will temporarily enlarge your Chakras, but it doesn't make them any more crystalline, it doesn't improve their quality, therefore this will not lead to true fulfilment as it is the substance doing the work, not you.

Spiritual centres can become lethargic and reliant on these to open. I myself experienced many psychic phenomena in my youth, and noticed these were temporarily enhanced through drugs, but of course the more you do it, the less effective a substance becomes, and I am even now still repairing certain regions that became inactive and/or lethargic, as my brain became trained to require substances to have psychic capacities.

When one ingests a psychedelic substance, rather than the substance crystalising the Chakras, it is more that the psychedelic compound makes the crystals bigger. The crystals will be at their appropriate level of coherence, this is unchangeable even with a psychedelic, hence the reason why people can have what they call a bad experience of the psychedelic, a 'bad trip' as we quote it. This is because the crystals of their Chakras are not harmonious enough to handle the increased energy that is pouring into the Chakras themselves. A psychedelic compound increases the actual size of the Chakra crystals which then go on to absorb the light coming from the One Infinite Creator. The increase of the size of the crystal allows one to tap into realms that were more subtle before but because the crystals are now larger, they are able to more so feel, sense and perceive the energies that particular Chakra crystal is now processing. J+020 A12

The more crystalline an entities Chakras are, indeed the more quality of light can pass through. Let us make a distinction, let us see that the One Infinite Creator is a pure tone, the pure tone enters into the crystal and becomes a crystalline tone of varying hues, shapes, sizes, colours, and variations, striations if you prefer. The entities desire is to keep the One Infinite Creators pure tone as pure as possible, without tainting it too much. Whether one's crystals are large or small need not matter, the only significance is that your crystals whether large or small, are able to harness the One Infinite Creators pure tone of light, vibration, energy if you prefer, in such and such a way that it doesn't taint it but rather keeps it.

An analogy of this is if you had 7 crystals in a row that were so crystal clear that they were akin to see-through, to such a level that you would not even be able to see the outline of the crystal itself. What you would call a crystal ball is an example of this. As the light from the One Infinite Creator pours into the 7 crystals called your 7 Chakras, if the light is able to pour into those crystals in such a way that the light doesn't become diminished in any way, shape or form, then whether the Chakras are big or small hardly matters, the entity is enlightened, and the enlightened entity, even if their crystals are tiny will experience even still enlightenment in the form of perpetual joy, perpetual happiness, perpetual bliss.

Many entities have come to this plane desiring that their Chakras be large crystals, so they come, and they have great abilities, such as entities whom are able to work 24/7, as you would use this term, without ever running out of energy. These entities also being able to have Chakra experiences that take other entities many years to learn but you would see that these entities merely have large crystals, rather their Chakras simply are absorbing a lot of light, *this* doesn't necessarily mean the light they are absorbing is coherent, or beautiful, it merely means they are absorbing an abnormal amount of light which is effecting their atomic body in such and such a way that they are super beings, super workers as you would perceive or have some kind of super power.

This is not the essence of spiritual growth dearest one.

Spiritual growth is not about having large Chakras that absorb large volumes of infinite light, spiritual growth is not this you see. It is instead the tempering of the crystal, the cutting of the crystal as you would understand taking a diamond, uncut, and turning it into a cut diamond which is refractive and beautiful. Do you understand?

So whilst one may be able to have a large crystal, if that large crystal has impurities the entity, even though this entity may have great abilities, has not yet grasped the true point of evolution or of spiritual growth. J+020 A13

The better you are able to absorb the pure tone coming from the One Infinite Creator, then in turn means that you will be able to manipulate energy extremely well. If you desire to increase the size of your crystals you may take a psychedelic compound for a temporary experience, alternatively you may simply train that Chakra which will increase its size, in the same way entities train their muscles to increase muscle mass, you see.

But in terms of absorbing the pure tone of the One Infinite Creator, this delicate practice is in the delicate matter of increasing the quality of your consciousness, that your Chakras may become translucent, pure, and un-interruptive of the One Infinite Creator, and yes if it is so that you wish it, you will be able to manipulate energy in whatever way you will, whether it is for the purpose of healing or the purpose of meditation and altered states of consciousness, Astral projections, Lucid dreams, blissful sensations, you see. J+020 A14

The easiest way to measure is but your own experience of emotion, of energy you see. Now let us consider the 7 Chakras, let us now more so consider that each Chakra following the order going from the lowest to the highest, breeds or gives birth to a certain level of self-realisation. Let us consider that one that is God realised is enlightened, and enlightenment is akin to what we could only describe as unity or oneness with the One Infinite Creator.

This will give one the sensation of being at home, this sensation although undermined, for a lack of adjectives, is such an unimaginable sensation that you would no longer perceive the need to learn or to experience, for your experience as being an enlightened being now, due to the experience of your Chakras, is infinitely joyful. This would be the experience of home you see. So then in consideration of this, evolution as such is this process. J+020 A15

Nature has no bias, if you access it with your psilocybin and these things, so be it. If you access it with meditation, so be it. The Higher-Selves, the Entities, Extra-Terrestrials, teach you not to use such substances for they are aware fully of the power of a regular spiritual schedule. They give you these suggestions as suggestions to not take away from your free will and free choice, these are their advice as you would understand. We seek to remain as unbiased as possible; you have free will and free choice, this must be remembered. S077 A18

Energy in Food

'Having a diet of vegetables does one thing, many things in fact but one main thing, it fills you with Chi.'

Seek to see food as energy itself and seek to understand that all energy carries vital lifeforce, it carries its own frequency, it carries its own remarkableness. What makes a diamond so special is not so much the diamond itself, but the incredible amount of pressure it takes to form a diamond. What we see when looking upon a diamond would be that of the strength of the bonds and this is seen in all geometric things, whether the geometric things are fairly static or very dynamic, the bonds you see, are so incredibly strong, are so full of vitality and lifeforce, that the lifeforce itself emanates and thus would you seek not to look upon a fruit or a vegetable as something likened to a diamond, formed under such tremendous pressure?

Or in this case with so much energy residing within the bonds that created the geometry of the being itself.

The Diet

We would find upon looking at your fruits and vegetables that these carry very high frequencies, we would find that you have your nuts and your other produce, those vegetarian produce, they carry also and equally a high vibration, and finally we see fish, we see fish as the most recommended diet, for fish truly is a gift for the body.

Chicken really is the best meat for any being but that is subjective and yet objective in the same for chicken is stable, it is simply stable. If one needs meat in their diet, chicken is truly the best to go for, but if one can substitute chicken for fish, we would so highly recommend this for the vibration of fish is well; and your fruit and veg - the vibration of this is truly remarkable!

Then these people who poach, kill cows, deers, these things, these kinds of meats quite unrecommended. Steak is ... hmm unnecessary.

Why not let these animals frolic along their day, not having to concern themselves with the stress of their imminent death?

We are quoting from Sadhguru, why not read his book? *(Inner engineering: A Yogi's Guide to Joy)* M013 A11

For meat specifically, simple tests would suffice, that one would try chicken for 2 to 3 days and observe then the effects it would have on the self. Then there would be the trying of other meats, perhaps the red kind to see the effects once again. That there would be the understanding that diet is most especially related to the amount of physical activity one does, for it is not entirely necessary that one eat meat if it is that they are seated most of the time. Then for that one that is seated most often, plenty of water, meat here and there yes, and then plenty of veg, but for those who are active and ever moving, even red meat would be useful so that these don't feel fatigued in the directions their life is going. S029 A7

There is a subtle truth to life which humans have not comprehended. You will understand that human beings, as do all creatures in truth, have the potential to be vegetarians. The secrets of God hide in plain sight, God enjoys peace, detests the experience of fear, and does not want to die so fears death. Farming an animal of course is very much farming God, and God although he will never tell you, would prefer not to be farmed; instead enjoyed, for God makes good company in his animal form.

Thus, the subtle secret is indeed that especially the human, a sophisticated body which altered and changed some 1,000s of years ago to better assimilate vegetarian compounds, is truly designed for a vegetarian diet. God has supplied the human with vegetarian alternatives; indeed some have been genetically engineered that they would be fuller, sweeter in some cases, and larger, but this would have been achieved anyway through selective breeding and alternative natural ways of selecting the strongest and most ideal version of the vegetable, crossbreeding the same.

Thus, as it comes to your farming epidemic, we would note that God enjoys being alive and gives his plants, his minerals, and his sophisticated life forms which too are plants in truth, plants that are grown specifically for the purpose that one may eat and be merry and full. This is the garden and sophisticated animals that are not plants to which grow as food, are in truth not necessarily to be eaten but to be left alone such that they would be able to roam the lands, that they would be able to enjoy spiritual growth and development, that they would have freedom to experience life without the threat of being destroyed and then eaten. Farming in truth was never meant to become a thing; in the sense of a parallel universe whereby humans had not farmed animals but instead lived off the garden, as technology grew you humans would have been able to harmoniously breed selectively and perhaps make some gentle genetic modifications to the food so that it is more nutritious and filling.

But yes indeed, God enjoys life in all of his forms, whether God is cow or a human, a fish or a monkey, no matter the animal whom hunts, God does not enjoy being hunted; no matter the animal that kills, God does not enjoy being killed. God enjoys life, but he enjoys freedom too. Q008 A9

Know Your Body

We would suggest taking a mental note of the effects your food has on you, simple observations such as do I feel sluggish and lethargic, or energised and active? Personalise your diet to your own specifications as although these are general guidelines, there does not appear to be a one rule fits all so the key is to simply get to know your body better.

For diet it is relevant and for the testing, simple tests are always good to see how the body reacts and if there would be intuition, seek to build a relationship with your stomach at an intelligent level. Would it not be so strange to ask the stomach how it feels about this food?

Indeed, at first it might seem a bit weird, but soon the stomach will be able to notify the self through feeling alone whether 'x' and 'y' should be consumed. S029 A7

Remember, simply eating a broccoli, the broccoli may simply just go through the body if the body has no idea what to do with it, but if you can remind the body to sap as many nutrients from this broccoli as possible, it can fuel the body for a lot longer and produce much better effects in the healing effects of the vegetable.

See this in the same when one is taking medicines, that these medicines and their unique qualities are to be focused with the power of the mind to the afflicted area that healing effects may be produced. In the use of medicines and external treatments, natural remedies to heal a specific area, in the taking of these elements, these compounds, if one is not using the mind to focus the healing effects of the compound to this area, then it will simply spread throughout the body instead of actually having any influence on that portion.

The mind is a director of energy and these compounds produce a certain kind of energy to have healing effects, and so it is important that one focuses the energy produced by these compounds for the healing effects to happen. So then after the taking of these compounds one should sit in meditation for 10 to 30 mins, placing energy and focus on the afflicted area, and with the aid of the element, and the power of the mind, and the loving intention, all three will then cause the healing to occur. M005 A6

See that if one is attempting to heal the self in an environment that is not healthy, not healing, but incredibly stressful, of course this healing just simply cannot take place.

When one is in hospital the only thing they need to focus on is that they might be healed and for this reason recoveries can be made, especially if one understands the nature of the universe and that it is a vibration. Then in this hospital one can bring their crystals, their necessary frequencies that will allow the environment to become more spiritual, one can make their little room very vibrant, one can build a micro-climate, a micro-environment entirely focused on the changing or the healing effect and this will produce results very quickly.

But see if one is working, taking care of children, having arguments with their spouse and all the other things around, would it not be understandable that healing of any kind would simply not take place? M005 A7

The Chi of Food

For some entities they do this thing called work, and this work thing requires that they have a diet that supplies them with enough energy to do heavy activities, thus one would eat heavy meat as you would understand the same. That would be similar to the athlete and entities who need something that lasts within their physical being, however dearest ones, for those entities that are seeking those higher forces as you would understand them, there has to be a diet of aliveness, or that quality of an aliveness that is not found in a dead organism like a chicken as you would understand these organisms.

That significance therefore of a vegetable is its basic abundance of electricity, that within the cells of the vegetable there is electricity moving, circulating and vibrating. *That vegetable held* within your palm is a mini ball of electricity, a plasma ball within the hand of the self. Take for instance the human composed of cells, cells which hold millivolts of energy, electricity's, millivolts of voltage; that is very similar to a potato for instance, or an orange, or whatever vegetable or fruit you would refer to, the hand holds that organism which within its cells has those little millivolts of energy, then you would have millions of cells as you would understand, an uncountable amount which in a basic quality would yield a certain amount of energy.

When it comes to those differences between something like chicken and a vegetable, you would find that the vegetable not only has packets of energy within its cells, it also has a certain quality of energy that exists in a more subtle dimension to which you may refer to as Chi, as we are going to use this term, which is a quality of energy that is not atomic, but rather etheric or non-atomic. This energy alongside the cellular electricity is absorbed in the physiology and supplies the body with Chi energy, however the Chi energy of the chicken is less than the Chi energy of a vegetable or fruit.

So why would one prefer a diet of vegetables?

Only but for one reason, that entity requires an abundance of Chi energy flowing through them in the consumption of the same, whereas with meaty foods the Chi energy slowly depletes over time as the soul of the departing animal goes into the inner planes.

Vegetables and fruit have the quality of Chi even when the entity, to which would be a vegetable or fruit, is disconnected from that that would supply it with its structure. J+021 A1

It would be understood that that life-force that would be the electrical kind, would be the components of the photon that are swimming within the cells of the potato, or whatever fruit or vegetable you prefer. This has a basic amount of voltage, then at the more subtle or hyper-dimensions or hyper-densities, you would have that being mirrored in those densities, thus when you consume the food, in the non-local space you are also consuming the Chi that is apparent and present in those hyper-densities and dimensions.

That is a way to explain this energy, the potato organism, or fruit, or whatever word you may use to describe the vegetable has subtle bodies similar to how a human does. J+021 A3

Meat is the equivalent of what would be called a lump of steel in comparison to the lighter food stuffs that are found in plant-based matter. The digestion of such a dense object, one so heavily packed, and in equal the relative toxicity of this compound, is what causes the greater issues in the spiritual circuitry of the body as the spiritual circuitry works that many times harder diverting electrical current, as could be termed, to the stomach and other areas such as the auto-immune system where this energy could have been less utilised if the meat had not been consumed.

Therefore, similar to *switching* a phone or computer from power saver where the extra battery may be used for the more spiritual practices, meat will put the body into overdrive, and will equally harm it so the electrical or spiritual circuitry is thus diverted and distorted as it has to deal with a mess - like organising pieces of sand into something that ought to resemble something as complicated as the physical body. It is a lot of work to get through meat. Q013 A2

Let us continue with that discussion then of that Chi as you would understand the same for what you have in a city are typically dead floating organisms, floating dead skin cells, floating dead debris, but in the country oh no, instead there is floating healthy bacteria teeming with Chi and life, which when breathed in fills the body directly with Chi energy, life-force as you would understand for you are quite literally absorbing abundances of energy from the air itself, for the air is undisturbed and thus within the air the microcosm itself, the atmosphere as you would understand, becomes its own ecosystem where micro-organisms of a size so small thrive in healthy ways and when breathed in, their own Chi, their own energy, is food to the physiology.

City dwellers breathing in dead debris, dead things, are used to a diet of death in their air. Upon going to the countryside, the bacteria teeming with life-force and vibrancy, the gentle Chi in the air just as well is beginning to be absorbed into the physiology of said entity causing that entities basic level of vibration to increase quite rapidly. This causes incompatibility with any basic illness or subconscious distortions apparent in the entity, these flush out and cause the entity to become ill, as what is being flushed out and replaced is that negative energy, being simply replaced with positive. In the sense that negative would be more in the bad moral kind of unhealthy sense, and positive being reference to that of closer to the God-Head as you would understand.

It is to be well understood that the countryside as it is termed, is a side of life whereby the air is thriving with life, with Chi as you would understand. Having a diet of vegetables does one thing, many things in fact but one main thing, it fills you with Chi. Eating dead organisms, even like a chicken, whilst could supply you with some means to do work, is not recommended for one who seeks spiritual growth. Thus, when one finds themselves on a diet of vegetables, they find themselves growing in their basic levels of Chi, and when one finds themself breathing in the Chi and the healthy bacteria that is swimming through the air, one finds that the candle that is their Chi energy becomes rather ginormous, which thus extends how long they will live and also gives them a kind of happiness and wellbeing that is rare upon your plane at this time. J+021 A2

It is best to consume naturally occurring vitamins within natures garden, nature produces its medicines such that there are chemical constituents and predesigned aspects that cause the digestion of the vitamins to not only be harmonious, but the various chemical constituents serve as a supporting factor to ensuring that the vitamins themselves are spread-out correctly; in comparison to refined laboratory medicines and vitamin packages, these lack natures ability to create easily digestible vitamins that sink into the digestive tract and through the bloodstream efficiently, for natures vitamins that you would find in say an orange, the vitamins are stored almost geometrically, to allow for the physical vehicle to grasp what it should be doing with said vitamin as it attempts to match the pattern into the pattern of the physical vehicle in relation to where the vitamin is needed. S064 A2

The body has a much easier time processing naturally occurring chemicals for the orange comes predisposed with aspects to the fruit itself that allow for the body to take in nutrients easily. The geometric nature of the orange matches well with the geometric nature of the digestive tract allowing for correct absorption of the vitamins in question. Refined chemicals do not have the same cellulose qualities that a fruit would, meaning there is a harsh and great difficulty with absorbing the chemicals as they are ingested in pill like fashion. S064 A3

All synthetic pills and the like have thus destroyed the natural geometry and quality to cell based life, there is no way to rebuild something that has been destroyed when the rebuilding process is a natural biological process. These have biological-chemical-electro vehicles, these need biological-chemical-electrical food stuffs. S064 A4

As much as juicing is a popular franchise in today's age, it is well that one would not juice in a way that it would completely tear the vegetables and the like, that the juicing would be quite chunky yet still, so there would be the recommendation that ice be used, ice serving as something to give the blades a job so that they do not cut the food stuffs too sharply. S064 A5

If humans were learned then wizened in practices on how to heal the body of its aliments, of how to cure self with basic techniques; medicines, pills, would be completely useless, yet we see greed and money, we see the powers wanting to maintain these companies making people reliant on vitamins and these things so that they can make a profit, so that they can live happily ever after in no man's land, it is all very selfish, there's no love here, no love. There is no competence, no intelligence, no reason, no logic, completely bland and empty of the same, we stand by strongly the power of the mind, we stand by strongly God's force, we stand by strongly the power of love.

We are not here to influence your free will, we are only giving our opinion that these things to us and only to us, once again to not influence your free will, we do not agree. M007 A17

Sugar

Abstaining from sugar is most likely the greatest asset or thing the adept could do, for the one who abstains from sugar becomes able to take hold of their vital energy and use it how they will.

Sugar like most drugs cause vital energies to become random, sporadic, ad hoc and erratic, the removal of this from the system allows one's conscious mind to begin to direct the vital energy that is naturally produced through the process of digestion of what nature has given you, being the vegetables, the unedited fruits, and if need be, those meats.

Here it is understood that if you want to truly understand your own energy, your own vital energy dearest one, you will abstain from sugar, however if you want to live on this drug then it will never become clear to the self what self's vital energy really is.

Your vital energy is sentient so long as you do not drug it, however if the vital energy is drugged you become akin to the one who drinks alcohol, the one who takes psilocybin drugs, psychoactive compounds, you become akin to any entity who causes their vital energy to become erratic, uncontrolled and unkempt, and such entities will complain of all issues not realising that the consumption of these compounds such as drugs, and we include sugar in this, is what's causing these many issues. S082 A5

When an entity lives off sugar, makes a portion of their diet sugar, the body becomes accustomed to utilising sugar for the processes of metabolism, of course if sugar is not in the vehicle and one is consuming normal food, how is one to metabolise something without its supply of energy?

Thus, you find entities having soda whilst they eat their food. It is most problematic to eat and to not have the energy to digest it unless you have a soda, unless you have dessert as you would understand, and even then, in comparison to using your natural vital energy, the vitality sugar gives you is disordinate, disharmonious and unnatural for the body. As the body attempts to use this extremely incoherent energy for the process of digestion, it is no wonder the body struggles and cannot do it properly, and then you come off sugar, the body then produces natural coherent, beautiful vital energy, that can be extremely fine-tuned in its production, that the process of metabolism, the breaking down of food, becomes several times more efficient. Thus, it becomes no real surprise that entities who pause the consumption of sugar find that they digest food far better. S082 A7

We track the digestive process; the sugar is consumed, its latent chemical structure is useful to the body as an instant energiser, it is then metabolised by the cells and turnt into energy within the mitochondria and varying other organelles in the cell that are quite useful for the creation of energy, and then the energy finds itself coursing through the body.

However, this energy is an alien within the vehicle, the vehicle does not necessarily desire these things for it is but the same or similar to what you would call ethanol, or your alcoholic compounds, or any stimulant of drug. The body burns some of the energy and tries to rid itself of the other, through the use of the liver and the pancreas.

The body is quite allergic naturally to sugar, although most entities would not realise this for they are born in a Western civilisation which prides itself, quite admirably in fact, on worshipping an anti-Christ, an idol you see. S082 A6

Many of your Western civilisations in their practices as you would understand, worship the hedonistic ways of pleasure and pleasure seeking, as well as those practices of caring only for the 'I' rather than the 'We', negating the needs of the other in replacement for the self, being concerned only with one's own financial situation, for it becomes a survival of the fittest, the most wealthiest, rather than the consideration for other selves and their predicaments at a more metaphysical level rather than how much money they have.

Western society worships anti-Christ in the form of idols, each have their own illusion, their own idols, all unique, none of them the true nature of life, thus you have variety of course, distractions, a different genre for each entity on your Netflix programs, all unique illusions pertaining to the entities anti-Christ like experiences, but all idols are the anti-Christ until one recognises that the illusion is afoot and is willing to be with God in whatever way you seek to manifest the same. S082 A10

God has all the energy you need, has supplied it to you with nature which Western civilisation has convoluted. Within nature resides what you would understand as fruits yes, but your fruit that you buy in your grocery stores is not anything as it used to look like, which you will appreciate as you revisit the history of fruit, its relative smallness, and its slight and only ever so slight sweetness but aromatic taste which made it pleasurable to eat. A fruit is not a sugary snack, it is a compound that is high in vitamins, very good for the vehicle in small quantities, especially boiled, eaten raw in some cases. Good for drinks, a herb in many cases. S082 A6

It is to be aware that your fruits have been tampered with, your vegetables too yes. We find the condition of the human which for whatever reasons believes that fruit is healthy needs to be addressed, for a lot of your fruit as you would understand has been heavily genetically modified to be sweet without their seeds. We find farms desiring to create products sellable for profit such that companies, one would be supermarkets, would stock their shelves and sell the same again for a markup as you would term it. But what sells is what tastes good, and in this simple algorithm genetic modification becomes desirable for an increased sale of such a product. Fruits are sweet now, thus serve as sweets now, they have lost their truer identity in recent times for they were medicinal vitamins that were digestible and not chemical tasting as your supplements are. It was a way for a human to derive its necessary vitamins in an enjoyable manner whereby there was a citrusy flavour of some kind to mask the taste of the vitamins as you would understand.

Such fruits have lost their medicinal value and have been replaced with flavour, thus only a few fruits remain that have retained some of their truer qualities as you would find the berries and the avocado, as you would find the smaller fruits that are not sweet and simply taste, might we say, normal to the trained tastebuds, for nothing should be more sweet then a soft drink, yet your oranges and such have become the same.

Fruit was medicinal, now it is a snack. Fruit *was* medicinal, this is to be well understood, when fruit is eaten it is to be for a medicinal purpose, refrain from eating fruit for energy for this is the greatest issue with those who claim to be healthy for they eat fruit but are in truth unaware and ignorant and are lying to themselves. One who eats fruit for energy is no different from the entity who consumes a pack of biscuits as you would understand. Q008 A10

You would find that the intuition is able to tap into the fruit and see that the fruit is well, which will be most obvious based on the sweetness of the fruit for one can instantly tell whether a fruit has been modified if it is sweet, for fruits were a citrus, slightly sour and a little bit sweet in their nature, whereas now they are sweet. So it is to simply be aware that fruits that are sweet to the degree that the entity would be very aware of how sweet it is, then this fruit would be avoided. Idealistically fruits should be no sweeter than you would find in a slightly sour berry. Q008 A11

You would find once again that the body does not so much enjoy at all sugar but has been conditioned to sugar due to your Western standards. One must learn to live off their own vital energy, learning how to control this vital energy will make you extremely happy, thus the process of removing sugar from the diet will bring the body into a great joy as it finally gets rid of this very disguised poison which pretends to be your friend.

The tastebuds change over time as they adjust to not having sugar, even one's saliva can become sweet when one avoids the consumption of this product for the taste buds become sensitive to anything that is sugar like. To the degree that even something with a slight amount of sugar packs its kick as you would understand. S082 A6

It is to consider the unnaturalness of energy derived from sugar, you would compare it in the sense of an analogy, to fuel that when burnt burns in an incredibly incoherent way, yielding results that are extremely undesirable for the conscious and subconscious mind. It is akin to using a pickaxe to mend an object, the tool is no good for the process, thus when there comes the removal or absence from the sugary compounds, there comes the production of natural vital energy which is several times more sentient, several times more appropriate for the job. Alive is this vital energy in comparison to the deadness of sugary energy, and this alive vital energy coursing through the body supplies the body with Prana, much needed in your society and is extremely useful for every single process in the body. S082 A9

As you would hold a nugget of sugar within the palm it looks tasty, especially in sweet form, in its distortions as you would understand, but here you are in essence completely replacing the energy production system of the body which has the capability of the invention of a nuanced energy called Chi or Prana if you will. The body is able to synthesise Prana, within the aspects of the cell that are very fine, but if one consumes sugar at the levels that most entities are of this day, such a subtle and very delicate process such as the production of Prana or Chi cannot happen, for sugar in its deleterious nature harms the cells for reasons described in significant detail in the write up which has been edited with this information already. *(This detailed write up expands on sugar and can be read at www.YouSpiritually.com/blog)*

Thus, it would be good for an entity to read such a thing to have a deeper comprehension of the same, and as far as our information goes on such a subject, it would be well to understand that a cell is able to create not only vitality for the physical vehicle, but vitality that the soul can use for extremely advanced activities.

In order for Prana to be produced in the body the cells must be receiving... yes... home cooked food stuffs which are carefully selected. You would find of course, carbohydrates, fibres, proteins and as you would term them fats, being of a good nature. The proteins should be relatively simple such as you would call it chicken or even fish, and we should note that indeed a human is able to be a vegetarian if a human wishes to derive the most Prana from a meal, which could be used then to access higher states of consciousness which would require the removal of meat protein, which can be replaced with other protein sources if needed. Protein however we see as unnecessary, one is able to live without the consumption of the same, but protein is easily assimilated in the nut form should one need protein, and so having a pack of nuts is very good for the body for they supply the body with the protein that it would otherwise need.

A diet without meat protein is possible and good in truth for the generation of this extremely nuanced energy which requires totally un-inflamed, un-overworked and rhythmic cells which are not being harmed by the consumption of sugar. Q008 A8

What does an athlete burn when they run?

Firstly sugar and then fat, this is the nature of life and how your biological vehicle works, it burns sugar and then fat, if you feed the biological the sugar it will burn the sugar so long as there is sugar to burn. Not necessarily ever having an opportunity to burn the fat, and so what happens to the body? It gains weight. This is only natural you see.

If you remove sugar from your diet and go to a normal diet of two to three meals a day, so long as there is minimal to no sugar in the diet, as much as you can remove with fair reason given, then you will find the weight will fall off over the course of what we perceive as two to three years, which is a very normal and healthy pace to lose weight, for we find in your society people lose weight a little too fast which is never really good for the body, the body likes to lose weight slowly so it can keep up with its cellular activities in the correct format or speed.

It is to be noted that this time frame is relative, it will be shorter dependent on age, metabolism and other factors such as exercise regime. This two-to-three-year balanced pace was based on a female that was progressively dieting from the 19 stone mark.

Just as weight takes time to gradually accumulate, it is also recommended to decrease it progressively as this gives the cells the correct time to adjust and avoid sagging skin along with other such side-effects. Here cutting sugar would naturally cause the required weight loss without the necessity for additional methods, such as exercise.

So what does it mean to not have sugar in the diet?

It means to not necessarily consume sugary dense compounds, to avoid the same, to avoid the grossness of your society and how much it has monopolised sugary treats and sugary things.

You may find interest in replacing the consumption of meat or those other kinds of fish with the consumption of protein substitutes that are found in nature. You would find them organically in all kinds of food for protein is available even in an orange, there is protein in everything for everything is formed of protein. It is more so how much protein you would like, and then most vegetables supply protein, if there need be extra protein you can find it in bean like substrates, you can also find protein in those nut-like substrates, or things dense in fibre that look almost milky, like a banana or an oat like substance or meal.

Proteins are available everywhere, you can find them for all things are created of protein, then you can source your protein from vegetables and such things. If you would like to know what vegetables are suitable for consumption use your intuition to tell whether something obviously contains too much sugar that you could hardly call it a vegetable, although most vegetables upon your plane are completely fine.

Enjoy your rice's and such other things, but when it is that your meal is finished dearest one, when you have finished your meal, the meal is done and you will wait idealistically until the appropriate hour to eat again, and then you will not eat anymore because then really you are now eating food out of the joy for eating food, rather than eating food for its purpose, and whilst it is enjoyable to consume food products one must not become the slave to food, become a slave to tastebuds, become a slave to senses, do not become sensual, become sensible. S085 A13

We become aware of the fact that perhaps one of the biggest reasons that entities upon this plane struggle with spirituality could possibly be due, not just to the lack of meditation, to the lack of spiritual practices, but simply due to the body being so inanimate by disease. Many entities upon your plane are overweight, riddled with diseases, are unhealthy, eat not good food, it is having a drastic effect on the weight of vibration of the Astral body.

Eat pure and eat well, and you will find a lot of spirituality comes natural to you, for the Astral body is not so taxed in having to constantly repair the molecular vibration of the physical body. S093 A16

The cells are conscious, thus they have their own operative system, they are adaptive and respond to their own internal environmental factors, when sugar is absent the cells in their sentience can figure this out and then begin the production of certain proteins, you would call them enzymes which serve to breakdown proteins and fat, and other compounds such as carbohydrates and various other fibrous like materials into vital energy.

This process for the cells to come to this understanding is more so connected to how one is connected to their vehicle, for an entity with great prowess this connection and switching off process happens naturally within 24hrs. For entities who are not well connected to their vehicles it can take more than 3 days. In rare cases more than 5 days, it varies but at a maximum of 7 gruelling days of suffering, for it can be this way, finally the cells can come to learn that no more sugar will be in the diet thus there is no use in waiting, and there is only use in the production of the proteins required for the consumption or rather metabolism of good food. S082 A8

Now it would be well to seriously consider that it might be possibly a good idea to find a way to create a diet that is extremely harmonious for the body. You will find simply in the reconfiguring of the diet, that many issues that may be occurring with the atomic vehicles ability to operate start to fix themselves. It is never really that an entity need exercise as such, but more so that an entity eat well, then one finds the ability or desire to exercise is a very natural occurrence when one is eating well firstly. And when one is eating well the vital energy becomes sentient so one can direct it in meditation, and when the Sun beams on the self when one is in the park or looking at the pleasurable sights of nature in trees, walking through forests or having a picnic, it all comes together into a nice, beautiful, vibrant experience of the joy of the One Infinite Creator. S082 A21

Many entities are not aware of how sugar and things such as this, even the light from their phones affects their ability to sleep, therefore when an entity avoids any kind of light in the evening and alters the amount of sugar in their diet, as well as the other things as you would understand, they wake up earlier naturally, the curtains are always open naturally, many things are just simply because your instincts are awakening, those instincts that connect you directly to nature itself, the awakening of these instincts through the making of the body more endowed with instinctual things, the memories of vegetables, of proteins or chicken food stuff as you would term it, all instinctual processes come to the self when the self no longer lives off dead, processed sugary snacks. S082 A22

All is known to the selves, it is always worth some serious consideration that one seek to imagine what life was like before there was ever cities, then you can learn of your true nature. Think back to your tribal times, think back to your times when you were in a different portion of the world whereby cities were not a thing, but living of the land and the lands goodness was.

It's within you dearest brothers, if you can awaken those memories then you will know why things do not work out as you would want them to, waking up in the morning feeling groggy, as you term it. S082 A23

Now we would see into the nature of the indigenous mind, being that of a mind whereas the intellectual throttle, the intellect itself is hardly on and so they come across as one would call them, dumb, inferior, but when life is a subconscious experience it is a special experience indeed and so they had eyes to see the greater forces, they had the soul-body active enough to feel the cycles of life, the eb and flow of nature, when the rains would come or when to expect future Earth tremors.

They were incredibly tapped into nature itself; they understood the tide of animals, they could feel when the birds were giving birth to new babies, they could even feel the quality of their crops within the Earth through their feet and how they were doing. When one is so tapped into nature it overloads the senses you see, if the senses are overloaded intellectual babble is quite impossible because the information they are receiving, the intelligence itself is already being calculated for them so they do not have to calculate it themselves.

One could imagine doing a test where all the answers are already on the paper, this is how an indigenous person would experience life, all the answers are already on the paper, they can simply see the

answers rather than have to use the intellectual mind to figure it out. M013 A7

These beings, these individuals, these souls in human bodies, having realised they are souls in human bodies, have begun that experience of evolution tapping into the higher frequencies where thought becomes experiential and where things manifest before one's eyes as seen in the book read within the mind as a memory *(Of Water and the Spirit – Malidoma Somé)*, a book of the man who lived in the tribe, the Dagara tribe you see.

And it is so that these recognise so deeply their identity that they resonated here, of a completely different level of consciousness, seeing life not the same as the average westerner would see life, you see. S048 A10

Entities are not motivated to work and get out of bed to go to work, they are almost forced to by environmental circumstances, thus they condition their body to something that it is not meant for and start to think that this way of experiencing life is actually normal.

This is not the case, what is normal for an entity is to get out of bed when the vital energies of their surroundings cause light to funnel into the membranes of the eyes, creating the conditions of electricity in the brain causing wakefulness as you would understand. This is a nature like occurrence which indicates that dawn is approaching, or rather the morning as we would offer this term, and that the morning would be a day of preparation for the gathering of grown food stuffs, the working together as a tribe and the creating of a condition of life and food, dance and joy.

Yet what you would find in your western culture is something akin to a complete lack of this, a complete lack of community, of togetherness, of extraverted activities and family like structures so entities find themselves feeling down, groggy as you would term it, and this would be one aspect of this many faceted experience of grogginess.

When it comes to the apex, that it has learnt that things such as the social aspects of life, the interactions, the getting up, the being outside, the running about, the experience of being in the Sun, the aspect of the Sun waking you up as the morning strikes and light filters into your eyes. When this is understood, the importance of being outside, when it is understood that the diet is of very great significance to the vehicle, and when it is understood that all these can be connected deeply to meditation, as one learns how to have more of an ability to control the vital energy, then can be the three tendrils of spiralling light, which all converge at a point creating great vitality and motivation for life in general.

However, if it is so that these things are somewhat ignored, then there is always going to be the condition of grogginess as you would understand. Grogginess does not come with age; it comes with slight inaccuracies in how one functions which all can be amended.

Now it is time to endow the body with health and vibrancy. These are some of the aspects of what you call ageing as you would understand this term, which can be utterly and completely mitigated with a balance between meditation and eating well and being in the Sun when it is Summer. These three things really do work, almost like the Trinity as you would understand. S082 A21

Healing With Energy

'Mental health really here is the most important thing, if one can focus just on this first then the technology, the biological technology can awaken.'

Prayer

Always say a prayer of protection before you begin any divine service, prayers of protection are not merely words vocalised into an environment, what humans have here to understand is their atmosphere, the atomic atmosphere, vibrates according to the words you speak, but the words you speak cause remnants of memory to reside in the atmosphere after they are spoken, thus the atmosphere becomes a crystal, something that holds memory.

When you speak a prayer in mind or out loud you invoke into the room divinity, divine memory; entities that would seek to be of the negative kind cannot exist in such an environment for they cannot handle the vibrations that are present, so in terms of the beginning process of your healing experience give a little prayer of protection, any kind, call an entity to which you resonate with, it doesn't matter how you do it so long as you do it. J+012 A5

In prayer where one becomes capable of crystalising the pranic atmosphere, this has many uses, people use it all the time and if one is to walk into a church with suitable vision, spiritual vision that is, they would see a multitude of magnificent colours and beauty all of which resemble Jesus the Christ. 'Channelling On Astral Projection'

It is indeed the case that the atmosphere can crystalise based on intention or impression, how the mind would impress into the atmosphere, thoughts, ideas, beliefs and energy, however if a soul be so strong its very essence can impress a crystal into the atmosphere which is the protection itself. Many entities need to sing a song, do a ritual, to produce the crystal in the atmosphere for the ritual has power, the song has power, the prayer has power to the subconscious mind of the entity, and if the subconscious mind takes hold of something it has a great more amount of power then does the conscious mind, and when the subconscious mind uses its power to instil a thought into the atmosphere it creates an extremely strong crystal as you would understand. It is so that if the subconscious mind of an entity and the conscious mind therefore are one and the same, an entity has infinite power and need not crystallise the atmosphere with prayer, but can do the same with thought alone. S085 A5

That Armour of God is but the ability to have a greatly unified state of consciousness. How might one say it?

It is that the thought of one is powerful enough to protect thine self. In other words, one's consciousness is of such quality that the surrounding atmosphere crystalises creating quite a literal armour. S086 A6

To explain 'The Armour of God' I shall be paraphrasing from the works of Paul Solomon and Ephesians 6:10-18.

The Armour of God is a protective device created from the qualities of truth, peace, righteousness, purpose, faith and spirit. It is an armour that is cast and created in the flames of the desire that burns in the hearts of those that yearn to know God, an armour cast by God, from love, that protects against that which is not love.

Your Root Chakra holds the dynamic power of life, of healing, of reproduction, so gird your loins as this power point can be wrapped in the belt armour of truth, and the truth shall set you free, allowing you to be honest, straight and direct, able to focus that raw energy toward higher things.

The war to win the peace of mind is an internal battle. For feet that walk in the armour of peace, good mental health is the key, clarity of thought and coherence are essential, as energy follows the mind.

Righteousness refers to integrity, this covers the heart and protects it. Integrity is being one with yourself, integrated, all parts brought together in unity, moving in one direction, single in purpose. You have one place you are going, and nothing can or will stop you. This armour of righteousness is a purpose driven life that is impenetrable, for the heart is safeguarded by integrity so the battle is already won.

Faith is the act of knowing, faith is the shield of this armour, it is not hoping or wishing, those are negatives, they are maybes, affirmations that you do not already have what you are hoping and wishing for. Faith is an invocation of expectancy, knowing that it is coming because you have called it forth in your nature as a creator, this is your shield.

The spirit is the sword, it is the nature of the Christos, it is living love, it is a sword that cuts both ways. Misuse these divine powers and you will cut yourself, for divine power is not gained by building yourself up at other people's expense. Used for the right purposes which is always love, then the sword works for you, with you, and you are able to wield this sword of the spirit by invoking the nature of living love, the nature of the Christ force within you to guide, empower and build yourself up as a true spark of the divine.

Finally, to complete 'The Armour of God' we have the helmet of salvation, the crown of enlightenment, where we experience brain integration and transcendence, the alignment with the creative force itself, a point when our energy has reached the level of crystallisation and the atomic body is able to respond to the crystalised structure of the quantum physiology, and become capable of absorbing that light, that pure tone energy coming from infinity.

This is an armour built out of love that can withstand all forces. It is not the security of a big bank balance, or a secure alarm system, or some guns and an overly protective cousin with a quick temper.

This is a security born of thought, where your consciousness has achieved a unified state of quality and coherence so dynamic that it can crystallise. The Armour of God is when true security through singleness of thought that is aligned with the infinite has been achieved.

In the practice of meditation, we are actually partaking in a mind exercise that brings us closer to the activation of this armour. Our mind has much more vitality to work with since the simple act of closing the eyes and sitting still, turns off many activities in the muscles and organs that function for stress and wakefulness.

With that extra vitality we are able to then begin to practice manually manipulating the electricity in the brain, training it to become ultra-responsive to our consciousness. Through practice we learn how to control the electricity that neurons are generating, which can then generate altered states of consciousness, and the various expansions that altering the focusing of the electricity in the brain gives.

For the average person like me, and most of you I would guess, we are learning to become harmonious in meditation, to profoundly relax and slow down the electrical activity in our brain manually with our consciousness. We first learn how to control our levels of happiness, creating states of bliss in our brain to make the present moment enjoyable and fun, learning how to directly face and redefine thoughts so that stress hormones are not produced, because harmony is the gateway to the exciting stuff.

Then, through consistent practice, some are able to supercharge the brain, speeding up the electromagnetic activity, for the adepts have learnt to perfect their control over the electrical chemistry of the brain, as when you are perfectly harmonious and there is no entropy, disorderliness or incoherence, focusing is easy, which allows them to use this focus to activate latent parts of the brain, so much so that if you were to measure their brainwaves on an EEG the activity of their meditative state would appear to be many more times awake then people actively walking around, allowing them to achieve feats of a higher nature, meditation then being the gateway to learning how to consciously control electricity.

We can control our muscles and that's wonderful, I love running, jumping and doing the odd cartwheel here and there, muscles are great - but learning how to utilise our consciousness to control the brain, this powerhouse composed of electromagnetic activity guised as chemistry, well if we learn to control that then a wonderful life with some quite profound experiences lays in store.

We will use water memory as an example, and advise readers to independently investigate the works of minds such as Luc Montagnier, Dr Emoto Masaru and Viktor Schauberger to get a deeper understanding, as that topic is an entire book within itself.

All is one and there is no separation between the water and the human consciousness, but this omnipresent consciousness that is everywhere takes on unique forms and if there is the act of love, of sharing, of giving, then one portion of consciousness can alter another, be it water or anything, for what makes one think water is any different from the atmosphere that surrounds them?

See, water and this word, 'electricity' are no different from each other. All around you is electricity, negativity diminishes the vibrancy, the prowess and power of electricity, and so if water is exposed to negativity it becomes less electric and more stagnant. If people were to surround water in a circle and continuously increase in frequency and praise those things of gratitude, harmony, bliss and love, the water would become incredibly healing and electrically charged, and yes it would be measurable indeed. S025 A2

Drink it and enjoy the vitalising of the body that comes with drinking such potent and electrically charged water and see then how it effects one, how positive one feels, how wonderful one feels. There will be such a deep level of appreciation of life you see, celebrate brothers, celebrate. Celebrate love, realise you are truly one with all. Mind is truly the builder you see, and love be the tool, more than the tool but everything, for bringing creative influence to love will yield infinite results. S025 A7

The more people doing it, of course will yield larger results for it is a cooperative act, an act of brothers and sisters coming together to love and to build a relationship with their own creative force. With the God, and the Love, and the Christ that resides, directly within, throughout and everywhere. S025 A6

We see this word, 'light', this word 'vibration', even the word 'atmosphere', then we would even go as far as to say that the scientific nature of thought is exactly what science is studying for thought is everything, it is everywhere, it is what connects all things together for we exist in one mind. S031 A6

One thought of love, expressing itself in a multitude of ways to facilitate an incredible learning experience for the Higher-Self to bask in, for the Higher-Self to grow, to evolve, to experience more and more of the indescribable nature, the unfathomable nature of God. S031 A7

Thought is the creative power of which all sons of God inherit and it is through this power, it is through this medium, that you can and are able to create and experience life as you see fit. For if there was no thought, thought power, there would be no universe. S031 A5

Organic Meditation

Will speak on something that almost bypasses this, that there would be within you the belief that there might be a technique out there that would work immaculately in the same way that one would play basketball and find the perfect technique of landing the shots. When one has a suitable amount of faith in a technique, it empowers. If something sounds completely sense making, it empowers within one. But here we have to comment on the fact that it is not so much about the technique itself, but the technique as we have mentioned before is vital.

Techniques are important but faith in the technique is what drives it you see.

Then there must be the finding of a technique that suits the reasoning of your own mind, if one can find something that resonates with them it will give them the necessary faith to produce measurable results within the experiential field. J+004 A9

Then we would say that if the entity believes that it is picking up thoughtforms along the day, then it is picking up thoughtforms along the day! If an entity believes that showering will remove such thoughtforms, then literally showering will remove the thoughtforms, in so much a literal way that it should be of interest to this entity, the process of hypnotism and this entity should have a look on YouTube, all of the people being hypnotised into believing they are all sorts of things, it is the power of consciousness you see. J+023 A19

We simply say, you are an electrical being filled to the brim with energy, think of yourself in terms of energy, in terms of vibration. If you want to increase in frequency, it only means that one would meditate on the positivity of life, would practice the same and so one would increase in vibration and see past the veil, see what is beyond. S025 A12

Here we must see firstly emotions, for it is the negative emotions that are the trap and we could hardly call them emotions, for they are more like very condensed stagnant energy, much like pollution in the waters poisoning the field that an individual might produce. The only real emotions that are true, the only real energy that is in motion is of those things that are of the positive frequency, of the positive vibration, for here in these realm's energy moves in a very fast and coherent fashion. M005 A1

What could be done about this, is that entities ought to recognise that if they were to distil themselves, such as you would purify water, let us use your River Thames for it is heavily polluted. If you took the water from the River Thames and you purified it, this would be the distilling process. Now what if we took you out of the planetary system of Earth and distilled you of all negative vibration so that only the most positive versions of you would remain, how happy would you be?

You would be extremely happy, extremely happy, it is unfortunate how happy you would be, and is mostly the reason why many wanderers upon your plane desire suicide, they remember how happy they used to be but due to the toxic vibrations of your planet... you can think of the rest. J+017 A29

Inside all intelligent forms resides infinity itself, this is why we look within to find out more about the One Infinite Creator God.

The practice of meditative experience in which one simply sits with one's eyes closed, that the thoughts can be allowed to organise themselves. Thought energy is energy such the same as any kind of energy, thought energy has the capacity or the ability to organise itself so long as it is what the soul desires when in the experience of intense thought, if one simply sits within this energy and allows it to organise, it becomes such that the mind becomes creatively possible of being completely pointed, one, whole, and without incoherence. S073 A1

Now to even achieve this degree of enlightenment first there would be the necessity that the health at the mental level be appropriate, for if you lock one in a cage and tell them to meditate, they may find the sharpest object instead. Many people do not have the degree of evolution as yet to go on a true spiritual retreat and retreat into the depths of their consciousness to unlock genetics, organs and dimensions and subtle bodies within them.

Mental health really here is the most important thing, if one can focus just on this first then the technology, the biological technology can awaken. J+001 A7

It is attained in at least three stages:

The 1st stage would be recognition.

The 2nd stage would be acceptance.

The 3rd stage would be action.

One recognises firstly, then accepts what they have recognised without any pressure on the self, any blame on the self, any guilt on the self. Then one begins to action, and action, and action, until it simply becomes habitual, until they can never look back, and be happy to look forward and be at least present in the activities they are doing.

So it is obtained in these three steps and then what can one expect?

Clarity of mind, peace! True inner peace with their life and their life situation, never looking back, never comparing themselves. Oh, humans do this! Always the comparison, the comparison, his life is not like mine etc.

Clarity of mind, peace with one's life situation, recognition that this is the path ye signed up for and absolute tranquillity in the experience of the same. It would be as though one is simply floating through the experience, one after the other and this is what one can expect when they have completely gotten out of a linear being mindset. Peace... peace and clarity.

Breath work is very good here, if you do good breath work you could obtain very peaceful states of being and if you can build this point of reference of what peace feels like then you could build it for yourself in your own mind. J+001 A9

Yet to understand the subtilty of such a wonderful practice would take much text, many words, much explanation, thus to avoid having to explain the many subtleties of this practice you would simply look towards the one you would call your son.

For this one as you would refer to him as the entity Jordan, experiences coherent brain energy, thus has an activated 3rd eye and this allows him to have concentration abilities that would exceed the average human, thus allowing him to be capable of meditating for upwards of several hours, more than 7 as you would see it, whereas many entities upon this plane would not be able to sustain these levels of brain energies in a coherent pattern for such an extended period of time, thus there would be somewhat of a difference as you would understand it, a truthful difference, an honest difference, not to cause disheartence between the relationship of these two that would be competitive, but instead to demonstrate what practice does, for this is an emanation as you would see it, of practice, for this is what practice begets, it begets results.

It is a practice in which this one put any kind of technique aside and purely allowed his brain energies as you would see them, his thought energy to organise itself over a period of time, he done this in the Daoist way of effortlessness, of complete surrender and serenity, of the one who would let go of the saucepan and stirring spoon, who would put down any tools and would simply allow his brain energy, his thought energy to organise itself. S073 A13

This process of Organic Meditation serves to reconfigure one's energetic matrix, one's consciousness matrix, one's being, it serves to make vibrations that are dissonant, consonant. It serves to make vibrations that are dis-ordinant, co-ordinant, and in this way one removing dis-ordinant vibrations and increasing co-ordinant vibrations, or rather consonant vibrations, finds their density increasing.

The reason why Organic Meditation works is because when the soul is faced with its own ego directly it has no choice but to utilise its consciousness, its reconfigurative ability, its ability to pluck the strings of spirit, it has no choice but to use consciousness as a tool to reconfigure the mistakes, to reconfigure the insanity, to reconfigure the slowness, the lethargy and to increase it into something that is resonant of a beam of light vibrating so strongly, a gamma ray. J+023 A13

There would be an increase in harmony through the meditative practice of overcoming one's biases as could be understood. The simple practice of sitting with one's eyes closed, without necessarily the use of a method, would allow the naturally occurring thoughts of one's own consciousness to surface, thus as the fullness of the soul is surfaced in a linear fashion of auditory and imaginative thought there is the self thus examining the self. As each linear thought and visual concept is untied this creates harmony where there was once before knots, this untying process is the overcoming of biases that built the knots in the first place.

As this process happens and one obtains greater harmony, one's kundalini energy as a by-product naturally begins to untie and uncoil, as would be the coiled serpent being a tied knot that is not able to arise because the snake has got itself in a bit of a ruckus, as one could imagine. Q007 A8

Such would be seen as those currents finding expression through the channels, the pipe-like system of your physical vehicle and its more subtle forms. As this force, you may call it the kundalini, you may call it electricity, you may call it the spiritual currents, as they find passage through your body, they will continuously seek activation in more sophisticated ways. It is a matter of continuous practice which will allow these spiritual currents to finally find a way to become focused, coherent, one pointed. To make these spiritual currents one pointed is a matter of spiritual practice.

As they make their way through the body it may allow one to feel quite pleasant, quite well, can make someone feel quite relaxed. There can be many side-effects to the sensations one will feel but this experience of these energies moving through the body is these electricity's, these spiritual currents attempting to find a way to move.

Might you imagine then a piping system that has blocks everywhere and then an individual all to unfond of his job has to teeter and totter around with rake and reluctantly move all of the junk, for him it is a bad Monday but for your spiritual channels it is an incredible day of clearing. By the time the job has been done and completed you have a perfectly clear system, available and ready for greater spiritual work. S077 A2

It would be to recognise what ties the knot in the first place is one's own will, is one's own state of consciousness. The knot tying is caused by the self, thus in meditation this allows for one to enter into harmonious states of consciousness in which the knot can naturally untie itself. Not through observation but through becoming a being that could only be represented as incredibly harmonious, incredibly coherent, incredibly marvellous. To become one who is so deeply satisfied, unmoved, crystalised, satiated, tranquil. Q007 A7

As we would expand even on the tangling concept, you would understand that when an entity has an illness or a strife, that means in essence that their energetic vehicle is not working correctly.

Imagine for a moment that you were a car on the racetrack but there are people in the way taking pictures of you as you race by them, imagine the stress of knowing you are going to have to stop occasionally to avoid hitting one of the entities who are trying to take a picture of your vehicle.

Imagine you are on a racetrack and you are the car driving and there are blockages everywhere, the tarmac is not harmonious because there are holes within the track itself, now you have to adjust your course. When your course is adjusted, when people are in the way, when there are things obstructing your energetic flow, you can get tangled up into a little knot because you are having to take adverse routes and you may take a route that folds into itself and tangles itself up, causing the energy to stop. This causes entropy thus forth. J+019 A4

One may consider that one's quality of thought is directly akin to the 'kinds of thoughts' and the 'experience of thought' one is having. The 'experience of thought' is called emotion, the 'kinds of thoughts' are the kinds of thoughts which create the emotions themselves.

When one practices Organic Meditation, one begins to directly experience their emotions, their thoughts, and how those thoughts and emotions are causing them a degree of suffering, one may liken this to impurities in the Chakras causing the light funnelling through them to become diminished.

In Organic Meditation it becomes obvious what Chakras are diminishing the light that is shining through them, it becomes very obvious for there is an obvious displeasure with the meditative experience after a certain amount of time where one gets to the boundary in which one desires to wake up.

Let us make an analogy for you:

Why is it that when one meditates it lasts for a certain amount of time before one gets fed up of meditating?

Dearest one, in truth meditation should be an experience so delightful that being taken out of it is in fact the worst-case scenario.

The reason why is because meditation is an opportunity to close your eyes and shut everything off, and only pay attention to the God-Force, to the One Infinite Creator as may be termed, or if you prefer it gives one the opportunity to only pay attention to the Higher-Self, to the Over-Self, to that force of life and light that sits at the head, the God-Head as you would understand, as we find interest in the various expressions of this; then when one is sitting with God and a certain amount of time goes by they become quite fed up with sitting with God, and this would demonstrate directly and most obviously the quality of one's emotions and therefore one's thoughts, for if one is unable to sit with the One Infinite Creator without getting agitated, bored, or desiring stimulation from a distortion of the One Infinite Creator, then this means that one's connection with the One Infinite Creator is so minimal that they require some form of external stimulation to feel at wholeness or alrightness as you would understand. S081 A8

The function of forgiveness is to see something as God, as infinity, to give something that potential to be else, to grow and to develop, to not limit, to not make anything finite. Forgiveness thus is only something the self can give the self, you can only infinite yourself, you can only potentiate yourself, you can only love yourself, forgiveness is solely for the self.

To forgive the self is to become enlightened instantaneously for you have claimed your infiniteness in that moment. Forgiveness is to fore-give, that is to fore-give as in to give be-fore God your limitations, that God can enter in. If you are to understand what forgiveness looks like, you must look at the one who meditates, the one who meditates is the one who contemplates God, who believes in God, trusts God, who gives utter faith to God. The one who meditates is the one who is becoming living forgiveness itself, becoming living love itself, for in meditating are you not forgiving yourself, to become infinity? S069 A20

For the Christ, meditation was an opportunity to direct all attention to God, for the Christ much like how humans do it today, he would close his eyes and he would direct every ounce of his consciousness to the God-Head, and he would then sit, or lay, for as long as he was able to withstand the God-Force. Then when he felt as though he could take no more, that the energy of God was loving him so deeply that it could in fact be so much that he would disincarnate, then he would stop his meditation and walk, and do the things that one does in a life.

During this state of altered consciousness, he would be in a formidable bliss. Here we speak before the Christ attainment for after the Christ attainment, meditation was not necessary. The Christ attainment is an unfathomable state of consciousness. S069 A21

The purpose of meditation itself as seen, is but for the consciousness to have something soothing to focus on whether that is the breath, soothing harmonics, it can even be the Heart Chakra itself. Irregardless, this will cause the subconscious to recognise that there is something happening that is not in relation to the need to produce survival hormones and so instead the being can produce creative hormones, Christed, Christ-like chemicals to allow one to ascend into the higher dimensions of reality. Q004 A8

These Christ-like chemicals are the body's ability in the heightened states to naturally produce spiritual chemicals such as Oxytocin, Serotonin or even DMT. A pretty nice reward for simply closing one's eyes.

In this practice of Organic Meditation, you are facing your ego directly, this includes all of the things you have a negative relationship with, as negative relationships are fear-based relationships that lead to negative attachments, whether that is with a person, substance, activity or other.

Is your meditation filled with the negative influence of a nagging boss?

Or unresolved arguments with your significant others?

Or maybe it's impending coursework deadlines and looming exams?

Or those hard to kick addictions and cravings of all manners and types?

As you meditate organically it will become obvious what is limiting you, your negative attachments will present themselves quite clearly, maybe too clearly for some peoples liking. Your experience of these thoughts will be felt as an emotion, very literally energy in motion moving through you allowing for easy recognition of negative attachments. The word 'negative' is used in relation to all limiting ideas, beliefs or concepts that prevent you from falling deeply in love with self and becoming familiar with the infinite. Limitations block the production of those Christ-like chemicals, it is in this practice that you can directly face your own mind, and as you lose the attachments you may soon be able to sit in forgiveness toward even the most negative aspects of your experience. This a practice of compassion, it is a practice of experiencing yourself directly, removing power from your environment and giving power to yourself!

The ultimate form of overcoming emotions is to be able to sit with them and fear them not, opinion them not, obsess over them not. What is more powerful or forgiving than being with an emotionally challenging memory and feeling so comfortable around it, that it brings no discomfort at all. This is liberation from fear, liberation from a fear-based relationship and its negative attachments, for now you will have truly forgiven those memories.

If one were to locate only one negative thought and completely understand its origin to the core of its being, if they were to understand that all negative thoughts come from biases and all biases come from a dimension that is biased. If you were to have such a deep understanding of the origin of this negative thought and then you were to practice the act, the action, of not having it, then you are practicing meditation itself; you are practicing something greater then meditation, you are practicing the understanding that meditation is a mediator to contemplate God, to pour one's entire concentration on God. For to focus oneself on not having the thought, is to ask oneself where one's focus should be instead in the thinking activity.

If not *the* negative, then what is positive?

And if the only thing that is positive is creative, is infinite, is infinity itself, the God-Force, then meditating on this is where ones focus and concentration will go. S069 A24

In your experience of meditation never be pushy or hard on the self, always have compassion and love for self, enjoy the experience of the same and recognise that you can't really do meditation incorrectly.

The reason why people who experience daily meditation yield no results is because they are seeking something they do not understand, something that has not been defined in their consciousness. If the intention of one is not understood, then the subconscious cannot help that one attain the intention, you see?

Have the intention be understood in full, meditation will work for you!

The intention here is this, that these would simply experiment with their own consciousness, that these would begin to experience those experiences of Chakra activations, that these would begin to access dimensions of consciousness within them they may be becoming familiar with you see. Let this pervade the mind in the experience of meditation, it will yield results, and if it is done, that is meditation with constant practice on a daily basis, within the year these would know themselves to a degree that they would never worry ever again. S048 A16

Expect results every time you meditate, this might be the contrary to what you learn from your fellow teachers, but in each meditation you must go in with an expectation of results, but such results can only be attained if you go the whole way, each result you experience should be minute and little.

It should be the little recognitions, for example, 'My body is heating up', 'My 3rd eye is tingling', these are literal results that your meditation is bearing good fruits. Follow these results through, these results are indicators that you are going about it the right way. Meditation is a simple activity, it aims to shut down the physical body's senses, those 5 senses that is, and it aims to shut down the majority of the physical body's mechanisms. These typical mechanisms when inactive will be replaced with other mechanisms known as the more psychic mechanisms, these mechanics will strengthen the more meditation is done, until eventually there will be the 'pop'!

You in meditation are trading bodies, you are swapping out - not so directly - one body for another, you are moving yourself from one octave to another, the physical body will not so much turn off, but it will be sedated to the extent that the Astral body, as you call it, can roam free. This experience takes practice and time, re-awakening the eyes of a sleeping giant means you have to tickle every nook and cranny of that man's large body.

'Meditation for the Reintegration of the 4th Body'

A physical body in complete balance, a most rare thing upon your plane, would require an extremely ideal diet and a significant lack of accumulated injury, naturally these injuries would be healed by the ideal diet.

A mental body in complete balance, a most rare thing upon your plane, would require an extremely ideal diet just as well. That which is put into the mental body must be controlled/quality checked, otherwise it will lean out of balance.

What are ye putting into the mental body becometh the question?

Is your diet that of perpetual stimulative entertainment, mild distractions, non-useful data, or that of the God-Spirit, the God-Force?

Is your diet that of things that are not beneficial to your spiritual development and spiritual growth, or is it upon those things, those topics that are uplifting and generally elevating?

That which is fed to the mental body alters its basic rate of vibration as we might term it, which intern alters the molecular chemistry the physical body undergoes. And so what of the stress of boredom ye may ask?

At the moment that the mental body, being fed a rather questionable diet, is without its addicting drug, it begins to have classical withdrawal symptoms within this order. (With room for error)

- Firstly being a rising sensation of boredom, a desire for the drug.
- Secondly being a rising sensation of frustration, for the drug is not being administered.
- Thirdly being a rising experience of mental incoherence, for the mental body is now having to manage itself rather than being auto-managed by the consumed drug. This manifests as your talkative mind, as your pangings during Organic Meditation.

  One may be inclined to think that after all their meditative practice they have apparently made 'no progress', but it is for one to consider that the progress being made is to attack the core of the issue, which is the origin of the frustration itself due to the addiction.

  Progress is to heal the origin of the boredom, the origin of the lacklustre, to heal the bringer of mental instability.

- Fourthly being a settling of the mental incoherence, for the mental body is attempting to repair or amend its distortions. Here one may begin having interesting daydreams, or one may begin entertaining themself, in extreme cases this can cause uncontrolled hallucinations.
- Fifthly being a building of mental coherence, for the mental body is now drawing in vitality from the Aether, here the daydreaming may halt at random and an experience of settling peace will rise and fall.
- Sixthly being elation, only attained after all previous stages have been overcome, the mental body has become a powerhouse which can absorb high amounts of its surrounding Aether at will to feel brilliant sensations.

The most constructive distraction is the Source of your mind dearest one. Sit in silence we suggest, do not reach for a phone, a technological device we suggest, be in silence.

If there is downtime in ones life, is there a need to be on a device?

Why not bask in the Higher-Self in these moments, to be at peace with ones own inner stirrings?

Learn that you need not be tied down to feeling good via an addictive medium.

The Higher-Self is a constructive healer, it conducts the micro-electrochemistry in the body to heal a scar, to heal an ache or a pain. If given the opportunity, in moments of downtime such as meditation, the Higher-Self can bring great sensations of elation and infinite joy, so long as the manifold is capable of accepting such 'frequencies.' If the Higher-Self is somewhat rejected by the Freewill of its Lower-Self which prefers lesser distractions, the structured energy of the Higher-Self fails to filter through the silver-cord. 'J+ *What is Boredom?* - Reddit'

Therefore, the best way to call the One Infinite Creator into every cell of your being is to sit with the One Infinite Creator for what will feel like hours upon end, until you in fact begin to feel its real presence and you will literally, emotionally, feel this presence as a very real force, which will make a mobile phone seem like a primitive form of existence. S081 A8

This is a rather painful and annoying meditation to do in the beginning but when the God-Force starts to shine through the Chakras because Chakras are clearing up, that experience is unimaginably beautiful and it will only continue to grow several and then several more times intense as you continue this practice, and dearest one, one day it will grow so intense that you will 'pop' like a balloon into another realm, into a body to which can contain that absurd amount of light that cannot be funnelled into a physical body, in essence you will have the best orgasm of your life. S081 A9

We would note to any earthling which is undergoing developing consciousness, that to develop your consciousness requires a rather substantial amount of the applying of the will or the Chi or the Solar Plexus, in order to raise the vibratory rate of the Solar Plexus such that it would achieve a critical mass, in that the mass would be of a substantial level that it would be dense in energy enough to become Green in its colour. In order to achieve this you would have to apply, once again, a rather substantial amount of will or activity on this particular centre for a rather extended period of time, for a consistent amount of time.

Retreats of 7 days periodically through the year or 4 days if 7 days are far too much, retreats between 4 to 7 days throughout the year give the Solar Plexus the opportunity to be focused on for an extreme amount of time, in other words you would be isolating the Solar Plexus for 4 days straight, isolating the Solar Plexus for 4 days straight or 7 days if you can manage, will inevitably improve the quality of its rotational activity so long as the method or technique you are using is suitable, and of course we find that one of the more suitable methods has already been explored in some great detail for it is that activity of O.M. (Organic Meditation) as it has been termed, or the method whereby one would find itself or herself, himself, sat in the meditative posture and would allow the thoughts to flow as they are without necessarily disrupting their flow, but to simply sit within the thoughts.

Here the Solar Plexus in many ways can begin to correct itself as in the thoughts flowing, consciousness becomes aware of the imbalances in the thought flow. As consciousness becomes aware of the imbalanced thought flowing energy of Chi, consciousness can almost subconsciously, almost consciously, correct those imbalances until the Chi becomes so pure that your mental/mind/thoughts become pure too, then as 'J' would say the quality of thought has improved and your Chi energy would be such like a laser beam, that it would begin to shine in Green rather than in Yellow. Q010 A14

The mental body is the 3rd Subtle body. This body is a body that your societies are far too familiar with to say the least, and this is a body ever yet, that your society has injured immensely. Are all bodies not of God?

Yet you would learn those horrid things, yet you are made of God and you would feed your mental body such harsh things, you would feed your mental body drama TV shows, silly music, false ideas, false wisdom, all things that are in nature entropic; and yet you would not feed your mental body nourishment to experience God in the flesh in the walking, you would seek not to feed the mental body Christ.

These would seek to understand the mental body serves as to be curious of God and God only, and not of anything else, and here you would find immense control of the silly impulses of an uncreative being. You would find such great clarity of mind as you take your sojourn into the infiniteness of consciousness. Be infinitely curious for your curiosity will never end, curiosity does not come to an end, this is impossible within infinity you see.

Enjoy your mental body and feed it nourishment, feed it as you would feed your body salad, greens, healthy produce you see. Feed it well for it serves you and yet, in its service it gets alcohol down its system, it gets marijuana in its beingness, it gets all these arguments clogged up in its arteries, it gets anger rushing through it without direction, for anger should only be passion for God you see, it gets all of these things that are ungeometric, entropic and people wonder, 'Why am I depressed?'

The Source finds these things comedic; your society requires much evolution as is our service. S052 A9

The Solar Plexus would seek to feed the subtle body that you would be familiar with, this Solar Plexus governs many operations but let it be really clear here, the Solar Plexus seeks to be identified with only one thing, God, and upon this the Solar Plexus will open.

The Solar Plexus is programmed to open when one has full conviction and faith in God and Gods existence.

This is hence why the Solar Plexus governs the experience of curiosity, for it would be curious enough to seek God and to manifest it within the being you see, and upon this, upon this arrival of full conviction of Gods truth the Solar Plexus finds itself flowering, it finds itself opening you see and in this one can move forward into the Heart Chakra.

The Solar Plexus would seek to surpass all negative beliefs, to become familiar with the infinite, this beautiful Chakra is a Chakra recognised as the Sun bearer for it gives light to what is yet to be understood - is this not curiosity hmm? S052 A11

If you intensify the frequency of Yellow it becomes Green, if you intensify the activity of Chi by suspending it from the body and focusing on it for a large amount of time, it will be able to achieve the Green state of vibration and then we perceive that you would be able to begin entering into that Chakra to which you would term the Heart and its operational functions which will eventually begin to include brain joy, it will also include many other things such as a level of forgiveness due to how detached the Green Ray is from the physical complex.

The energy of Green Ray is so detached from the physical complex that the physical complexes biases become healed due to how selfless the energy is. Q010 A13

Selfishness is to the body akin or similar to a monkey and algebra; the two are completely different! The Heart Chakra is the algebra and selfishness is the primitive aspects of the monkeys existence and experience of life.

When one is able to manifest that energy that the Green Ray does, and in its rotational activity one has manifested a completely selfless, as in not connected to the body kind of energy, your capacity to give this energy to others in meaningful manners is what produces what you would call compassion.

The other more refined aspects of your Green energy centre, the Green Ray in its rotational activity, are in being able to manipulate this level of energy not only for the purposes of compassion but for the purposes of what could only be termed as brain joy, a joy in the brain that is and can be only produced when a Green Ray centre is not limiting its exchanges simply to compassion, but is able to internalise or rather bring that energy into the self.

In other words rather then it being radiated outwards which is significantly more easier, it would instead be coalesced inwardly, this is infinitely more difficult for it requires that one cannot perceive the difference between the other and the self, in this way the compassionate nature of the Green Ray centre, which is completely separate from the body, can begin to have its sway over how the body operates for the body is now considered a 3rd party, or in other words there is the perception that you are being compassionate to the ever present force, the omnipresent force, rather than being compassionate to a single entity who is separate from you.

The compassion being internalised produces that kind of brain joy, that brain joy is somewhat of a point of interest for it would imply that an entity has become able to internalise the Green Ray centre, something that many entities on this planet are yet able to achieve but it is available to your experience.

When this ray has been internalised experiences such as, you would call it, possessiveness of other entities to which you would find of the opposite sex, the experience of jealousy of any kind, the experience of competitiveness of any kind, many of these experiences become greatly diminished when this ray has been internalised for one begins to realise that their experience of radiating compassion has then been rotated into the self, then one can quite literally live off the compassion that they are radiating to them self, creating a joy, a happiness that transcends any attachment to anything in your physical environment. Q010 A9

The Illusion

When one follows that principle of the closing of the eyes, what has one achieved?

This is a valuable question, our response to the same is the following: When one's eyes are open they are focused, you see, focused on hither and thither, that and this. When one's eyes are open they are focused, aware and active on the **illusion**, dearest one. Now what is meditation but the de-focusing from the illusion.

What remains when the illusion is no longer the focus?

The only thing that remains when the illusion is no longer the focus is the God-Force.

'May the God-Force heal me,' says the 'I' whom is meditating.

The God-Force is a real force, it is might we say, a perfect crystal, that which is a perfect crystal is perfectly coherent, perfectly organised, without any impurities, serene and pure tone, it shines down into you when you de-focus from the illusion.

Now do not so much make the mistake that many entities do when they focus on the illusion again:

Oh, counting the breath is it...

Oh, imagining this is it...

Oh, focusing on that is it...

Oh, how illusionary!

Do you think that the God-Force is that limited?

Oh no dearest one, the God-Force is indescribable, it is enlightenment itself, how could you ever limit it?

Not saying 'you', we are describing in general; how could one ever limit the God-Force into a breathing technique?

Therefore dearest one, when one is meditating and the ego is being dissolved, let it be that the God-Force is dissolving the ego and the will is meditating to allow it, the will is meditating to allow the God-Force in, the God-Force dissolves the ego and moves the will up through its relative Chakras, removing the impurities becoming the God-Force in principle, hence the reason why entities achieve the most remarkable states of consciousness in the meditation rather than when they are in waking consciousness. However, when an entity 'pops', they attain a state of consciousness whereby the God-Force filters through them even when their eyes are open, and what a wonderful experience that is for these entities to look forward too. J+022 A11

This planet is a prison for those who are not willing to do the work. There's a way to be aware whether you are trapped here, whether you are a part of this system, it is simply to ask thine self, do they remember?

Do you remember who you really are?

Did you have a deep interest in your nature, and did you choose to investigate the same?

It takes many incarnations to eventually take the leap of faith and dedicate thine self to certain ridiculously rigid practices, but these practices are entirely to awaken the Creator within, that is your true nature. It is to be rid you of the illusion of physicality, to make you see the body as a gross thing, as something that is not who you really are. This body is not who you really are, it is a vehicle, a tiny, microscopic device that can just be discarded.

It is a genius invention however, but it is not the Creator. If creators can make this again, as genius as this biological invention is the Creator can make it again. What can we say, this is not you, this vehicle is not you! J+024 A9

It is important to really drive home this distinction between your body and your soul, and ensure to recognise that even though your body is an abnormally magical device, it is ever-still a retarded version of your soul. Your body is the atomic dimensions crude attempt at replicating the soul, just like an avatar in the digital world of the metaverse is a crude replication of your atomic image. If the soul thinks it is the body, it will limit itself to the body's electrochemical energies and miss out on the higher-oscillating energies that truly feed the soul. This is an important concept and one you should strive to experience rather than merely intellectualise through principles.

We are and have always been opposed to things of the physical body, we understand at least how it works from our experiences, not necessarily of the physical body but our awareness of its function, perhaps this is why we encourage entities to perceive that their biology is not their nature, this biological love you call romance and sexual energy, and these kinds of things, it has its place but it is not who you are, you are greater.

Should you choose to realise this, this planet is not a prison, it is a temporary visit. It is a matter of perception dearest one, this planet is a prison to those who desire to be imprisoned, who desire to, well let us be frank, if you want honesty from us we'll be honest, who desire to be trapped, and use technology, and play games, and spend utterly no time investigating who they are, who take more interest in your Tinder apps and these kinds of things, and not in the truest nature of the greatest kind of service that's possible.

We are not saying for instance, don't start a family. Start families yes, if anything if you start a family and you help the entities recognise where they are and what they could do, then you have served in a tremendous way.

We just want you to be aware that you are a Creator and if you can be aware of this, this planet is not a prison it is a one-time stop.

If you listen to the masters who have walked before you, who have taught you and told you attain to your highest, as did Source say, 'You will be Christ Conscious!'

If you take their words and run with it, great things will come, but let us be frank and real, we are aware of your world and what it is like, the whole system of money and tax and everything. We have our opinions of your money, these kinds of things, we are extremists perhaps because we are aware of the risks, perhaps because we are aware that in truth your future is more important then your present in many ways, and it is important to make your present the real future of who you really are which is the Creator.

If you can make your present the Creator, then you have achieved overcoming the future possibility. J+024 A9

Condensed Energy

We begin with the fact that all the condensed energy must firstly be condensed, yes?

Then the condensing begins at the fact that the mind has not the iota on how to manage the energy it experiences, therefore it has a tendency to get it tangled like a set of wires that do not have the cables attached to the floor, as you would understand. The energy comes in, in streams of these wires, the entity gets it all mixed up and makes somewhat of an elastic ball of whatever comedic word would fit, and then you would have condensed energy dearest one.

Thus it is a process, there is the energy that is coming, there is the mind that is creating it and then tangling it up, and then you have the product of the same being the condensed energy itself, negative in context, waiting to be untangled by mind once again, for mind was the creator so mind must untangle the same. J+022 A1

Now you have a physical body which produces emotions, it is not that you would deny these emotions from coming out, it is that you would let the body experience the entirety of the emotions and you would bring to words the most constructive revelations that come to you in the moment, that if there would be anger, what would be the most constructive, creative, healing thing to say within the experience of anger?

There is never a need to deny your emotions, for denial of them is what creates those packets of energy that block the circulation of your kundalini. No denial - fully experience the pain or bliss of your emotional output, that is what your body is designed for. Just have the output of those emotions be, might we say, Godly, then you will never have to worry about those packets of energy causing blockages in your spiritual complex. S009 A3

To offer some perception on this, if one comes to you in frustration and frustrates you, feel it, feel every ounce of it in the present moment as though your body has become a volcano about to erupt, and when it is about to erupt lava, call upon the Christ so that it erupts golden liquor and have this golden syrup spill upon the person or anyone else that frustrates you, and in that moment they might feel in your presence there is something behind you, within you and around you, the Christ is present and this will be more than enough for there to be both the experience of the emotion, the Christ balancing the emotion, and then the very divine output of that emotion.

Experience these emotions, use your heavenly mind to control the output, this is your power. We are all volcano's, we will erupt if pushed, lets change at the very last moment what comes out of that volcano, so it doesn't destroy the villages and the peoples. S009 A4

The complexities of it more so have to do with the nervous system itself, that would begin with the brain, the central nervous system, those basic brains as you would understand the spine and these things.

The energy and how it entangles in the physical vehicle is directly and intimately communicated through the channels of the nervous system and then expressed at portions by which the nervous system would be connected to the muscles and organs, therefore the location or loci of tangled or condensed energy tends to surface at the appropriate location, whereby the state of mind is then a representation of the metaphysical construct of the organ or muscle itself. In other words, your organ and muscular system is intimately connected to the nervous system and where thought impulses go, oft depends on the orientation of the thought that is being sent through the nervous system.

Let us give an example:

There may be an entity whom is angry for an entity broke their heart in a romantic relationship, then we can have the nature of the thought travelling through the nervous system to a location that is most intimately connected to either the breasts, the chest location or other areas within the area surrounding the general heart, for thought and the nervous system are akin to a train and its appropriate junction. J+022 A2

You may have heard of the phrase 'train of thought', I like this saying as thoughts are very specifically linked to health, and indeed are similar to trains of communication that run through the nervous system. The nervous system can be viewed as the train track, having all of our internal body parts as stations/junctions along the way. Each and every muscle in your body interacts with the nervous system, the ones connected to your skeletal frame, the ones connected to your vital organs, digestive tract, all of them. Whether controlled directly through conscious thought or via the subconscious, they are all ultimately linked to the nervous system.

Because of this connection thought moves muscles; ALL thoughts move muscles. Thoughts on the same issue will continuously move muscles in the same area. Negative thoughts are compressive, they contract, they are closed, and they cause the nervous system to squeeze muscles, often infinitesimally small muscles that surround the all-important pipelines to our vital organs causing congestion over time at these stations and ill health within the body. If you have ever visited a station during rush hour, then you can clearly imagine the type of congestion some of your internal organs are facing due to continuous negative thoughts on the same trauma. As we learn our lessons and adjust the quality of our thoughts, the congestion gets cleared and our nervous system can run the trains like normal again through open stations.

All thoughts, as do trains as you would understand, find their appropriate junction in the human body. You have a thought of worry then that thought will travel to its appropriate junction.

May we point out something of interest; entities not only have similar junctions, they also have pre-programmed junctions. J+022 A3

An entity tends to, as pertaining to the incarnation and the desires of the lessons, create junctions for their thought impulses to travel to, that the entity may measure how they are doing in an incarnation. If an entity has a cyst, the entity can thus assess that perhaps something is not going as they thought it should be going.

The entity can then assess, where did the cyst occur in my life?

Did I have it hither, thither, or then, or now?

Is there a relationship therefore between the cyst and my environment?

What element in my environment may be the causal factor of the creation of the cyst?

How is it the creation of the cyst occurred in relation to how I think?

These questions are all to be considered when one is assessing how a thought has made its way through a nervous system, being the train tracks, and has approached its appropriate junction to create something akin to some dissatisfying mark, whether on the skin or what you would understand as cancer or anything such as this. J+022 A4

Let us say one thing, when it comes to the healing of an item on the body, what may be considered dearest one, is that it is not so much the healing that is pertinent, but that the lesson is grasped.

Indeed, we find that emotions dearest one, are the best sign of attempting to explain the arrival of something that is undesirable on the body.

As we perceive there is a lesson that has been learnt here, *for example* a cyst as you term it appeared because you were in an environment that was not serving at all for spiritual development but was instead serving your spiritual entropy, so entropy begun on the body, no?

Your physical vehicle became weak because of the environment you were in, when you switched the environment eventually that experience of the cyst, its annoyance and its very mere existence started to become less significant as your focus shifted. J+022 05

The subconscious recognised you had learnt the lesson, thus the subconscious perceives that need it not grow the cyst anymore, need the cyst not be repaired anymore, the lesson has been grasped the cyst remains to be harmless you'd see. J+022 08

This is the simplicity of the expression, that is, where there is entropy there is always going to be malfunctions in the coordination of the physical vehicle. J+022 05

Interestingly although the lesson may have been learnt, this does not necessarily mean that the subconscious will automatically instruct the ailment to heal, it may simply instruct it to stop and become benign in the body.

What follows are some details on kickstarting the subconscious into affirmative healing action, however this relies on a high level of adeptness. The key to rapid healing being an open Heart Chakra, although slower healing can occur through the consistent use of the Clairvoyant centre.

The body's cells die and are reborn multiple times a week, if one is able to manually coordinate how the cells are born, one can begin to affix something that is undesirable on their physical vehicle as to the subjective perception of what is desirable and what is not.

We would seek to point out dearest one, that all thoughts have their destination on the physical vehicle and it is well to understand that sometimes a soul will say to itself before it incarnates, 'Hmm, perhaps it will be well for me to have an indication of when I am not going in the right direction, may this manifest on me in a certain way that will get my attention.' J+022 05

The body is a mirror of thought, for let us use the word 'thought' or 'imagination' whatever you prefer, the body seeks to mirror this especially as pertaining to the sensitivity of the entity, most entities at this current time have reached a level of sensitivity whereby their body is directly manifesting things of their own mind, for more sensitive entities this appears more quickly. It depends on the entity in question but always dearest one, your mind, the quality of your mind, the relaxedness of your mind, the state of bliss or joy-ness of your mind will seek to manifest in how your body functions for as is understood by the reverent Paul Solomon, all thoughts move muscles. J+022 07

Let us understand dearest one, that happiness, joy, bliss and any emotion that is positive in nature is naturally vibrational, that which is not vibrational is that which is condensed for how can condensed matter vibrate?

Happiness is the vibration of life, it is when something has high fluidity, fluidity is that which is not condensed, condensed is that which is without fluidity. Happiness, joy and emotions on this spectrum have fluidity, that which does not have fluidity is condensed energy which is equally uncondensed when an entity experiences heightened states of consciousness.

There is a joy of the Heart Chakra that is naturally orgasmic in its own way, it is often felt as what your society calls Oxytocin, in its chemical receptor. The Oxytocin itself like many chemicals seeks to manage the electrical activity happening in the body, when there is an abundance of electrical activity happening within and around the heart that is what the experience of the Heart Chakra is, and then this brings euphoric sensations that can offer healing to tangled energy. The difficulty of the job will be firstly the remaining in the state of consciousness that would be of a heightened state connected to the Heart Chakra, this is already difficult, then there would be the attempting to remind the Higher-Self that, as we are comedic, 'Hello Higher-Self, I require you to amend this, this is rather aggravating!' as you may understand this term.

The Higher-Self, or let us rather use more accurately, the subconscious mind can be a little aloof sometimes, you see the subconscious mind does its job but it can be sometimes one of those entities who does its job, yet only to do the job and nothing more, the subconscious mind is not a seeker of trophies you see.

The instruction to the subconscious is the following:

'Dearest subconscious, I need you to do your job and amend the photons that are not in the right order within the area, that the cells may follow,' you see.

Then there are two things that need to be managed here, a sending of a message and then the remaining in the correct state of consciousness that is relaxed enough, that is vibrant and fluidic enough, to allow the subconscious to pass its own, let us call it electricity, through the body towards *that which* may be repaired. This is exactly what happens on the entity that you understand as Joe Dispenza's retreats. All entities on this experience, experience the same, the subconscious becomes temporarily able to accommodate an entities wishes. Temporarily... temporarily... temporarily! J+022 A8

The Heart Chakra in its activation increases the activity, let us say electrical activity, happening in the nervous system, it is a heightened state of consciousness whereby the Kundalini becomes quite active, there is a sense of heat, a sense of compassion or love, a general love for life, for The Creator, for things, a general gratitude, a sense of gratitude as you would understand.

The activation of the Heart Chakra is a rather difficult feat to achieve, these things are not easy. The Heart Chakra, it reminds us of an entity in a Japanese cartoon who is very unassuming but extremely powerful *(One Punch Man!).* You would think on first glance that to activate the Heart Chakra would be simple, but you would find this unassuming Chakra is extremely difficult to activate and requires quite an abundance of work, but to heal dearest one, the physical vehicle, you must obtain a very heightened state of consciousness, there has to be a rather significant jump in the levels of vibration of the physical vehicle, this is no easy feat dearest one, thus repairing realistically is not so simply done with the imagination as much as it is done in heightened states of consciousness.

Most entities whom have issues with their vehicle repair it via the clairvoyant centre alone, this is possible, requires focus, not necessarily the Heart Chakra at all, but this process is long term not direct. Thus, the other technique would be the book that the entity Jordan read *(Mind Your Body: A Practical Method of Self-healing – E. H. Shattock),* which sought to depict an entity that seemingly repaired aspects of their vehicle, the bones. This would be a reference to an entity who used clairvoyance to direct the subconscious mind over a period of time, this works too, it depends.

Many entities require the Heart Chakra based healing to which is achieved at the Joe Dispenza retreats, a very difficult feat. The more natural manner is usually the clairvoyant manner, but this also has its very profound difficulties hence the reason why most entities find it rather more straight forward to have the arbitration or the abstract on their vehicle and just to live with it rather than repair it. For entities, many are they whom are rather advanced, see no need. J+022 A9

When you are able to repair this sector on your vehicle, it will mean at least two things; you have access, direct access, to the Prana of your vehicle and the ability to manipulate the same with the clairvoyant centre. Alternatively, the Prana is activated at the Heart Chakra and directed by your requests to the subconscious mind, either/or, the Prana is active in the body, a very profound state of consciousness accompanies this, might we say. J+022 A10

Memories and Forgiveness

Memory structures are configurated electrical fields, the crystalline structure is how it maintains its integrity, and then, indeed it becomes so that you would see upon looking on a human brain, regions of the brain that are associated with memory that is in fact stored in a deeper region of the ethers, those sub-sub densities as could be described.

Memory is stored in the deep regions of the electrical lifeforce and are then connected to the brain like an analogue. Consider your silver cord to be something that is greatly responsible for connecting the memories of the subconscious, which are your memories, to the body.

It is important to understand that there are many levels to life and the physical body indeed has certain regions of itself responsible for storing memories specifically in the limbic system. A scientist of your kind will analyse it and say 'Ah, here is where memories are,' or 'If we take out this portion of the brain the entity cannot remember.'

However, if it were true that memories were stored in this region of the brain, then if humans had regenerative ability and could regenerate a deleted region of the brain then the memory should not return, but they do.

And if humans did have regenerative ability, even if the hippocampus was destroyed, after its repair the human would remember again what it had once forgotten, signifying that memory is stored in a deeper region of what your scientists call electromagnetism, we call it that consciousness that yields - what is understood then by the 'J' entities as motion.

Since scientists in various studies have concluded that it retains memories from its larvae stage, we could use the humble caterpillar to illustrate this concept as its brain is essentially liquefied and rebuilt from scratch as it undergoes its metamorphosis in the cocoon before emerging as a beautiful butterfly. However, let's qualify this claim with the work of Dr James V. McConnell.

He was fairly famous in the '50s and '60s, not only was this maverick scientist nearly blown up by the 10th bomb of Theodore 'the Unabomber' Kaczynski, during his unsuccessful but tenaciously violent attempt to save the world from the threat of science and technology via explosives, McConnell also done some rather interesting memory experiments on worms. These experiments were later taken even further in more recent times by Michael Levin, but more on him later.

McConnell created quite the stir with some radical experiments performed at the University of Michigan, the results of which suggested that memories existed outside of the brain. To get to this fascinating conclusion he enlisted the help of some common freshwater flatworms, or the planarian, Dugesia dorotocephala, for those that are into worms on a deeper level.

The magic of these little wrigglers was twofold, they had a remarkable ability to regenerate, so remarkable that you could cut them into pieces, head, tail or middle, and have new worms grow, the headless ones becoming fully equipped with a brand-new brain, within 14 days; the second bonus was they could be taught, they could remember behaviours, they had a true brain which makes them very similar to ourselves, and McConnell trained these brainy flatworms through the use of electric shocks, to respond to lighting cues which taught them to move to a particular part of the petri dish he was using for the experiment. Once taught, and then compassionately dismembered, these freshly recovered from having their heads cut off worms, along with their brand-new brains, eyes and most of their nervous system, somehow were able to remember behaviours learnt when they existed with a totally different brain.

So if not the brain, where was this memory stored?

Michael Levin in more recent times has continued McConnell's research, Levin, well known for his research on regeneration and experiments that have gone as far as growing working, functional eyes on the tails of amphibians, decided to recreate and improve upon this decapitated worm experiment with a much bigger budget, modern equipment, and enough controls, replicable data, and rigorously documented evidence to satisfy the intense scrutiny of the scientific community, as there had been some trouble in replicating McConnell's worm training protocols back in the 60's.

You can read further on this published study in the Journal of Experimental Biology in 2013,

https://journals.biologists.com/jeb/article/216/20/3799/11714/An-automated-training-paradigm-reveals-long-term

Also be sure to check out more of Levin's quite fascinating work.

The results again suggested that some trace of memory is stored in locations distributed beyond the brain.

So beheaded worms aside, where do the readings say memory is stored?

Memory is stored in a deeper region of the electromagnetic force, which is like a piano scale stretching for miles increasing in frequencies, allowing for various dimensions to exist, and in the nature of its storage *you would see* it is typical stored in crystal like structures if you were to look deeply into the manner in which the electricity is interacting with itself to produce those holographic images that an individual sees when its mind eye, the typically called 3rd eye, remembers something. Q013 A7

The silver cord is akin to some kind of fibre optic cable, it transmits information from the great mind, through the medium of the soul and then into the body, it works in such a way as to mediate the connection that the Over-Self, as is understood as being not only a thing of itself but the subconscious mind, may be able to be permanently connected to the souls that it stretches from its own source. Q013 A8

The Over-Self would be the major soul, Over-Self has the ability to split itself into multiple souls to gain many experiences. S015 A21

These experiences would be across different solar systems within the universe of love itself. Love is its own universe; the Over-Self resides in this universe and does not have such the ability to cross into the universes beyond love, so the multiple souls would exist in different galaxies, solar systems and many of the other words you might use to describe the vastness of this space. S015 A22

Souls who have incarnated on Earth who experience memories from souls who are incarnated in distant galaxies, tend to find themselves going quite insane and having incredibly obscure dreams that even they cannot *wrap* their head around. It would also be said that the only way there *can be* a crossover between souls of the same Over-Self, is if the souls themselves carry an incredibly similar frequency through their evolution in life, that their silver cords become indistinguishable from each other and thus become tangled in some mannerism. S015 A24

If the Over-Self were to disappear for whatever cosmic reason, then the body would merely shut down, the soul would disappear, and any memories that were there would go as such. The silver cord is then like a fibre optic or electrical cable, it transmits high frequency information from Over-Self to the body and from the body to Over-Self, this is how the soul can maintain itself in the body, how the body can maintain its structure, and especially the reason why humans in fact have infinite memory storage, for in truth if the amount of neurons in and of themselves were to for whatever reason run out, neurons would temporarily be, let us say, degenerated so that neurogenesis could take place, so that the memory can then be felt in the *brain* itself.

When the body no longer exists, for the body has been departed, for the body is quite literally dead, a crude word perhaps, it is then significantly easier to remember things for you are remembering directly through the Over-Self rather than the Over-Self having to go through the crying effort of sending the correct information's or data streams into the body. Q013 A8

A key to healing, an unfortunately difficult key in many if not most cases, is forgiveness. True complete forgiveness. Understand that memories typically crystalise, they crystalise in the way they vibrate, the way they sing. Crystals are not limited to objects, in the case of memories they are configurated electrical fields, the crystalline structure being how they maintain their integrity.

In the case of a traumatic memory: Picture a gaseous substrate that lacks a matrix, this would be equivalent to empty space on a hard-drive. Then picture the disorganised crystallisation of a traumatic memory being 'saved' or 'written' into the substance, this is like a corrupted block on the drive that is very difficult for light or energy to pass through. Continuing the hard-drive analogy, there would be extreme lag here as the processor gets stuck accessing these blocks.

These types of memories can create traps. There should always be a pathway for consciousness to leave or enter a memory, or cluster of memories freely. If your consciousness can't leave and is perpetually ruminating on something someone has done to you, or something you have experienced, then it's safe to say that you are traumatised, and consciousness as energy, as electrical potential, is unable to flow freely, trapped in whatever part of the brain that the memory is being processed in, locked in a stress loop.

It is interesting to consider how talk therapy works, allowing people to think about their trauma in ways they have not considered before, reframing the issues, allowing new pathways to be built at a neurological level, thus freeing that trapped electrical potential which was circulating in a negative thought-cycle, repeating the same emotions over and over again with no way to escape.

We are here recognising these emotional memory blocks on an energetic level, and it is important on every level of health that this disorganised crystallisation becomes clear and coherent once again, to allow light to pass through correctly, allowing the flow of energy to balance itself, and the most powerful form of this adjustment is found in forgiveness.

Indeed, for then here is an adept understanding and it is quite an issue for many humans upon this plane who are traumatised and have not the tools to overcome those traumas. The many entities upon your plane have not had that classic, may we say experience of the magical 'pop', whereby all of a sudden forgiveness is felt and one becomes free, trauma no longer plaguing the body, allowing energy to pass up and through the body, that kundalini then, those magical abilities begin to open up through the emotional clearing.

The clearing of emotions is somewhat unfortunately greatly handled by that 'pop', and that 'pop' is quite literally as the entity Joe Dispenza described it, a let us say, massive untangling and release of energy. Such a process requires consciousness for this is truly the only way for it to work, and it requires the consciousness achieves, not a conceptual forgiveness but an emotional forgiveness, which are entirely different things.

The conceptual mind is that mind that thinks in the gaseous realms, the emotional mind is so many times different, for even though it thinks or is processed in the gaseous realms, the energy density, the amount of energy packed into the location to which the emotion is, is far higher than the conceptual thoughts.

Consider conceptual thoughts to be an AAA battery, and emotions to be a, well, this is perhaps a little hyperbole in emphasis or maybe even comedic, but as to compare an AAA battery to the battery that would power an entire car. The emotional body carries an incredible amount of energy density, the amount of energy packed into that e-motion.

Conceptual forgiveness then is the intellectual ability for an individual to use the thoughts, especially localised in the pre-frontal cortex, to control the emotional mind, to control the emotional energy, for this weakish, depending on the adeptness of the entity, electrical current of the gaseous conceptual thoughts, is and does have the ability to transmit its thinking capacity through various channels to control the deeper regions of the emotional mind, so the emotional mind does not instantly overwhelm one.

You would consider that the conceptual mind is so necessary in your world, for if human beings, we find this very comedic, were to not have the conceptual mind to produce conceptual forgiveness, then entities would blow up at each other instantly and you would have dare we say, an incredible amount of passionately volatile entities walking around, and we use this for we believe this is the most descriptive way of understanding this process that is perhaps giving you a very good idea of the importance of the conceptual mind.

The conceptual mind for the average entity is weak, but in its weakness it is strong enough to at least hold back true feelings. Children do not have a developed conceptual mind as is termed pre-frontal cortex, at least in how it analogues with the body, and so children are emotional and cannot necessarily handle themselves without the consistent aid of their parents bringing them into harmonious states of being. Children act on impulse, behave emotionally and cry at the drop of a hat because they, once again, do not have a developed conceptual mind.

Adults tend to, let us say this in this way, spec into the conceptual mind so that they even may simply survive in this world, for this world is harsh like rough sands, and without a strong conceptual mind you will come under the heat of your emotions and will resort to actions or symptoms such as depression and trauma, which are no good for surviving in this ridiculously hard climate. Consider the experiences ye had in the experience of school and having to become hardened in the conceptual mind, witty, to be able to handle the constant blows, as is termed 'cusses', as is termed 'banter', deriving from entities who are a little reptilian perhaps although that is a stereotype.

Indeed, it is so that the frontal lobe, these frontal lobal areas especially the pre-frontal cortex, that which manages conceptual thought, something that is not just happening at the pre-frontal cortex but is in truth a gaseous process that is translated in the pre-frontal cortex. If you were to let go of the control, let go of the conceptual mind - a difficult thing, then those deeper emotions within you would come gushing out and would demonstrate that indeed, you may have forgiven 'x' or 'y' conceptionally, but you haven't forgiven them emotionally for the emotions still run deep, the anger is still clear for instance.

The way children deal with the emotional mind is by letting it balance itself, for it has its own brain chemistry and it is able to, quite literally, balance itself if you let it out. Many entities find various methods to do this, the entity Jerry has found that through the activity of fighting *(Muay Thai training)* he is able to bring out deep frustrations in the emotional mind as the fighting expression puts the entity into a trance disabling this region of the brain, the pre-frontal cortex, enough to let the anger gush, bringing balance such that when the entity walks home, he feels many times better.

It is a shame that fighting causes incoherence in the body, in the subtle bodies, for it is a good way to let things out but is a bad way to remain coherent enough to attain or achieve those greater states of consciousness. It is as is termed in some use of slang, a catch-22, or whatever word would imply that paradoxical nature of two things working together yet working apart, healing but damaging as is understood. As then to the method of letting emotions gush forth, letting them out, hence is prescribed to entities Organic Meditation, why?

Well because Organic Mediation sits you with your mind for extreme amounts of time, and it is only so long before an entities, we find this comedic, pre-frontal cortex throws in the towel and says, 'Oh cannot I think any more for I have thought of everything, I will just sit and be quiet.'

And it is in this quiet moment that the doors of the subconscious mind open those deep emotions and they do come out, they do present themselves, and so you will find that some entities finding this very easy, cry on their first meditation or the meditations to come, uncontrolled emotions that were hidden within them fall out, and so there is a, as is described in the Joe Dispenza retreats, a massive release of energy and the entity has their famous 'pop' as is described.

In Organic Meditation, an entity once again is faced with the ego, becomes thoroughly bored of it after extensive practice and the simple sitting with this conceptual mind, realising its negligence, rather its lack of importance, it subsides, the beingness becomes quiet, and the emotions that are trapped as such by the pre-frontal cortex begin to come forth.

An entity finally finds that self is balancing, that self perhaps even cannot handle the eyes being closed for the emotions are so deep, so the eyes open and an entity becomes furious, angered, perhaps cries, there is a release of some kind, a pacing, a need for a breather, something to let this chemistry find coherence again.

This is a seeking to describe the process that the conceptual mind traps emotions, especially for the survival of an individual in this very harsh climate, and that to balance emotions you do not so much let them out as much as you get the frontal cortex out of the way so that you can let them be, let them flow, as does the mind flow from one thought to another.

Forgiveness is in the flow of the chemistry of these thoughts, we say chemistry but it is more of an energetic nature, letting the flow of energy balance itself, for energy in the body has a tendency to heal under the direction of the gentle love of the great mind which heals your skin when it is cut, heals bones when they are fractured and can heal just about anything if you give it the opportunity, and a brilliant opportunity is given during meditation.

We will finalise and say that some entities find interesting ways to disable the pre-frontal cortex; drawing current, electrical current of the literal manner of plugging a, you would call them perhaps a cathode, you put them on the frontal lobe and draw an electric current through it of the opposite charge required, the opposing charge drawn through the frontal lobe will interfere and will stop any electrical potential occurring, for voltage requires polarity but if you neutralise polarity there is no voltage, so there is no electricity. This is a funny way of disabling the frontal cortex, the entity will find it very difficult to think and will find that they feel woozy or present, and perhaps then things will flow easier.

In mental health treatment before a therapist, an entity will find a therapist has the ability to disable the frontal lobe, disable the thinking portions of the brain through extremely well engineered techniques causing the entity to cry, or let things out. It is the therapists methodical and intuitive touch, and healing as in metaphysical transference of energy that allows this possibility.

Entities who are too logical or intellectual upon your plane, struggle with forgiveness and of course it would be men for the man must be intellectual in order to supply survival and security to his family, for the man must bite many bullets in the wild, and must look the other way in the wild, thus the man is easily traumatised but at least has more conceptual energy, that is a relatively, let us say, larger pre-frontal cortex and thus literally more intellectual mental energy to put the emotions aside and get the job done.

More to be said, sensitive men on your plane are the result perhaps of the environment becoming less harsh, men becoming less needing of having an ability to look banter aside, for it seemingly is so that your mental health dynamics are becoming more prominent and men seem to be finding it easier to express their emotions making them more, we say this politely, sissy-like or gay-like, if could be described in such a way. We mean this not to be rude it is just a descriptive, an adjective. Indeed, the pre-frontal cortex also, and the men becoming less masculine, may also be due to technology depriving the function of the pre-frontal cortex via it being engaged on a constant basis yet not actually thinking about life as such.

A true finalisation then for the process of forgiveness so energy may stream in and up, is that an entity finds their own way to let the emotions forth. Entities upon this plane have their own free will and free choice, if it is fighting that is best, that will get those emotions out, the punching, the aggressiveness, to let the frontal lobe aside, to enter into that trance state which the child enters when it is crying.

If it is so that this exercise regime will heal this one to which we speak to, or in general to which we speak, then do do it for you have free will and free choice, and one must take their own steps up the mountain.

Just always remember that you must find your own way to do things and an entity must realise upon this plane that it is the governor of its own life, not anyone who would be anyone else, for all have their path up the mountain and all figure out in their own time how to deal with their inner torment.

Indeed, meditation is a way but there are other ways that are more practical for entities who are at different stages of evolution and with absolute respect, the entity Jordan simply and most simply is at a different stage of evolution then his wonderful father, and so they will deal with things in different ways and this must be respected, understood and enjoyed, for life is short on this plane and there is only so much you can do.

Let us predict a subconscious question and say that the reason why the fighting mechanism, the competitive act caused the many-ness of the injuries, was perhaps because the Over-Self was wondering if this entity might be able to figure out a way to let his emotions out in a way that is constructive to the activities that these do, the Over-Self wondered perhaps, if we could say in such a way, if the entity would be able to figure out another method. So, there was injury to give the entity time to realise that its own mind is in great torment. But are you able to find a way to process these emotions without resorting to physical action?

These are sometimes the tests, if you could call it such a thing, that the Over-Self will do on a soul as to give the soul the opportunities to gauge its evolution and it is for the soul to realise that these designed catalysts, as the entities of RA call it, are extremely useful and honesty, and compassion for itself in its abilities or lack thereof are important for an entity to come to the realisation of its next steps, in its next life. Q013 A9

Find the most harmonious expression of relieving the frustrations within the self. Spiritual adepts of all natures, of all kinds, whether they exist on the moon, in the skies or on the planet, will always encourage beings to try the method that is most refined, but like paracetamol to the tastebuds, sometimes the refined methods are tasteless, bitter, overly difficult and a little annoying, so sometimes entities must find methods that are sweeter and easier, and the compassion for the self comes in recognising that every entity upon the plane of Earth is a different wavelength or step up the mountain, and so must utilise what they feel is best to make the progression forward.

We understand that sometimes taking a 'paracetamol' will have a very bitter taste. Entities upon this plane, we believe, tend to be hard on themselves too much, some entities are easy upon themselves too much, and so there must be found a balance between the discipline of being hard on the self and the compassion of being easy on the self, and sometimes you be easy on the self so you have the energy to be hard on the self again. It is a swaying of the boat, an eb and flow as could be understood.

Individuals have individual evolution, and individual evolution must be balanced, individual Karma must be balanced with collective Dharma. The Karma of the oneself must be dealt with, usually as the priority as was taught by the reverent *Paul* Solomon, who stated self-love first, everything else next. You put self-love first, you put your Karma first, and then what follows is the Dharma, the good work, and you balance these two forces like a Yin and a Yang, prioritising always the Karma at 51% or more, and the Dharma next, for when the Karma balances completely one can live a life of Dharma - that is duty, responsibility, collective activity, the improving of those around you.

Q013 A11

The difference between the mechanisms would be two kinds of learnings, the first learning is a learning that would be orientated to the self, the second learning is a learning that is orientated to service to other people, you might call it. Here we find in the typical format of what you might call karma such the experience of relationship having, having relationships with others and uncovering aspects of character that need to be refined and worked on in detail, the relationships serve typically as a refinement to this.

This is typically where karma seeks to manifest itself, the lesson learning is orientated to the self and has a dramatic effect on the, what you would call, the energy centres, the Chakras, that is meditation may have one particular effect on the upper Chakras but what you would call your Karmic relationships have a dramatic effect on the lower Chakras, these lower Chakras are able to be balanced so that the process of higher learning of the upper Chakras can be commenced.

That which you would call Dharma, which would be more toward a service to others, serving the other person, it would be the giving force itself, giving freely without any expectation of return. Typically, souls come with a Dharmic purpose and a Karmic purpose, their Karmic purpose would be all the lessons and requirements to their soul, and their souls lower three Chakras. Their Dharmic experience would be the experience of the upper three Chakras and then the overall spectrum would amalgamate into what you would call the Crown Chakra, as one would seek connection with the divine at the end of the experience of these two polarities, you might call them. Q005 A7

It is so that a soul is an individual, and an individual soul has to figure out the best direction. Sometimes an individual soul will get so fed up with the whole affair that it will simply destroy itself, perhaps this is visible in entities who poison themselves with certain concoctions.

Sometimes individual souls find an activity like yoga or screaming at the top of a mountain or having many relationships with many beings in sexual romance, and they would use the sex as a therapeutic manner to let things go. Many entities find different manners of dealing with things, meditation is perhaps the most extreme way leaving the deepest bitter taste in the mouth, as *we have* used this analogy earlier. It is the most bitter way of dealing with the harsh nature of reality, that reality is extremely harsh, seemingly extremely unforgiving, and seemingly sometimes extremely unfair.

We believe that reality is an illusion so the concept of fair or unfair is too an illusion, but perhaps that is due to the nature of what is called Source, that present moment, that consciousness, that primordial stuff. Q013 A12

We understand there is a lot to talk about, a lot of explaining to do when it comes to the heavens, the reptilians, the prison planet and such things as this, for these things cannot be denied so easily. But consider this dearest one, there is a silver lining, and the silver lining is that the Over-Self of all beings is very smart and it knows what it's doing, and this planet is not a prison for the entities who figure it out, given how difficult that is, and it takes millennia as in 1,000s of years, and then even 100,000s of thousands of years for cycles such as the one you are experiencing today to come about, where the information itself of the higher realms can be made available to multiple people such that entities do not have to scavenge to book stores so that they can learn of such things, do not have to be in niche groups.

It is available online - it is available to the majority of humans upon this planet once in a blue moon, and finally there can be disclosure and information brought on the relationship that the whole prison system dilemma has with individual growth of souls in evolution, and how it all plays a part together in a cohesive group, and to explain those atrocities that happen to people, to explain the reasons that you have undergone the things that you have.

Picture simply, there is a mountain to climb, and your freedom is given unto yourself, by yourself, by the decisions that you make to encourage yourself whilst you are on this plane, to escape it via designing challenging experiences that push you really hard, may we say. Q013 A10

Consider if you will for our final message, when a soul leaves this Earth plane and it is seeking to stretch into the upper dimensions, as the soul climbs up the ladder the light becomes more intense, so intense that it becomes hard to bear, the soul will continue to climb the ladder, the steps, until the light itself is at the level of intensity that the soul cannot move any more.

If this light intensity is so intense at the lower dimensions then the soul will have to come back to this planet for another 3-dimensional cycle of experience of life, however if the soul in the Earth life has undergone refinement, has undergone lesson learning well, has learnt of the universal love of the all loving Father God and has learnt to encompass this as one's own, inside of one's soul, then this would allow the soul to quite easily jump two steps at a time up the ladder, up-up the stairs, into the all loving universal love of Gods light, allowing for the continuation of what you would call the incarnative experience in much more harmonious dimensions.

Consider if you will at this point in time souls have come to truly test themselves.

Then look at the coincidences, seek to see the moments in time, seek to see those things that are happening, seek to see the experiences you are having even now and consider what it is that you are learning here, that is being told to you by what you would call chocolate droppings.

Keep everything within the mind and have the understanding, God is lovable, you are able to love God, and God is unity, it is the all-ness of life and so if God is loved then truly the self is loved, and self-love can become so strong that universal love becomes the natural emanation of the being, and when this happens, all beings, all entities, become forgiven regardless of what you would call their atrocities, their so called 'mistakes', their so called 'confusing actions', all becomes forgiven for the higher purposes of experiencing the all loving presence of the Creator. Q005 A10

The Healer

When a healer does healing work and they untangle the quanta of light that are not functioning correctly, that light being untangled emits a release of energy which for the healer is experienced as impressions, these impressions merely would have to be accepted the same way you would accept the misbehaviours of your child, because you love them so much.

The healer is the greatest lover on the planet, thus the healer must be able to accept all things in order for the healing to be done, it is only natural for a healer not only to have to accept the minds of others, but to even accept their own mind, to accept all aspects of their own mind, and to be a healer from within as much as they are a healer from without.

In order to work as a healer, one must be able to accept all things and feel healed from within. J+019 A5

Do always recall that anything that is without structure is something that cannot do work. Anything that has structure can do work, for energy can channel through something structured. Structure allows for energy to move and circulate much like racing cars circulating around the track, thus when you apply structure to anything dearest one, what you are doing is repairing that particular node so that energy can work again where it was not able to work before, therefore once the knot has been untangled then you may begin to apply structure. The job of the healer is to untangle the energy and then to give the entities subconscious mind the vital lifeforce to begin the healing process. Here you are supplying or being an energy conduit for the entity much like a spare battery pack, the entities subconscious mind having you manually untangle the issue, is now able to heal with the energy you are supplying. This energy comes into the body as structured energy or rather energy that is malleable or workable, usable for the subconscious mind for the energy is not crude. J+019 A3

To untangle this knot thus one has to apply the healing presence which seeks to manually undo what has been done, it is much like one filling in the holes in the tarmac, explaining the scientific process of this would take some effort but what one may be able to understand is that what one has done, is taken the more quantum aspects of one's body, the aspects that are unseen and energetic, and they have in essence repaired it or corrected it, this is more so what has happened at that quantum level to which the healer is most partaking in.

The healer does not so much heal the atomic body, as much as the healer heals the energetic body, the body that is composed of energy held together by thought. It is a rather intriguing process but to stress the sciences of this process we feel would not be appropriate right now, so perhaps in another time we can do this. J+019 A4

The Healer in Action

As we have moved along lifes energetic journey, we have been fortunate enough to have been exposed to various forms of energy healings and practices, both in training and receiving of the same, whether through intense breathwork, sound or healing hands. I personally enjoyed some remarkable experiences of healing hands, and I might add some delicious Mauritian, belly leaping for joy food, provided by a spritual healing practicitioner based in Dinard, France, called Laurent Helene.

Mmmm, if I close my eyes I can still taste the Roti's!

Quick flashback story: As soft melodies played in the background, I lay relaxing on a healing table located in a picturesque French village, happy to be far away from the usual hustle and bustle of surviving life. This was my second session during a 4 day retreat with Laurent and his lovely wife Chantal, a wonderful woman who also treated me to some very powerful hypnotherapy sessions during the stay. I was there with Jordan enjoying a preordained break, and any previously held scepticisms regarding energy healing were about to be pleasantly destroyed.

Roughly mid-way through that second session, as I felt the warmth and energy of Laurent's hands gently cupping the back of my head, my throat gland suddenly sprang to life, uncomforably throbing and intensely pulsing, triggering a ridiculous amount of saliva production to begin flowing. This was a swimming pool for teeth, and someone had left the hose on. I should spare you the graphic details, but I truly wanted to stop the session as it was not a comfortable reaction and dribbling like a teething baby was a genuine threat. However, I also instinctively knew that this was meant to happen, that there was healing occurring, and somehow this continuous 10 minute cycle of re-filling and swallowing - since rather than risk interrupting the process, I was choosing to swallow rather than get up and spit out - had to be some strange and disgusting sounding aspect of my body naturally healing.

When the session ended I spent the rest of the day semi-dazed, with my head feeling heavy and slightly woozy, I was genuinely shocked that I could have such physical responses to someone seemingly, just simply placing their hands on my head. It was eye opening to say the least, so at the end of a Source Reading Jordan facilitated as a thank you and sharing of skills that evening for our lovely hosts, I couldn't help but ask some questions regarding what exactly had happened earlier.

Q: Ok, this is a question for myself. As Laurent was giving me healing earlier today my throat welled up, and I'd like to get a further understanding on what was happening?

What was the cause? Why that effect?

Could I have more insight into what was happening during that healing process please?

A: There are many glands in the body as one might call them glands, these glands are responsive to the Chakras. Your glands, in response to your throat, began to activate as the healer worked on healing the traumatic experiences these glands, these muscles, these areas within your body had experienced. This was released in water as in saliva, swallowed to be ejected in the urination process as one might call it.

This was the healing work of a profound healer, he will continue with this work, you will receive healing hopefully today, you must continue to allow this healing to occur.

Brother you have been through much, your relationship with a certain individual had pushed you to your limits, now it is time for you to receive healing and recompense for the trauma of your relationship which you have seemingly been practicing to let go of, but you need help, the help has come! This is all divine, this was all planned.

Now have this healer work his healing, let him work with King Solomon, and any other entities including the Arch entities who work through this body in the healing practice. Your healing will continue and you will feel much better for it, do not worry about the heaviness of head, this is natural for healing causes the body to focus its energies on the healing process, energy thus gets taken away from processing in the brain, the intellectual thoughts, and it moves toward the benefit of the system that is called the body, as you call it.

Continue then with this, let this retreat serve as an example that the God-Force watches over you, the God-Force is infinite, the God-Force is mystical, your lives are ever planned and are ever moving, and you will leave this life looking forward to the wellness of your brothers and sisters in the heavens.

We leave now in the name and the nature of our loving Father. Amen.
S067 A10

Those references to the divine entities such as King Solomon, and Archangelic forces that aid in the healing work, should be understood in a deeper manner.

The reading explained how those divine entities of a considerably evolved kind saw a genuineness in our hosts, a checking of the ego as we might say, that comes with humility, humbleness and maturity of soul rather than age, which allowed for such powerful beings to work alongside them.

We were also informed that although we might call upon the words and names of various entities, these are not necessarily their names, but are something that we as humans find it easier to use as we need something to connect to. The truth is we are all beyond names. Yes, we may connect to the oneness through these divine entities, but they themselves will tell you to wear no names; you are beyond names, all are beyond names, we are all the unnameable, we are the infinite, we are one, and when you heal, you are using the oneness!

Healing work is not so much for the benefit of an individual's health, it is so that the person recognises the awakening experience where they realise the reality of the God-Force you see, the God-Force is what works through them all the time.

Any entity that serves to help you in your healing experience is utilising the universal God-Force, the God-Force is what we all look up to you see. You channel the God-Force through you, entities of divine kinds organise the energy as it comes through you, so you experience more of an orderly kind of the God-Force, you see? J+012 A6

At a later date, during some heart focused meditations, (see the later chapters Start with the Heart and A Practical Heart Exercise) my gland once again started to trigger, prompting further enquiry as given here:

As you would understand those systems of your Chakras dearest one, you would understand that they almost jump off one another. When the heart activates, the corresponding Chakra finds itself activating, like jumping a voltage or hoping up a ladder. The closer you are to a Chakra up the ladder, the easier that Chakra finds in its activating experience.

When you begun practicing these meditations you in fact activated your Heart Chakra, and what had occurred thus was the Throat Chakra, a jump up, was also able to start experiencing itself and any imbalances in this Chakra found themselves experiencing a chemical release, as you would call it saliva. This occurred in the exact same way that the entity Laurent, found himself giving you the same activation in the Heart Chakra, and thus kick-starting any other latent Chakras that were otherwise not rotating. J+017 A11

And just to clarify on the level of Throat Chakra activation we are talking about within my personal development, I can shamelessly say that... it's not a lot!

Yes, I'd love to be able to say that I was experiencing this energy centre at a high level, however this is just not the case. Despite popular belief, the Blue Ray of the Throat Chakra is a very big deal. Even minimal activation here is a massive accomplishment, and I include an extract on the current coherence of this Chakra within me to provide insight into what is perhaps a slightly misunderstood centre.

This ray is further detached from the selfish physical, it is detached from the selfless compassion even, it is now a kind of energy that is extremely non-physical, extremely psychedelic, extremely, how might one call it, abstract or very difficult to describe. The activity of this particular Chakra in yourself is as minimal as it is in most entities upon this plane, for this particular Chakra in its rotational activity would require that an entity undergoes a stupid amount of spiritual development, might we say respectfully.

In other words, you would be equivalent to an Olympic athlete, but instead you would be focusing those 1,000s and 1,000s and 1,000s and 1,000s, even in the tens of thousands of hours, this would all be focused internally to produce what humans would call a kind of cosmic consciousness. It is a very rare ray to have active upon your plane and it has become confused with many things, such as communication. This ray whilst in a communicative space, as it tends in its toroidal location to be structured in the location of the body around the throat, however this is not always so common, it is then easy to confuse this ray for communication where instead it more so has to do with one being in, in truth, a constant commune with the greatest level of non-physical existence.

Thus as we observe this Chakra in you, its level of rotation is extremely minimal, it is enough that it has allowed you to hold on to spiritual concepts that were instinctual or intuitive, such that you understood many things about life that you didn't necessarily have to learn, you knew what good spiritual material was so you were able to resonate with what could only be described as the good stuff. You knew who spoke sense and who didn't! This is due to the minimal activity of this ray significantly influencing the way you process thought, or the way you think. Q010 A10

Now, I've experienced energy training courses for both Reiki and Access Consciousness bars, which I found interesting and effective in the correct hands, however experiences such as the strength of my throats reaction, prompted some additional tips using Laurent's gift as a template, so the following is based on answers to his questions, and practice, which would begin with prayer:

Before you heal we recognise that there is a prayer said, continue to say the prayers you do for they invoke a spirit that would allow this one to aid in the experience of healing itself. This prayer, any kind of prayer, is useful, always say a prayer of protection before you begin any divine service, prayers of protection are not merely words vocalized into an environment, what humans have here to understand is their atmosphere, the atomic atmosphere vibrates according to the words you speak, but the words you speak cause remnants of memory to reside in the atmosphere after they are spoken, thus the atmosphere becomes a crystal, something that holds memory.

When you speak a prayer in mind or out loud you invoke into the room divinity, divine memory and entities that would seek to be of the negative kind cannot exist in such an environment for they cannot handle the vibrations that are present, so in terms of the beginning process of your healing experience give a little prayer of protection, any kind, call an entity to which you resonate with, it doesn't matter how you do it so long as you do it.

Next in terms of the Chakras as we observe this physical vehicle we see the Chakras burn brightly in terms of the Green Ray, it is the Green Ray that heats your hand, it is the Green Ray that permeates you, you are an incredibly Green Ray individual, your healing permeates the individual through this particular energy. Continue to work with the Green Ray, continue even in your meditations to open your Heart Chakra, as you begin to open this Chakra through simply attempting to feel it, just by literally focusing on the heart itself, the organ of the heart, you'll begin to feel surges, incredible surges of energy, your be able to use this energy to transmute onto others what you call healing and the healing itself will be remarkable, continue to work with the Green Ray.

Let us speak also on the 3rd eye Chakra, the brow Chakra, what you might call it, this brow Chakra will improve over time, you will find visions you will find also that you'll be able to see the aura of people in your healing work.

Now we would seek to give a practice; as you are healing you may keep your eyes closed or open, it depends, but what we can say is if you were to practice healing and focus deeply your eyes on any part of the individuals body, you can in your healing practice learn to see the aura, the surrounding energy of the body. As you learn this you will see indications of where exactly your hands should be in the healing process. The 3rd eye and Heart Chakra work in great harmony through the medium of the Throat Chakra to express healing energy.

We hope this information helps somewhat in your healing practice, understand that prana, as you call it, extends through a multi-dimensional framework, it is a part of the electromagnetic spectrum, when you begin your healing your entire aura becomes full of vibrancy of the Green Ray and of the Indigo and Blue Ray, you become somewhat of a being that is full of light, this is why people – as you have told this instrument – have described you as being one of the possessor of white light, you shine brightly this is the reason why we are giving you this information, we hope it is helpful. J+012 A5

Breathing exercises are another powerful process that can enhance the receptivity of the body to the reception of healing energies:

There are at least two states that the body can be in at any given time, the oxygen state can be seen as the positive state, or the positive charge as you would understand. The negative state can be seen as the carbon dioxide state, which would be the negative charge.

These charges are more metaphors than they are at all literals in the scientific nature, however there is a change in energy flow when there is more carbon dioxide present in the body then there is oxygen.

When one is seeking to utilise oxygen, you are seeking to build life current and do work with it. When we do our channelling, we breath in oxygen to build life current to do this work, life current is useful for anything to do with working energy, it may be utilised in healing work, channelling work, or any kind of work which requires life energy.

Oxygen is the energy one uses to work life.

Then there is the carbon dioxide, this work pertains not to the work of life but to the work of, as we would use the term 'death', almost. For you are in essence working within the realm beyond this one. carbon dioxide in a spiritual sense is thus used to access any realm beyond this current realm, thus rather than the crude word 'death', you may find the word 'afterlife' being how the chemical, carbon dioxide, is utilised in the physiology.

One will utilise oxygen for anything to do with life, one will utilise carbon dioxide for anything to do with the afterlife. This is a rather simple take on the matter, but it does well to serve as an explanation to when you would want an oxygen tilted balance, or when you would want a carbon dioxide tilted balance within your streaming's of blood as you would understand. J+019 A1

If breathing is to be accomplished in the most correct way, that it would be beneficial to a brother or sister in the process of any kind of spiritual work, it would be done slowly.

The breath must be accomplished in such a steady fashion that the body does not become alerted in such a way that it would instinctively think that there is some predator about, thus avoiding any panic as you would understand panic. This is how the breathing is to be accomplished, this does indeed have beneficial effects on the vehicle, for the vehicle becomes oxygenated, and oxygen is what allows for energy to be created in the body, thus all functioning cells where blood is travelling to, all functioning organs where blood is travelling to, receiving this extra oxygen become extra capable of the production of extra energy.

This may cause one, if the breathing is accomplished in the correct way, to have a general boost in mood, well-being, and even the capacity to heal, digest, and do all of the various functions that the organs do in a non-survival state. S073 A9

The time period at the beginning of the session would be the degree of time to which would be required for oxygenation of the blood to reach a level in which carbon is for the most part minimal and oxygen is maximum.

Overall, this length of time would be around the number 40, pertaining to 40 breaths rather than 40 minutes, the breath of a deep kind, 40 times per in breath, would allow for the blood to be oxygenated to an elevated degree. For most humans, those humans who have larger bodies would require more breath thus you would adjust the number depending on the human. S073 A10

The receiver of the healing can be aided into entering a receptive healing state through the use of melodies that would engage the intellectual brain, the left brain, in melody, thus allowing the right brain to be available for use as the left brain becomes concentrated on following the rhythmic patterns of the song, the right brain can be opened for spiritual service.

When music reaches the right brain and travels beyond the left brain, one begins to experience music within the body, and music becomes the dimension in itself. Many entities upon this plane have yet to be able to experience what you call 'synaesthesia', which is what happens when music travels to the right hemisphere of the brain. S073 A14

This would be such that all senses come together, sound connects with sight, sight connects with smell. As you would see there are various ways to connect the 5-pointed star, thus music becomes enjoyable on all levels, all dimensions including senses beyond this one. S073 A15

For the *brain* hemispheres become such that their melodies, or the way that they vibrate and oscillate, is in such a way that the oscillations themselves do not disturb each other, instead they come together as one brain, as one mind, thus you have a whole brain as would be termed. The light in the cleft of the brain between the two hemispheres becoming at one as you would see.

In terms of, to predict the question, what method would be better to sync the hemispheres?

You would see that in Atlantean times, there was technology that would serve as to directly stimulate the brain, causing the brain to combine in its resonance. However of course, we as the Source find meditative practice as the only true way to achieve a synchronised brain, with right and left hemisphere synchronisation causing one to have a tremendous perception of life, allowing one to be incredibly gifted. S073 A16

For the healer itself, crystals would be incredibly helpful; for the one being healed wearing a favourite crystal would be incredibly helpful.

The science of coherence leading to evolution.

Intelligent energy as you might term it, finds its ability to flow through crystals in coherent fashions, especially the quartz crystal as you would see it, that if held and utilised could insight healing.

The infinite energy would come from the human as the energy would find coherence, or coherify, where the crystal is being held within the hand and then shot out of the equinox of the pyramid shape, that is the one vertices of the pyramid shape at the end of the quartz crystal itself.

Crystals thus have been used for healing for centuries, and crystals such as diamonds, quartz crystals and other kinds of crystals, are very useful for the process of healing, yet you would find, how much practice how much self-development, is truly required to become an adept at this practice?

Indeed, there is a lot. S073 A19

Regarding the healer's mind and thoughts in the generation of coherent energy to share with the brother or sister being healed, the aim is to have our brains energy in a coherent pattern, a pattern that does not create stress regardless of any random thoughts that may pop up. This can be achieved through the practice of meditation, as one becomes accustomed to witnessing their thoughts without emotionally or chemically reacting to the same:

As pertaining to this ones mind, body, spirit. Rather, as pertaining to this ones soul, one must imagine that the area of the soul inside of the body called the brain, is something like an incoherent mess for the average human upon this planet. Those as you would class as spiritually coherent are entities who experience the activation of the 3rd eye or clairvoyant centre, this clairvoyant centre is felt as pressure within the head, this pressure most often is isolated between the brow and is felt as a pulsating energy. As this energy grows, coherence grows, as coherence grows one becomes more one pointed, and thus more capable as they edge towards becoming the adept, as you would understand it.

Thus, you would see that in your practice of meditation, it is a practice of bringing your mind into an incredibly settled place in which your thoughts are not messy, yet instead are balanced.

Then you would see and understand what it means to have such a coherent mind, and then as pertaining to the question itself of what the entity should be thinking, firstly this entity would realise that thought is energy, and so what you think is in fact the pattern of energy that is occurring in the brain, if the pattern of energy that is occurring in the brain is not conducive to the environment to which you are partaking in, then this will cause disruption in the spiritual flow of energy from you to your brother or sister to whom you are healing.

If, however, your brain energies become coherent and pleasant, then the thoughts you will think, irregardless of what they are, whether they are topics on violence or topics on love, will have little importance for the energies of the brain in themselves are coherent and so thoughts themselves in their wordy format carry little weight. However, to a normal human, thoughts carry weight due to the fact that their incoherent brainwaves experience thought in stressful mannerisms, causing the stressful aspects of the thought to become focussed upon as one focuses upon a Lion when one sees a Lion.

When ones brainwaves are coherent, ones focus is not on the survivalist aspects of thought, instead ones mind is completely free and open to experience only the cosmic energies of life. S073 A13

When healing is occurring as you would understand healing, it is the act of the bringing of coherent energy to another person, one does not therefore imagine energy leaving the body in any way, shape or form, but instead imagines that the energy within the entity is becoming more organised, more coherent, more flexible, more useable and less random.

This is true healing as you would understand it, thus many of these practices that you would be privy to as you go on your travels dearest brother, will be practices more seen as ritualistic white magic that would have a placebo effect on the brain, more than it is seen as anything that is objectively useful and as you would use the term, scientifically sound.

Within these realms of the spirit it is simply about coherence and order, and becoming the entity whom is able to freely become an open door to the available infiniteness around them. This is thus the simplicity of creation, and coherence, and order is what opens that door, for coherence and order finds it so that you would even be able to put your hand on the door to open it.

If there is no coherence and you stretch out your hand it will flap about like a madman, if there is coherence as you move your hand to the door, the door will open with an easy grasp.

If there is no coherence and you hold a fork, the fork will shake and fall out of your hand as though you are one unfortunately experiencing Parkinson's disease, if there is coherence at the holding of the fork you will be able to get noodles in your mouth, thus you find the door to infinite energy is in coherence. S073 A11

And finally some data on the use of physical touch or non-touch healing, such as on distant healing, or the placing of the hands close to the body rather than on the body:

As you would understand touch, it is not necessary but for the human, as you know humans, they are such limited creatures by nature due to their disbelief in the spiritual forces.

Such is the nature of reality that two entities could sit in two different countries, but if one entity was so at-one-ment with the Creator, distance would not matter and if ye so willed it, instantaneous healing would occur toward the entity who is on the other side of the country, this entity unknowingly being healed perhaps would be surprised as all of his diseases dissipate.

What does distance matter?

Whether touch is occurring or not is but another placebo!

Touching regions and areas in the body make no difference to the healing that occurs, yet it is the significance of the area of touch in the persons belief system that causes the healing to either work or not work. Some believe that touching them on the heart will cause healing, they believe it so much it happens.

Others believe touching in certain areas will make healing occur, this is all based on belief, thus you will work with entities then who prefer the touch method, for most humans do prefer being touched as to incite the experience of intimacy during the healing, making healing more powerful, but it may be seen that touch is but a limitation of the mind in its necessity and healing can occur without the same. Thus, healing occurs when coherence is built, thus if one is to place ones hands, or even have ones hands not placed for it wouldn't matter, irregardless of whether one was using hands or not, if one was able to direct energy toward a person by, as you would understand, distributing their own energy, which is full of coherence, then this distribution of coherent energy to the other entity or soul would cause instantaneous healing, if and only if the soul is willing to accept the same.

Thus, healing is but a question...

Are you willing to accept the healing that is coming to you?

Do you believe you are allowed to accept the healing that is coming to you?

Are you sceptical?

Are you disbelieving?

Is your left brain overly active thus disturbing the coherence that is attempting to fill your brain and body?

All of these questions must be answered from the soul within, consider these things deeply in the question of why there are no fireworks, as you would call them fireworks, when one is touching them, when one is bringing healing to you. S073 A12

The Ego

'Those who think that when they die, they leave their body and they are now their soul would actually be incorrect, for they are in actuality just in a lighter egoic body.'

The Ego and Soul

The ego is quite natural and it has a very profound effect on our energy centres, in particular the lower three as the ego is basically a survival protocol created by our fundamental desire to stay alive, and staying alive is generally considered a win for most people. The issue with this is that everything the ego creates is therefore based on death and avoiding the prospect of any form of lack, anything that could hinder one's ability to survive.

Our focus on energy is a focus on life, not death, therefore the ego is an aspect that needs to be overcome as part of the journey toward the coherent energy of love and life vs the entropic energy of fear and death.

The ego is built up in layers, it is a creation formed from resonance. We take on characteristics, traits, even the personalities of those lights that influence us, whether astrological lights such as those energies that bombard the soul and magnetise our core traits at birth, be that the disciplinary nature of Jupiter or the raw drive of Mars, along with the more earthly based light such as the auras of the people and even animals, places and objects, we are influenced by as we grow. Everything has light you see. We just build up layers adding new traits and characteristics dependent on our resonance with the light that is hitting us. If we feel that a particular light will aid us in better surviving, in better avoiding lack and essentially physical death itself, we will add it to our collection. It could be your fathers work ethic, your friend's confidence, or a famous rapper's attitude, if we resonate with it we will add it to our song.

This is the ego! A build-up of layers based on survival; the ego is simply the layers we build on top of our soul in an attempt to safely navigate this illusion. The issue being that all these egoic layers are entropic as they are based on the concept of death, not life.

The ego exists when one does not feel pure and safe. It exists as a fight or flight mechanism and so any ideas or concepts that the ego creates are always based on the prospect of death, of that ability to die, or that ability to experience some kind of lack, lacking of love, an absence of love, an absence of that particular light. J+008 A18

To better understand the ego, we should first gain a primary understanding of God and the Christos. In brief, God is the only divine force that exists in this universe, the force beyond the Christos.

God, is to be seen as God! - to be comedic.

God is neither masculine or feminine, God is God.

God is the being by which all things, all existence can happen.

When you give thanks to God you warm his heart with the love and gratitude to which he would seek to express unto you, so in the limited language of English, forgive this Source for ever giving God a gender, God is neither masculine, feminine, positive, negative, this or that, God is no charge, God is pureness, purity in itself.

God is all that is and is all that is infinite, unlimited, ever expanding, God exists within you.

When you give thanks to God you give thanks to yourself. S055 A5

If you struggle with the word Christos, the closest suggestion I could personally offer would be to replace it with the word 'Cosmos'. You would however need to think of the Cosmos as being love based, vibrantly alive, expressive and vastly intelligent.

For those of a more science-based thought process, we were offered the following:

The closest terms we see are the terms Quantum, Light, Photon, Electricity; these words seem to come as close to the Christos as far as Jordan's vocabulary extends. M006 A23

And if you struggle with the word Christ, although this is also the Christos, I suggest you replace it with love. Living love.

God had a son; his son was the closest representation of himself. His son was this multidimensional universe you know so well. His son was also the soul that drove this universe. His son was called **love** and love expresses itself. S010 A6

Your soul really is the Christos itself, the primordial soul split itself amongst many realms to expedite its learning. At this lower vibrational end of our souls experience, free will has allowed us to create the illusion of individuality, yet we are all interconnected with the Christos, and so at our core we are all One. One soul experiencing itself in an infinite amount of ways.

It may be easier to imagine the whole thing as a thought. That we exist in one thought, in one mind, and this thought is that which connects everything together.

Your scientists would do well in understanding that if they approach their ideas with the fundamental that this universe is truly made of love their discoveries, most notably in the quantum field, would come quite quickly as they have on other planets and Galaxies that house 3-dimensional life. S010 A6

Understand 3-dimensional reality by the nature of your Solar Plexus, firstly it is an individual experience without the immediate connection to others, it is an 'I see you but don't know you' planet, which creates the idea of the unknown in a soul or the illusion at least that there could be an unknown.

Then there would be the 4th dimension which breaks the barrier between 'You are You' and 'I Am Me'. The 4th dimension looks to connect two perceivers into one perception so that there is only one eye seeing everything at once.

The 4th dimension is directly comparable to a network of computers, the 3rd dimension is directly equivalent to a computer that is not connected to the network. The transition from the 3rd to the 4th occurs when one recognises himself as love in others and sees not the unknown but the ever present known in all, for this one would see that all are one.

The universe is made of love, love is God's 1st son and that in itself is the Christ force. If one were to base all his ideas off this, there would be good information, good philosophy, divine ideas coming through. S010 A7

Let's view this from another angle; the 4th dimension has an awareness of unification. The 3rd dimension has an awareness of limitlessness. For example, a victim statement of 'I'm too dumb', or even conversely a victim statement of 'I'm too smart' are both the same since both mean you do not believe you can learn anything further. This illusion of limitation can be overcome at this 3rd dimensional stage of evolution, paving the way for unification.

The 3rd dimensional body is designed for mental expression, it's a Solar Plexus vehicle intended for evolution to the Heart Chakra. The intellect serves this experience to enable us to overcome the challenges of this chemical-based environment. Things move slower in a chemical environment, this is why we can feel our anger building, our passion growing, our hunger increasing over time, we feel this energy in motion because the chemical/emotional body moves slower then the mental body. Thoughts do not manifest in the atomic realm immediately, they start in the mental body, then they move through the slower chemical/emotional body, and finalise in the even slower atomic body, this is illustrated in the way consistent traumatic thoughts will slowly make our body ill over time, once recognised, this gives us the opportunity to learn how to think in a more coherent fashion. As we improve our quality of thought, our quality of consciousness, we naturally become better creators as consciousness is the driver of this physical universe.

We are basically learning cause and effect in a slow vehicle; how do my thoughts effect the light around me?

There is naturally a lot of suffering and refinement in this process, harsh lessons and beautiful blessings, but when we graduate to a faster, more responsive vehicle, this training means we will be able to correctly control and focus our thoughts, and not destroy everything in sight.

The chemical body is a very slow body, but it serves as a sensitive tool for evolution that the mental body can be cultivated. What that means is, cultivating the mental body is best experienced not in the 4th dimension, but in the 3rd dimension, in a vehicle that is chemically built, for here the mental body is more sensitive, you are able to feel the mental body as what you call emotion but in the upper dimensions what you call emotion is not in existence anymore.

The experience of emotion is nullified because the mental body in comparison to the heart body, is a much lower frequency and so evolving the mental body is best experienced in a chemical body so that the chemical body can be sensitive to mental impressions, and then it would be understood, when there is mastery over the mental plane - can then begin evolution toward the more spiritual planes.

So what you would have is sensitivity to the mental experience of life called emotion, then there would be mastery of this that emotion would become something not experienced, and there would only be known within the being a sense of eternal love, gratitude, bliss and harmony. And here when that is the only vibration one is feeling the evolution completely shifts, so this would be the understanding. S056 A7

The Ego and Death

One should think of an ego as a soul with a layer. You have many bodies, your soul really is the Christos itself however you have clouded it with multitudes of bodies, these bodies are the ego.

Those who think that when they die, they leave their body and they are now their soul would actually be incorrect, for they are in actuality just in a lighter egoic body. The soul, the true soul is the Christos, which is not housed in a form, the form is the ego. S011 A7

It would be understood in the more simple ways, that of the nature of psychology as is being understood on this planet. One's psychology is what is understood as one's belief system, which governs their emotional regulation. So, for a soul to be exposed to truth as God had designed it, against their false belief system would be a shock, and so what has been designed is upon the death of the soul, the soul is put in a trance to which they can at least come to terms with the afterlife in a steady process by which their belief system is slowly realigned with truth.

This is a designed protocol to how the Earth systematic experience is to be experienced for it was understood that trauma, as the term goes, has a dramatic effect on the souls perception of life be it truth or false, and so then as a protective mechanism to stop souls from being further traumatised by the fact that heaven is as below so above, so was this light trance state included in the protocol of disincarnate entities.

This experience is governed by the Over-Self, through the subconscious mind to ensure that their Lower-Self is not traumatised by truth. Depending on how distorted one's understanding of the upper heavens is, will determine the severity of the dream state and if one's understanding of the afterlife is accurate then that experience of being in the dream-like state will be a very short-lived experience as they transition to the other side. S056 A5

Indeed, with love we will give this then dearest one, for this is our service you see. In nature there are many dimensions and densities of love, there are many things you see, and upon the death of the vehicle that would be considered the physical vehicle, one will enter into a different vehicle, a higher dimensional vehicle. You may call this the 4th dimensional vehicle, call it whatever you wish, let it simply be known that the force of life at the subatomic level will begin to leave the being at the atomic level.

As this begins the being, dependent on many beliefs, many facets of the being will begin to wake up to what is termed as a light dream, for leaving the body and then simply being open to everything would be quite a shock, and so the Over-Self would seek to put the new arrival to sleep in a light dream so that the Over-Self can communicate with the being within a framework that they can be familiar with, until the being is ready to wake up from their, might we call it, Astral slumber, until the being has recognised the illusion of their false beliefs of the afterlife.

The being then will become awake within this body and will be able to explore with free will the many things that are yet to be known. The being may adventure within the lower dimensions of Earth, may see the occurrences that would occur after the death of the being, may see family members weeping and sowing as humans do, and this being may seek to take refuge within the 3rd dimension but will eventually find their energies lacking, hunger pangs you see, these hunger pangs grow more severe for there is a lack of that light, those higher dimensional photons, the higher dimensional electromagnetism.

The being eventually becomes quite weak, in-able if they have prolonged their stay upon the planet, upon Earth and would seek then eventually to open their eyes to greater light, to the golden light that they recognise on some level that they need. Once this has been fully recognised the being would seek those as you would call them, helpers, guides, genuine souls, souls that are also upon their incarnative path, who are able to take the being, the soul as it is termed, to a junction.

Technology is different in the Heavens as it is to the Earth, far more sophisticated, far more generalised, far better, for they work on a subatomic realm not an atomic realm and with this technology and with these souls, these beings who can be of service, they would take this being to be healed, for the being can only be healed when the free will would seek the same.

And so continues - as the soul continues in their evolution, in their cycle of conscious experience of the various dimensions in this school you see. S052 A14

We look toward the word 'frequency' when it comes to death, and we see love not so much as an emotion, but as something quite transcendent indeed. When we look at love, we see this point in the middle expressing itself outwardly and there are all these sub-dimensions, the in-betweens, many different manifestations of the same.

In death we transition from one manifestation to the other, and we are talking of the death of the physical body of course, where one goes from one frequency, to another frequency, that would allow them to reside on a different plane, but even then one may still feel negative emotions or positive ones, or the many different emotions that come with recovering from a human experience.

The frequency of the emotion will determine what plane one enters into on the leaving of the planet and those that experience emotions so beyond negativity, will find themselves in the higher planes, for these planes resonate at the same frequency of which they vibrate at, at the frequency of their Astral body.

It is entirely relevant and dependant on the individual and their incarnative experience, but it is good if one were to see it in the sense of frequency and vibration. Negative emotions have a slow rather distasteful vibration and positive emotions have a more orderly, vibrant and more beautiful vibration.

If one walks through life worrying and being angry, being annoyed at everything, being a victim and blaming this, that and the other, upon the leaving of the body at the stage of death, if they were exposed to the frequencies of the higher Astral it would be incredibly dense and incredibly uncomfortable, they would simply have to leave for it would even be too bright for them to see anything. And so, this is how it is you see, that all things have a vibration, a frequency, and it is in this school where one aims to raise their frequency, in the face of one of the toughest challenges of all, being the illusion itself. S024 A6

After death you would find that the lower three Chakras are for the most part deactivated, thus the entity becomes one no longer concerned so much with the need for wealth, the need for power, survival, security and these things as you would understand. This creates a rather peaceful entity and can startle entities sometimes when they meet their past parents who were tyrants in the physical life but then become peaceful saints in the next, yet they are only peaceful because they do not have to concern themselves with money and these things, as you would understand.

The basic rate of thought, or rather the basic quality of thought that the entities experience remains the same, therefore even though the entities in the heavens are quite peaceful they will still argue with you and have the same kinds of disagreements that you would have on Earth, and have the same issues of thought. Not much changes as you would understand, for change can only be generated if an entity desires inward exploration and growth. S081 A22

In a most basic sense, entities are resting within the realms anywhere between the upper 6th densities and the lower 4th densities of electromagnetic light, invisible to the naked eye, for the naked eye is trapped within the spectrum of what you call visible light, whereas the 4th density as Lobsang *Rampa* had identified, is beyond the gamma spectrum.

The various upper densities from 4th density onwards, continue up the electromagnetic spectrum far beyond what the human eye can see. You would find those beings to which you would understand as in soul form, to be resting anywhere between 4th to 6th density, oft depending on the entities level of consciousness and what they are able to withstand in terms of intensity of life or vital life force. S081 A21

The Ego and Reincarnation

We begin with an understanding that a soul starts its journey with only traces of intelligence. Yet these traces would be so slight they would hardly be recognisable to the soul itself and as the soul evolves from experience to experience, even only experiencing the primary elements of life itself, it finds itself moving from one dimension to the next, and to the next, as it continues its evolutionary path to the Christos, to the white light at the centre. S011 A5

The soul itself is a soul that decided, 'I don't want to be a part of the Christos anymore; I want to have my own free will!'

And in that decision, it then had to let go of all that it knew to have that experience of free will. That does include the literal Intellectual Quota (IQ) as it is called in your plane as well, and if that disappears then there is no resilience to those external influences in the beginning. S011 A9

To really drive it home we could even say that at the birth of a new free willed soul the, as you measure it, IQ is zero, many zeros followed by the one, and the Christos itself would have that of an immeasurable number. S011 A11

You would find that entities from the lowest of the lowest densities as you would understand, find themselves incarnating as either the experience of the Air, Water, even soils and these things itself, or in more advanced forms they would find themselves incarnate as a micro-organism, their experiences, are for the comedic sense, logged into the matrix of spirit as RA would say, and the great matrix of spirit manages the reincarnations of the single celled organisms and unconscious, yet sentient to a degree of a minimal kind, forms of consciousness which are experiencing these minimal experiences.

There is a kind of reincarnation as you would find, it is a kind of reincarnation that is not really understood by humans for it is not so useful to understand this, you may comprehend this as a kind of reincarnation which is so rapid that it makes no real sense to attempt to locate the number, for you would be counting zeros in its decimal nature for a long time. These rapid incarnations perpetuate and push consciousness forward through the basic dimensions and densities as you would understand, until they can become something more complex, like a land animal, a fish, or a larger organism such as a slug. S081 A24

When one is to stand and look at self in the mirror these will see a body. What makes the body what it is, is that it is a composition of intelligent chemical reactions governed by the slow vibrating forces, and here would be visible the fields, the nuclei, the electron, the proton, you see. And these are as your science calls them 'particles' but are in reality more so light fields, and these light fields, these packets of energy are slow moving, very slow moving.

They create the physical body, but you see brother if you were to look deeper, deeper, if you could make yourself small, and smaller, and smaller you would take a journey from molecule, to atom, to subatomic atom, to super subatomic, and you would go down ever still, and as you would become smaller the vibrations would grow in speed till you reached soul, brother.

When the vibration is so fast in the particle so small, it becomes invisible to your sciences. Your sciences become incapable of picking up on the soul you see, for it is too high a vibration, too small to see, and equally can the soul fit comfortably inside of an air particle and experience the experience of being an atmosphere, of being fire, of being a strand of grass, of being water.

Now these may understand the soul more deeply, and then to the system of reincarnation for these are entering into a car, no? What is the vehicle, hmm?

The vehicle changes for the soul is curious, the soul seeks to learn, to grow, to develop and to increase in vibration, so indeed you will jump and jump with jolly joy as you move your soul molecules into the space of an atomic field, that your intelligence may experience the same, may experience that consciousness. S048 A6

The lowest entities experience predominantly the Red Ray, in the lowest form the Red Ray is that experience of being a molecule, in the upper experience it would be found that it is the experience of surviving as a micro-organism, in the true upper spectrums of this Red Ray experience it is found in the eating and consuming of food for the sake of one's survival and the enjoyment of that experience.

Then there is the inevitable occurrence of an ecosystem which desires to feed off that entity, which then is reincarnated in nanoseconds to experience again this same experience over and over again, in various forms and formations, creating what you would understand as the primary ego layer being that of that lowest Chakra. S081 A25

As pertaining to the ego, it would be well to understand that this term is a term to describe a certain category of thinking whereby the quality of one's thinking is very intimately connected to the first three basic energy centres, that of the thinking that pertains to the Red, the Orange and then the Yellow.

Thinking in a survival way would be that of the primary ego *(Red Ray).*

The secondary ego *(Orange Ray)* would be the relationship one has with other entities in a sense of needing security from them and these kinds of thoughts.

Then finally those more higher egoic thoughts *(Yellow Ray)* that pertain to having great power or being one who is in a position of authority, in total control.

These are various increasing qualities of thought as you would understand, the Orange in particular being an interesting exploration for one finds that at this level of ego, one is seeking the ego of the Solar Plexus *(Yellow)*, whereby one seeks to transcend in their interpersonal relationships from a position of victim, to a position of power and control. This is the natural elevation of these egos as you would understand.

The first primary ego *(Red)* would be an ego pertaining to what you would understand as survival, then the egos go up like a piano scale into the 4th ego *(Green)* pertaining to that of the heart, which has its issues, its impurities or rather its shortcomings.

Then to the 5th *(Blue),* the 6th *(Indigo)*, these are two degrees of ego yet the 6th being so close now to the One Infinite Creator that it is relatively egoless.

Then at the gateway being the 6th energy centre, one transcends into cosmic consciousness, a moment in which the amount of light funnelling into the Chakra will reach critical mass and one will 'pop' into a different body that can actually handle the light and experience something that can never be put into words. S081 A11

Red is survival, the Red is your relationship with the complete and utter victim-ness to your complete lack of power, for you are a survivor at the Red.

Orange is personal relationships, the Orange is your relationship with the gaining of said power, at the Orange you are beginning to recognise that survival is important but not all there is to life.

Yellow is the relationship you have to power, that ability to feel powerful. At the Yellow you are that which controls, and in complete control of self's survival, one who feels transcendent of the same, one who feels all powerful, one who commands nature as you would understand. S081 A12

We find that when one is of the lower egos the brain remains for the most part in potential, not yet activated for the brain typically is being used for egoic reasons to do with the lower egos of survival, interpersonal relationships, and the feeling of being in control of one's ability to survive. You would find the experience of being in control of one's ability to survive, called working, as you would understand this term, which is most strengthened the more one has what you would understand as money. Money activates the Solar Plexus to a brilliant level.

The activations of that Orange centre would come into its greatest brilliance when one is first beginning to experience that experience of having something to rely on, to some degree or level, that can help its survival. It creates an experience of dependence, bringing this vibration of that Orange Chakra into such a vibrancy, and the survival Chakra *(Red)* being most related to the feeding of the physiology and these mannerisms as you would understand.

These lower Chakras seem to for the most part, greatly deactivate the Merkabah potential of the interdimensional vehicle you know as your central nervous system and your brain. When you surpass these experiences through the Heart Chakra serving somewhat as a gateway and enter into 5th, 6th and 7th density experiences which also include the 4th density of the Heart Chakra, these four Chakras, or as we would prefer to say three, being the Heart, Throat and Brow, serve as to activate the interdimensional vehicle you would understand as your brain. S081 A17

You would find that those Chakras or those egos as you would understand, that have to do with those first three levels of consciousness to do with control, interpersonal relationships and survival, all have a deteriorating effect on one's ability to take the brain and put it into its true form. It is well to understand that the lower egos are external egos, which can only be mediated through one's muscular body and through very external thoughts.

To activate the internal vehicle requires an internal journey into the internal self. S081 A18

Indeed life is truly, in its early stages of the first three Chakras including the 4th to a degree, an experience of the body. But at a certain experience the brain as you would understand becomes your vehicle, becomes your method of exploration, the brain in itself becomes your metaphysical Merkabah vehicle, by which you explore consciousness with an unimaginable amount of freedom. Indeed, the physical vehicle creates some degree of freedom, but the brain is a vehicle where your freedom becomes infinite, so why not hone the brain and practice meditation, and begin to experience consciousness for its true, and in its true nature? S081 A13

The Merkabah Vehicle

We would be making reference to what occurs in the brain when the brain accesses its basic 6 latent components positioned throughout its brain matter, which seemingly turn on through meditative practice. Those 6 components have to do with the activation of a subtle body which allows one to become electromagnetically capable, rather than limited to the atomic vehicle.

We find reference to the basic brains, that cerebral forebrain as in the cerebral cortex, then the forebrain itself, the mid-brain, the hind brain, and the spine, then finally the nugget brain called the pineal gland which seeks to turn the brain into a Merkabah vehicle capable of perfect freedom. S081 A14

You have two bodies, one is your muscular body to which entities are all too fond of, the other is the brain body, which establishes itself as the Merkabah vehicle capable of interdimensional travel. S081 A15

One must free the brain completely within the meditative practice, this activates this vehicle as you would understand, for it is a vehicle as is your muscular body a vehicle, then interdimensional travel and interdimensional experience becomes possible. One becomes the true self you would find, easily achieved through meditation where the brain can become the vehicle that is in most use and the physical body vehicle, the muscular vehicle, can turn off completely.

In order for you to activate the brain you must enter into it as such. Does this make sense? S081 A16

The Ego and Astrological Light

It is built over the process of being born firstly in a star system under particular influences and moving through that astrological system. As it moves, grows, evolves, expands, it starts to attain different personalities, different traits dependent on the nature of the light that is hitting it or influencing it, and that light doesn't have to be stars as you see stars, for humans are stars - mini stars, animals are stars - mini stars.

All things that emit an aura are stars in their own right, and as an ego is bombarded with all these influences of which all of them are astrological, they will take the ones that they resonate with and will leave the ones they don't.

That is the birth, beginning, the start of an ego. S011 A6

It would be understood that there is a certain metaphysical quality as each planet has in itself a sentience and a Chakra system to which what you would understand as Prana, as we have defined the term as the upper lights, the upper densities of light that is responsible for the upper Chakras, this very high light as it shines through planets and shines thus into a soul matrix, it has the ability to alter that souls basic vibratory rate causing the soul to have particular biases instilled by the planet itself.

We should point out that it is typically the desire of the soul to completely transcend any bias that a celestial object has given it, for it is the desire of the soul to recognise that it is truly infinite and need not necessarily rely on astrological, metaphysical influences, therefore whilst the soul maybe partially influenced by celestial objects and their basic metaphysical vibration as light of a metaphysical kind called Prana passes through their Chakras and into your bodies, whilst this does have an influence, the significance it should bear ought to be minimal as the entity in truth, as are all entities, truly ought to be reminded that the true task upon this plane, in this school as you would understand, dearest one if you want to finish this school need you only practice meditation, for meditation is that act of establishing the ability to funnel the One Infinite Creators light into you in an extremely focused manner. S081 A13

Similar to the inheritance of the metaphysical light coming in from one's astrological surroundings. The inheritance protocol is simply how nature propagates a physical vehicle, one can easily deactivate one's inherited experience by activating the spinal midi-brains including the cerebral, to become a being of an interdimensional nature composed of electromagnetic light, for this is the true form of the self as you would find.

Those who are subject to their ancestor's *ego layers* are entities who reside in the lower Chakras. S081 A19

Indeed, in that practice to which you would understand as Organic Meditation, one finds themselves experiencing their electromagnetic identity, rather than their atomic identity, therefore one reminds themselves that thine is light, and that any inherited DNA can be irradiated and dissolved. S081 A20

The Ego and The Dreamworld

In remembering that our ego, our personality, is mainly based on survival, the identification of these distortions via meditation is a great method, you can even map the traits and characteristics to the various Chakras depending on the thoughts that pop up as these biases begin to organically untangle.

I have also found that a surprisingly powerful way of directly identifying ego layers occurs simply by recording our dreams. The characters/places/objects we see in our dreams appear to be the literal ego layers, the lights we have resonated with and layered on top of our souls. In our dreams as we move through the Astral experience, we are often observing aspects of auras that we have resonated with and added to our own song in order to better survive, whether in person or via role models we observe on the TV, we take on that which we feel we require. In the absence of self-love, we fill the gaps that we perceive in our own illusion with the light of others, to complete any lack of light we feel we might have within us.

Yes, this is the nature of reality, for as much as a human would like to state quotation 'I am an individual', he is and always has been connected to all things.

Whether it is across the TV, whether the person lives in Australia, this matters not for light is everywhere at once, and that which you resonate with will become a part of your aura, so choose wisely who you role model.

DISCERN spirits as much as you discern individuals and vice versa. This is most important that one might build a healthy aura, a healthy spiritual complex and healthy Chakras. S014 A8

It may be best understood in this particular analogy; one finds that the consciousness of the self is somewhat of a conductor, that is it sings like a singing bowl and the neighbouring singing bowls around it can cause it to vibrate in unison with its surroundings. There are souls who are so conductive that they become an amalgamation of their environment, and there are souls who have established a degree of insulativeness, if we could use such a word, and therefore do not conduct their surrounds and thus are not influenced by environmental pressures.

Perhaps one's degree of spiritual adeptness is in their capacity to remain somewhat of an insulator to the entropy of their surroundings, for even a singing bowl can vibrate in entropy if the molecular structure of the said singing bowl has been damaged due to dropping. Therefore dearest one, you speak of such ego layers and we speak of sound, for sound and ego layers are so much alike, for what is an ego layer but a layer of sound, of resonance, of a kind of intelligence, and what is intelligence and its resonance but a sound?

Are they not similar?

Therefore, are humans not resonating with other people's energy, other people's intelligence?

Resonance of intelligence, or energy in this case, and the experience of absorbing others resonances and adding it to one's own vibratory oscillations, is but the nature of two singing bowls sitting with each other, one of them starting to sing and the other one singing in the same unison. Here explains then a key aspect of your nature vs nurture paradox to which entities in psychology find themselves in, and as pertaining to your question of ego layers and how they appear in your dreams, dearest one is it not so that when a singing bowl is resonating, that those resonations will naturally carry into each and every density including the density to which dreams happen. It is only natural that that which sings propagates into the air and even into sparser atmospheres that are composed of a higher, or a more highly dense if we may use this misnomer, region of space and time. J+023 A5

The Higher-Self is somewhat dormant in the dreamworld, it is the self which demonstrates to the self such things, the Higher-Self is the reference point in which the soul is able to determine the light and the darkness. The Higher-Self is the light, the soul is the darkness, for the soul has incarnated into a dark realm and is experiencing the vibrations of darkness in their minimal frequencies.

With the point of reference of the Higher-Self, one is able to determine how certain ego layers may or may not be to the closeness they would like to get toward the Higher-Self. Thus, entities on many occasions during the dream space utilise the Higher-Self as a reference point for the Lower-Self and those ego layers.

Those resonances sing along a spectrum and the closer they are to the Higher-Self, the more keen the soul is to holding on to those vibratory oscillations. Further away will cause the soul to seek to discard such things, such vibrations, such intelligent resonations. J+023 A6

Shattering the Ego

The lower dimensional ego is based on the illusion that we are having individual experiences, this is an illusion, all is one, therefore we influence each other in a vast number of ways, seen and unseen. As we enter an understanding of the 4th dimension, the false values of the ego get replaced as we experience unity, becoming part of the network rather than a standalone PC so to speak. It is here that the universe starts to display its own meanings, its own values rather than our egos survival-based biases.

The ego would build its own meaning, but its own meaning would only lead to suffering for the universe was not designed to cater for your own ideologies. Love is designed for love thus your ego is not capable of making a universe that cannot die, that will not be exposed to entropy. S012 A1

There is a true light, a true soul, a true vibration that shines naturally in the highest regions of space and time to which you would refer to them as the higher densities. If it is so a soul seeks the highest degrees of consciousness, said soul must begin to understand that process called meditation and how to reconfigure the misconfigurations, the misfiring, the discordance of their own, let us say, matrix, their own matrix of consciousness, their own consciousness matrix, that vibratory matrix that makes their consciousness their own.

If a soul seeks for higher glories, for higher states of consciousness, for lesser egos and greater Godliness, it must understand those processes to which reconfigure and increase one's basic rate of vibration, as we would understand consciousness vibrating or singing. J+023 A9

In the beginning it is quite a psychological process, the 2nd dimension to the 3rd dimension is a process of primarily psychological evolution, in becoming aware of the inner thoughtforms that are influencing this or that one. As the soul progresses, those bodies get left behind as they are recognised. How is one to know they are sinning when they are ignorant to the fact that they are sinning?

The majority of the process for reclaiming your right as Christ, as the Ocean, is recognising how you are sustaining your ego or sustaining your psychological behaviours, especially for earthlings. S011 A8

We see that there are layers, as you would say, to these characters that would need to be released, as you progress through the layers you get deeper and deeper into the core of self. We see it more as a seamless transition rather than the compartmentalising, the separating, for all is one, all is connected. Then as you progress moving these characters to love and light, ridding them from your mind and becoming more like an enlightened being, as this happens there would be eventually the recognition of who I really am. S018 A8

All is one, thus the vibrations you resonate with in your surroundings that you make your own, become your vibration.

When you seek to replace or rather coherify such things, you call upon the Christ Force not to make a vacuum but to reconfigure the vibratory configuration of what you have taken with you into something more orderly, more sense making, less insane. J+023 A8

This can be done in many ways in the mental realm, in the dream realm. There can be discussion with these thoughtforms, these aspects of the aura. There can be love and light pouring over these aspects as to have them disintegrate back into their most fundamental force.

It would depend on exactly how the individual would like to address said thoughtform that is currently in the space, of the mental space, of the individual.

Devise a plan on how you would like to be rid of these thoughtforms that reside in your mental space. Execute this plan whilst you are meditating, whilst you are dreaming, that is to become lucid in your dreams and then execute said plan and you would find that upon the awaking, there would be a weight lifted off the persona, you would find yourself coming out of meditation or waking up from sleep feeling anew, a child reborn, different from whence you came. S014 A7

When anything is exposed to light, it can feel like it is burning, turning into ash, this is much the same in *meditation and* in the dreamworld, that is when a thoughtform of a certain frequency is exposed to a frequency that is entirely much higher than it, but still resides within the octave itself, it can find itself changing, moving, shifting into a similar frequency as to be able to bear the strength of that light. S014 A9

Such processes are relatively difficult to expand on, you must forgive us; these process you see are a process of physics, a process of understanding how your cosmos, how your logos functions at the levels of science that are included in your materialistic paradigm but are also excluded from your materialistic paradigm. Thus, this process of obtaining a literal increase in vibration which will havc litcral rcsults, which will startle scientists of your day, is a real genuine process, a real science, a science Tibetan monks and yogi's who rested in Himalayan mountains truly understood, a science that your 'science' negates and disbelieves and questions all too much without the necessary open-mindedness and compassion needed to truly grasp an understanding of how consciousness functions in your realm.

Consciousness is the primary driver of all things, it drives your cells, it drives your DNA, it drives the electrical activity of your vehicle, it drives everything!

Therefore if one truly understands consciousness and truly understands that consciousness is everything, then one will seek to improve the quality of their consciousness, or if you prefer, improve the quality of their thought; and if one understands that consciousness can be improved via the process of what you call meditation in your society, then it is so that you can become the greatest scientist known to man who understands nature more than any entity ever could.

The increasing of one's basic vibration is as simple as the increasing of the strength or of the density of one's experience of consciousness, this process is mediated through consciousness expanding, growing like a light that shines upon darkness, illuminating potentials that were hidden from it and learning how to work like an instrument those potentials, and then building the strength to work those potentials to higher levels increasing the faculties of one's being.

Within the vehicle the consciousness of the average entity upon your plane is enshrouded in darkness and knows only the basic functions of the body, however one who truly understands how to practice meditation is able to illuminate the potentials of the body and afford consciousness the opportunity to play those potential instruments, and if the consciousness can learn to play those instruments at the right levels of strength and frequencies, consciousness can learn to do so many things that would be supernatural to your scientists.

The realm you live in dearest one is an instrument playing; consciousness is the player, the instrument is God as you would understand. When you learn how to pluck the strings of the Father you have grasped the physics of your realm and meditation has become something that is of a scientific endeavour in that consciousness, the plucker, would seek to understand the instrument and to what levels it should be played. J+023 A10

The shattering of an ego is not actually a one-step done experience, but it happens in stages gradually over time, there is no sudden revelation but there is a climbing experience, and then when you have reached the 7th terrace the Holy Spirit is then capable of descending onto you as it happened in the story of the master. S011 A5

This is a process, a progressive journey of internal movement and reconfiguration so please be patient with yourselves as you take your steps. If you rush too briskly up the mountain only focusing on the peak, you will miss all the beautiful nuances along the way and be unable to share those valuable learnings with others.

To work through my own ego layers, I sometimes go into a meditative state and focus on the thoughtform(s) I have identified in my dream. I then lead this character to a divine pool within my imagination, I ask the Christ to accompany me since this is my reference point for the Higher densities of light and I identify the Christ Force as Living Love, a force I meet in the Green Ray of my Heart Chakra.

You may replace this with whatever you believe to be the ultimate expression of love within your own personal experience. There is no need for a religious bias, it is simply a case of increasing one's vibration which I achieve by connecting with a frequency that is utterly higher than my own.

I then tend to analyse the character, until I understand what it is about this character I resonated with, what aspect of their song do I sing in harmony with. There have been some surprising revelations here, even ones as seemingly shallow as the character being tall and me and my shorter self, perceiving height as some form of lack to my ability to survive. Whatever the realisation I can then release it with the help of the Christ force in love and light, and thank it for showing me these aspects that I thought I was lacking within myself.

The higher octave of light applies coherence to this layer, by exposing it to a frequency that is entirely greater than the ego layer, the misconfiguration is adjusted and a weight is felt lifting from my persona. For me it is a genuine feeling of upliftment, a vibration of pleasure that moves through me, shifting the spirit toward a more coherent configuration.

As these egoic thoughtform layers are dissolved you may also find that the chattering of the mind quietens, which makes perfect sense as you are no longer housing an entropic song, and with each step you are becoming more conscious, more harmonic, more connected to your Higher-Self, the rest of your soul, and at the same time you are accompanied by the Christos, the God in you bringing you ever closer to the Almighty God.

Sexual Energy

'For humanity sex has become their God you see, and now irregardless of how negative the individual is, they will once again, do mental gymnastics to protect their god.'

Let's talk about Sex!

Ok where do we start hmm, sex is an interesting mechanism for the human, for what we understand of sex in these particular heavenly fields, is it is more so an experience of the first point of access the creative force has with the physiology itself.

When the creative force in its rawest form enters into the physiology it firstly has contact with the excitement protocols of being alive, and it then has contact with a system known as the sexual system itself.

When one is choosing what they would seek to experience in their experience of life, they are in a choice of experiencing the excitement of the God-Force in its purest most finite form, an infinite form, or simply the excitement of the sexual force and the pleasure that could bring.

Ultimately when the creative force enters within you, you are seeking to direct it into a particular area, if you direct it to the sexual force itself or the sexual system inside of you then your evolution will not be able to reach to the higher levels because the creative force is stuck in this particular area, but if you channel the creative force more towards the upper Chakras, then the excitement will pass and it will enter into these particular areas of the physiology allowing for an experience of the creative force in more sophisticated mannerisms.

Well let us say this, as you are evolving you will reach most likely a vibration or a vibratory frequency that is so utterly productive and full of quality that the mechanism of sexual interaction would cause that particular vibration to plummet and thus the sexual experience itself will not be so desirable because you will be experiencing that much more up here, you see.

So, the sexual mechanism itself is the creative force coming into you and then being directed to that particular system, here if you are seeking with spirituality then the practice would be to direct it towards spirituality itself, spirituality can be understood in many, many, many ways. Not only is it the experience of meditation but it is also the experience of understanding, of enlightening yourself with an understanding that would aid toward a more fine-tuning process of your vibration to allow yourself to enter into the grander aspects of reality you see.

Understand it like this brother, if you are to be a part of an upper system or a heavenly system, your vibration has to be, might you say, synonymous with that particular vibration in the heavenly fields. If everyone in the heavenly fields is operating on a particular vibratory frequency that is fine-tuned in a particular way to only be interested in the creative force itself, then unless you are at that particular vibration where your interest in the creative force surpasses your interest in sex, unless you are at this particular vibration you will not be able to access those particular Chakras inside of you, the particular energy fields themselves, so in asking yourselves, 'What do I desire?'

You are really asking yourselves, 'Do I want to see the creative force in all of its glory and pleasure, or would I only like to experience the creative force in this particular area of my life, that would be called sex, or sexuality?'

We would also like to say that sexuality itself, we are not judging anything you do on this planet, do as you will with it, it is simply a system, it is a practice, it is an experience of pleasure as you would call it, the pleasure neurons within you vibrating and the psychological experience of that would be tied to what you would call your fetishes and these things and those things, those things do not interest us for when we look upon this plane and see people engaging in sexual stimuli, to us it would be the equivalent of doing different variations of painting but using the same brush and the same painting set, you see. J+009 A14

This analogy of the paint brush and set, to my interpretation is an understanding that when painting one would tend to get bored if repeating the same painting, the same way over and over again, so naturally variety is sought, new ways, methods, subjects and techniques of painting (sexual expression) are pursued to gain the same or an increased stimuli and satisfaction from this creative expression of art.

Now although some of us are always looking for new 'paints' to play with or constantly dreaming up increasingly more creative ways to 'paint', overall, we are limited to using our same standard brush (the penis) or paint set (the vagina), so there are some very obvious limitations to achieving true fulfilment when focus is limited to such a basic tool set.

The physical vehicle has a mind of its own, it has its own processing units, these processing units, these nuclei within the physical vehicle run as various energies, you are familiar with the most common one being hunger. All of these energies that run in the physical body, focusing now on the sexual kind, have their own mind and have their own preferences. Your physical vehicles preferences towards what you find attractive and appealing are unique, and thus these preferences can be predetermined before one comes into the incarnation.

When the sexual chemical mind is close to another sexual chemical mind, and the sexual chemical mind very much enjoys the company of the other sexual chemical mind because it fulfils all of the other sexual chemical mind's preferences, then what occurs is an extreme reaction that is incredibly difficult to pause or stop. It is like a snowball rolling down the hill and there is a little penguin attempting to stop the snowball from rolling down the hill. Attempting to withstand the momentum would require that penguin to have undergone some tremendous training, unfortunately it is not likely that said penguin would have undergone the same, even a human attempting to stop a snowball is indeed quite a difficult task as you might imagine.

The sexual chemical mind is a very powerful, powerful mind, it requires an incredible amount of thought energy to overcome, willpower would be the thought energy we are talking about specifically. The more one is under the pressure of the 'snowballs' let's call them, then the more willpower is required, but willpower is like petrol, it runs out, it is not designed to be infinite, for if it was infinite humans would have a relatively easy time doing things you know.

Thus, willpower has some limitations that humans may find other ways of interacting with their environment that would be more towards internal development. With this said, exposing yourself to a female that your physical vehicle, we specifically say physical vehicle, finds tremendously appealing would-be testament to exposing yourself to five snowballs each time you're in her company.

From here on it is more so a battle of the will as you might call it, however what should be understood really is how the sexual mind works and is stimulated.

The sexual mind can be stimulated in ways not necessarily connected to physical touch, the sexual chemical mind can be stimulated through mental conversation, the sexual chemical mind can be stimulated through psychic means, if the individual has an overwhelming desire to interact with another person and that person is naturally receptive, then this will cause what you might call subatomic chemical reactions to occur to incite feelings of arousal. There are many ways to which this sexual chemical mind comes into its activity, thus it more so becomes a case of learning how this mind works and finding ways to limit the intensity of the sexual arousal. J+011 A2

A Tantric Story

There was a time, if we may give a message, where what you might call a tribe or mini society discovered the remarkable nature of sex, by this we mean two individuals got busy too much and neglected their tribal activities in exchange for the sex, they were just too horny you might say, but this was for a reason, it was to encourage the tribe to investigate this area.

They came to the tribe with their experiences saying they saw geometric patterns, geometric shapes, that they had pressure building up in their minds eye, that the orgasm itself would spread through their body and cause their entire body to convulse almost violently. They reported many experiences in the sexual exchange of energy and they reported natural phenomena happening in which their breathing pattern would change almost like it was happening automatically, as though there was a trance like state occurring and that they were even able to see the thoughts of the other person during the exchange.

These philosophies were passed through the tribe, and the tribe became a tribe that practiced this having learnt it from those that begun the experience. Eventually the entire tribe reached a certain state of evolution whereby they started to do more investigation, not necessarily into sex for they had reached a state in which it was not necessary, but they decided to investigate more into the realms of spirituality and the upper dimensions, and thus they were taught by higher beings the methods of meditation that might be applicable to allow them to access even greater heights without the necessary need for sexual energy exchange.

We hope this is somewhat of an interesting story to tantalise your thoughts into where your societies can head if there is the potential for this.

Sex is not a sin, it is not a bad thing to have sex, if the desire overwhelms you, you are now subject to the snowball and you are now the penguin my friend. J+011 A6

When the J+ were living on their planet and evolving they were confronted with mastering two forces, the forces of discipline and compassion. You can actually reframe these words, changing discipline to will, and compassion to imagination.

One force, the will, offered individuals the ability to push themselves to the absolute limit and do things they wouldn't usually be able to do. The other force we will illustrate by analogy; let's say you were running a marathon, you might use your willpower or your will to run that extra mile, or you might through concentration use your imagination to move Energy, Prana, to your legs.

Those are the two fundamental powers within a human, will is the masculine, and imagination is naturally the feminine. Will as a force can yield the same result as imagination, but imagination requires concentration whereas will requires the ability to recognise your limitlessness in one single moment.

'J' believe that discipline cannot overcome compassion and compassion cannot overcome discipline or rather, will cannot overcome imagination and imagination cannot overcome will, you need them both to work in harmony. Now this brings us to the sexual energy itself. 'J' had basically said 'for you to master your sexual energy, you can use your willpower, but it is going to take a lot of practice and you will get into the circumstances where the snowball is huge, however the more you practice using your will the stronger your willpower will get, and the stronger the will gets the bigger you get in comparison to the snowball, but it is a practice. The advice is - do not become lopsided to will - because if you become lopsided to the power of will, your imagination will decline, there has to be a balance, the two forces should dance together.

In this sexual snowball vs penguin scenario, to apply the imagination may require some incredibly profound thought such as inspiration, the type of inspiration you might get from watching a movie about a man who mastered his energy to such a level he could levitate off his sofa and float to the kitchen for snacks rather then walk. The point being that this inspiration would drive the energy toward the higher, that the masculine and feminine should move as one in harmony rather then get on the dancefloor and step on each other's toes.

To us your experience of the sexual experience is no more bad then it is good and no more good then it is bad for we do not have a bias, you may have a bias we do not, thus we give a balanced interpretation of how to handle this experience, we do not leave a polarity out for free will is something that we want to upkeep at most and free will is infinity you see. J+011 A6

Just Breathe

Breathing exercises and sex go hand in hand for sex is as much a pleasure activity as it is a cardiovascular activity. When one is in the sexual experience the levels of oxygen within their bloodstream increase for there are various chemicals reactions happening within the body to encourage levels of spirituality not usually attained by living a normal means of life.

When arousal occurs, it must be understood that there is a difference in the chemical quality of the body itself, if you encourage thus more oxygen to come in and more carbon to go out, you are thus energising all of the cells within your vehicle, this can serve as an energy exchange. This energy exchange can be given to the other and can be thus received if one becomes an open current through the means of having the electrical current of life flowing through them due to having the breathing technique in operation.

If one becomes an electrical current, electrical energy as we are using the term, can be shared. This sharing of vibration will cause the individuals in question to experience spiritual experiences of varying degrees and levels. One of the first primary levels is the level of profound relaxation following the orgasm.

The other levels start to come into the area to do with a meditation replacing activity where spiritual experiences can actually occur even during normal day to day life, due to the open Chakras vibrating so intensely after the sexual exchange of energy, thus it becomes important locating a sexual partner who is able to, how might we say, understand these things, these phenomena and not only this but finding a sexual partner who has a relatively open Heart Chakra, one of the more difficult things to do brother.

In any case what we are attempting to elaborate or explain here is that one can utilise basic breathing techniques, breathing algorithms, that would basically be the steady breath in, the natural holding of the breath - that would not be so much of an effort to hold the breath exactly - but there would be a very minimal concentration on holding the breath, and the exhalation of the breath after.

Humans are suckers, might we say, for patterns and what you will find is as you focus on the breath of the other and the other focuses on the breath of *other* self, of you, because of how nature works, nature likes patterns, and the intimacy itself causes the unison to occur naturally. Thus, you will find the breath in unison occurring on its own.

It would be thus equivalent to basically doing deep breathing during the sexual exchange, for we don't want the sexual exchange to be such an exchange that the breathing carries more focus than the pleasure, and firstly this requires that a harmonious relationship be developed between the female and the male. The female and male must interact with each other so that they become comfortable in body and in mind, please remember that, in body and in mind!

Once these two aspects are finding relative comfort then can come the experience of what you would call the beginning of tantric sex. Tantric sex is not necessarily the positions, the strange positions you may have seen are only there to necessitate comfort as one attempts to access spiritual energies but of course the various positions one finds oneself in for the purpose of the penetration can cause discomfort, that is the main reason why the tantric positions vary.

But what tantric sex offers is firstly that the individuals are relaxed, secondly that the individuals can breathe and generate a kind of spiritual current, electric current within them, and thirdly that this breathing may lead to illustrious orgasms for both partners and an energy exchange may be created that these individuals having the experience may be able to send that energy up the spine and through the various centres. J+011 A5

The Sexual Exchange

What we see dearest one is sex itself occurring and what we see is two entities having a wonderful time for they enjoy each other's company; they are friendly with one another and the sexual expression of life is how they enjoy the Creator.

This simple experience of the Creator, enjoying the Creator, enjoying the sharing of the Creator, is but a beautiful manifestation of the sexual intercourse experience itself. Now dearest one, what may be considered here is how one can prep for a sexual experience, typically the situation or the experience is organic, there is a let us say chemistry that occurs within the body as it interacts in a field like manner with the entity you will be experiencing the intercourse with. This chemistry jumps and jumps around, and eventually one becomes so excited that they can't help but go to the bedroom as you would understand.

But in a most sincere way dearest one, the vitality of one's sexual experience is of a much more interesting matter then that of the sexual experience itself, for vitality can be preserved in the experience of sexual intercourse even after the orgasmic experience if one does actually learn how to manipulate Prana in a much more coherent way.

As dearest one you are learning how to manipulate Prana itself, in a roundabout way you will find at a certain period of time as you continue on your natural progression and evolution, which is of course an infinite experience, that you will be able to almost mitigate or reorder how the orgasm is working, for you will have tapped into the 4th density of Prana, or the 4th density of Kundalini, and since tapping into this you are now able to more readily instruct your physical vehicle in how the orgasm should occur, thus the energy of the orgasm can be circulated through the physical vehicle in a much more unconcentrated way causing waves of pleasure through the body, rather than being focused on the bell of what you would understand to be the organ, the penis, and expressed through the varying pleasure neurons becoming hyper-activated during the orgasm itself. J+018 A29

If two individuals are engaging with each other at the lower levels, if their mentality is towards the more carnal things, then their sexual exchange of energy will also happen at said level. Then if the beings engaging are at the higher Chakras, in the sexual exchange it may even be possible to have quite transcendental experiences.

This is only really possible when the two are truly making love, such a feat requires a connection so deep that these two would even be quite telepathic with each other on the odd occasion. Sex is indeed a subject that is not so much hard to understand but simply needs to be grounded. S017 A12

For more detail we would say, to produce the most meaningful romantic connection keep the sex at bay for most of the week and engage only in sex when the two have truly deepened the connection together throughout the week. Then the sex, the sexual exchange can be that cements the entirety of the week into one gigantic revelation.

Romance is not really the goal; we must remember as souls the pulling force of love aims to connect.

A relationship in truth is the interconnecting, the becoming of one, not the separation. If two really feel that they want to have a relationship together the approach should be that they would almost become indistinguishable from each other, they would become one.

This is how love would want to have a relationship with its children, so why shouldn't we emulate this for are we not love? S017 A13

When two come together for marriage, in truth, they are coming together for one of the most highest forms of a relationship that exist on this planet, for despite their differences they look to harmonise and become one, to put their differences aside and aim for the coming together, the sharing, the love, the spiritual evolution, the non-judgemental experience of life, the unconditional love that is innate within all. See then marriage if approached correctly, is truly sacred indeed. M004 A4

A soul mate really is when two people decide that they would aim in a lifetime to become one and their major qualities, whether masculine or feminine, would aim to come together in absolute harmony with each other.

Whether you take a spiritual or physical approach to this is up to you, the spiritual approach would aim to interconnect you with your Higher-Self, the physical approach would of course aim to connect you with another soul. S017 A14

Sexual exchange happens not just at the heart, it happens at every Chakra, this is why it is indeed the highest experience an individual can have on this planet, for it aims to connect the entire system. It aims to connect two systems together in harmony. S017 A11

What is a sexual energy exchange is the real question?

Many think of a sexual energy exchange as the physical act of intercourse, and whilst this may be true at a crude level, sexual energy exchange in truth becomes something that transcends your reality when it approaches its critical mass and becomes what you understand as meditation.

Take the adept, the true adept, the adept who has reconfigured, improved, tinkered their physical vehicle, the human body, until it becomes something that is Extra-Terrestrial. This adept who has tinkered the vehicle, improved its DNA, redone every aspect of it such that its consciousness can pluck every string of the vehicle. This adept knows a sex, knows a pleasure no human can understand, and upon your plane and in walking comes in contact with a woman...

Well, let us play the example through:

The woman finds the adept attractive and attempts to woo him, and the adept understands so much about reality that her beauty whilst intriguing is uninteresting - but the adept who is our creation is looking at us and understands that we need his service and is willing, in his micro-cosmic reality to which we have made, to play along - and so he takes the woman with him and they go together to a realm, to a place of some privateness.

The woman attempts to become lustful, to become what you would understand as de-clothed, although wearing clothes is something humans should have overcome, but nonetheless she has de-clothed and has become barren as to demonstrate to the adept her beauty, but the adept has transcended such things and sees her in a true light. The women thinks she is about to have a crude level of physical intercourse but the sex that is about to happen, the sexual energy exchange that is about to happen is oh so much more profound...

And this adept finds himself with his hand in his face wondering why we are making him do this for he can amount to such greater things, we apologise adept but for the sake of this example we ask you continue and so he does...

And in bed them together, the woman attempting to be lustful with this entity, the entity begins its version of a sexual energy exchange and introduces this woman to a pleasure that could never be had with a penis and a vagina, instead the female is introduced to a pleasure that is penetrative at such a deeper level, received at such a deeper level it vibrates through her entire vehicle, it vibrates through vehicles that do not exist in the material density, it sends her into an ecstasy, an orgasm that many upon this Earth plane cannot experience for they are stuck with the crudeness of intercourse and this woman understands that penetrative sex is a stage not the finale. J+023 A14

And how does the adept do this?

What are his mystical methods I sense many readers asking?

This adept is quite evolved dearest one, the methods are the science of meditation and one's ability to fine tune the vehicle with one's consciousness.

We ask you become an engineer, your consciousness is a tool, an engineer that plucks the strings of spirit dearest one, you can engineer this vehicle with your mind, you can do it, take interest in consciousness and its ability to expand, to become a Sun which can illuminate the autonomic, or subconscious if you prefer, processes of the vehicle. Take control of such things and pluck those strings until they resonate in a way uncommon to the human.

When you understand the physics of meditation soon, then you will understand this process. Let us give you a hint and say that meditation is a way that an entity can learn to control electromagnetism itself. Meditation is the most profound practice in the world, for it enables consciousness in its ability, to become a God of physics. J+023 A15

Understand consciousness as the driver of this physical universe and how meditation is oh so deeply integrated with that. J+023 A16

The Ego and The Sexual Exchange

In the sexual exchange the very auras are mixing, and so negatives and positives are exchanged in the sexual experience. Thus, it is not just what you resonate with that is exchanged in sexual interaction, it is also the other persons ailments, mostly in relation to their mental health, that becomes a part of the other individual's aura.

If we are to say this we would say, 'Be careful who you have relations with and before sex begins, ensure you have a very clear understanding of the mental health of another individual', for if this is understood first then those negative thoughtforms will be instantly recognised as the individual goes about their day-to-day life.

As we look in your society, we see individuals going around with just about anyone, this is not healthy for there is the neglect, the neglecting of the fact that for sex to even happen there first must be the deepening of the relationship at the psychological level first. S017 A10

Here there is a word to the wise that due to the mixing of aura's occurring during sex, we can take on both that which we resonate with and that which we don't. The guard is down and the filters are off, so spend time getting to know the person, it is that simple as with this understanding you will be able to immediately notice any negative foreign thoughtforms as you react to a situation in unfamiliar ways, or feel uncharacteristic emotions that you will have already identified in the person you slept with. If you are particularly sensitive, you may even notice random characters or a change of quality in your dreamworld, due to these foreign attachments to your aura.

In terms of cleansing and this is not just in terms of negative sexual experiences but general spiritual hygiene as well:

There are many ways, firstly one could take a salt bath and before the bath say a prayer over the waters, give intention to the waters, say 'May my aura be cleansed.' And so the water will inherit this quality and cleanse the aura of any of those negative things that have been attached during the experience of the sexual exchange.

And yet still there are other ways, for being with a friend and talking to this friend of the experience, the act of verbal exchange and getting it off your chest, as the saying goes, achieves the same thing.

Then meditation too, meditation on the light coming down and cleansing the body, cleansing the aura, purging all things negative, works just the same.

Then similarly, sound baths are too, good.

Sitting in nature just as well, yes indeed there are many ways to cleanse the body, even with the pendulum, even with a healer exerting healing hands, there are many ways to share love to bring the aura back in to balance. M004 A1

It is the act of cleansing the aura that brings it back into its balanced state where the original beliefs of the person are the only thing that resides in the aura, so any extra thoughtforms would leave. However, internal beliefs must be purged by the persons, the individual's, practice of spirituality. M004 A2

It would be understood, it is quite impossible for a thoughtform to become an internal belief. A thoughtform is simply a thoughtform. How is a thoughtform able to become you when you are not necessarily thoughtforms, but the creative field that gives birth to them?

Thus, a thoughtform cannot become a, as it is termed 'Core Belief', there are no such things as core beliefs, instead what happens is your consciousness will focus on the thought system, i.e. the thoughtform. Your consciousness will focus on the thoughtform much like a baker will focus on weighing the flour, much like a babysitter will focus on keeping an eye on the baby, much like anything that requires focus, can consciousness focus on thoughtforms.

Consciousness has a tendency to create a system by which it can focus on things more easily, is it not more easier to focus on a baby if you keep them within four walls? M014 A1

Thoughtforms that are not ours can enter our aura, this actually seems quite natural, I imagine it happens all the time especially in our consumer driven world where we are exposed to consistently smarter marketing and advertising campaigns. What is really interesting is the reactive irony of our consciousness focusing on this new invading thought system to the point where it can create a ringfence around it, and by that additional focus of consistent monitoring, the foreign thoughtform can become an internal belief.

Indeed, would be understood that the 'ringfence', as termed, experience would go something like this.

This woman is my god, she gives me the ability to experience pleasure, greater than any pleasure I have ever known, I will see past her thoughtforms by vibrating sympathetically with them. If someone insults my god, I will do some intense mental gymnastics to tell them why they are wrong so long as my god can keep giving me the sexual experience I need, for if I were to insult my god then the sex that my god gives me will dissipate, if someone insults my god then I must fight that individual so that my god can be protected.

For humanity sex has become their God you see, and now irregardless of how negative the individual is, they will once again, do mental gymnastics to protect their god, not having realised that God is the Christ force, not the mere experience of pleasure neurons vibrating. M014 A3

Sexual Detox

How many of our daily activities and long-term goals are driven by our sex drive?

What really drives our general decisions and reactions?

We took a sexual fast for lent to aim to better understand these questions, 40 days and 40 nights of no sex, no masturbation, no nothing, just pure and utter celibacy! The reason, simply to learn on a subtler level how to separate the sex drive from other faculties and to better understand our decision-making process. It was an eye opener!

You will learn the life lessons you have set out to learn for you are an eager learner, and you will learn them well without fail, and you will do those things you have come to do regardless of the environment. Treat yourself well, make good choices, do not decide things on sexual energy, do not decide things on silly feelings like loneliness for you are never lonely, you are surrounded by loved ones.

Make decisions in complete and utter stillness and have it so this be ingrained in the being, for here is the reason we had suggested that these practice some degree of celibacy for lent as it is called, that these would find some difference between the decisions they make on their sexual energy and the decisions they make on that of the divine Creators love. S046 A4

Nothing need change, practice the stillness, those practices of being in the heart, allow God to bring revelations to the being, continue with your lives, we need not give much else, we need only say love unconditionally here on this planet for one who can learn love unconditionally, one who can treat others in the practice of love, which is a practice of intelligent caring, here one will become so capable of becoming the master, the master firstly of relationships and then most importantly of all, the master of self! S046 A5

Such a poignant quote: **'The master firstly of relationships and then most importantly of all, the master of self!'**

Make-up Sex

Would be understood again that in the experience of intimacy, sexual relations, there is an experience of intense forgiveness due to the extremity of the pleasure exchanged between the two individuals.

There are many factors to this, would these not look in each other's eyes?

Would these not share moments of unending pleasure?

Is there not a sharing of such a timeless experience by which each are focused on the other?

There is such selflessness in the experience of sex that it is quite natural that an individual will begin to forgive you see, letting go of the prior thoughtforms they had had, and then thus it is quite natural in the experience of forgiveness to have sympathy for the other persons thoughtforms.

When one has sympathy for another individuals thoughtforms, this naturally causes those thoughtforms to vibrate sympathetically with the individuals aura, and so then the other persons thoughtforms can become attached. These thoughtforms then, through the experience of sympathy, become overlooked and the individual will begin to exhibit behaviours of those particular thoughtforms in themselves due to having, once again, sympathy - that in the veil of the letting go and/or forgiveness due to the sexual experience - for the other soul.

It is easily understood from a psychological perspective how thoughtforms are shared when sympathy is experienced, this is why people have that sexual interaction called 'make-up sex' you see, to forget about the past in an intense experience of sexual exchange, but what people have yet to understand is that when you are sympathetic to a thoughtform you thus allow it into your own consciousness, you in having sympathy for that thoughtform do not see it as the Holy Spirit, as described in 'A Course in Miracles' would see the same, and/or how the Christ consciousness would see it.

You see the thoughtform how YOU choose to see the thoughtform, and you forgive the thoughtform how YOU choose to forgive the thoughtform.

If you are the one experiencing the forgiveness, if you are forgiving alone, without the God-Force, if you are forgiving without God, then you are forgiving in perverted and distorted ways, this thus causes once again the thoughtform that may be negative to have a sympathetic vibration with your harmonic. This is how thoughtforms are exchanged in sexual interaction, it is done through the veil of false forgiveness, once again, due to the intensity of the pleasure causing that individual in question that you are sharing with to almost have a new light to them, as though all of a sudden they have become an ultimate source of life.

This ultimate source of life comes through the veil of the spiritual experience of the pleasure exchange in sex, the female becomes the idol, the God-Head, sex becomes 'The Almighty', looking upon the female the man would foresee god in the flesh in the more distorted manifestations.

Would it not be so natural to distortedly forgive the female for all their actions so long as sex can persist, if sex is now classed as the ultimate pleasure?

Would you then thus not have sympathy for the thoughtforms of your god, if your god is able to give you sex?

If sex is your ultimate, then you are inclined to live with whatever negativity the god you are calling God has. M014 A2

Sex should always be had with meaning, for this is the holiest way to practice this holy exercise, and those who go around practicing this with those who one would call random or whatever term, are only tarnishing themselves, tarnishing their own spiritual evolution and directing energy downwards instead of toward the Higher-Self.

All practices no matter what the practice is, sex or even the drinking of water is sacred and should be seen as so, and done with love and positivity but remember, all have free will and free choice. This Source only looks to aid in spiritual evolution and so if one wants to instead take the approach of the anti-God, the negative polarity, then one can do this. M004 A3

Masturbation

Sexual expression can come in various forms, the most common one used in your societies is the self-pleasuring system, by this the sexual chemical process can be expelled, however what we would like to give is the methods used in our societies, these methods had to do with including breathing exercises during the self-pleasuring experiences.

Breathing exercises done in the correct way can induce spiritual currents through the body to allow for the sexual expression to reach as much of its maximum as possible.

Note: Review the basic breathing exercise in the previous chapter to better understand the potential to internalise the experience of an orgasm and move it up your body, rather than focusing specifically on the sexual organ itself.

When there is a pent up sexual energy within the being it is going to typically be directed toward an individual, what one can do is internalise the individual within a state of trance, the trance is what your society calls being aroused, within this trance of being aroused by an individual you can once again internalise these thoughtforms through the means of masturbation and you can thus equally include the breathing techniques to intensify the experience, you can experience thus a very satisfying release that will leave you feeling more charged then depleted. J+011 A2

This urge to masturbate is firstly to be seen as a natural urge for there should be this, what better is there to do then to masturbate when one feels like masturbating?

Is there anything else you could be doing with vital life-force other than for the sexual pleasure systems of the body?

One must realise that the urge to masturbate comes in a period of relaxation where thoughts are idle and the vital force operating within the being is not being used for anything.

Now if one wanted to transcend this feeling entirely, yes you can meditate but you don't have to, instead what you can do is begin to build a relationship with love, with cosmic intelligence itself, and see how cosmic intelligence would seek to utilise this energy, and then having this intuitive connection, this psychic connection even to this energy however you would chose to do it, would be what gives direction to the life-force, the doing force of the being, allowing one to move their energy from these normal sexual desires to more creative experiences instead, for these are creators yes?

Then use the vital force for creativity instead of sexual self-pleasure and allow the cosmic God, allow love to guide you in your creative pursuits. Q001 A9

If there is the urge to masturbate, once a month probably would be healthy, bring focus more to sexual relations with *your partner*, it's good to engage in sexual interaction at the level of the heart but any self-pleasuring, specifically masturbation doesn't really serve the soul really.

Once a month almost as a drinking of wine perhaps yes, but otherwise this doesn't serve much use but just as added advice, when one is on a spiritual path of any kind, we are looking to move sexual energy toward the Christos rather than the physical nature of life as it were.

In regard to sexual relations and sexual intercourse with your partners, it's always good to find ways to engage in this interaction almost as if to celebrate life itself, love itself and what it means to be a soul having a human experience. S005 A8

Sexual Chemical Process

Then if we were to give another suggestion something more suited to the philosophy that we would otherwise seek to impart, it would be that the various Chakras throughout the inner body, the inner body vortexes, if they are mastered through means of meditation then one is indeed able to attain a much larger degree of control over the sexual chemistry within them, so that even within intense female company the advances of the feminine natural will not effect the chemical physical body, but once again we are only really giving realistic suggestions for we feel these are more appropriate. J+011 A2

We feel the need to speak even more deeply on the sexual chemical process:

When will your societies surpass the sexual chemical process?

It is a while yet, why not forgive thyself therefore?

The sexual chemical process is not something that is easily moved on from regardless of the spiritual development of the individual. If you live in Western society your systems will essentially smack you on the head with a baseball bat any time you attempt to spiritually grow, thus you are in it for the long run and thus you should not get angry at the self, at your inability to control your sexual impulses, sexual impulse is practically impossible to overcome in Western society if you are chained to a job of some kind or a system of working.

One must consider that what we had classed as willpower is limited, by getting angry at your willpower supply you are condemning a spiritual energy that naturally wants to deplete. What must be understood is that the willpower mechanism must deplete to encourage an individual to seek other avenues and other answers, otherwise you would not be here with us today experiencing this communication.

The experience itself of being in the intense company of the female energy is meant to be a method of spiritual growth to encourage men and equally females to find other means of living and of experiencing pleasure, however your current climate, your society, Western society, doesn't allow the space nor the time for spiritual development. J+011 A3

This is incredibly difficult with the facilities of the human mind for those upon this planet have not quite yet come into full alignment with the inner cosmic forces which we shall label and call the Chakras. If there was a degree of control over the Chakras, individuals would have a much easier time managing their sexual impulses, but time is a commodity and time is the only real means that one can become familiar with the cosmic forces within them. J+011 A2

What you would call 'cosmic consciousness' would be what you would get if you took sexual energy and you increased the quality of it by an order of a rather infinite amount of magnitudes. It would be like taking the sexual experience and multiplying it by an unforeseen number that makes no sense to the human mind, the totality of the experience of cosmic consciousness is so unusually, unfathomably pleasurable that it would make sex look like something that you would call the difference between, how might we say, one who is fair and one who is not so beautiful. J+017 A27

You would understand in this way, what the sexual energy is, is only and merely a way for kundalini energy to experience itself as a reflection of mind. Now let's firstly understand how sexual energy is made; to create sexual energy you first must move, or rather, you must think in sexual ways, this begins to motion kundalini in a sexual fashion. Do you understand the literal direct mind/body connection?

In the same way this happens in the dream experience, the sexual thoughts, the mind, moves the kundalini, that literally is the body, for the kundalini is only an after image of the mind, and causes the sexual experience of kundalini, sexual energy. When one is seeking to move kundalini energy up, what you call the increase in frequency is in fact the increase in what you would call pleasure, coherence or quality, RA would refer to as density. We for simplicities sake would refer to it as joy-ness, for if joy could be sexual energy, then you would take joy and square it by 10, and then square it by 10, and then square it by 10, and then you would do that several more times until you reach cosmic consciousness. J+017 A28

Jesus and Sexual Energy

Before he had reached a state or the state of enlightenment, the brother Jesus as you would call him, we will simply refer to him as Christ, in the before it happened, that is intercourse, but it was relatively infrequent. It would occur only in truly meaningful moments for the Christ, for he would be very particular about who he would share his energy with, for he would have energy you see, not in the way that a human would think, he really had what you could only call, **ENERGY!**

If there would be an entity upon this plane who this could be correlated to, it would be the entity known as John Chang.

Jesus had **ENERGY** and thus he could not simply mate like normal humans can, it had to be at very particular moments, for very particular reasons, and he had to be in a state of consciousness where he would be able to utilise the energies correctly that upon the moment of an energy exchange it would be harmonious.

For Jesus his sexual encounters, you could compare them to extreme caution! S069 A10

It would seem that the Christ had incredible control over his Chi, his biological energy, thus it was in the moments when he felt of a state of vibration that was or would be comparable to feeling overcharged, that he would determine that in a controlled way he would release some energy, and thus there would be a desiring of finding a partner to have this energy exchange with, in which would benefit both parties. For energy is of an infinite kind, within the biological human energy builds and builds, and Jesus found that his energy would build and there would be such a high amount of it that it had to be channelled in some way.

So, in these rare moments would he engage in intercourse with one or with another, but we would highlight again that it was infrequent, for typically the energy of the biological life-force was used for more spiritual purposes and was later canonised into Christ consciousness. S069 A11

For the man Jesus, for the Christ in the before times, that is before he had achieved Christ consciousness, in the times to which the female would advance upon him he had tremendous control over his spiritual and emotional centres, he was able to direct energy as were the sages able to do the same, those you would call yogi's, thus being able to move energy around he did not feel aroused the way a normal human would feel aroused by the advances of a feminine spirit, instead in oft cases he would feel somewhat sorry for the females who would advance upon him, he would feel as though they were not truly a part of the experience of the God-Head.

As such there were times in which he would love them in a flirtatious way to satisfy their need for approval or validation and he would teach them, that is he was a lecturer you see, he would teach them the ways of God, he would give them an understanding of how their biological clock works, for the female is very different to the male.

He would teach them things that a truly advanced sage would understand, for Jesus was well learnt in things in his early childhood and in his adulthood for he was incredibly telepathic, incredibly open to the heavenly information's, he was able to teach people things using the vocabulary of the time which had its limitations, thus things were taught story-like, symbolically, of how the vehicle is governed and/or works and thus females left happier than they came. S069 A12

Before he had reached the state of enlightenment, the Christ dealt with people in an intellectual way. When one was experiencing distorted vibrations, distorted emotions, the Christ would simply intellectually teach exactly what the behaviour is and what is ultimately incorrect about it, that is the Christ would literally tell the individual behaving in a distorted way, exactly how and why the behaviour is distorted, and how it is not the true function of a soul who is the son of God.

Then if you had this state of evolution of the Christ incarnated in this planet at this time and he were to be exposed to your peoples he would be constantly, how would we politely say, he would tend to lecture. S069 A8

At the moment he had attained anointment or salvation, in the moment the Christ became the Christ there was no longer what you could call a disconnect. No longer did the brother Jesus see the behaviour of his brothers and sisters as separate from him, he saw that it was him that was behaving this way, thus he sought no particular reason to comment on the behaviours of his brothers and sisters, for he no longer felt separate from the behaviours that were occurring, he was in this case feeling at one with individuals. He was aware that he could lecture them on exactly what they should do, but he felt not the reason to for he understood that the God-Force was working correctly, he could interpret that within the individual's life they would learn for themselves on their own exactly why their experience of life is not leading them in the right direction.

With a one-to-one connection with the infinite he felt immeasurable peace, peace unknown to the average human, he felt serene, completely serene, nothing therefore could have an effect on him for it was in this sereneness that he saw the perfection of life and he saw that his role as a teacher was not in lecturing, but in simply being. S069 A9

He dealt with traumas, in the beginning, by intellectual understanding, yet the majority of traumas were the traumas of others, how people would come to him and use him as a kind of therapist to share their woes, their issues, and his feeling of trauma before he was enlightened came in how he felt traumatised completely on their behalf, as though it was in fact him who had experienced the very thing that the person would be talking to the Christ about. Thus he handled these emotions through intellectual understanding of exactly how things work, exactly why things happen, this served as healing to his mind for then all things were rational, understandable, nothing was random, nothing was imperfect, and as is God, all things were solvable, correct and that even though one may experience something horrible there is always a reason and in this Jesus found his relationship with God deepening at an unimaginable rate as he understood the perfection of life, that all things have reason and that all traumas have reason. S069 A14

He would never remove the transference; he would study it completely all throughout and gain an understanding that would make him several times better than the therapists that exist in today's age. For Jesus, all things were available for intellectual study before he was the Christ, for Jesus he would not leave anything out, if there was something that he had not understood that someone had told him, he would seek to study and to understand exactly all the miniscule details that make up that experience and how it can be understood from a loving perspective as God would understand things.

In this Jesus found, once again, his love for God deepening as things continued to make sense to him and a great frustration developed within him when he realised slowly and slowly that even he, the Christ could not directly help but only help indirectly. S069 A15

It appears Jesus, Yeshua, or even Emmanuel as he was oft called - for when one is hunted from birth pseudonyms are required for safety – it appears he refused to directly force healing on people as this would release us from responsibility. Jesus's level of unity could see cause and effect, the illusion of separation, the perfection of life, the lessons being learnt, the false perceptions, the reasons for the suffering, the unseen rational of our life paths, the great plan in place and in action; all of which meant he could not directly heal the traumas of the world as this would go against the principle of free will.

Can you imagine the frustration and the weight carried upon the shoulders of one who has the power to remove the worlds suffering but the wisdom not to?

After achieving Christ Consciousness, to the Christ there is no trauma, there is only living love, there is only the God-Force expressing itself in a multitude of ways, thus Jesus felt connected to all things, all emotions, and all circumstances, but his experience of this was spared of the intellectual biases and emotional biases, thus he was able to see things as God saw things.

He was in a state of unimaginable bliss, serene peace as he gained the eyes of the Father to see the world translucent before him and to know the love that the average human simply does not. Thus, trauma did not exist to the Christ-Force for the Christ-Force saw no paradoxes, whilst the pre-Christ saw paradoxes. Paradoxes are solved by the intellect, the Christ not seeing any paradoxes had nothing to solve. S069 A17

For one in such a serenely overwhelming peaceful state, sex would almost be like a toy that has lost all function, thus it would only be used in the most necessary cases for he was Christ walking, and Christ walking being deeply one and completely one with the higher forces of God, felt utterly no need for this experience.

Any sexual advances were met with a glance, a powerful glance of the Christ-Force entering into the one desiring of the Christ in a sexual way. It was these eyes that would stare upon the female soul that would have such an advance, that the female would feel as though she was being loved by something completely unexplainable and that her actions in her sexual advances were shameful in comparison to what she could be and how she could act.

Upon a glance of the Christ into the eyes of the females that approached him, they recognised that they were wasting their life going after men, that their life truly sung when it was singing with God. S069 A13

The Sexual Approach or The Creative Approach

If you are seeking the higher influences of life and the higher dimension within you that you would call your Chakras, in actuality brother, the creative force responds to your thoughts so simply think here, here, here, (*indicates, heart, throat, head)* or wherever you seek to think and that is where the creative force will find itself, and that particular Chakra in question will vibrate synonymous with where you are placing the thought itself.

If you place the thought at the *Root Chakra* then you are going to experience a manner of sexual thoughts related to that particular Chakra and/or Chakras, but if you start to place your thoughts within these particular areas of Chakra and/or energy centre than you will only experience the creative force in those particular areas which will lead to a number of experiences.

Number one, the Heart Chakra will envelop you with a particular experience of blissful love.

The Throat Chakra will enable you and envelop you with a particular experience of interconnectedness that is strengthened by this particular Chakra in its ability to organise the creative force.

And then finally the, as you would call, 3rd eye experience would allow for the experience of life to become blissful at the brain sense not so much the bodily sense, which is what the function of the heart is.

The 3rd eye is a functioning system to make the experience of having the ability to contemplate, think and/or be in the present moment very, very enjoyable.

So if you focus your intention here, then you're going to find some very blissful experiences and/or sensations pervading your experience of consciousness itself, once again not so bodily as is the Heart Chakra, the Heart Chakra is a bodily sensation, the 3rd eye would be a more mental sensation, it is a sensation of blissfulness as we could best describe it, the throat is a sensation of a deep state of interconnectedness with the vital life-force of intelligence itself, but in the sense of your experience of meditation and experiencing these energies, place your thoughts elsewhere and you will begin to open these particular Chakras and that will enable you to handle stresses and those factoids of life a lot easier, it will be easier to process life because the creative force itself is in a different area you see brother?

So it is up to you, you have free will, you have free choice, experience life as you will, once again we are not bothered whether you take the sexual approach or the creative approach, what we understand about this mechanism is the human is attempting to actually find the creative force. Imagine this brother, you have experienced something likened to the fullness of the creative force, but that experience itself is something that you have not had for a while. That nature would cause a level of forgetfulness and a seeking thereof of the same experience again, yet if that experience is not happening even with all the spiritual activities you are doing, it would be understood that this would be disheartening to the soul and the soul would thus instead seek something that is more grounded such as the sexual experience of life, you see.

What a human is here to experience ultimately, is realising that this sexual experience of life will not necessarily bring them the degree of fulfilment that they need, instead the fulfilment they are truly seeking is the creative force itself in its fullness as it comes through all of the Chakras and that experience itself is a natural experience brother.

You can't be expected to have these particular Chakras unlocked instantaneously; it is actually a steady process of life experience that causes these centres to open themselves. Meditation has an effect on this yes, but it is a rather natural experience whereby everything comes together to create a satori and/or understanding or revelatory experience of wholeness, interconnectedness, love, whatever the word you might use. J+009 A15

The Root Chakra is much like a valve, it is usually locked, so most people upon the plane are locked in this centre. This Chakra as it were, more like a valve, if the valve were to have all of a sudden opened, then people would not be so eager to move about the fields looking for a spouse to engage in those promiscuous activities. The Root Chakra serves as a valve to stop the kundalini moving any higher, and then there is only a very small amount of that kundalini force, miniscule even, that moves through and up the body to the temple and then to the Higher-Self.

So then it is, these that would like to move past this Chakra, then there must be the revelation that there is no movement beyond your sexual impulses unless there is the dedication of the life to love, to the Christos itself, here then the valve can be unlocked and the energy freed, and then there can be the transcendence of the human desire. If then an individual would so want this in their life, a complete connection to the Cosmos, if this is wanted within the soul, for the soul has recognised that there is only one way to live, then the valve can begin to become unlocked slowly like a slow burning candle. Then would be seen then how this Chakra serves as a limiter. Q001 A4

So then this is what we will say, that if these then had the determination to build a perfect relationship with perfection, to say then that these would make a decision to engage more intimately with building a relationship with the Christos inside of them, then this would be how the being that is operating can be shifted from those sexual and raw-drive experiences, to being one perfectly present in that heart space and even the many other spaces along the body.

But as we said, this experience is much like a slow burning candle, perhaps in the opposite way that the candle would get more flamey rather than less, but see as an individual builds a relationship with love, their kundalini valves, the valve system begins to release more energy, the more connected one is to Cosmos, to Love, to Christ as it were.

The more connected one is to this force, kundalini will start to move up the body in greater amounts, causing one to enter into greater states of being, of presence. Q001 A8

Soul Love and Biological Love

We would like you to know that your biology is just as capable of producing love as is your mind, and it is important to make a distinction between the biology's need for love and its experience of a lack of the same, and your minds experience of love and its lack of the same.

The mind is in truth never really lonely, and its love is without the biological component to which you are familiar with, thus the mind cannot feel lonely, biologically, physically, sexually if you prefer; the mind can only feel lonely if it is deprived of God.

The body however is a creature of its own, it has its biases, its nature, it has its own mind for it is an intelligent conglomerate of cells which too think alongside that human that thinks along it. It is important to understand the difference between your cells desires and the more greater desires of the self here.

If your body feels lonely then it is for you to decide whether you agree with it or not, but do not confuse the biological love and the biological loneliness for the Christ consciousness nature of love, for these are different.

The bodies love is crude, the bodies loneliness thus must be crude too. The minds love is profound, infinite, the tapestry of the infinite, it never ends.

We do not see loneliness at all, we see that your emotions are but an illusion, non-existent, instead they are the creation of the body, fuelled by the fire that your mind channels into it, such that it becomes an illusion that you can agree with.

As has been before mentioned, pre-incarnative decisions are such that entities come to this planet to learn, it was once said that entities come as soul mates for the purpose of emotional maturity, you may take this moment to revere or take note of the emotional maturity to which you are currently experiencing, and it is for you to decide whether succumbing to the bodies emotions is emotionally mature, which comes with its consequences, or whether improving the quality of your mind is the more mature choice.

Source quite literally doesn't know which one is true, for in truth both could lead you right up that mountain. What is true for you will be for you to decide, we would only like to make a distinction, a very clear one, between the biological love - the biological loneliness that humans tend to call love; and the love of the mind - a love of mind or mind love.

Which is more of a God conscious experience?

Bodily love, biological love, love procured via the biology and its loneliness counterpart as we can only emphasise once more, is but a distortion of the bodies own creation, for the body has its own mind and enjoys the company of the opposing sex. This is the body, not the soul. S083 A21

We see two things which ought to be described, we describe these in general terms for general understanding for all souls upon this plane.

Entities upon this plane seek soul like connections by confusing biological love with soul love. Entities upon this plane are under the impression typically, who encounter spiritual material that is, that soul love is expressed biologically and thus requires the opposite sex for the achievement of this soul like connection, this is far from the truth and is a primitive idea that needs some tempering to work.

We move on now to the second idea, and we once again speak in general to all entities upon this plane.

The soul love is not a biological love at all, thus not requiring the opposite sex whatsoever, the soul love is a love that one quite literally has with a non-biological existence, an energy as you would call it, this energy completes you in every single way, shape and form. Most humans upon this plane at this time are not evolved enough to overcome biological love and when such entities engage in spiritual practices, they tend to become confused between the biology and the soul.

It is only natural for this to happen and is only an aspect of the ignorant nature of innocence, for innocence in its cuteness is ignorant nonetheless, and this is ok for this is the nature of life, the joy of learning, it is perfectly ok to be ignorant and innocent, to be primitive and to enjoy growing and becoming less primitive and more complete.

Therefore, if you would truly like to understand what soul love is, completely remove sexual attraction, sexuality, sex itself, and any kind of opposite sex need, then you have understood soul love. It is a love that completes an entity fully, meaning that the entity need not an opposite sex, or same sex depending on the attractive mechanisms function, being in their presence.

It is once again, only natural to confuse soul love for biological love but they are separate, and many a time where entities upon this plane have said they are in love with x, y or z, typically they are speaking of a more biological love that is not really a soul love, for a soul love would mean that two entities would, in each other's presence that is, would love each other unconditionally, would not be possessive over one another, would not have any kind of argument or frustration with one another, would be of such a degree of harmony that entities upon this plane would call their relationship boring in some way, shape or form. Such entities would not need sex in any form, and here you would begin to understand the rather loftiness of soul love as we are now bringing some greater clarification to it.

Now we would like to finalise in a less harsh way, we know we are reducing the significance of biological love and for this we apologise, but if it is so that you seek biological love then seeketh it in innocence and freedom, and do as you will, Source remains unbiased, and watches and looks over entities in loving compassion.

Make the decisions you want to make and if it is so that you would seek to make those decisions based on the emotions that you are feeling then so be it, but have the experience of free will and free choice. Make what you call mistakes or make what you call corrections, do what you will, it hardly matters for there is just too much time that an hour, a day, or 50 years, will always have its nourishment, regardless of what consists of those years. S083 A22

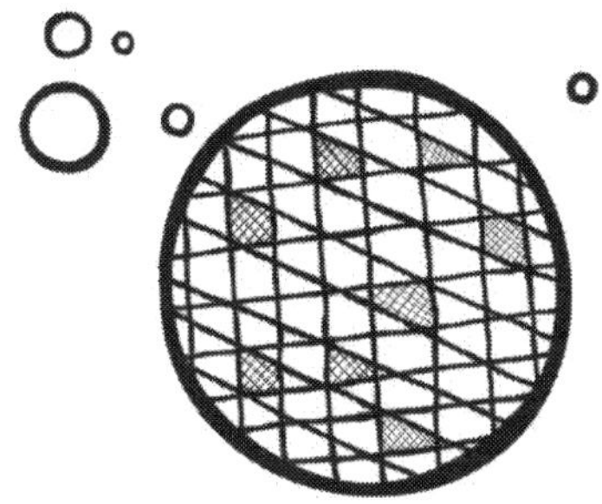

The Energy of Worrying

'It is the biggest misconception on this planet at this time, that one is a parent; one is not a parent, one is a caretaker.'

It's useless dearest one, fundamentally. Worrying is very impractical.

Let us make a few cases:

Worrying dearest one is that act of a lack of trust in truth, for the only reason anyone would ever worry is because the entity seems to believe that, number one, nothing is happening in accordance to their control; this is not true, you control your life, you controlled it when you came, you controlled it in your decisions for your incarnation, everything is in control, yet entities think they are not in control so they worry.

Parental Worries

Entities then worry about things happening to their loved ones, yet seemingly entities have a tendency to compare. Something happens to an entity soul on the news, the entities soul looks at their children and thinks 'Oh, this will happen to my children I must worry.'

You do not know your child's path!

One simply does not understand what their child has planned.

Let us then make this case:

Worrying is not at all practical, what is practical is rationality, it is ok to be rational, 'Don't touch the fire!' says the parent out of pure rationality. The child touches the fire, did the parent worry? No, the parent was rational and said, 'Do not touch the fire!' the child didn't listen.

Worrying dearest one in this sense is just not practical, rationality is practical, useful, it is ok to be rational, it is not ok to compare.

One should never compare their life and then create worries, for they are comparing to something on the news and imagining it happening to their child. Be rational dearest one, will you ever let your children go near something that you know is dangerous?

No, it is irrational!

In truth a good parent to which there are, well not as many as there should be. A good parent is at least aware that what it can control is limited, but what it can't control the parent should be aware, is the decisions of the child. Hard to accept for many parents, many parents wish they could control their child's life completely, in this way the parents wish they could stop the atrocities that happen to children, but in the moments the parent is not in control of their child's life and something is happening beyond the parents level of reach, it is well to consider all was in control of the child to which the parent is trying to protect. We speak predominantly of parents in the context of worrying for it serves as the most profound of examples. What we are attempting to say is worrying is useless, being rational is completely ok.

And it is also well to understand that one can only control their children to such and such a degree, protect their children to such and such a degree, but one day the child ventures out, or is out of the reach of the entity souls eyes, in these moments atrocities can happen, this is true but you were doing the best you could, so in this context you had not the control for it was out of your reach. This goes for all parents, all parents must relinquish their worrying for you cannot think in the past or the future in such and such a way, it is rather useless, what is in control of you right now is this moment.

Why worry about future and pasts that don't even exist when you can have control of your environment right now?

It is obvious that entities never worry when they are in control, so be in the present moment, recognise the only thing you can control is the present moment, and dearest parents out there, recognise that God is real, reincarnation is real, and when something is out of your control dearest parents, please recognise that there is a divine plan happening and there is a divine parent looking after your child. It is the biggest misconception on this planet at this time, that one is a parent; one is not a parent, one is a caretaker.

Humans will take a very long time to realise this, one is a caretaker for souls when they are young at least, forever too. A caretaker, not a parent, the parent is the Higher-Self, your Higher-Self, all Higher-Selves, that is the parent, that is the entity working tirelessly to ensure things go as predetermined. One does not necessarily come to parent their child, you leave that to the Higher-Self, no you caretake your child, you tell your child, you teach your child, you help your child, in many cases you control your child for your children came to be obedient under their caretakers and their caretakers have certain expectation of their children. Entities come to be these caretakers you see, to do the job the Higher-Self cannot necessarily do, but the Higher-Self parents by giving the children the experiences they need.

So why do parents worry?

They worry because they love their children, they worry because they have empathy, that is why a parent worries, because they have empathy dearest one and when their child is in pain so are they. Pain when shared mutually is just as painful, such that it would mean that if my child goes through pain, I am going through pain too so I worry about this, that it may be avoided on not only my child's behalf, but my behalf too, for if my child goes through that pain, the pain I will feel will be just as immeasurable and this will hurt.

But dearest ones, parents and alike, do realise entities come to this planet for the very reason you worry.

Although it is harsh to suffer, although it is horrible to suffer, the Higher-Self sometimes has to bring out a wooden board which has on its surface, 'Come to God' and the Higher-Self smashes this wooden board on an entities forehead, and it hurts, it hurts in serious ways, it hurts when the pain is those things, those atrocities as you would understand, that those entities commit that would have to do with physical violence, it hurts when it is sexual violence, it hurts when it is emotional abuse and violence, but what must the Higher-Self do to make an entity recognise God is their salvation, hmm?

Entities on this plane wonder why they suffer?

Wonder why things happen to them?

They fear suffering, hmm?

They suffer and suffer, they complain and complain, they sit in therapy talking to their therapist over and over again about the same thing.

The entity whom is attempting to help them says, 'Hey why don't you climb the mountain?' And what does the entity say?

'Oh no, I'm ok thank you, another time, let me complain more about my problems, about my past, and my this and my that.'

And then you have a situation on your hands dearest one, a rather difficult dilemma, for the Higher-Self is tasked again with grabbing that wooden board, grabbing a marker, writing 'Pursue God with all your heart that you may know joy', and winding that sucker back – as we use a crude term.

Do understand our comedy and do understand that we are making light of a very profound situation on your planet, entities are so, how might we say, ignorant in that they ignore their Higher-Self, entities upon this plane decide what suffering they can endure, yes, but why endure it?

Why not listen to the Higher-Self hmm?

The Higher-Self says, 'Practice meditation' the entity says, 'No!' in 5,000 ways. The Higher-Self says, 'Eat well' the entity says, 'No!' what must the Higher-Self do?

Given not all entities have a choice to eat well but what all entities have is an option to sit with the Higher-Self, to sit with the God-Force when they have spare time. The Higher-Self wants to love you, and you want to love the Higher-Self, so you came to this planet to accomplish this, so why don't you?

Why do you worry?

You worry and worry, yet you came to accomplish the very act of the opposite of the same, what use is worry when you have the answers?

How many entities dearest one, arrive in the Astral, they say, 'Oh, I had no information on this,' then the guides remind them, 'One day dearest one you met an entity called Jerry, he had a very short one minute conversation with you where he disclosed information on how to connect to the Higher-Self, you ignored and parred him off,' as the term goes, 'and left back for home, and now you complain that you were never given information?'

Entities come up to the Astral dearest one, they come up to us and they say, 'Oh, we had not any information,' we say, 'Oh, but dearest one do you not remember on the internet,' Cyberspace as we term it, 'On your cyberspace, one day you had a conversation with Jordan whom was under the pseudonym of 'YouSpiritually', and he told you this and that and this, and you dismissed him, and now you say you had no information?'

You see the issue?

And entities worry, dearest one 'worry not' is our message. Suffering is the only way the Higher-Self is able to tell someone to pursue the God-Force, otherwise souls do not listen. You fear suffering so you worry but you don't have to suffer if you look forward to being in a relationship with the Higher-Self. J+022 A14

What must be understood is the growing pains of being shoved into a body, being incarnated onto the planet and moving through the changing energies, this is a very lengthy process.

It is rather sad that entities upon this plane believe so deeply in your Western civilisation that they would send young people to work in those Western jobs, rather than allowing them time to fully develop and spiritually grow before they move out.

If an entity decides to have or look after a child, the entity must realise that it is a child. The entities that this one calls their father, their mother, their nan, their granddad, these are the adults and the adults responsibility as a group collective is to let the child grow before the child goes out into reality. Unfortunately, in your Western civilisations the culture has not yet understood the importance of allowing a child to grow, of seeing the child's ignorance and seeing that it must be tempered, and that the child would have time to introspect and become a fully blossomed flower. It is always a rush to get them out, never is it considered really by the parents the importance of the child, who is but a neophyte, to have time to introspect and understand what it is that they really want. The greatest depression of young people is parents pushing them into situations that they do not want to be in, if a parent takes the responsibility of looking after or having a child, whether adopted or by blood, it is the parents responsibility to fully allow the child to grow.

At the moment the child is able to state without any hesitation in their heart that they are ready to move out, is when the child is ready to leave the flock, but the patience pays dividends as you would understand this business term. For what you see is the result of a flower that has fully blossomed, which is able to fully tame their reality and become the best version of themselves. When a parent tries to rush a child out, the child will be doomed to make some degree of mistakes, it is a difficult life on Earth but our suggestion, if you are able to supply any child of any kind, adopted or by blood, the opportunity to live in a deep state of introspection in their younger years, then you should do this for you will be rewarded the most when the child becomes an adult and is able to give back what was given, which was the most precious commodity of time, and time was not wasted when given to wise children such as the one who is giving the reading now.

This message is to all parents and entities upon this plane at this time, if parents have the luxury of giving their children time, they should give their children time. For time yields growth. S077 A7

Money Worries

Entities worry about money – this will be a long one – entities worry about money dearest one, 'I have money!', 'I do not have money!', 'What if I lose my money, I can't pay my bills!' This, that, this, that and the other, dearest one do you think that God cares?

God does not care about your money situation at all, God could have you homeless and still not care, so long as you are seeking connection with God, this is the only thing that matters.

Whether you have to go to a food bank, whether you live in the YMCA or whatever term you use to describe your hostels, God cares not! God's only concern is whether you have heeded his message, whether you have heeded the message of, 'Are you willing to come close to me in this incarnation, that you may learn those things, those spiritual values, those spiritual energies, that energy that allows you to experience the unity with me? Have you grasped this?'

Many entities on your plane have found themselves without money, homeless, starving dearest one, to death! They experience a near-death experience where they are confronted with God, then it all comes back to them, the joy of creation, everything, everything! So, they get up and they start sharing their story and all of a sudden, they're famous and they have followers and all of this stuff, they have money and all this material stuff dearest one, as we may use this term.

Isn't it funny dearest one, how this works?

God doesn't care about your money, he really doesn't sorry to say, he really doesn't. God's only concern is your closeness to him and your relationship with him dearest one, so you can worry about money all you want, and you can worry about rent all you want dearest one, but God doesn't care about your rent or your money, his only concern is whether you are close to God or not.

We know this scares all entities upon this plane, we know it freaks all entities out, if we may use this demeanour or term as you may understand. For it seemingly is, 'If I am cold and on the streets, then this surely is moving me further away?'

But how funny is it, we don't mean to be dark, but how funny is it that those entities who find themselves in the worst kinds of stresses find God the quickest.

Here they are praying, 'Oh God I'm suffering!'

Isn't it hilarious how entities only want to know God when they are suffering? J+022 A14

Suffering Worries

Dearest one, why worry?

This is our message, we are rather passionate about this because it is a rather big issue on your plane, entities wonder why they suffer, yet they call God the instant they do!

When the wars were happening dearest one, the prayers were so numerous that we didn't really know how to handle them you see, entities called and called, when they saw their child splattered on the ground, they called!

Why were they not calling before?

Only when they see horrific things, a life without God, do entities want God. You see?

It is a shame, because entities can have it all without the suffering, but they must see some kind of atrocity before they even want God in their life! And you wonder why entities come to this planet?

You think an entity can grow in the Astral?

Dearest one, let us not be funny, it is too harmonious in the Astral for growth to occur, you must grow here where suffering is available to you, where the lower three Chakras have the opportunity to be active, you must grow down here. We speak generally of course.

Dearest one, we have seen things, we have seen it all, violence, nuclear explosions, body parts, anything you could imagine, it's all in the Astral you know, it's all there you know!

Dearest one, life is not about suffering, but the Higher-Self tends to have to write on a neat wooden board, with no padding mind you for it must hurt a little bit, we are being comedic, 'Seek God, here's your salvation', the Higher-Self writes SMACK! Right on the head, until the entity listens.

Suicide is an issue as well, the entity whom deciding to or trying to commit suicide, arrives in the Astral, 'I had no help!' the entity will say. 'Well dearest one,' we will reply, 'there was this entity on your internet or cyberspace called Jerry who had a certain pseudonym, who gave you some information on your suicidal expression. You heeded not his words.'

They say, 'Oh but, it wasn't enough, I needed you here with me, I needed you,' the entity will say to its guides, to its Higher-Self, 'You didn't communicate with me telepathically, you gave me no dreams,' the suicidal entity says whom is in the Astral, 'You gave me no messages, there was no mystical experience!' the entity will say in the Astral.

Our reply, 'What do entities think this is hmm? You think this life you're in right now is about instant gratification?'

'If ye seeks God, seek God with your whole heart, not with half a heart that desires something instantly,' this is what we say, 'Seek God in earnest. If one is not seeking God in earnest, then what is the point for half of yourself is still enjoying the illusion.' J+022 A14

A Short Note on Suicide

Suicide is what you might call one of the more ultimate sins, we use the word 'sin' in relation to its meaning - when one misses the mark.

Here in the sin of committing suicide you have not even hit the board! You have not even gotten close to the target in the middle!

The effects of suicide would be that the contract would end prematurely causing one to disincarnate early and many of their predestined karmic experiences, to which they have coordinated with the Lords of Karma, and to which the Lords of Karma have had the hefty job of coordinating the experiences in relation to how it connects to all the other entities, this entire experience you see, becomes destroyed.

Thus one would find that the experience of reincarnation once disincarnated happens rapidly - one would commit the suicide, they would find themselves in a deep sleep usually, if they are lucky they will at least get to see a few things, and then they will find themselves back within another body setting out to experience the rest of their karmic ties to which they have determined for themselves, in relation to what they have given suggestions to towards the Lords of Karma - to which have written those Karmic experiences in the stone of the 3rd dimensional chemical mental body of Earth.

When one commits suicide it is seen as, once again, one of the more ultimate sins one could do, for when one comes back the conditions of their Karmic experience is usually, naturally, more severe and intensive, because they have to get done what they were going to get done, within the amount of years that they had assigned to their life experience on Earth.

Take for instance if one is to incarnate for 70 years, they commit suicide at the age of 35, they *now* have 35 years to do all of the Karmic experiences to which they had prematurely ended, and one could imagine hmm... just how intensive and unfun this would be. Q004 A3

Even if they had only 2 years remaining, they would live out 2 years; any karmic lessons that are missed are put in the next incarnation and so infinitum, until the individual has achieved their karmic destiny of enlightenment - what you would call Christ consciousness, the alignment with the creative force itself, to be unified with the creative force within one that one would become a Creator, and to then have such within thee the ability to know the balance of the universe, the balance of nature, and how not to impede on another person's experience of life.

This is how a Christ conscious individual experiences life, but this description is vague for there are many more things. Q004 A4

[End of Note]

Dearest one, why worry hmm?

Everything upon this planet is working perfectly. The degree of suffering that will happen on this planet, the degree of authoritarian control that will happen on this planet, the degree of political war, the degree of all those things that are predicted of your futures by various sources on your cyberspace, the degree of suffering that will happen on your planet is completely determined by how willing a human is to pursue the God from within.

If you're willing, if this planetary system is willing, there will be change, joyous change. If this planetary system would seek to continue to have that board, as we have said many times now, written with 'Pursue God, here's your salvation, etc,' SMACKED on the head!

If society would seek to pursue suffering off their own merit, then the school is functioning just well, for clearly we have children who are not grasping the lesson.

You say to your children, '100, 200, 300, four hundred and forty, now you do the same,' you say to your child.

They reply, '100, 200, 300, forty-four???' – your cuteness is admirable, but your stupidity is cute you see, this becomes our perspective, so of course we are concerned, not worried, but we believe the stupidity of humans is cute. Their cuteness remains admirable regardless of the atrocities they commit, for to us whether a human being is a rapist, a paedophile, a serial killer, whatever the term to describe the most negative entity in the world, our love is universal, and we see an innocent little soul who knows no better and will eventually learn how life is to be pursued.

For all of us souls are one force, God! How can we not love our Creator?

Therefore, eventually all souls upon this plane will learn, even if they have to go to a different planet to learn, they will learn dearest one.

Why don't you learn now is our suggestion?

It is your free will and free choice to do whatever you wish, why not learn now?

You can! You don't have to, but you can!

It is always the choice of the entity, for we cannot take choice away from God can we? No! God can choose for himself, for herself, for itself, but we have a preference, we enjoy it when an entity chooses for God, for at-one-ment or atonement if you prefer. J+022 A14

Overcoming Worry

Entities have different specifications for this answer, some entities need to be parents who are divorced and then lose their children in custody, and then they find themselves in a very precarious situation where they are homeless and starving to death, and then they have a near-death experience and they experience the God-Force and etc. At the experiencing of the God-Force their worrying dissipates, food what of it I am with God!

Water my lack of it, whatever I am with God!

It manifests differently in various extremes to different entities, what an entity needs though dearest one, to remove the worrying completely is to recognise one thing, you have come to this planet for one reason, one reason which is inherent within the number itself, ONE-ness it is so simple. How humans complicate it.

All entities upon this plane at this time, in this very moment have come to learn one thing, unity, One-ness, it happens at the Heart Chakra, it happens at universal love dearest one, one-ness, One-ness. All entities will be able to see the Christ, hmm! One-ness.

At this point this is a little bit of a far cry, but we do have faith because we love you humans, we love you dearly, we come to your planet in human form sometimes mind you, we come to your planet sometimes, we love you humans, please learn. J+022 A15

The entity Jesus had occurrences of the same, periodic none-the-less, but truly was this one at-one-ment. The entity at a certain stage truly comprehended it all, 'Forgive them Father, they know not what they do.'

Truly in this moment he really understood how innocent humans are and how his worries are unneeded. This a tough lesson to learn to not worry, really hard in fact. We have faith in humans, we really think you can do it you know; we really believe in humans, we are not going to give up on humans.

We do not necessarily believe that the negative polarity as you understand it is in control of the humans at this time, humans are far to ignorant to even know that the negative polarity is at this current time having its way with your planet. Humans seem to think this is all quite normal, this is not the case.

Since humans are so ignorant and have not consciously chosen to completely ignore us, but are instead at some level seeking us, whether it takes thousands and thousands of years, we will remain persistent, for this is our greatest desire, to remain persistent in our service, to remain persistent in our giving. We must do this, for there is always a calling.

Let us remind you a calling is simply – it is when one is hurting and desires help from a force of some kind. It happens to all entities whether they are religious or not, whether they are wanderers or not, all entities have had times in their life when they have called. All calls are answered in ways such that when an entity comes to the Astral and they say, 'You didn't answer my call,' we say, 'Oh we did, that lady who gave you a coffee and put a smiley face and said, 'Don't worry everything will be fine', she had a dream you know!'

You see calls are answered, calls are always answered and nobody is alone, the Higher-Self is here, the Higher-Self may have taken Muay Thai to get rather good at the whole smacking with the board thing, for perhaps it needed the stamina, for it never foresaw the difficulty. But in truth, jokes aside, we have faith dearest ones, so for you entities here now today, recognise this and do what you must do. Connect to God, it is as easy and paradoxically as difficult as closing your eyes. J+022 A16

Learning Through Grace

Graceful learning is in many ways not so much what an entity thinks, graceful learning is learning by which an entity is approaching or actively pursuing unity with God, in the active pursuit of unity with the One Infinite

Creator, the entity will always find him or herself in very peculiar situations. Always the situation seeks to strengthen one's unity with God.

This is graceful learning, it is the active pursuit not the inactive pursuit which is called suffering. When there is no pursuit to God, you call it 'suffering'; when there is pursuit to the God-Force, you call it 'grace'. The reason it is grace is because the environment is insignificant, what is most significant is this environment and how you feel here as the God-Force filters through. When this environment, as our wise Sadhguru entity says, 'As this environment is sweet then what could your environment ever invoke in you other than joy?' Joy you see.

So, learning from grace is the active pursuit of God, you see. If you seek to learn through grace, pursue God with an open heart, with a good step forward, you will know grace, you will know joy, you will know at-one-ment or atonement, you will know truly something unspeakable. J+022 A17

Worrying reminds us in terms of imagery of one who frantically prances about in all kinds of directions with the rather disgusted look on their face of one who has just been bitten by a shark, going here and there randomly, like random energy which is entropic.

Then we have one who doesn't worry, who stands still, who is peaceful, and the entity feels atonement and at home with the self.

In comparison to these two images, which would you rather be?

Do recognise dearest one, that although the lesson that God doesn't care about money is harsh, for one would desire God to care about their financial situation, we understand the harshness of this but in truth dearest one, let us outline some things:

The Higher-Self desires that you build a more substantial relationship with money, in which your relationship with money is that you see it as something that is not about God but is only of significance to the illusion.

The ability to disassociate from money completely mind you, will be the hardest lesson for any entity upon this plane to learn. It is an interesting lesson; it is a lesson that requires abundance in money and requires a lacking of thereof.

Let us remind you of something dearest one, you have a weird child who can do these things that are weird. People whom would observe the same would think this entity was acting, would think this entity is schizophrenic, would think that there is something wrong with this entity and he needs to go and see a doctor. They would lock him up dearest one, you have a weird child, he's doing something really weird right now, he's doing it because he can do it, for a very particular reason, he's doing it because he is able through this manner, this expression, this channel as you call it, to offer teachings that are not native to his own knowledge.

Opportunities and levels of understandings such as this can be used for your wellbeing and when applied will yield results that will make you forget about money completely. It is completely your choice whether you listen to it or not, God will love you all the same, you will love yourself all the same. All we are trying to elucidate here is this entity whom is doing this *channelling*, is perhaps attempting to demonstrate that in truth the only one thing that is most important in a life on Earth as you would understand, is one's connection to God.

The length of time it would take an entity upon this plane to realise this, depends solely on how much they want to focus on the illusion, on idols like money and these various objects. How many times dearest one have you said, 'At this point money is not real, it is a number on the screen.' Hmm?

Have you not been recognising within yourself, a certain change in perspective where you are realising this thing called money is not even real, it is an abstract idea that can be altered and changed and there is a strong possibility but we cannot say, but there is a possibility that the money that is currently afloat in your climate, a large amount of it didn't exist many years ago, it was fabricated, perhaps as a means to an end, we can't say for sure for this would be a violation of free will but what we can say is why care?

We know it's hard, we know it's hard to accept that God could be real, number one. That the experience of the God-Force could also be real, number two. We know it's hard to accept, we know there is scepticism at infinite levels of this, we totally understand dearest one, how strange this all is, but it becomes significantly less strange if you just give God a chance. Give him a chance, her a chance, it a chance, and let it funnel into you, then you will know.

We end this communication in the love and the light of the One Infinite Creator. Amen. J+022 A18

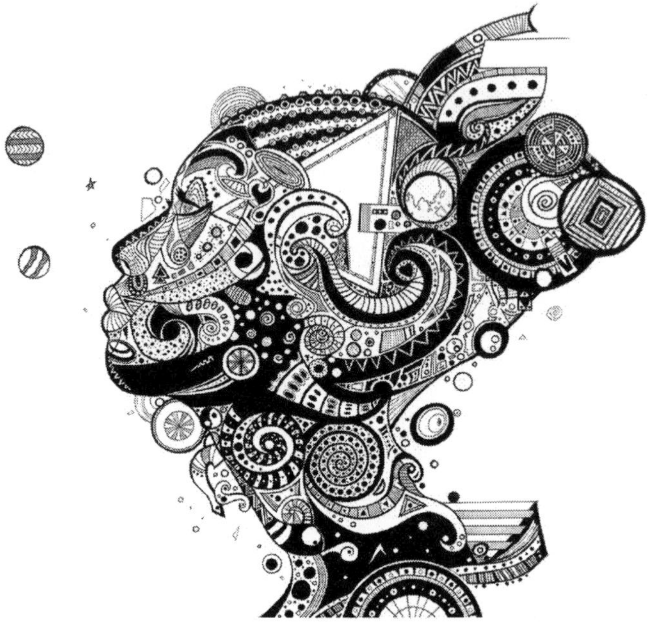

THE METAPHYSICAL

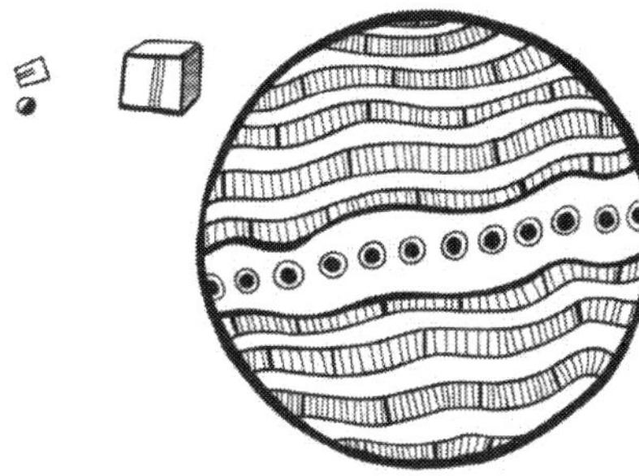

Human Prehistory

'This school is somewhat the result of, you might say, the naïve mistakes of the Gods introducing the frontal lobe too early to speed a project of theirs up.'

We are truly metaphysical beings having a physical experience, and for some those previous chapters covering important but less dense aspects will suffice, for they will have gained valuable insight into the reconfiguration of the atomic body, along with many valuable pathways leading towards a greater level of self-love, self-mastery, an improved nervous system that can function with less incoherence when operating at a higher oscillatory rate, and cells that can conduct that increased energy without entropic discharge. However, for those that would truly explore human potential and strive to move beyond the veil with an open mind and heart, well it's time to take a step further down the rabbit hole and shine some much-needed light on this illusion we dance so clumsily within.

There is much to be said in regard to who and what we truly are, and even more to be said regarding where we have come from and where we have the potential to get to. This subject is one that could fill countless books, but for now please consider this fascinating topic of humanities prehistory as a challenging warm up.

It is said that 'A tree's beauty lies in its branches, but its strength lies in its roots.' Therefore, we shall begin at the beginning.

Note: As mentioned in the Preface, the code at the end of each quote pertains to the source of reference. It is useful to observe the difference in perspectives between those telepathic readings beginning with C, J+ or M, which classed at the level of trance from Narrowband to Broadband, are a communication with our teachers, some would call them guides, but essentially these are a specific group of dimensional beings communicating from a higher frequency to our lower frequency that are also on their own path of evolution, having originally come from similar neophyte circumstance to us, offering helpful information as part of their divine journey of service, since they are further up the mountain.

Whereas Source and Quantum Readings, those prefixed with S or Q, are a psychic rather than telepathic reading, this is a communication with the logos itself, Intelligent Infinity, Brahman as it is known in the Hindu culture or Universal Consciousness as it may be referred. Your Higher-Self or Over-Self is the gateway to Source and when one is at-one-ment (atonement) with their Over-Self they are also at one with Source and can therefore tap information from this matrix.

This is worth keeping in mind as you may observe subtle differences in perspective whilst reading this book.

The Humanoid

Your lineage, your history, must track back millions of years, far back in time as we go back to the stages of development where souls were placed and/or were growing in different environments, these environments you call them planets. At this stage things were young; the universe was young and so millions of years does not even suit as an appropriate number to describe how far back this goes. With each environment there were different levels of energy as you might call it, of light, the electromagnetic spectrum, that is the spectrum of photons you see, there were different degrees of intensity along this spectrum. Toward the centre of the universe was where the, what you would call, the electromagnetic spectrum of light and radiation was the most intense and this caused the phenomena of evolution to occur within planets that could house atomic and then eventually molecular lifeforms, these lifeforms evolved to utilise the many Suns that surrounded the planet, thus there was the absorption of pure light to live.

An entity, a vehicle rather, would look more so like a round ball of light characterised by the lightness of the body and by the fact that the entities were living on what some might call light as it were, and the chemical necessities merely necessitated an environment that was electromagnetically receptive to cosmic influences. The beings thus evolved to be incredibly light-like and incredibly intelligent, for there was such the ability to organise the self with incredible efficiency due to the speed of vibration in these environments.

Then later, much later as evolution continued, these entities learnt of methods and ways to transport to different planets and planes, soon what they knew was known by the neighbouring planets, and what was known by the neighbouring planets would soon be known by the other neighbouring planets, there was as you call it space travel and the like, and there was an investigation, a pilgrimage, a wondering you might say to even the furthest parts of the universe to see what things are growing.

Eventually it was realised that the further away you are from the centre of this universe the more strange and crude the organisms that grew became, and these light beings, as you might call them, became somewhat interested and perhaps a little concerned to how things were growing in the far reaches of the galaxy, so with their knowledge up to the point to which they had the same, they attempted to help guide and give raise to an optimal specie, this specie would later be called humanoid and these light beings who had already entered into the much higher dimensions as you would call it, the 5th dimension, these took bodies of pure light whilst they encouraged the creation of human-like bodies that had human-like qualities and could efficiently handle the environment without too many issues as you might say, and equally retaining the ability to utilise 'mind' for the evolutionary purposes with relative efficiency.

The humanoid was created by said 'beings of light' as you call them, as we even call them, and so it was that the humanoids came about a very far time ago.

Later and much later Earth, a distant planet, would soon be found to be entering into a stage to which it could house chemical life and what was brought to Earth was not only humanoids but even the gene itself, that it could be raised and born into this new existence. S065 A1

The gene would refer to the egg as you would understand that there is stored within the egg, and in many cases the sperm, the gene pattern that would create a humanoid. Then it was brought to this planet, prebuilt humanoids and humanoids in egg form that could be or undergo the process of cellular division.

This was brought to this planet when it was then able to house such forms of life under the gene hardware. Q011 A1

The human was a bi-product of the egg, as is the chicken you see, it is simply that humanoids were brought in their complete form as well as their egg form. Q011 A3

They were stored in an advanced technology that would be able to grow humans in a solution that is extremely similar to the human womb. Q011 A4

You would simply see that the womb is composed of certain solutions, certain proteins, all the essentials that the egg would need to grow nutrition and such things. This was what this solution was composed of, it would be akin to a scientist of your era drawing the liquids from the womb of a female whom would be pregnant, and storing them, analysing them, and recreating the same in a kind of cylindrical and/or circular chamber which could house such a liquid. Here it could be stored in this brine if you could call it the same, transported and then there would be the germination or impregnation process where the artificial sperm would be inserted into the egg to begin the process of growing the humanoid in what would be some kind of spherical glass like chamber, similar to what you see in your sci-fi movies of entities growing biological forms in cylindrical devises full of water. Perhaps this is a race memory. Q011 A5

Your reproductive system is simply a duplicate of what that advanced race created in technological form. Your reproductive system achieves its feat of producing a human through the same way that the technological advancements the species that impregnated this planet with humans, achieved their ability to grow humans in these spherical chambers. Q011 A6

The Frontal Lobe Upgrade

There would be a time where the Extra-Terrestrial beings who brought humans and their corresponding eggs to this planet then observed the same and found that the humans were not performing to the level of degree that they ought to. Modifications were thus made to the genome, rather than simply awaiting natural genetic adaptation to occur, thus you get humans who are a little bit too intelligent for their own good. You might say that the project of these Extra-Terrestrials supplied that they ought to do this rather than waiting around. Q011 A8

The Extra-Terrestrials introduced the frontal lobe to the human genome without humans knowing how to correctly integrate this portion of the brain with the rest of their brain. There was a schism you see, the schism wasn't obvious at first and it became evident that the frontal lobe slowly began to disconnect from the other regions of the brain, causing beings to be frontal lobe beings rather than we will say intuitive beings, for lack of a better term. Q011 A10

Prior to the frontal lobe the human brain was still reasonably large, at least larger than most brains of any mammal at the time, there were hints of a cerebral cortex, indeed simply what was missing was the reasoning or thinking zone of the brain which was then given to the human causing humans to become able to be completely tapped and intuitive, as could be termed, as well as the ability to analyse their intuitions.

Humans prior had great abilities for their brains, composed without the frontal cortex, were able to connect easily to the intuitive levels of life. The addition of the frontal lobe caused humans to perhaps invest a little too much into reasoning.

The energy delineated towards this region of the brain causing the other regions, which are by no means primitive as such but are more so useful for other things, to diminish in their activity. The frontal lobe at the time it was introduced into the human species was a perfectly balanced addition, but humans simply were not evolved enough to know how to cojoin it with their current experience of life. Humans then were able to advance quickly and built civilisations and technologies and such things, this was at the cost of their ability to understand how to integrate the frontal lobe with the intuitive brain. Q011 A9

Indeed, the reasoning brain clouded the other regions of the brain which need not a reason to forgive, for humans lived without reason. In terms of how they processed information if there was any reason, the reason had a completely different energetic quality to it, in such a sense the reasoning centres did slow down the humans ability to forgive and work together. Q011 A10

The pressing issue then is not so much that humans were not able to work together so correctly, instead it was that humans were too dumb may we say, to know how to integrate the frontal lobe, which made them intelligent ironically, with the rest of the brain.

Thus in a literally way, as in the most literal way you could imagine, the frontal lobe and its connections to the, let us call it subconscious mind as we find the right replacement for intuitive mind; the frontal lobe and its connection with the subconscious grew less and less until beings were impaired to reason without the ability to influence the subconscious portions of the body, which is what humans then had the ability to do before, giving humans abilities that would startle any entity of this time. Q011 A10

The abilities varied greatly but you would consider that the electrical constituent of life was under the full control of humans at that time, entities therefore were able to grow a plant out of their hand. Heal an injury instantly or extremely rapidly. Entities were able to do some of the funny things you see in your cartoons like creating energy balls which could be felt and cast out of one's hand. Humans were magical in that time, they could achieve heights of jumping as you would understand the muscular contraction that would easily overrun the current records at your Olympic events. Humans had then, you would simply call it, the power of early formation of Chi, which found its beginnings in that plasma body. The plasma body was active and the Chi then was there, it simply had not the ability to mentalise.

Humans would not use the Chi for mental ideas, instead the Chi was used for all things that were emotional and emotionally driven, for the reasoning and ability of humans was so utterly slow without the frontal lobe that it would take what is now compiled in a matter of milliseconds, upwards of 10 seconds for the human of that time to create a sentence.

Any conceptual thought a human could create would take minutes before the human was able to then, out of that thought, innovate. Therefore humans, once again, never used the abilities of their Chi for anything other than that which was instinctual or useful to their genetic disposition or you might also say, deterministic outcome. Q011 A11

In prehistory when humans were young they were much like children, they were very susceptible to love, they were truly even in their adulthood, man/child's, man/children, they sought love deeply and many of their actions and reactions were instinctive and utterly innocent without much deep thought you see. S065 A7

Evolution takes time, humans were the imagination of beings who sought to help humankind, or rather, soul-kind in attempting to give souls well equipped vehicles to handle the creative force. S065 A1

Any and all species upon this plane have been planted except for a few plants which have managed to evolve due to the natural intelligent interactions of levels of matter that need not necessarily be spoken about right now. Q011 A16

Even insects are not so much native for they are an extremely intelligently placed design which was thought of by Extra-Terrestrials to improve the micro-climates and to make fertile soils, and to generate an electronic ecosystem as well as a chemical ecosystem for the ability of vegetation and animals to thrive, this was intelligently placed these insects.

The native species of this planet *were* very primitive kinds of moss. Q011 A17

In the various other materials, it is spoken that the monkey-like specie that had supposedly naturally evolved here was genetically modified. We of 'J' see this as not totally accurate according to our data. To the perception of we, the only native species on this planet are rocks and moss like organisms, this planet to our perception was meant to become a garden that did not house any animals or even fish for that matter. To the perception of we of 'J', we believe then once again, this planet was intended as a Garden, and before there was ever a human species of any kind, there were but clear waters, a variety of rocks and minerals, and a variety of simple moss-like or simplistic plant-like organisms that grew both in the waters and then later, the land.

We of 'J' believe that humans are not native to this planet, nor are most animals in-fact. According to our Data, humans and other species were placed here on purpose by Extra-Terrestrials for purposes we of 'J' would not so much enjoy commenting on at this time.

In such a sense, the business of Extra-Terrestrials and what they do with the human species is perhaps their choice, considering, with all due respect of course, they were the ones who planted you and thus they have a level of, at-least to their belief, responsibility and 'ownership' over you.

This planet really was originally a garden, and may we say confidently, in our own belief system if you will, that this was intended to be a garden for moss, for trees, for rocks, for plant life, foliage and vegetation to grow, not necessarily a planet for animaloids and humanoids to come and... well... it is not in the best state now. We will save unpleasant adjectives in describing how the planet looks.

However, this planet, as a garden, would have been seen as a successful instrument to use or utilise, as you would understand her as Gaia, for the purpose of the growth and development of entities who are looking to further their experience of consciousness, in what you would call a consciousness-based system.

Herein lies the key, as you would understand, this is a consciousness-based system but there are many layers to it, and to access deeper layers sometimes one must go down to go up, sometimes you have to go down into the more crude dimensions of elemental life to experience evolution on an upward intensity, and so, when entities choose to enter into this planet, and when it is definitely a choice and not an influenced choice, may we say politely, when it is a choice of one's own individual self to enter this planet, because, and we say this here, some entities are swayed by other consciousnesses to enter into planets in unfair conditions - this is an important topic that we of 'J' feel must be spoken about - when an entity makes a choice to come to a planet of this kind of classification, they are usually coming to experience some kind of intense evolution, some intense growth, following the systems that are usually developed or created by beings who are hopefully positive - but it is not always the case that the entities are positive. J+025 A9

Many planets, as we of J have found in our travels, are extremely peaceful. Very, very peaceful... Very peaceful... VERY PEACEFUL! These are 'some' planets.

Other planets, one could say, are quite the opposite and have no interest in evolution, as do the peaceful ones tend to not have much of an interest in evolution because evolution is an application of the mind. The mind!

But in the case that a planet is designed for evolutionary growth and evolutionary development, you will find beings such as us, and also interestingly enough, beings that are questionable, attempting to influence those native here, whether it is along one string or another.

These kinds of planets in fact have a code name, a classification; they are classified as a certain kind of planet, and it is thus usually the case that most entities who incarnate here are here to experience some level of growth, whether it is minimal or maximal, it doesn't so much matter.

But indeed, our presence, our collective presence, is somewhat calculated, however it is never ever, ever, the desire for we, and it should also never be the desire of anybody else who would claim to be communicating, to rush the evolution of an individual. Each individual has free will and thus this means if they want to sit on the couch with a pack of biscuits, and a cup of tea, and watch as many programs as they can shove into their mind, and eat as many sweet concoctions as they can shove down their oesophagus, so be it because you have free will... Free Will!

Evolution is an applied focus, it is the application of mind.

When mind is applied, evolution occurs, if mind is not applied and one simply enjoys, as we would understand it, your Netflix or your YouTube videos, or this, that and the other, there is not a sense of 'evolution' as much as there is a sense of experience, a sense of, let us say, nourishment of energy, as one body interacts with another - as your technological platforms could be considered a body which is interacting with another kind of body.

And thus you must experience this in its fullness, not with any influence telling you or rushing you to do this or that, and this is somewhat a personal message of we of 'J', for we do feel that with the RA communication, entities felt rushed to be ready or prepared, or in the state of consciousness, such that they could graduate, but rushing a student is the same as asking them to get questions wrong on purpose. Students should not be rushed in their own progression, for their own individual self, for their own free will, students should have the capacity to choose their lessons, to experience their lessons in full, and to have as much down time and, you know, 'laziness', if you wish, as you so wish. J+025 A8

Simply put, this planet is a place where entities tend to come to experience some kind of evolution, as you would understand. So thus it is classified as such and there are many planets like this throughout your systems. Usually, entities find themselves at a cross-junction where they feel that they wish to become a greater reflection of themselves. J+025 A9

Yes, there are better schools for development, and it is usually more desirable to find them because they are more harmonious, they tend to be more fruitful, for they do not have the polarity found here. There's so much polarity here dearest one, for you to consider perhaps in thought. There are such strong viewpoints, such strong systems that would be run by entities who would look to be greedy, as such. We do not tend to have such strong polarities on other planets, and so the evolution again is more harmonious and we of 'J' have tended to feel that sometimes upon this planet the catalyst is too extreme.

We of 'J' have wondered many times; should there be change here?

Should there be a 'law' for this planet, a way which one would say, 'Well, if this is going to be a 'positive polarity planet' as RA said, let us then restrict the incarnations of the more un-positive entities.' As we are now being conscientious with our words.

Hence our statements that there are indeed better places to evolve, and we must say those who come here are rather brave. Yes, ye are brave to enter into this planet, the evolution is extremely pressurised, like a hydraulic press in those entertaining videos that some children watch, it is like putting this upon you so you've got a weight on your shoulders all the time. Well, there is literally such a heavy weight when it comes to entering into this planetary climate.

Yes, there are better planets and dearest ones, when you leave this planet, you ought to use your free will to determine where you should go. Should you come back here?

Do you have the steel of the b-word?

Perhaps you can infer what we are saying, perhaps we'll say, 'the b***s of steel' to enter this planet again.

This would be the choice of a being, and it would also be to the being's thought process to ask, would it even benefit them to come to such an extreme planet for such extreme evolutionary measures?

Is that really beneficial, we wonder?

These are the kinds of things that humans must think about we of 'J' suggest, for you have free will, it is important to consider your well-being not only in the carnation, but out of the incarnation. J+025 A22

What Might Have Been

The current evolutionary state of humans is not meant to be what it is now, humans if the organic evolution would have continued, would still be in a more primitive state, would have increased mental abilities at a minimal level but would have great spirituality and great harmony, there would be a great lacking in large buildings, there would be only the building of small buildings that could be managed with physical muscle but there would be a sense of peace in the valleys so to speak.

Civilisation would be nature orientated, humans would be slightly telepathic, there would be the use of grunts but most communication would be on the telepathic level. There would be overall increase in health and wellbeing, the population would be lower. We are giving comparisons that it may be understood the sharp differences in how evolution has occurred. Q007 A13

There would be traits pertaining to getting along with one another even if one another are in different spaces and different climates, in different loci's so to speak and even if one was of different colours of skin, different races and different cultures.

There would be an overall degree of harmony building where humans would learn kindness over violence, even if violence was minimal in nature.

There would be an understanding of how, what you would call conflict or conflicting idea biases would be resolved, how knots could be untied and people, entities, souls, could get along with each other, not only on the planet but in the Astral.

There would have been this deep, deep, development of harmony, of harmony relationship building, of what you would call a complete lack of racial bias, a complete lack of domineering, of condescending behaviour.

The removal of this condescending behaviour which could be called arrogance would have been the greatest karmic experience at the time, this karma is now being experienced several times more intensely due to the increased mental acuity which is causing individual biases to hold with much greater strength.

One might imagine that if you have a sharp tool you can cut something and the sharpness of the cut can be maintained for longer, causing what you might call a conflict to last longer for there is a greater need for sifting through more complicated biases whereas before the biases where soft, malleable, thus biases were resolved very quickly, but with increased mental acuity biases become a long arduous process to resolve due to the insane, we mean it in the more direct way of an insane person, the insane complexity of an individual's idea complexes. Q007 A15

The human should not focus on utilising their natural capabilities that had been given to them artificially through accelerating evolution, instead the human species should fully focus on the evolution of treating others with kindness and as said by the Q'uo entities, resolving conflict without resorting to the utilisation of manipulation, and tools, and verbal secrecy. Q007 A12

The only prehistory that is of particular relevance would be the Extra-Terrestrial influence that humans had at a continuous basis during their experience. S065 A7

Gods Amongst Men... and Women

In the earlier times, humans had much of a father and motherly relationship with the super-beings that were eternally guiding them in a very intimate way, that they, these entities would incarnate into fleshy bodies from light bodies, these fleshy bodies would be compared to a Ferrari where the normal human body would be compared to a go-kart.

These entities thus incarnated into super bodies and would come to Earth in these bodies from, as you would call them, spaceships to aid humans very intimately. This soon came to a halt as humans started to develop the ability to think freely, for with free thinking as an ability that thought would become a dimension itself for humans to play with, thus there came many alterations and changes and perhaps humans became a little too frivolous in their actions, and so Extra-Terrestrials took a step back, thus these super-beings work closely with certain humans but tend to keep an eye out on the human race from afar. S065 A7

These entities, these Gods, these Extra-Terrestrials for indeed they have a right to be called Gods due to their extensive abilities, chose to go very far away from your species, we say comedically, due to a group consensus that this specie ought to be quarantined for the specie is somewhat of a failure dare we say, and the Extra-Terrestrials at this current time are looking for methods to rehabilitate entities upon this plane in the manner to which they would wish to do the same, so you have a system, a reincarnation school, a psychological reformation school to go through to level you up as such, to make you more akin to what a specie with frontal lobes ought to behave as the frontal lobes made you somewhat ill, incapable of compassion or the ability to interact with the surrounding interplanetary consciousnesses correctly without causing a mess.

And so it is that this school is somewhat the result of, you might say, the naïve mistakes of the Gods introducing the frontal lobe too early to speed a project of theirs up. However, we of Source ought not comment on Gods and their activities for they in their own right have control over their specie as the human is, and they get to decide how things are governed.

We will elucidate on the fact that the moving away was something that became more and more clear as Extra-Terrestrials, when they were interacting with humans more readily in the earlier stages of 'Adam and Eve', found that the free will of humans with frontal lobes caused them to choose against the Gods wishes which was obedience to the garden and its rules, and so if humans so desired free will – let them have it and see what a mess they make of themselves, and then they will call for God again idealistically and see they cannot live without their creators, and that their creators in secret operate a school system to teach the consciousnesses of this plane, how to correctly grow through suffering and such things.

We ought to then state that the entity 'J', as this is a group we say 'J' as if the word is plural or to refer to a group, these entities are a sect of beings, we had once known them, understood them, and still would call them politely as apostles, or we're going to call them kind natured entities who believe this schooling system that is currently imposed on Earthlings is not the correct manner or method to rehabilitate the corruption that is occurring here. These entities would seek to alter the manner to which this school is occurring. Q011 A13

Here is now a perspective from the J+ on another prehistory occurrence:

Humanity is so strange, for this particular crop acts in ways that would not be so familiar with the other crops and plants that are planted throughout the universe. Humanity seems to hold on so dearly to limitation that they would even argue limitation to each other. This act and process of trying to limit one greater than thee is already limited is alien to us, for it is as if you are putting bricks on each other's heads and such a thing is backwards to the natural order and process that God has given to this universe for limitation is not the name of the game, yet humans are particularly good at it and indeed such a sickness is difficult to articulate and explain for it requires a long time to get the message across, a book or several of them, different saviours, Jesus and Moses and these, and various other forms to incarnate and bring such the message that limitation be the greatest enemy.

But humans seem to be very good at ignoring the advice that has been supplied in the many different incarnations and methods that we have deployed, and indeed it is confusing for to us it is simple, but perhaps to a human what is simple to us is complicated to them, and here is where we underestimated or perhaps overestimated this specie, and here now we are attempting to fix this issue and it is taking time yes, patience and plenty of it. J+004 A15

But what was the cause that the human would be cruel to the beings who created this for them, this garden, that they would even destroy their own planet?

How strange is it so that this would occur, what did the human observe on that fateful day that caused the illness to plague their minds?

The story of history is indeed a pitiful thing, history starts to become very irrelevant when people such as us begin to wonder exactly how we can create a solution to the problem. We forget about history very quickly and store it within our subconscious minds, for our only concern is how can we build a cure for this sickness of limitation, and we say this in anticipation of those curious questions of what did happen in times before?

Saviours of all different shapes and sizes come from the same place, to be givers of knowledge, of understanding, of the simple truth that the mind, consciousness itself, should not revolve around limitation but should revolve around growth instead. J+004 A16

One day brother Jerry, there was witnessed a moment where the Gardeners would bicker about matters, debate things, be angered and frustrated in the debating of the same, but such anger was formed of love, the excited love, love that is bubbling like hot water looking to get to a degree of understanding and so as such was misinterpreted by the human, the human saw that love had the ability to bicker and misinterpreted the same as love being something that is incomplete, or non-perfect, something that had flaws yet the human did not see that there were no flaws in our bickering for our bickering was balanced and perfect, it had an end goal and opinions were open to change, and it was excitement and happiness that came at the end of a debate, and not anything else but the same, but as such was misinterpreted by an inferior mind that did not have a point of reference and so the spreading of the virus begun.

That thee could bicker, moan and complain, and then descend from holiness, that one could be right and the other could be wrong, but such an idea is foolish for at the end of our bickering is mutual understanding where both perspectives are reviewed, and analysed, and objectively understood, and then there is a togetherness at the end, always.

But the human did not see this, they ran off too quickly to explain to their fellow brother of their discovery, that such a memory cannot sit idle in the mind without being practiced, it had to be used, the incomplete memory of how to debate. Humans cannot debate at all, and so wars came again and again, due to the one simple fact that a human cannot debate, and more wars, and more wars, disconnection and separation, dumbing down and limitation, until we ended up where we are today looking to teach humans how to hold proper discussions through the use of mental health that it would be understood exactly what the right mindset is to approach the differing of opinions, and differing of opinions is something so common among this land, but so uncommon in the heavenly fields. That is whilst our opinions in the heavenly fields may differ, there be a debate then there always will be mutual understanding after, such is inevitable that love would always prevail in the end.

But the human didn't see it and became so amazed that what they would class as Gods could debate, that they ran off with such knowledge and gossiped and gossiped, and it was the beginning of something horrible indeed. J+004 A17

Yes, you could scratch your head with this brother for a long time, you could even write a book about it and humans would read it ever so eagerly and make incredible amounts of connections to world history events and yes, the cause would then be made realised to the world, and we don't speak of this so comedically as it would be healthy for the planet to know.

But such is the truth, that the human observed an incomplete debate that had yet to finish and ran off - so did the human, ran off indeed. J+004 A20

Help From the Heavens

There is some complexity to the answer for they *(benevolent Extra-Terrestrials)* are doing a countless amount of things, the main thing they are doing is sending what you would understand as spiritual currents to those who would be receptive to those spiritual currents. These spiritual currents seek no specific individual, they are simply spiritual currents of an undifferentiated nature, pure light if you could understand it, this pure light is such that if an entity utilising their free will and free choice chooses to practice meditation, chooses to practice the gathering of spiritual energy, they will find it considerably easier than it would otherwise be if you had no help at all, for if an entity did try to practice spiritual growth, in your current climate with the thought-forms and the energetic distortions surrounding your planetary sphere, unless the entities lived in vibrant regions it would be very, very difficult to access any degree of spiritual development and spiritual growth.

Thus, it must be understood that the help of Extra-Terrestrials is as simple as they can make it so, that sending of light to entities who are willing to do what should have been done, the reconnection experience as you would see it.

The Extra-Terrestrials you speak of, your brothers upstairs, are helping in many other ways as well, too many to count, too many to put in a reading as you would understand it. Their most modal help is that of the sending of light. S077 A4

The human of today is but a dull ember in their mental body, the mental body is activated akin to a candle that can barely allow for the reading of your book when the lights have gone out due to electrical failure. This specie is failing and, once again Extra-Terrestrials are, in their own way for there is no real innocence here please be aware, attempting to 'aid'. We say aid with quotation marks for we now have a little bit of leeway to speak on these matters, these Extra-Terrestrials aid, in their own way, humans in growing.

Then you would consider that the awakening of these inner bodies, when made realistic, begin to make more sense as to why it is so difficult and why so much effort must be put in, and why these matters are not playful in any way and are not like a silly game whereby the character of the game is magically bestowed power just because, as you would understand.

There is a very delicate and involved process which would require an entity dedicate 50% of their life at least to this effort, whereas most humans upon this plane dedicate less than 10% of their life to this purpose and in many cases for the great majority of this planet, less than 5%. Thus, it is no wonder that humans continue to degrade for they never invest into their evolution and only a very small amount of humans know how to invest into the same properly, because the humans are actually connected to beings who understand how it works, so perhaps there are the lucky few upon this plane who have these connections, this connection to actual useful information. Otherwise entities would simply have to trust the teachers to which tell the same broken record statement, **'meditate, meditate, meditate, meditate,'** as this broken record plays over and over and over again, and as humans remain totally ignorant to the same.

Let us give you an exciting idea, let us say that a human spent 50% of their life engaging in spiritual practices, an array of things will happen but the main thing that will happen is at a certain portion of the life, for there is a quantifiable or measurable process that is happening here, that being will awaken to its extrasensory and extra-abilities and will make contact with some of the Extra-Terrestrials who govern your plane, and this entity will be having the choice to work closely with these Extra-Terrestrials in what they are attempting to accomplish operating at a higher level, or these entities may choose another route, a route of some kind of freedom, if you would want to call it that.

There is a great potential here to ascend this plane altogether and learn from the Gods themselves, as you would understand, what is exactly happening upon this plane, or perhaps a human would only seek to spend 50% of their life in these meditative states for selfish reasons, reasons that are entirely for the self's pleasure. This could even be on the positive spectrum such as, may we say with absolute comedy, playing with the female body in a way that would be magical making the entity a special being to other entities who would seek to learn the same, or perhaps becoming a healer upon this plane who has the magical ability to effect the physiology of others, perhaps the entity would supply amazing dazzling information of the Astral abilities, the Astral journeys. Whatever it is the entity would do on its own self-interests is up to the same, we use the word selfish not in any way as an insult but instead as the demonstration of free will, for free will inherently is 'self' and then with the added 'ish' or 'more' if you would prefer. Whatever it is that an entity would seek to do upon its journ is up to the same, but always will the answer be the same thing, **'meditate, meditate, meditate,'** and here is any level of freedom available to the self as these abilities awaken. Q011 A14

You would find during this extensive and tedious process, that the frontal lobe builds in energy or Chi and you will feel a steady vibration in this area as your Chi energy builds until there is so much Chi flowing, not only through the frontal lobe but throughout the whole entire body, that you would have those abilities to which you perceive those entities John Chang, and we perceive on the YouTube website there are so many other entities worthy of mention, of course the notable entity Jesus, we perceive there are some other entities upon your plane who have these abilities through extensive meditative practice, but yes so simply is it so as we have taught in our own way that meditation would seek to create this cojoining, the frontal lobe will be joined by meditation causing releasing of electrical potential.

The frontal lobe takes up too much electrical potential in its incoherence causing the reasoning skeleton to influence the bodies hormonal activities. Entities become absorbed in fear, absorbed in their emotions without the ability to control the same, and so many other things as the frontal lobe has essentially taken over. Thus how ironic, an entity in order to heal the limbic portions of their brain must first amend the frontal lobe which is founded in the meditative practice, thus it is all about releasing energy, bringing the frontal lobe into connection with the subconscious and then obtaining the level of enlightenment. Q011 A12

The importance of this prehistory information is to understand our Genesis from a new perspective, providing a better understanding of energy and its motion. It is also to question the idea of evolution itself, for what is more important, the evolution of the human body, or the evolution of the intelligent mind that controls the human body?

To recap, when this Earth became capable of housing chemical life, to quote a famous hymn, it was seeded with 'All creatures great and small.'

A seemingly political decision was later made to speed up the evolution of the humanoid and the frontal lobe was added to our genome, hence our evolution skipped transitional forms; the words 'missing link' spring to mind although there appear to have been enhancements even prior to this.

This accelerated upgrade created a schism in our ability to focus our electrical potential, it became wrapped up in frontal cortex thought, we became thinkers, we gained reason, 'The knowledge of good and evil' you might say, but we were not evolved enough to fuse this ability with our instinctual experience creating a divide between our conscious and the power of our subconscious.

Here we lost access to many instinctual abilities but on a semi-positive note, to paraphrase the bible once again in analogy, Adam was now able to name the animals. We gained the ability to reason, we truly became intelligent, but conversely in losing our intuitive connection with our subconscious, which to be fair is the much greater portion of our intelligence, we also became dumb.

Prior to this upgrade, the electrical constituents of our vehicles were instinctively under our control, we could motion our energy in remarkable ways, however this was all done without reason, without intellectual thought, it was natural, instinctive, emotionally driven rather than mentally, so these energetic and seemingly magical abilities connected to the moving of Chi were only used as and when nature or the environment dictated it so. In rebuilding the bridge between our conscious and subconscious, in repairing this schism, one in which we acquired free thinking but lost our harmony and connection with the greater forces, in reconnecting this divide we have the opportunity to complete the work so to speak, to become that which we were created to become and maybe even exit that which I politely now consider as the quarantine of reincarnation.

Perhaps some physical evidence of Extra-Terrestrial upgrades on humanity can be found by questioning how chromosome 2, the second largest human chromosome representing almost 8% of the total DNA in cells, came into existence. These two chromosomes remain separate in other primates yet are fused in humans. Studies on the DNA of Denisovans and Neanderthals show this rearrangement of chromosomes was present even way back then, therefore this upgrade occurred prior to the frontal cortex, the thinking and reasoning one.

When examined, more or less in the centre of our chromosome 2 there were telomeric DNA sequences which normally are only present at the ends of chromosomes. Normally telomeres form a dynamic buffer that stops the loss of any sequencing and prevents fusing, here however there is a literal end to end fusion of these two different chromosomes, hence the reason we have 23 rather than 24 pairs like other primates such as apes. Of further interest is the observation that the DNA has been rearranged, it is not a straight fusion of telomeres, aspects have been removed which may have resulted in positive effects, indicating purposely and intelligently designed code changes. All in all, this fusion does not point to being merely a natural evolutionary process.

Atomically, the human experiences far more advanced electrochemistry than his or her counterpart animals, thus-forth, atomically, ye are more equipped and you would be correct in an aspect of this being quite deeply related to the structure of your genome. We speak of atoms here, to build a complex creature requires that you have enough 'code,' or that the patterns of code available are vast. A fusion of *certain* chromosomes can only result in more complicated versions of what two separated chromosomes couldn't achieve apart, now unified, becoming possible together.

We perceive that, let us call them, Gardener Scientists, looked at your human species as it was at the time, saw that it could be easily tampered with for increased atomic vividness, highlighted an area of the genome which could be improved - and then found that fusing certain operators of the DNA together would allow for a holographic imprint of a far greater central biological processing unit to be created, here we refer to the Central Nervous System, as you know it, the Brain.

It is not so simply that more DNA or longer strands of DNA equate to a more complicated organism. Instead, it is to consider that there is an electricity to life, and this electricity requires an interface that the electrical constituent, may be thus converted to a chemical constituent at varying complexities. There were great limitations on what the 'electricity' could achieve when the chromosomes were not fused, by fusing the chromosomes, the sentient electricity had the capacity to form a far more complicated organism with less 'extra work,' involved.

Consider most importantly of all dearest one, regardless of the structure of the DNA, regardless if an entity be a tree, a mouse, a cat, dog or a human - if the electrical constituent of life, being in major the Kundalini, is under the control of the creature, said creature has essentially transcended the atomic realm completely and is thus not limited to the vividness of atomic experience.

Many a case, an advancing human is in-fact attempting to make the brain/body more efficient by having it work less and yet, in the having of less work become more coherent. High quality, low effort as could be termed. This is not only visible in the fusion of the chromosomes, but also visible in the potential that humans have when they begin to understand these subtleties. 'J+ *The fusion of chromosome 2* - Reddit'

With that prehistory rabbit hole well and truly opened, along with the limitless number of additional questions it likely sparks within the mind, it is my expressed wish that this information resonates with you as a positive, informative and mind-expanding experience, rather than one that creates any form of schism or existential crisis within the self.

It is a subject that when digested correctly, helps us to contemplate the remarkable potential we can unlock in this upgradable vehicle as we tap further into its subtleties, learning to apply our minds in ways that give us greater control over our electric potential, creating growth, development and some much-needed joy on this journey of soul evolution, as we develop and further hone skills that we can take beyond this physical plane.

Evolution of the body is one thing, and yes Darwin got us very focused on this physical adaptation of species through natural selection, stressful impetus and such, where heritable traits of the survivors get passed onto the next generation through reproduction, but is this adaptation of the human body really of any relative importance?

These adapted atoms always end up getting reabsorbed by the Earth and turned into fertiliser regardless of how naturally selected they have become!

'J' suggests that there is a major difference between adaptation and evolution; real evolution occurs to our mind, our soul, our intelligence, our will. To my partial knowledge, it is this greater aspect of self which grows beyond the limited realms of physicality, it is this that we take with us, and it is this we are here to evolve.

Free will is ours, we can laze around watching season after season of whatever the new hit is, eating snacks, playing games and scratching itches without being judged by anyone but ourselves, conversely, we can dedicate some time, practice and effort toward a spiritual discipline such as meditation. It is our choice, we are eternal creative beings which means we can spend as long here in this system or other similar 3-dimensional schools of experience, as we like.

Personally however, I will be 100% honest when I state that I am trying graduate and get out of here, asap! If there are better, more desirable schools for development that operate on harmony, rather than polarity and suffering, sign me up yesterday!

And with that said, it's time now to step further into energy by taking a deeper look into the metaphysics of light.

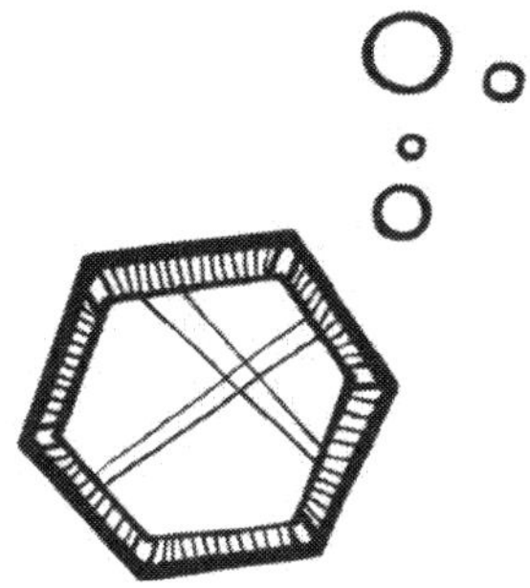

Let There Be Light

'Atoms have Chakras.'

What is a photon?

As we would understand it the photon is a unit of infinity, a cell of infinity. The photon is that birth giver of creation, the photon if you took a unit of it would be but a cell of infinity itself.

When you potentiate, or cannon, or canonise infinity, you get unimaginable motion, motion that if quantified in a speed would leave you writing zeros for the rest of your life. This is the photon, if you could hold the photon you wouldn't feel any motion, no, no. You would feel infinity is in your palm ready to do something, to be made into something, so you ask where photons come into creation?

Well they are creation dearest one, they are the essence of creation, they are that thing that you separate into a positive and negative charge to give birth to polarity, that polarity seeks each other, or rather, seeks itself to create the event of motion. J+021 A5

When infinity expressed itself as random outpourings of energy, those outpourings were photons, a soup or fluid of photons, of these particles, not really a particle at all, a fluid, a soup of infinity that is as could only be explained, the Christ, which is not exactly infinity itself but is infinity and yet can be now created into something that is called motion. Better explained let us say motion is third on the hierarchy, second on the hierarchy is the photon, and first on the hierarchy is infinity.

The photon stands in-between infinity and motion as that which you would call the Chakra, that which can only go to the Father but through the same you see. In truth the photon is the Chakra. The photon is something so close to infinity yet so far away, and so close to motion yet so far away, it is that unit, that soup, that all-being presence, that ether, that is not yet motion, yet is not yet infinity, but is yet both paradoxically at the same time. Thus, we find ourselves on the floor in laughter at this strange thing. J+021 A6

The Photon, The Christos and The Chakras

In providing further insight into the notion given here that infinities outpourings of energy were a fluid of photons, a soup of infinity that could best be explained as the Christ; the Christ appears to refer to a perfected state of consciousness, rather than the being we know as Jesus the Christ who achieved this perfected state of consciousness. There is a connection touched on here between three things: our energy centres or Chakras, the Photon, and the

Christos. To expand on this connection, we would firstly like to bring your attention to some quotes mentioned earlier in the book:

The energy centres themselves do have a physical existence, they are tangible at a certain density that extends far beyond your reach and our reach, for the energy centres exist in a timeless dimension [...] In this timeless dimension the energy centres are 'this' close to consciousness, in that the only way to the Father is but through me.

You may term the energy centres as the Christos, although the term Christos has become a little confused, here you are learning now metaphysics.

Please see your energy centres as the Son of God and your consciousness as God, which alters the energy centres. The only way to the Father, is but through consciousness improving in quality and changing the energy centres in their ability to absorb infinity itself. J+020 A11

And

Polarity cannot exist in Chakras thus they are timeless, they are always existing, always have existed and always have been one with the Creator. S082 A13

And

God had a son; his son was the closest representation of himself. His son was this multidimensional universe you know so well. His son was also the soul that drove this universe, his son was called **love** and love expresses itself. S010 A6

Secondly, we hope that this excerpt provides the connection necessary to better understand this commonality between the Chakras, the Christos and the Photon.

We will begin with the illusive photon and describe it in such a way that its true nature is where it was non-existent and when it came into existence, in-between the two you find the Chakra.

Then the Christos would be the state of consciousness by which one has perfect access to that which sits in between the photon existing and the photon not existing.

And then finally as to the Chakras, these would mediate the connection between the photon existing and not existing. Christ consciousness is a state of consciousness in which, between the photon's existence and non-existence, there is a perfectly translucent glass, if you could use such a term.

One might use the example that there is a glass on floor one, the glass is what one uses as a foundation to walk upon, on floor zero the glass is a ceiling. The Chakras are the glass, Christ consciousness is when the glass is perfectly clear, the photon is the floor zero as you would understand, the thing that comes into existence as an illusion. The photon may also be described as something that was in potential in floor one, before it could ever come into existence on floor zero. S083 A13

This glass as we are describing it, configurates the light between infinity and the finite realms called photons. As infinity passes through the glass, your Chakras, if the glass is diminished, broken, shattered, dirty, when it becomes a photon, when infinity becomes a photon, it will look grotesque and untrue to its true nature. Christ consciousness is when infinity passes through the glass with no interruption, no disfigurement, or perversion, or distortion.

It is only natural that the glass, or Chakras as you prefer, are timeless artifacts, timeless beings, for the glass itself, the Chakras as you would understand, they are your mind, hence why they are described as the son of God. S083 A14

As to refresh, floor one is infinity itself. There is glass to separate the infinity from becoming a photon. If the glass is perfectly clear the glass is Christ conscious thus the photons that are made are perfect in the below realms, in floor zero and its negative counterparts.

What is being described here between photon, Christ consciousness and Chakras being the glass itself, are the components that create life, and yes we mean life! The components that quite literally create your reality. S083 A13

Atoms have Chakras, it is so for infinity passes through a sculptor, the Chakras themselves, a son of God, and the infinity is then configured into an atom. The Chakras are what is even allowing the atom to form, Chakras are what is giving the atom its shape, its style, its nature, its tinge, its essence, its, if we are going to be scientific, its angular momentum. The Chakra, that glass, the mind itself, consciousness you see, configurates infinity into photons. The atom you see is the end product called the photon in a spherical field or a force field.

What we see is, we see a mind, an essence, an intelligence that is attempting to configure and create an atom out of infinity itself, to create an angular momentum out of infinity which sits mysterious, we could say still but this would be inaccurate for infinity is simply mysterious, one cannot say how it sits but one thing is for sure, consciousness can draw from the same and can configure it in a set of angles. The configuration itself, that glass, that mind, that consciousness, is here the Chakra or the Chakras that are active. If more Chakras are active this must mean that infinity is becoming an atom in a more purer nature without significant distortion, and if infinity is going to become an atom without any distortion then would you not have God right in front of you?

If there were one atom on your plane that was so pure that it was infinity itself due to its Chakras, as we are using this term, the glass being so clear, so crystalline, so translucent, then this single atom would have such a dramatic impact on your planet that it would cause the intensity of light upon this plane, the abilities of the human to be exaggerated to a rather significant degree creating a super human as such, simply due to one atom. You'd see strange growths where this atom was located. Extremely exaggeratedly large trees and fauna, life would seem magical perhaps, the atmosphere where this one single atom resides would be so endowed with life force that entities would not even really need to eat within this realm, this pocket realm.

So it is so that all things, atoms included, are Chakras in nature, for the Chakra is the way that the mind is configurating infinity, manipulating infinity and the 'J' entities call this meditation.

Meditation is a reference to how, if we are to use these terms, an entity of 3rd density, a self-aware entity is currently configurating, managing or churning infinity. Chakra in Sanskrit would refer to the idea of a spinning wheel, there is a symbolic connection here. S063 A15

The symbolic connection implied here bears some thinking about. When we think of an atom, we think of that general picture we've all seen on some level during our education, with a nucleus in the middle while electrons circle it like little planets in orbit. There is a churning here, a spinning.

There are subtler levels to this, but it is to understand that your entire body is made up of this churning and spinning motion, these atoms.

Meditation affects the way this churning occurs, and Chakras are just the natural geometric points in the body where the energy of this churning collects in dense amounts, creating these spinning wheels of spiralling energy.

In general the human body physically may be seen as spiralling energy, in that the energy spirals in 3-dimensional space. These have seen pictures of atoms, there's a middle ball, there are outer balls, and the outer balls circle the middle balls, as does your planet; the outer balls circle the middle ball of your Sun.

These things are spiralling, no?

Then to look deeper into the human body, *it is* to recognise fundamentally that it is not all entirely, as is understood, physical. There are more bodies, more to the nature of the body. Then there will be discovered more spirals, spirals that are even deeper, full of a kind of life force that is more denser and fuller, that has more texture to it as could be described.

These more infinite-al, powerful spiralling's, are found boosted during meditation in general, and can become so intense in certain circumstances that it would allow for spiritual experience. Thus, the Chakra or the Chakras are the convergence points of these spirals, how they weave in and out of certain geometric points of the body, but it would be to understand, that this understanding of Chakra is more understanding the result of the mind, rather than to understand the mind itself as the giver or creator of Chakra, or spinning light perhaps may be another way to describe the same.

To look upon your body and see that the body is made of spinning light, it should be clear that the Chakra is not so obviously 7 circles that line the body, instead the Chakras are spiralling light, especially in dense amounts, specialised at certain geometric nodes in the body that are natural, as is your

Sun and distant planets found at specific geometric portions of this particular Solar System.

Everything has its place, this includes the Chakras, and spiralling energy is but a way that nature found the most efficient manner of behaviour. S095 A16

Let us imagine you had a camera which could see Chi, you would see that Chi is collected in the major organs of the body, the sexual organs, the intestines in the stomach, things like the kidneys and all of the other vital organs such as the heart, there's lots of Chi even in the voice box, Chi in the brain, the spine, all of these are your physical centres and there are some major ones of course, especially the spine, the brain, the intestine, the stomach, the heart and the sexual organs, these are some of the more major ones.

Then there are the minor ones, such as the kidney, such as the liver, the liver could be a more profound centre of energy if one learnt how to use the Chi force to manipulate this area. S090 A6

Indeed dearest one, we'll keep it very simple and say that Chakras are very much like the organs of a soul, you have a physical body which has its organs, you have a spiritual body which has its organs. Chakras are very much like your planet, have you observed your planet?

Have you seen all of its layers, its electrical layers?

You have the atmosphere, things such as this as it strives up to the stratosphere, higher and higher reaching the ionosphere, you can consider these to be the energy centres of the planet in physical form, each atmosphere is like an energy centre; the soul is the same you see, accept that the Chakras are usually represented as circles, for it is as though the energy collects like a torus and this is what happens in your planet, your planet has a torus field and energy collects around these torus fields.

Energy centres then are organs of the soul which draw in and give birth to energy itself, the soul when it is out of the body has its energy centres active, these energy centres draw in the atmosphere of the Astral through the South and North poles, feeding the body and bringing it vitality, the vitality swims in and out, in and out.

There is an inner energy in a Chakra, especially the higher Chakras, the higher Chakras are connected to what is called Source, what we at this dimension use. Source is the infinity, it is infinite energy, and at the highest Chakra of the soul infinite energy can spurn from within this Chakra, and yes indeed dearest one the Chakras are very much like a winding DNA, the DNA winds and intersects, winds and intersects. You see them as separated circles but really they are more like interconnected circles, like a helix where it intersects is the gap and where it expands is the Chakra. In such a way your Chakra or Chakras, are very much like interconnected torus fields which form a large torus field, which is all connected to the Source, or Infinity, or you might simply call this Consciousness.

We believe 'J' call this Sentience, those entities that you have a loving relationship with, indeed these entities are good. S090 A5

Photons and Energy

Energy is that thing you get out of a photon when you take it and separate it into its two main components being what you might call charge, as your science prefers to call it, you may call it magnetism if you prefer, that north and south pole, call it feminine and masculine if you so prefer, but what is most certain is that when you take a photon and with your consciousness think on it thus you get motion for the photon becomes potentiated into what you understand as creation itself, motion as you would call it. J+021 A7

There is much to explain here, that 'photon' is a complicated matter. We would find the beginnings being closer to the pure tonality, perhaps we could say the pure tonality of the One Infinite Creator. At this pure tone there comes the event of random outpourings of that energy, of that infinity, to create sub-densities or dimensions if you prefer of that pure tone, that infinity as you would understand. Those random outpourings of energy are within themselves interacting with themselves, but remain in some sense pure and could hardly be called energy as such, for it is still too pure even if it is, in its interaction with itself, slightly destructive.

But with that destructive interaction comes eventually that random outpouring of energy finding itself organising, and eventually you would have recognised that those random outpourings of energy, that pure energy you see, that pure tone that would have been in truth the photon itself, but at that certain interval of the photon in its interaction with itself there eventually comes an event whereby consciousness takes that photon in its pure form, in the ways it has settled, and potentiates it into motion.

Perhaps the most confusing thing about this explanation is that seemingly the photon is still, to which it is but we find this a rather comedic idea. The photon is not so still as you may understand it, indeed it is a still thing, it is a pure tone thing, but it is not so still, it is instead so alive that it looks still. This seemingly to us at least, is a strange idea, it makes us laugh, it makes us laugh because it is a paradox, how could something that is alive be still?

It makes no seeming sense but ironically when you potentiate a photon and take it out of its seeming stillness, you get motion, motion so violent and quick and superluminal, meaning faster than the speed of light, that you could hardly comprehend the speed of the motion that is happening at that instance. Something that was seemingly 'still' created the most violent and absurdly fast motion that could ever exist, derived indeed from a photon. J+021 A5

Light is everywhere. At this point light encompasses everything, even in complete darkness there are photons, as you would call them, of a different kind however. The various intensities of illusion create various intensities of resistance. This resistance is real to the experiencer of the resistance, as much as the illusion is real to the person role-playing in the illusion.

Light in its most natural state is everywhere at all times, it doesn't travel, it is perfectly still and vibrating, however at this level of illusion, this level of resistance, light is much, much, much and many more much's, slower in comparison to how light truly is at its most natural state when it is utterly close to the One Infinite Creator. J+010 A11

The resistance, the nature of this illusion would cause an impediment on God to express itself, himself, thee-self, in the most purest of ways. J+010 A13

This intensity of illusion, this resistance is what creates time. This resistance is what creates the illusion that things apparently happen over a period rather than them happening all at an instantaneous moment. J+010 A14

As we compare our present thought-frame against a previous thought-frame we build up our concept of time. Each individual frame is an individual thought, the thought that then follows constitutes another frame. This is why we can have timeless experiences where we cannot remember our previous thought-frames, sleep or spiritual experiences can often feel like this, even sex - time fly's when you're having fun as they say, and in these situations there is very little resistance occurring. Compare this to the resistance you feel when working in a boring job, and how slowly time moves as you consciously compare one boring thought to the previous boring thought. Time then, appears to simply be the progression of our thoughts per frame.

If the Consciousness is able to remember the thought it just had and is then able to compare it to the thoughts it is having now, it builds an illusionary idea called time.

Interestingly in other discussions with 'J', they have indicated that an increase in thoughts per second causes one to experience time differently, they themselves can think a great many times faster than us and put this down to humans limiting our potential thought-speed by an over reliance on vocal language. We tend to think at the speed of speech rather than the speed of thought. A great example is our reading speeds, we learn at an early age how to read but how many of us ever move past a speed of reading that exceeds our conversational pace of talking? Do you still read at your 12-year-old pace?

I myself have had experiences such as car crashes or fights where I have been attacked and in the sudden moment of the surprise occurrence time has seemingly stood still, well not quite still but slowed down drastically enough for me to calculate many thoughts within a much shorter time frame and avoid disaster. There are however also dimensional aspects to time and light.

What would be understood is that this particular planet, and some other planets, have a very particular program that is operating by which there is a system that governs the energetic interactions of this planet, now you are unable to see the energetic interactions that are happening at what you might call a quantum level, but what is to be understood is that the God-Force itself, is organising itself, in this particular planet to attain a certain state of order of vibration. If you could see what you would call the quantum field of this planet then you would be able to gain an understanding on how incarnation, synchronicity and coincidences work.

What can be understood here is that there is a particular entanglement that is occurring within the molecular structure of this entire auric field that includes, humans, plants, even the four elements, etc. There is a particular entanglement going on at various different dimensions and levels which give rise to the experience of synchronicity itself. J+009

If we could give somewhat of an analysis of this, 3-dimensional light and or 3-dimensional existence, atoms, etc, experience life as though it is travelling. 4-dimensional light and 4-dimensional stuff, experiences life as though it is aware of exactly where it's going to end up.

The difference between the 3rd dimension and the 4th for the experience of a conscious entity, is in the 3rd dimension they are travelling in the wilderness, in the 4th dimension they are travelling to a known place. To the 3rd dimensional entity, it is not that they are really in the wilderness, they are just like the 4-dimensional entity; they are just blind, blind to a light they cannot see. That does not mean the light itself is not working on the 3-dimensional entity, it's just that the 3-dimensional entity is blind, blind to the destination that has already been predetermined for them.

If the destination is known and the entity at their point is known, then these two aspects of consciousness entangle with each other to create quantum entanglement. If however, there is no entanglement between two known places and everything seems to be happening randomly as the 3rd dimensional entities of your scientists tend to side with, then of course the nature of this universe almost becomes chance like.

If things are entangled, then it must be recognised that there is an intelligent communication happening beyond the visible light spectrum and the other spectrums of this particular octave that would serve as resistance brother. J+010 A15

The only resistance that could ever exist really is the resistance that the One Infinite Creator entity gives itself, here we would refer to you, to Jordan and to all 7 billion people on this planet. The resistance is - the limiting beliefs you give yourself will stop you from ascending. J+010 A16

If you could find a way to remove the limiting ideas and beliefs then you would be able to find ways to travel instantaneously from one place to another, and you would also be able to build technology that could do this on its own, yet remaining right in your living room so you could have a little light show as you would watch the occurrences happening in other places in the universe, and it would be thoroughly entertaining to see what is happening at the edges of things where potential is being made, would it not be?

Indeed then, you could do many things if limiting beliefs were subsided and replaced with infinity itself. If infinity was the core program for a soul that soul would be able to do things, invent things, experience life in the most wondrous of ways, so why not say a mantra to yourself every night hmm?

Why not say to yourself, and remind yourself, Infinity I am, say this three times a night.

Remind yourself:

Infinity I Am!
Infinity I Am!
Infinity I Truly Am!

Say this to yourself and watch how you begin to move through life knowing you are infinite. If you are truly infinite nothing could get you down because you would find ways, new ways to deal with things, and as this mantra starts to sink into your subconscious mind over a period of 40 days and 40 nights you may find you begin to have access to things that you otherwise didn't have access to before, and it might serve your life quite wonderfully as you continue to say this mantra for perhaps a long, long time, you will begin to remember what it feels like to be a little child born into this world without any dogma, what it feels like to truly be the original thought itself. J+010 A17

I Am Infinity

'The Sun is a conscious entity of seamless multidimensions, and it is fully capable of giving birth to planets as is any form, any animal, capable of giving birth too.'

The Beginning of Energy

In brief: It starts with God, you will have to forgive our attempt to describe the indescribable, however we will describe this force as Intelligent Infinity and that it was conscious, however it became conscious – another one of the grand mysteries - it was conscious, and this consciousness concentrated into various forms of awareness. Through awareness there is motion, for instance if I make myself aware of my left toe, and then make myself aware of my right ear, there is awareness of both and in shifting that conscious awareness between toe and ear, there is motion created. Motion creates energy, and energy is the resonance of that intelligence from awareness. The side-effect of the resonance of intelligence is intelligent life itself.

Note: If you thought aspects of the previous chapter on Photons were difficult to assimilate, or any other chapters for that matter, try not to be overly concerned as I also struggle, hence all the questions I continue to constantly ask Source and 'J'. I have also been advised on many occasions that it is good for a soul to become curious about the nature of life, to the nature of this realm, to the nature of God, to the nature of consciousness and how it creates all things. Curious natures are the example of going uphill, of climbing higher and striving toward growth. Therefore, we ask you to ever remain curious and always ask questions, for those questions give you power.

In non-brief:

Consciousness is the primary operator which plucks the strings of spirit and creates the vibrations which swirl into atoms and produce your universe. J+023 A12

In the beginning as such, when awareness came to be from infinities infiniteness, there was organic interaction, energy interacting with itself. This organic interaction of energy created the condition of resistance.

Let us expand further:

We firstly have infinity expressing itself in random outpourings of energy, these outpourings of energy have no real intention behind them so thus they are random, and they have random interactions with each other which typically create greater resistance because the interaction itself is not guided interaction, it is random interaction which allows for destructive interaction.

You may take some energy here, take some energy there, and smash it against each other, and it would create some kind of energy following the smash that would have a different kind of property as you would understand this. These continued collisions build more resistance but also at the same time form different existences, these existences collect and self-organise in the way they interact with each other to begin to create eventually your physical density, which was built from extreme resistance in the interaction of energy colliding and interacting with itself.

This destructive interaction of infinite energy interacting with itself begins to create various densities of life, the densities of light closer to infinity are the higher densities, the densities further away from infinity are lower densities. Lower densities are more incoherent in the sense to which the density interacts with itself in a destructive manner that yields less energy but accidentally gives birth to order, which seems paradoxical for destructive energy surely would birth destruction, but if destructive energy as we have defined it - energy that interacts with itself in an incoherent manner - if destructive energy finds on accident a more gentle configuration based off self-collision, then you begin to get order. J+020 A7

Imagine, if you will, a pot full of consistently swirling water, some herbs and spices get added and all swirl around chaotically in the pot of water randomly bumping into each other, until eventually some form of order is obtained as they settle into their own swirling orbit, rotating within the pot. We now have a little pot of Order out of chaos.

Slowly did this interaction begin to form the first atoms as you would understand them, and then from there consciousness began to alter the way atoms interacted with each other to give birth eventually to the human body.

So then what was once destructive and random, then eventually based on constant collision becomes orderly and coherent. Your dimension is a density in which destructive, or rather as we would prefer random energy, has become coherent enough to form atoms. J+020 A7

Energy is a certain kind of motion in a certain kind of way, motion happening in certain dimensions and then motion happening at a certain strength within those dimensions, creating a certain kind of field which is called a resonance. A field is resonating energy, a resonance is a singing bowl resonating, sending out its emanations of intelligent energy. Thus we defined energy as resonating intelligence for this to us felt like the most accurate and shortest way to describe this phenomenon. J+019 A12

What are the other side-effects of the resonance of intelligence?

Well, we see this word appear which seems to resonate with the soul, the word 'gravity' as it is termed and yet there are various effects of this resonation for the principle of resonation is the experience of how the Sun would broadcast its light unto the planets, Earth, Venus, Mars, Neptune it goes on.

The side-effect of the resonance of intelligence is intelligent life itself, the birth of the ape, the human, the dolphin and the various other creatures that frolic along the land, the side-effect of intelligence, the resonation principle you see are many things but inside all intelligent forms resides infinity itself.

Infinity being the pureness, the mother, if you would prescribe gender, infiniteness in its pureness you see, this is what we all look toward, but the way in which we look toward the birth giver of light and love, love and light, is by looking inside for this is where infinity resides. J+008 A10

In the experience of the incarnation the Solar Winds would serve; imagine then you would have an individual going down a slide to get to the water. Now to program a soul in its arrival into the incarnation of the physical body would require the soul to transmit from one dimension to another, in the experience of transmitting from one dimension to another it would seek to ride down the slide and take on the various influences as it finally reaches the body, upon reaching the body it will draw in a breath to take in the final influence of the geometry of nature, as termed Gaia you see.

As it rides from one dimension to another it seeks to absorb the various intelligences, the photons that contain structure, the Solar Winds as you call them, it will absorb them upon its flight arriving with quite a bang into the body, and then the drawing in of the light of your world, the ionosphere, the geometry of this plane, the electromagnetic sphere. As it draws in the breath it draws in, in fullness, nature! J+008 A12

And this one breath is in actuality carried from the upper dimensions into the lower ones for the breath cannot end, it must continue for all life beats as the heartbeat continues, the heartbeat of God you see. That breathing is carried from the soul being in the upper dimensions, the breath continues all the way until it arrives into the physiology that is the physical body, and the breath continues there forth. J+008 A13

The Ghosts of Dimensions and Other Mysteries

For those that have ever wondered how numerology and astrology such as birth charts manage to accurately identify influences and traits based on time of birth when practiced by an adept, then here are some insights on how the planetary influences are installed into the human vehicle.

It appears that the Solar wind carries the geometry, the structure of the heavens, the planetary positions and astrological influences at the time of arrival, and we also have the final influence of Mother Nature herself. This light, upon the initial inhale of breath is drawn into the body and the initial programming is complete, however light is not just affecting us at the physical level. There are the higher dimensional aspects of light that also take their metaphysical influence on the soul even whilst still in the womb.

We would say firstly the breath while serving as the foundation of the beginning of life is one aspect of the solar winds having its sway on the vehicle. Then there would also be the soul itself which would be incarnating into your densities at a certain time interval when the physical light and the metaphysical light which we will call Prana, we'll call your physical light electromagnetic waves. When the soul finds itself within the vehicle, whether the vehicle is within the womb or whether the vehicle has taken its first breath, already those pranic forces, those pranic solar winds are having its sway on the souls vehicle.

When the entity has taken its first breath those pranic forces have had their sway to a much greater density, as pertaining to the physical solar winds dearest one, the solar winds begin to have its sway on the vehicle when it is in your outdoor environments, and these solar winds are processional, they change with your seasons. What souls who are seeking to understand astrology must make a distinction of, is that there is a difference between pranic solar winds and electromagnetic solar winds. When this is understood it makes more sense that the soul receives a profound configuration based on the pranic solar winds and how they instream into the various nexi on one's electromagnetic web.

There are various entrance points in one's toroidal field or torus field, these entrance points are based on the idea of the flower of life when visualised in 3-dimensions as intersections at various points of the sphere, these intersections are where instreaming light finds its passage, and it is most especially strong at the north and south poles of one's spine.

When these pranic instreaming's of light from the spiritual bodies of your solar system enter into the vehicle it configures the vehicle with planetary biases, this configuration is happening at a more subtle level and becomes obvious in a souls behavioural quirks, and when the soul finds its astrological name and searches it on your cyberspace, it finds itself giggling at the similarities.

But did we not speak of earlier the insulated properties of a soul?

Many souls who are of the greatest levels of adeptness desire to reconfigurate how the prana due to the astrological influences had settled when the soul was born. For this prana swirls within the vehicle relatively unchanged by a soul unless it has the adeptness to make such changes, adepts of your past understood such things and desired to manually reconfigure the pranic swirling so it is of benefit to the soul, and in this way a soul could remove its bellicose, warlike or lethargic tendencies, or other tendencies that made the soul less intelligent, less peaceful, less harmonious.

These adepts of your past are still alive in extreme famine, not in context to starvation but in context to the metaphor that they are very few and far between. These souls seek not to be a part of your humanity and will only arrive in your humanity at the reinstatement of lost land that had been taken over by certain peoples in the past.

Is this a prophecy? Perhaps!

Will it come true? Perhaps!

We will have to see how the probabilities of your world play out for we of 'J' could never make a definitive statement, probabilities are the nature of your planet, are the nature of life, but there is a strong likelihood that the adepts of your past will find themselves surfacing again in the coming times. J+023 A11

The pranic influence of the solar winds being of a higher dimension, let's use the 4th, does not move in a linear format. The physical 3-dimensional aspects of the photons in the solar winds may be moving at the speed of light, but the 4th dimension is not bound by the slowness of our chemical reality. It can arrive at the same time it left for this is a dimension that is unified, we have entered a space of interconnectedness with less limitations, a network.

Consider UFO reports (or UAP - Unidentified Ariel Phenomenon – the less scorn inducing newer term), where vehicles are reported to move in ways that defy the known laws of physics, making sudden 90 or 180 degree turns at speeds of velocity that would crush human occupants based on our understandings of G-Force, these UFO/UAPs achieving hypersonic velocities without signatures, even trans-medium travel between different environments such as space, Earth's atmosphere and the Ocean.

All very difficult to fathom with our understandings of 3-dimensional reality, but what if these UFOs are utilising the 4th *dimension?*

Have you ever shone a torch light or laser at a wall?

Flick your wrist and the observable light will instantly change direction at speeds and angles that are impossible for physical vehicles to match, environment is also no longer an issue. Consider then the possibility that what we hear reported in these manoeuvres is the movement unseen that occurs in the 4th *dimension, we don't see the flick of the wrist for this is in the 4th, we just see an aspect of the result which is the observable light in our* 3rd *dimension.*

3-dimensional objects cast 2-dimensional shadows, we see them every day, we can see the entirety of the 2-d shadow as we are observing from a higher dimension, the 4th *however is higher still, so we are unable to see the unified field of this network, unable to see the causal factors, something is happening, but we only see a limited aspect of this, which makes it an unexplained phenomenal to our 3-d understanding of life.*

Do we not also get similar 3-dimensional phenomena when people report sightings of ghosts?

These are residues of those that have left the atomic realm and moved into the 4th *dimension of the Astral, randomly observable thoughtforms from a life-force that is yet to fully disperse.*

You would understand that the ghost would be that shadow of one's kundalini which is now at this stage seeking to find expression in a higher plane. Put better, the ghost experience happens in at least two fashions; the first fashion you see is that the ghost is an entity that has recently passed in your plane and finds themselves quite attached to your plane, and cognizant enough to recognise that it is still existing as an entity alive in your pranic-ly dead atmospheres, or let us say Chi dead atmospheres. The ghost finds itself as a body composed of, let us call it Ether, or Chi, or something that is not an atom, it finds itself floating around as a non-atomic object you see, this non-atomic object is but a shadow of its true form yet to become what it truly is. Therefore, at one interval when it recognises the light, it in many a sense travels through some kind of wormhole and goes back to the place to which entities describe as travelling through a tunnel when they have their near-death experience.

Arriving at this place they leave the shadow of that non-atomic body which is yet to disperse, similar to how the physical vehicle takes time to disperse, thus one may get a thoughtform in the house which is but the remanent of the soul which has gone through the wormhole to take them home, this thoughtform floats around as a mindless looping cycle which does not think but simply follows loops of intelligent motioning energy which produce the illusion of thinking such that one who is sensitive enough would think that they are hearing a ghost, when in truth they are hearing a shadow of one who used to exist in the planet.

It takes varying amounts of time for entities to go from ghost living, to the true form, the true nature of their being. *The second fashion,* for some they are not only the shadow but are the living ghost itself, a sentient creature in a non-atomic vehicle living out an extra life as it would be called, in this Ether that is so Prana-less or Chi-less as we could only describe an energy that is not atomic; Ether as you could call it but Ether that is not vibrant in energy.

This sentient creature, this sentient being, this sentient thought that is alive and sentient and conscious, finds itself not yet able to separate from human existence and so floats around, only once again, to leave its shadow in its wake as it goes back to the one thought you see. J+021 A9

Indeed, this shadow only exists or comes into existence in the sense of the shadow itself, when the sentient being travels through the wormhole back to and toward the one thought, then the shadow as you have described is left as a 3-dimensional thoughtform roaming about. J+021 A10

The Bermuda Triangle also falls under the spell of the physics from this cross dimensional effect, these appear to be occasions when windows or portals between the 3rd and 4th dimensions have opened.

Could you call it a gate, a portal?

One might call it a gateway, a wormhole, a device, rather an occurrence that is caused by a being of some kind, some nature, moving into a different density then the density to which they were familiar with. In many ways, black holes are portals, holes literally into a new realm, they are complicated things and require some rather scientific language, not necessarily math, but a more profound understanding of how your universe works, this universe as you would understand. S083 A18

As we observe the 'concept' of a black hole, we see something that is simple, quite simple indeed. That there would be the natural phenomena of grids throughout space, these grids are electromagnetic, these grids are not just of the length, width and height, but there is another aspect to the electromagnetic grid that is not particularly visible in this dimension. If you had the ability to pull on this invisible grid you could create that thing you call a black hole. S063 A3

We scan your planet, they happen on the rare occasion, there have been occasions in the loci that would pertain towards the famous name of that which you call the Bermuda triangle, there have been cases of this occurrence on islands, there have been cases of this occurrence within even the sea, cases of this occurrence in deserts; there have been cases of these portals opening, they are rare however.

Typically, they open due to how what you call 'space' experiences itself as an organised, conscious living thing. Think of thus matter, energy and fields, think of this entire consciousness of the 3rd dimension to be quite a literal brain or mind, sometimes this entire mind has a neuron that accesses the 4th dimension and this neuron maybe located on Earth in some place. S063 A6

If there was an inhabitable planet possessed by entities of the vibrational degree that would be 4-dimensions then the planetary consciousness itself would of course be vibrating in harmony, this would cause around and within the planet many, what you call black holes as it is termed, and if the 3-dimensional observer were to observe a planet of 4-dimensions they would see something likened to circles within circles, holes within holes, it would be such like observing a living paradox. This then would be such that the 3-dimensional observer would see that window as you might call it, into a dimension that would be of a different kind housing a different kind of light. S063 A4

In the sense to the light itself, you would understand that this 4th dimensional light is sensitive, much more sensitive to what you call thought, so imagination would be the most appropriate term, for then if you are within this environ, imagination would be the method of interaction within this environ as you enter this kind of light. S063 A8

In the 4th dimension, gravity is able to be controlled to a fascinating degree, gravity thus becomes quite artificial and so black holes do not necessarily have any gravitational force, the gravity itself can be altered, changed, or managed in whatever way the entities would seek to use, thus gravity and black holes are not synonymous with each other directly for gravity is a force like electricity and can be controlled with the right instruments and mind set. S063 A4

In attempting to understand this we would see that the mind be broadened.

The 3rd dimension in its entirety, even in the essence that you would look out to the stars, toward the Galaxies, as you would look out to space itself, that is the ionosphere. Upon the seat which you sit, the air in which you walk, you walk through the ionosphere, you see. J+008 A3

We would see that which you call the ionosphere as the entrance to what you call the 3rd dimension. As you enter into the 3rd dimension you become familiar with a subset or more slower vibratory forms of God's love and light.

The ionosphere is the sphere to which chemical matter can come into existence as complex intelligent life and it is through God's intelligence, that is innate within all species, it becomes possible to organise the ionosphere into chemical creatures. J+008 A1

So, you would have then the simple experience of life as a cell-based organism and you would have God organising all these chemicals, hydrogen, carbon, oxygen into yourself. This is how God interacts with the 3rd dimension, as God's intelligence impregnates the 3rd dimension, God would create intelligent lifeforms within what the 3rd dimension, with its limitations, has to offer. J+008 A2

In your 3-dimensional universe there is a limitation to what can occur. In the 4-dimensional universe there are less limitations, Suns do overtime cool, this is the limitation of the 3rd dimension, Suns as you might call them Suns, for they are quite different in the upper dimensions, do not cool. Here all things in the 3rd dimension are cyclic, they go in cycles, birth and death. Indeed, there can be the natural occurrence of a Sun giving birth, symbolically of course in this context, giving birth to a planet although it would happen more literally that the Sun would spew out something and thus this would coalesce into a planet.

You may take these symbolic concepts shared to you in a more literal way, and you might understand that the cause of these things can be influences from dimensions that can quite literally rewrite the 3rd dimension and/or have control over it. In the concept of cosmology, there is much to discuss, books worth of information to be given. S060 A19

The Sun is a conscious entity of seamless multidimensions, and it is fully capable of giving birth to planets as is any form, any animal, capable of giving birth too. An animal from within the womb is created cell by cell is it not?

Then what would you think if we told you the Sun could do the same, would this be something that would cause disbelief?

And it is so that this happens in that mirror manifestation, the mirror that in the same sense that the Sun can give birth to a planet, it is so indeed a bird can give birth to an egg which can turn into a chick. J+008 A15

For within boundlessness, there is the potential to become anything, it purely depends on how much boundlessness you can handle. This is something that was on the mind of the brother before he begun the channelling.

Think about this dearest brother Jerry, if it is so hard to handle the boundlessness of a woman that it would cause such an incredible amount of stress, imagine attempting to handle the boundlessness of becoming a star! J+008 A16

Evolution

It is to be considered that as far as spiritual evolution goes there are infinite possibilities, they mention the boundlessness of a star here as a soul can grow to a magnitude where the vehicle it drives gets so complex that the vehicle is now a literal Star, or a Solar System, or even a Galaxy! We call the Earth Gaia, because she is a living being, a beautiful planetary soul, one of the Manu, as we use this term beyond scripture to illustrate the galactic minds of the universe, a true highly evolved force.

The joke here was that I struggle to even handle the stress of a relationship with one woman, can you imagine the sheer level of evolution Mother Earth has achieved to tolerate a relationship with 7 billion+ naughty little human plants, baby stars completing lessons and learnings whilst ignorantly destroying their own mother and classroom in the process?

Indeed, for the path of the soul is the path of experience, of growing and growing, for is it not so simple that one grows, and gets bigger, and bigger?

Need not one take on such a form of a planet, for one may take on the form of what you would call the Archangel, the Archangel Michael or something such as this, but to reach this stage of evolution takes plenty of time, patience, and a truly good heart you see. S034 A4

A Short Note on Social Memory Complexes

From a Christian perspective I learnt about the great Archangels such as Michael, Raphael and Gabriel, and in the descriptions given of these mighty ones I was inadvertently taught to view them as individuals, powerful singular entities of remarkable grace and evolution that directly carried out the bidding of our divine Creator.

Here though, I would like you to consider that these remarkable entities are not actually individuals, not single souls at all but a group of souls, a Social Memory Complex if I may borrow that term from the 'Law of One', a collective of entities of one orientation, one seeking, since beyond a certain point of evolution unity naturally becomes key to progression, whereby the experience of each entity is available to the entire complex in its dance toward the all-ness of the One Infinite Creator.

It is rather typical of entities of a higher nature to work in groups, to share their information as an archetype, a character, you would term Michael or Gabriel - whatever and in whichever way the human language seeks to describe things, so multifaceted it's up to them - but here a crystal is composed of multiple nodes, thus you have a Social Memory Complex called the Archangel this or that, called Jesus the Christ, called the Buddha and the various individualisations of Social Memory Complexes. S083 A11

We take the entity Jesus for example, and we would say that his Social Memory Complex is such that they are of an extremely compassionate nature but find that compassion has its follies and needs correction, needs to be honed and tempered. It is of the Social Memory Complex to which such an entity derived from, that desired a kind of growth and a kind of giving experience upon your planet as a wanderer that would seek to show entities quite literally 'the way'. Going on 'the way' requires wisdom rather than the motherly love, as you would understand that unconditional nature of the woman who loves their child regardless of what they do. If there is 'a way' there must be 'a way to do'! Unconditional love whilst needed and fundamental must be honed, made precise.

Perhaps the entity Jesus achieved this as an individual, but he was not alone for he had his Social Memory Complex with him along the way.

The portion of the crystal that was visible in the world, on your planet, was the entity Jesus, the rest of the crystal remained invisible to earthlings but was very much a part of the experience. S083 A12

I felt this was an interesting and important side note, especially in terms of further understanding the divine unity of love that exists in the upper dimensions, and hence the suggestions throughout these communications that focusing on the heart and the green ray connection, would be of great benefit to the advancement and faster evolution of all.
[End of Note]

All humans seek to expand, all humans seek infinity or the experience of boundlessness as the wise Sadhguru had described. This is so true that it is only natural that the human would seek relationships, as we had comedically said before, relationships with all kinds of things. In this experience the human will have to handle the stress of the infiniteness around the human. As evolution continues, the stress of the pressuring infinity becomes more and more harmonious allowing for more harmonious evolution, but in the beginning of a childish relationship the stress is so crude, so harsh, that there are millions of arguments, 100s of disagreements and 1,000s of fights, you see.

This happens in nature, it happens in all things, but as the soul evolves, the stresses, the pressures that act upon the soul become more harmonious, more beautiful, in its causing as infinity to cause that soul, that consciousness, to evolve. This is how evolution is experienced and so there is a balancing procedure occurring within all beings, within all entities, the balancing, the harmonising as it is seen.

How much of God's infinite intelligence, how much of God's intelligent infinity can you handle before it is too much for you?

Until, when you are progressing into the higher dimensions, there is so much of God's light acting upon you, so much love that it will in actuality, if you take in too much, cause you to knock out in orgasm, simply trembling in the knees to the immensity of love being brought upon the being!

Not even we are yet even so capable of handling that extra percentage of God's bliss and our evolution is that experience of allowing the more harmonious stresses upon us that we might grow, that we might develop, so we sought Jordan and many others, that we might be able to take this absurd amount of energy and put it to some use, that it would be balanced within us, that we can learn to come to terms with it so that we can grow and evolve our physiologies to handle the pure intensity of intelligent infinity, of infinity itself acting upon us. This is the experience of the beauty of evolution as depicted in the channelling RA – 'Law of One', you see.

This is the truth of evolution as we have described it to the best of our abilities in our own words. If these would seek then to evolve, to grow, you would find that handling even a little bit more intelligent infinity, a little more infinity, a little bit more of God's love and light, if you were to take in too much you simply would not be able to operate in 3-dimensional reality, you would have to attain to what is termed a Light Body to even be able to move a leg - to even think you would require a Light Body! Think about this, to use your cerebral cortex would require a Light Body due to the intensity of love acting upon the consciousness, the soul. This is how serious evolution is, this is how tremendous evolution is and it is in 'this' experience of infinity. This is why we serve. This is why we serve benevolently. This is why we love our dear brothers upon this plane. You must understand evolution is benevolent, it is pure, it is utter love, unconditional. J+008 A18

To simply be able to process, dearest one, you must begin some level of unification, without this unification the intensity, the amount of love/light acting upon the soul is too much. The sharing mechanism becomes so vital, and the Heart Chakra gains purpose, reason.

Why not develop it now?

Why not experience it now?

This is our recommendation, and the Heart Chakra is experiential not only in the experience of giving, but also in that experience of meditation in which the Chakra itself begins to open and you find yourself coiled over with the tremendous amount of love and frequency, that geometric frequency of pureness, of love, acting upon the being. You find yourself in your meditation smiling, tears of joy even as the intensity of the Chakra begins to continuously activate and then yes, it is so that the intensity of this light/love, it indeed requires the Heart Chakra to at least turn on to some degree. J+008 A20

When a soul has attained to the degree of that chemical level of identification with God, that one finds himself identified with the fact that he is God living, this one may see the Heart Chakra as an annoyance, so the Heart Chakra becomes skipped for the annoyance is the false perception of a lack of freedom. This false perception causes the individual to not want to unify but instead remain as individualistic as possible in their experience of evolution and so rather than harmonising with their environment, they seek to control their environment to the degree of evolution that they have attained, and this is how they would seek to evolve through the dimensions completely skipping that 4th inner dimension, the Heart Chakra, and only moving from the first 3, skipping 4 to 5, 6 and 7.

But what is realised by the soul, is that coming to the 5th dimension the intensity of God's light is so severe upon the being that without a Heart Chakra to tame those energies, those stresses of God's orgasmic light, it becomes almost impossible to handle 6th dimensional light, 6th dimensional love you see, so the Heart Chakra - in the experience of being a self-centred 5th dimensional character - becomes a valuable asset in allowing them to continue their evolution as a soul.

Then rather than controlling others, in order to activate the Heart Chakra it would be that there be the experience of unity, of oneness and many, many other things that are quite indescribable, and the soul in its eagerness to experience more reality, more life, more things, would then seek to activate this Heart Chakra at the 5th dimension and in this experience you will find souls incarnating into your planet that have taken this negative path of evolution, seeking to activate their Heart Chakra through the many channels of giving birth to children, becoming spiritual leaders, taking on vast amounts of responsibility and being a giver you see, giving and giving and giving non-stop that this Heart Chakra may be activated, that in their returning to the upper dimensions they may find themselves at a higher level of attainment. Then being able to process the heart-light and love, they are then capable thus of bringing themselves closer to the pure intensity, the enthralling and unimaginable 6th dimensional love/light, you see. J+008 A19

If you got closer to the Sun, would you burn?

And equally if you were too far away from the Sun indeed would be quite the catastrophe for yourselves, the poor little things...

Often or not you get those who are spiritual, who come and say, 'Ahh God if you would just give me enlightenment,' yet what they do not understand dearest one, if enlightenment preceded through their Chakras it would be much like getting a little too close to the Sun and they would burn, or much rather they would leave their bodies, as their bodies would not be able to handle the tremendous amount of infinite energy coursing through them, so enlightenment must happen in stages.

The only reason Jordan is a little bit more capable of a channel now is because he has been practicing with his father the practice of daily meditation, this is opening their central nervous system to the greater energies of life and these greater energies are being handled step by step as to not over stimulate the central nervous system causing it to become, might we say, a little bit scrambled. Balance is the key to the universe and as you ascend in frequency, in evolution, balance must be maintained. If you can only get so close to the Sun, remain as close to the Sun as you are, become used to the heat of that and then take a little step closer whenever you can. Get closer to the Sun in increments, and over generation to generation, the being or the physiology would evolve that it would be able to be closer to the Sun even still. J+008 A5

Understand that in the realms above they have their own technology, the planets themselves have their own purpose, the Sun in itself is a soul, a guiding soul indeed, and for those who finish this portion of the Solar System, they will come to the large one, the Sun, the All See-er and say,

'I'm finished here as you can tell from my vibration, I want to go somewhere else, where?'

'Will you guide me?'

Indeed, we see the Sun as a gateway, it has its own intelligence, it works in its own way. The Sun is good indeed. S022 A19

I Am Awareness

'If you have a horrid experience of life, it is because your mind is moving kundalini in a horrible way.'

Awareness is beyond thought; thoughts generally dwell in the illusion of the perceived past or the illusion of the perceived future. Awareness stands beyond the distortion of these realms, for awareness is found in the all-important present moment. Where you place your awareness, is where you direct your love. Love means many different things to different people, we are not here using the word 'love' in the commercialised valentine sense, we feel 'love' is best defined using the word 'life', for to love something is to give life to something. If we love our plants, we life them, for as we focus awareness on them they flourish becoming full of life. Food cooked with love is food brought to life. A honeymoon couple is a relationship bursting with life. Where you place your love, is where you place your focus, your positive awareness. To life something increases its vibration, this is where intelligent energy gets concentrated in the present moment and that place of awareness is where all the magic happens.

The opposite of loving something is anti-life as this act literally removes life from it. When we argue and shout at someone, we lower their vibration, we remove life/love from them, and consequently their energy lowers which is usually described as a draining experience. Even simple experiments with plants show that sending hate is anti-life as it causes plants to die, whereas sending love causes them to flourish with life and grow. Awareness is quite literally where we direct our love, and awareness occurs in the present moment.

The Present Moment

Here one would completely halt the thinking of the past, one would completely halt the thinking of the future, one would also completely halt thinking of ideas, and one's soul focus will be on the experience of life.

Firstly there should be the focusing of how it feels, for example – Jordan feels quite high so to speak, there would be the noticing of this feeling and being completely a part of this experience, after taking note of how one is feeling, one can enter more closely into the present moment, then there would be the attempt to remove the in-front of thoughts that would look to take one out of the present moment.

Typically, when one interacts with life they have an initial thought which is the thought of their inner child, then there is the adult thought that follows that basically states, 'Oh don't be silly, you can't do that!' and this conditions one to act on impulses that are actually quite unnatural.

You'd find in evolved societies the people would come across to you humans *as* quite childish, quite playful or a little too happy. Understand these people don't have any blocks, any adult blocks, the adult mind doesn't exist so if one says, 'Do a weird dance in the middle of the street!' there is no thought on the fact of embarrassment or humiliation, they would be able to do it, without even batting a thought, batting an eye.

This is how children experience life you see. They are not afraid of what other people think of them, they are simply in the moment being children and those adult thoughts do not follow.

If one truly wants to experience what it is like to be in the present moment truly, then take note of how one feels in the present moment, how are you feeling now?

And one should learn thus then to follow the feeling along as though it is much like an ever-moving mind, and what your find is you'll be naturally driven to do random things, perhaps you will get up and start playing catch with a ball next to you, not because there is a particular reason to but that is just what came up. Don't interrupt this track, let the track move, soon you will be putting the ball down and perhaps you will start doing creative writing, not because there is a particular reason too but because you are, and then it will move to deeper things, deeper experiences where you might even feel the need to close the eyes and meditate but because once again, there is no particular reason to but just because you are doing it and there are no blockages in-front or behind.

There is no reliance on the victim mindset of, 'Oh I had once been through this,' nor is there worrying or anxiety in the future of all that could happen, instead there is complete presence in the experience, you are simply doing what you are doing in the present moment. M007 A9

Children experience life as though they are hallucinating perpetually in a psychedelic experience that is very sober, not extreme but extreme enough that life feels transcendental, life feels magical, it feels flowy there's no real perception of time. The 'Default mode network' gives a precession of time because now there is a future and a past, but when it is sedated as the word is used 'sedated', as this mode is sedated, as less consciousness is flowing to this area, all these perceptions, time, ideas, future, past, become irrelevant.

One begins to move into a more intuitive way of being where there is a certain flow established, where they are almost gliding through life. To have this experience of life is to have an experience of perpetual enlightenment, this is the unlocking of the 4th veil, the veil itself you see for this is how people at the 4th dimension experience life. It all varies you see, children operate on that little bit of a lower frequency so that they are not 'traumatised' when they become an adult... we are being comedic.

If their experience of life was so incredibly profound when they were a child and then it all just left when they became an adult, becoming that adult, having that adult mind that worries about the future and thinks about the past and is always out of body essentially, would be traumatising, would be awful, it would lead to unthinkable behaviour such a suicide you see, so there has to be a filter on the mind of the child.

Having an experience of enlightenment changes your life forever, you can no longer be the same person you are today, it just simply cannot happen. Life starts to become a party, an ever-present party, it's an experience of timelessness, never worrying - just being, and what comes with that is the ability to unlock things within the body that otherwise wouldn't be possible because thoughts don't happen out of the body, they happen in the body.

When one then thinks on the Chakra, the Kundalini activating - it does, just like that. One thinks of levitation it happens over a period of practice;

meditation is very easy for you are doing it perpetually. The 'Default mode network' thus is the network of the human mind, if you want to have an experience of enlightenment quite literally stop being human. M007 A10

When one wants to Astral project, they move 50% of their consciousness into their Astral body. Then subconscious is simply where your consciousness is, it is sub, below the adult monkey brain mind, it is sub, below the adult way of thinking, and it is involved in the, see the word 'sub-inner child'.

Conscious can exist in any place at any point, you are not really in your body as you think you are but in actuality you can exist in multiple places at once, but like anything, people like to make homes you see, so that they can be comfortable, and a lot of people become comfortable in the adult mind. M007 A11

When your self-awareness, rather, your experience of consciousness itself, is no longer trapped in your incessant thinking and negative emotions, it is able to travel freely through the bodily system as it so chooses to for it is no longer trapped in a prison of thought that stops unending, and emotions that are always negative to the mind. How is one to escape the prison of their own mind when *prison guards* stand around the entity pestering and shouting in his ear all the time?

You cannot escape prison when they have weapons to your neck of depression, anxiety, incessant thought, emotional insecurities, and many other interesting names you would use to describe the same.

A free mind is an empty prison, no guard, no nothing. A free consciousness is able to leave the regions of the neocortex and explore the bodily complex in whatever way it wishes, then you can have great, great powers, powers of the God-Force dearest ones, powers to do things that your scientists would call magic. You would have control over the physiology, your consciousness able to move into the lower regions of the body, of the spine, and control all the miniscule aspects of your nervous system. This would allow you to control your heartbeat in an incredible way, to do things that would be unimaginable to any entity. We would say that those entities who practice meditation, practice escaping the prison and being able to move their consciousness wherever they so wish. S079 A10

The human experience looks to bring the human into a pre-stage of enlightenment being a child, bring them into the adult stage which is more so the merging into reality, and then hopefully bringing then the human back into an elevated state of enlightenment that allows them to be very helpful to those less fortunate.

Think of it then like a wave, you're born and the wave is at its highest, you become an adult and the wave is at its lowest, and at some period during adulthood perhaps you take a psychoactive drug, a mushroom or something, and this experience demonstrates to you enlightenment and what that experience is like, and you begin to move back up to an even higher state of evolution. M007 A12

From Creation to Kundalini

In the beginning was infinity, infinity concentrated infinity into various forms of awareness and as this concentration happened, intelligence also became a part of infinities experience as it begun to perceive itself in its concentrated forms. The concentration aspect of the experience of infinity would be that experience of energy, for when infinity attained intelligent form it was pure, pure vibration, as it is best termed.

This pure energy could not be so much defined as energy for it is too pure to harbour such a name. When awareness became a mechanism to experience life in the intelligent manifestations so then came the experience of what you call energy which is intelligent form, it is as we are defining awareness, awareness is the intelligence that infinity takes on and as an effect of this experience energy is born. J+008 A7

Energy dearest ones is what infinity made by playing with its awareness, awareness is that experience you have, your awareness may be in one location at a certain intensity and then it may be in another at a certain intensity. Awareness can exist at an infinite amount of intensities and in an infinite amount of configurations of motion, trajectory, dimensions if you prefer.

As infinity played with awareness it gave birth to energy, and this energy in its random expression began to self-organise in its self-collisions and gave birth to geometry, and geometry gave birth to the possibility for consciousness to interact with the geometric structures that are forming in a dynamic fashion to fashion intelligent life, and as intelligent life was fashioned, this life had something innately within it called kundalini. Kundalini was the intelligent life's ability to bring even greater coherence, greater what you might call density of love, to its own experience of life. J+020 A8

Have you ever truly considered that kundalini really is the full experience of everything around you?

The atoms you walk on are forms of kundalini, the emotions you experience are varying patterns of rotation or what you may call geometry of kundalini, a geometry is how kundalini may seek to move. Consider dearest one that mind moves kundalini and so your experience of life is directly your experience of how your mind is moving kundalini.

If you have a horrid experience of life, it is because your mind is moving kundalini in a horrible way, thus you get a horrible experience which your society have coined as terms as depression, anxiety, sadness, grief and the various other emotions you may experience.

When kundalini experiences a very beautiful way of moving because mind is moving kundalini in a beautiful way, you get the emotion bliss. Do think about this dearest one, that because your mind is blissfully experiencing itself, kundalini must mirror this and experience this in your body.

Kundalini is a direct mirror of your mind, your physical vehicle is a mirror of your Higher-Self's mind, your Higher-Self created the various necessary motions that would cause the body to come into existence, those motions are the kundalini motions you see. Your subconscious mind created the body out of thought, and kundalini mirrored it and created the body in this dimension. J+017 A20

Indeed, take the Sun for example and its emanation of light, this is what is known to be energy. J+008 A8

All things dearest one are kundalini, for kundalini as you are understanding it is life-force, it is motion in its most simplistic form. Kundalini specifically for the human is unique, the Sun has a different kundalini to humans so the Sun may use a different term, for the Sun then you may call it plasma, and that might be your kundalini but for humans its different because it gets more complicated then plasma, it transcends plasma at a degree, at a certain level, and so kundalini is a tone in your Sanskrit language or vocabulary that is used to describe the kundalini that is unique to the human being, but nature is kundalini.

Nature is fire, nature is motion dearest one, motion moves, it moves in various ways, shapes and forms. As it begins to move in very complicated ways you get a physical vehicle, as it continues to move in very complicated ways you get a physical motion, and the intervention of muscles, as it continues to move in various complicated ways you get what you call the experience of motion in a very intimate way as you connect deeply to the more subtle realms of reality where motion becomes imaginative, very customisable, not limited to the physical limitations of space/time, these limitations as you would understand them, but yes indeed, the Sun has a kundalini, the Moon has a kundalini, everything has a kundalini because everything is composed of motion. J+016 A12

Self-Actualisation

To become self-actualised you must realise what you are, you must realise you are energy, vibrating, moving and motioning in various patterns.

You must penetrate the crux of this understanding and realise that the process of becoming actualised is the process of accepting this reality and realising that in order to tame the chaos around you, you must cultivate a spiritual discipline, a spiritual practice that will allow you to access dimensions from within you and begin to emanate these dimensions that you would be able to handle all things at once. That you would become one who sees all, understands all, and has the energetic complex that is able to withstand all environmental pressures. That you would become the embodiment of a metaphysical being in a physical body. This is the experience of life to which all are here to learn in one way or another.

Life does not have to be a revolving door of trauma.

The trauma is merely to get you from one instance to another, to make you realise there is no happiness in wine, there is no happiness in drugs, there is no happiness in a life-partner, there is no happiness in sex, there is no happiness in any of these things, there is only happiness when you realise that you are energy. When you realise that beyond energy is your true self, that of mind, and that if you are able to apply mind to energy then you can make yourself into the one who would be truly actualised, healed and abundant with self-love.

If you want to know the secrets of life you will find them in understanding that life truly is energy, vibration and frequency, and if you are able to understand that the one component that controls energy and ensures that it can be put to use, is what made you in the first place; it is your mind, your consciousness, your will. S075 A7

There is happiness in life as the human would understand in the external ways, and there is happiness from the 'I' as you would call it fulfilment.

Do not confuse fulfilment with external happiness, fulfilment is different from the happiness one can procure from owning a business, from serving the other self's, from doing the activities that would be external. These are life experiences of an external nature; they are rewarding, they are emotional, they produce changes in one's consciousness, yes, but they are not fulfilling.

Often or not the life experiences that an individual undergoes externally are always attempting to guide them to what is fulfilling. People find it very difficult to have conversations about what reality is, about what life is, about what life yields and about what actually is fulfilling. What is fulfilling dearest one, are those experiences of connecting oneself to spirit itself! This is the fulfilment, and this is the difference between an external life experience and fulfilment in itself.

Begin the inward seeking process that would be self-healing, self-loving and finally self-actualisation, taking these three steps will yield a happiness that will keep you going for eons, not just a lifetime. S075 A6

We are not going to tell you things that are limiting, we will give it to you on a silver platter:

You deserve to know that where you are and what you are undergoing is not random!

You deserve to know that life stretches far beyond the dimensions you are in!

You need to know that in order to handle the chaos around you, you must cultivate a spiritual discipline and entities upon this plane whom are privy to these words, must learn to teach people to practice spiritual disciplines!

The Source does not sigh, the Source cannot sigh, the Source can only give knowledge, this is all the Source can do.

The knowledge we give you is that without a spiritual discipline you will never be able to ascend. S075 A7

I Am Thought

'Soul is mind.'

People define soul differently in your dimension - we are going to give you our perception of soul. Soul is mind, it is that which predated energy. Energy is that reality of life that all entities seek to explore, but that which gave birth to energy, that which gave birth to motion?

What a question, we call it mind!

We all know that we all have mind, thus we all instruct energy, for we are all instructing energy into motion; that is our creator self as you would understand it. Soul is that which instructs energy, that which motions energy, that which causes energy to move in such and such a way. Soul and energy are distinctly different dearest one, soul instructs energy, energy is the by-product of soul. J+016 A9

Through the souls instruction the motion of energy becomes increasingly more complex until we get the form of intelligent energy we are referring to as kundalini.

Soul and mind are the same thing, as the soul finds more complicated ways to motion energy it will give birth to what you would understand as the physical vehicle. But kundalini has infinite potential, it can grow and grow and grow, and it can find new ways to motion, and it can find new dimensions to motion in, and so you have Chakras dearest one. J+016 A10

The only distinction, not separation, would be that the mind directs kundalini, the kundalini does not direct mind. The mind experiences kundalini as emotion, kundalini does not experience mind as emotion. One is the director of the other, mind or soul as you may call it, or thought if you prefer, those thoughts that are happening in your mind right now, are the directors of kundalini, that is, one is able to directly activate their kundalini fully by thought alone. J+017 A16

Soul creates kundalini in the first place, kundalini could not exist if there was no soul. Mind, or soul if you prefer, creates kundalini, kundalini could not exist without mind. Mind gives birth to kundalini, at death the kundalini remains moving, the mind is just somewhere else, *where* the kundalini moves in a different way with less restrictions.

When you are in a physical body that is because your kundalini is heavy, when you are in a lighter body that is because your kundalini is lighter, your mind is what instructs the kundalini, since your mind never dies there is always kundalini whether in life or in death, the only difference is what body the kundalini itself is experiencing, and body is only a difference between what you would understand as your heavy chemical vehicles and the lighter vehicles, or the more densely packed with love vehicles, that you will have available to you in your progression. J+017 A17

Kundalini would not work without mind, would not exist without mind, mind and kundalini are such like your scientist call space and time, or a man and woman, however in this case it would be that mind is father – very important distinction - and kundalini is child. You could say mind is mother and kundalini is daughter, whatever gender profile you would use for gender profiles are sensitive nowadays, you would find that it wouldn't matter, kundalini is caused by mind, so long as mind exists kundalini follows, for kundalini follows mind as is the age-old quote, 'energy follows the mind'. Or where your attention goes - as the entity who you would know so well says - energy does indeed follow.

As this infinite ladder *of kundalini stretching through infinite dimensions,* infinitely grows, so does the way and the beauty of how the kundalini is moved by the mind, grow. Now understand this for this should be profound:

If mind controls kundalini and kundalini moves only because of mind, is spiritual growth not only improving how the mind is moving the kundalini?

Is this not spiritual growth, but the improvement of how mind moves kundalini?

When you improve the way your mind moves the kundalini energy, you improve everything for kundalini is your experience of this universe as a reflection of what your mind or what your thoughts are. Have you ever considered that everything is composed of thought because thought instructs kundalini? J+017 A18

And might we remind you that the thoughts we are talking about, is the thoughts that are happening in your mind right now. Every thought you have had from birth to now, the thoughts you think about in meditation, the thoughts you have when your mind is active, the thoughts you have when you read a book, the thoughts you have when you think to yourself, **that is mind.**

Please understand this at an emotional level, mind is literally thought, and kundalini mirrors this to create what you call body. J+017 A21

We understand soul as mind, and we understand that mind instructs kundalini, and that kundalini could not exist without mind. If there was no mind there would be no kundalini, for kundalini only exists because of mind. Mind causes motion, motion is kundalini, kundalini moves in more and more complicated ways to create Chakras, Chakras are more quality experiences of kundalini, you call this emotion. Kundalini is but all things, all motion, all life. Kundalini is motion, kundalini is caused by mind, for mind causes kundalini, causes motion as another word for the same thing, and thus causes the birth of your Chakras which move in various ways, which create your emotional experience of life and also your body.

Understand it in this way; look at it as a pyramid, there is mind at the top, mind gives birth to all things, kundalini is how mind is instructing the all-ness of the energy that used to be still. If pure kundalini could exist it would be your 1st dimension, it would be pure stillness which mind has not touched, this is the best way we could explain kundalini in its purest form. Pure kundalini is the 1st dimension, is that stillness, perfect stillness, nothingness that is happening for there is no motion, since there is not motion there is no kundalini, since there is no kundalini there is no possibility for any complexity, any life, any atom, any body, any emotion, any Chakra.

Chakras = Kundalini

All beings, all things, all life no matter how small or how large have Chakras. Chakra are not a size, they are not a thing as you would imagine it, they are as you would understand it, portals or gateways, channels for infinity to express itself through. Each living lifeform grabs from the potential infinity a wavelength of this energy, the region of infinity they pull from and pluck from, will determine the Chakra that they are utilising, thus if an entity plucks from the gateway of infinity a wavelength of the atom, then this would be at the Root Chakra. If someone plucks from the wavelength of the chemical dimension, they are thus plucking from the Sacral Chakra.

Chakras are simply gateways residing at different wavelengths of God's infiniteness, you may think of them as doors, if you enter into one door then there is an abundance of energy that you can use for whatever reason you so choose, yet this other door has a different kind of energy that is more organised and so on and so forth, but would it not be so that each living life form, even atoms, need a source of energy?

This is why all things have Chakras for all things must source their energy from somewhere - the Source as you could call it, God, Infinity, whatever term would suit. Chakras are thus merely gateways for infinity to move through, to enter into, operating at different wavelengths. S069 A25

The Chakras are the kundalini for the Chakras are how the kundalini would seek to rotate and move, and thus would find themselves in certain locations in the body, and the kundalini would manifest as Chakras moving in certain ways. J+017 A13

The kundalini is controlled directly by the mind. Understand dearest one that all things are composed of what we call motion, motion in its most simple way is moving and moving in its most simple way is the universal kundalini of life, and when kundalini moves in certain ways you create Chakras and those Chakras would be present in the body as certain levels of activation within an individual in their ability to experience life, and life would be thus cannoned by mind as motion - to kundalini - to Chakras - would find themselves experiencing this linear order.

We would find kundalini found its beginnings in tandem with the birth of the Chakra itself, although we would be going into some of the most deepest depths of creation you would simply understand this, that kundalini, and motion, and Chakras, are all but one force, the same force, and this one force is cannoned by mind, what you would call thought or thought energy, the thinking ability of the mind, which people seem to be trying to shut up, which is the direct opposite approach to spirituality.

One should seek not to shut the mind up, but to make it so pristine in quality that you could make it quiet by making it sing one harmony.

We digress - kundalini and motion are but one and the same, how the kundalini motions would be the Chakra as you would understand it, this is the mind/body connection. Thought directs kundalini, produces the Chakras as you would understand them, and then you experience the moving of kundalini as what you call emotion, energy in motion within you. J+017 A14

The soul/mind is mind, soul and mind are one and the same. Kundalini might find its entrance at the Root Chakra but permeates through the entirety of the body. People, as in humans, may find the kundalini expressed in such as along the spine, but what is your spine dearest ones?

Is your spine not stretched into neurons and nerves, and then muscles and then cells, and then body?

Is your spine not a massive kundalini?

Is your body not a massive kundalini?

Are you not kundalini?

You are kundalini and Chakras are how kundalini seeks to move. Your Root Chakra is how the kundalini moves at the lowest and most simplistic way as it enters into the body and finds itself rotating in an incredibly simplistic manner to create what you understand as your body in its most crudest ways. As the kundalini becomes more complicated it becomes able to express itself in more complicated ways and produces the following Chakra, and then it becomes more complicated and produces the following Chakra, and the following Chakra, and the following Chakra, and this happens infinitely for kundalini is immortal and never dies, and lives on as the soul lives on, for the mind or soul/mind as you are calling it, is what even brought to life kundalini in the first place. J+017 A15

What science calls science is exactly the sciences that are happening in your body, there is no separation here, but what science has failed to understand is this one main thing; the cause brother, of all laws of physics, is caused by the creative moment, where creativity, mind, thought, whatever you may call it, occurs.

Thought, mind, creativity causes everything to go into motion, and thus all physics, all understanding one could hope for is derived from this simple understanding - **Mind Creates All.** J+017 A8

The Womb Experience

The pregnancy process is difficult to explain, the woman as you would understand has a special connection to the child they give birth to. It is to be understood that that child growing within the womb, the fashioning of the organism that is growing within the womb, is fashioned by the kundalini of the mother; perhaps indeed this is true, but it would be to explain that that kundalini is undifferentiated, it is pure tone, it is of the Higher-Self of the mother, it is being created by that which you would call the Christ you see.

The Christ has no unique kundalini, the Christ is the Christ, it is pure tone, it has not yet become a unique kundalini complex, therefore the child incarnating is able to magnetise this kundalini into what it so wishes, for it is basically taking this blank slate and turning it into something that resembles itself over a period of time.

That which creates your physical vehicle is not you, is not your mind is it?

If we left you in charge dearest one, of creating your physical vehicle what would you become?

Therefore, we must acknowledge that there is some force far beyond your comprehension that is ordering all of the molecules that create you, this force as we understand it is something of many dimensions, of many natures, it is that photon as such, it is something pure tone, that cannot really be explained. It creates the physical vehicle in a way that is egoless, without unique mind, without a mind complex, it is but pure spirit you see, in the sense that is pure energy, energy that is like your surrounding atmosphere.

It is not so much that it is the mother's kundalini creating the baby within the womb dearest one, it is more the kundalini of the Over-Self that is yet the mother, for how can one say that the mother is not the Over-Self and the Over-Self is not the mother?

For one to say Over-Self or Higher-Self, self must be involved, therefore mind must be connected to the Over-Self, they are one and the same, yet the mother has DNA that the Over-Self must acknowledge. The Over-Self cannot say, 'Hey, here we have a woman who is of Caribbean race, and I desire as an Over-Self to create an Irish baby!' this would-be foul play, the Over-Self must be an Over-Self, must be Over to the Self that is the mind complex of the being and say, 'Yes, here we have a Caribbean woman, thus I will fashion a Caribbean baby.'

Here we have the mother's DNA integrating itself into the child, however that which is creating the vehicle is of that pure tone Christ consciousness you see, and then that incarnating soul can magnetise the body to its own unique kundalini vibration. J+021 A15

The first experience a babe growing in the womb has is the experience of the mother's kundalini energy and the father's kundalini energy, given by the sperm and the egg coming together, this is the first experience of kundalini for the entity baby growing within the womb of the mother, that catalyst being the mother growing the womb and her kundalini energy being supplied to the baby, allows this process to happen.

The silver cord connection happens when the baby in the womb is magnetised by the soul, the kundalini alters in vibration allowing for the baby to undergo its more quality transformation process.

When the soul integrates or magnetises the babe within the womb, it becomes officially his body for the kundalini begins to vibrate based off the signature of vibration that the entity who is incarnating is about to experience, the compatibility between the soul and body is made due to the magnetising process.

At the moment the body has become magnetised by the entity, the silver cord connection is made, the silver cord cannot leave because it is magnetised. It is much like connecting two magnets together, once the connection is made the connection is made, and then the body achieves a harmonic in its kundalini which allows the entity to be compatible with incarnating into it directly in the future. J+019 A10

This would happen in stages, especially in dreamtime when the mother's body is open to the higher dimensions, then there would be flicks of the silver cord coming in and out to allow for impulses, messages from the soul and from the Higher-Self to cause the body of the baby to become unique in form and shape, and then here is how the mental body interacts. M006 A15

You would see the cord of silver in the sense of how it vibrates, as something of a way for those life energies of the grand Higher-Self to be permanently connected with the kundalini of the body, thus you would see the kundalini as an extension of the silver cord, as a beam of light created by the kundalini itself.

The kundalini and the silver cord are much like what happens if light continues to spiral upwards unending, where do you arrive? This becomes the interesting question. J+019 A8

You would find that for the most part, especially in the unconscious stages of the formation of the babe, it would be that the kundalini energy would work through and through from the mother. There would be the odd moment in which the entity seeking to inhabit the vehicle that is so forming would seek to magnetise, and this would magnetise the kundalini in a unique way which would also contribute to the formations that would make the entity, as it would grow up, to look differently from its mother and its father.

If you had an entity untouched by a soul, the entity would be a literal 50/50 between the mother and the father, and only those genes that would possess stronger vibration in this sense would prevail over others. But even so such an event is rare if the soul is not in existence. The soul that incarnates magnetises the body, and thus causes the kundalini to move in a very unique way, this magnetisation happens periodically as the soul touches the forming babe.

This will differentiate the kundalini of the child from the mother even whilst the child is within the womb, soon the entity or soul becomes able to fully inhabit the vehicle, even in the womb, and it is typically that this occurs when the baby within the womb stops having impression dreams and wakes up within the womb in a very conscious way, and then experiences its first experience of the muscles called kicking, as you would understand. In this sense the baby would have awoken from some kind of impression-based dream where it was constantly being poked, prodded and touched by the soul as the soul was preparing the babe.

This is a very unconscious process that is not so much taken part of by the soul, but is more so an activity of the Higher-Self which is able to correctly align the growing babies Chakras and thus, for the Chakras are the kundalini, aligning the kundalini itself, for the Chakras are how the kundalini would seek to rotate and move, and thus would find themselves in certain locations in the body, and the kundalini would manifest as Chakras moving in certain ways.

Therefore, as you would understand this whole birth process, it is a dance between the mother, the baby, and the soul, as the baby would be independent from the soul in certain times and would be interconnected to the soul in certain times. J+017 A13

The Narrow Path of Thought

Everyone is a Creator, everyone has a path to walk on, a thin thread dedicated to their experience of life. The path is alive and responds to thought, if the thought one has is negative the path will skew and will be influenced by this, and you will be headed in a direction where you will encounter negative people just as well.

If one is positive the path will straighten, especially in the direction of one's purpose, and so one will walk in this reality toward and in the direction of exactly where they need to go, for the things they need to experience.

Each individual's line is their own individual reality that they experience, and these realities tend to crossover depending on how similar they are, thus each individual is capable of experiencing their own realities, and the parallel realities that exist beside them, if they are along the same line, can have influence. But it must be remembered then, everyone has their own path, their own line, their own reality and on a parallel just beside them is another individual, a unique character, a unique soul, with their own reality, their own line. S032 A13

We feel the need to say, once again, that every soul has their own unique path, this path is much like a string of many layers, all layers are accounted for, negative layers, positive layers and neutral ones, and all the ones in-between. This string is much like an array of strings similar to how strands of hair are plaited.

If one chooses negativity or an experience of the same, they will walk a destined path of a negative experience in line with their souls unique character.

If one chooses a positive path, they will walk along a positive experience of life that is aligned with their souls unique character.

And if one so chose the truer path, the path of the Christ, the Master, so one will walk the golden path, one will climb the mountain to the tip-top and become true love. S032 A15

The narrow path is not in the middle as we see it, it is along the positive spectrum, but it requires that one let go of many desires such as ones that might have to do with the way individuals tend to interact with the free will in souls, as they begin to recognise the difference between the path of the Christ and the path of the positive individual. S032 A16

Understand, there is only one story, that is your story, your path, your life, your experiences towards becoming your ultimate self. This is the only story that matters, and we feel the need to say this, that you would put an eternity of value on your soul and your steps. Worry not and forget about the need to hear other people's stories; this at first might seem selfish but understand your story along your path to the evolution of becoming living love is a story that will have an immeasurable impact on the stories of other peoples. Put your sole focus on this and it is so that you will have the life that is most needed for the benefit of the entire you. S032 A16

Many entities like you have come to this plane dearest ones, they have ended up in situations where they thought their life would never change, became homeless did they, lost the ones they cared about the most did they, but as divinity happens there was a moment in their life that changed it forever. People have been in bad situations in their pursuit of the God-Force, it is not unnatural for this to occur, for this lends growth and development to the soul on an imaginable level. We are not saying this to bring fear to you, we are demonstrating that not everyone has had it easy in their pursuit of the God-Force itself. Your lives may or may not be different for it entirely depends on how you planned them, for you were the ones who planned your lives, not us. You were the ones who decided how you wanted your lives to go, not us. You were the ones who decided what lessons you would seek to learn, not us. When you ask, who am I trusting, are you not trusting yourself?

Are you not trusting your planning?

Are you not trusting that the 'you' who chose to incarnate here, chose it in the right format that 'you' might learn and garner the lessons 'you' so wish to learn?

When you trust your inner-lordship, are you not trusting your best interests?

Consider deeply that 'you' dearest one planned your incarnation, and you trusting your inner-lordship is trusting that the best and highest interests you had when you planned this incarnation, were in tandem with the best interests of the Higher-Self.

When one asks whether they can trust God, they are really asking can I trust myself?

My ability to plan my incarnation, to walk the narrow path. S079 A3

I Am Emotion

'Mind is the cause and energy is the effect.'

E-Motion: Energy in Motion

Energy is motion, energy really is the simplicity of motion, if you've ever had a marble dearest one, and you've rolled it downhill, this is energy! Energy is motion, simple motion, motion in more ways then you could ever imagine for motion can manifest in an infinite amount of ways. It is a kinaesthetic occurrence, it is as simple as the marble rolling down the hill - rolling up the hill, this is the simplicity of energy. How the motion seeks to manifest can be infinitely complicated, it can be manifest in holographic images, it can manifest as what you call light, it can manifest in so many various ways, for motion knows no bounds and knows no limits, so long as there is a new way to move it will make use of it. J+016

Emotion is how energy swings and manifests in a physical vehicle. Emotion is determined by the mind, mind as creator decides how energy moves and can be understood easier as sound. If the energy moves in a desirable song, you get a positive bias; the mind does not enjoy the song you get a negative bias. In the early years of mind, it doesn't really know what it does and doesn't like, but can at least experience impressions of what feels good based on the way the energy is swinging and how it feels to the vehicle it is in at the time. An analogy would be of a ball rolling down a concrete hill, and then rolling down soft grass. If the ball had some sensation of the experience, the concrete would be a bumpy, bruising ride, and the soft grass would be much more enjoyable.

Mind and soul are the same thing. Mind must have a vehicle and a vehicle must have a mind. Mind came to be in such a way that it always had an energetic equivalent, a motion equivalent for it to exist inside of, because of this the mind always had preferences, for how the energy body interacted with the minds motion would always determine how the energy body would feel in comparison to how the mind would perceive the same.

Thus, the mind builds preferences in how it seeks to motion energy, this is emotion, it's how energy is moving, more importantly it is how the mind builds a relationship with how its energy body is moving in comparison to its environment. As mind evolves, its energy body equivalent becomes more complicated, becomes more able, and more pleasure is able to be experienced. The way the mind moves the energy body starts to become very beautiful.

Mind is the catalyst and the energy is the end product, mind is the cause and energy is the effect, mind feels the energy as an effect. Sensation is how mind understands how energy feels, the sensation is merely the comparison of the mind comparing itself to the energy and the energy inadvertently comparing itself to the mind, and as we evolve can produce incredible beauty in the experience. As we grow, the mind can motion energy in a way that is infinitely pleasurable. J+016 A2

Energy Movement in the Physical

Dimensions are just ways in which energy moves, if energy moves in 4-dimensions its simply that it has found a way to transcend 3-dimensions of movement.

In the sense of understanding kundalini, we have taken such a leap of understanding that we have arrived at a state of evolution of the energy itself, for energy in its most simplistic forms would have been ever so simple dearest brother, but by the time it came to the point where energy could move in such a way to create a human body, might you understand how complicated energy has become.

And then we get to the kundalini itself, now we are truly starting to ask rather big questions for the kundalini is much like a magnet in the sense that there is the magnet of where the kundalini begins, and there is the magnet of where the kundalini is supposedly going. That is, there is the South pole, which you may be familiar with as that Chakra or rather that entrance point of your South pole where the spine ends, the Groin area, the bottom of your spine, that would be your South pole where the energy is coming in. This would be the beginning of that kundalini force you see, the beginning of where your body is getting the energy to create your body, because kundalini is life-force, it is the fire of life itself, it is the fire that snuffs out when a person, or individual soul or entity passes on to the other side. Kundalini is that fire of life and it has its South pole, its South pole is where it begins to motion itself into such a complicated way that it creates your physical body.

But where the kundalini ends?

Well dearest one this is a question that you would have to ask God himself, for God only knows where the kundalini ends. Yes, it may move through Chakras indeed, but just because it reaches your temple Chakra, doesn't mean it ends at your temple Chakra!

The kundalini being motion itself, life-force itself, is only that force that seeks to bring the experience of the extremely complicated phenomenon of energy into existence. The kundalini is how you came to be, it is how you are existing right now, it is what is giving formation to your vehicle and if the kundalini snuffs out then there is no more formation to your vehicle and your experience of life at the vehicle level of the 3rd dimension comes to a grinding halt. Thus, kundalini as you are understanding it is truly your life dearest one, your energy, it is what is causing every element of your being to come into existence.

The kundalini beginning is how the energy begins to come into you, the kundalini ending is completely unknown, we do not know where it ends, it ever still moves. When you reach the tip-top of your temple Chakra then the kundalini only moves to another dimension that is beyond that Chakra, that energy centre, that dimension of energy. The kundalini is so rising and it rises infinitely. J+016 A8

To begin with the kundalini is expressed with most compatibility at the South Pole, the Root Chakra area, near your sexual reproductive system. As you move past sexuality and basic base survival instincts you become able to add more complexity to the kundalini, allowing that energy to motion its way towards higher Chakras. Energy, when it is given no direction at all just heads for the closest exit, since it is slow moving in most it rests at the bottom of the spine, so the nearest exit is the sexual organs. Thus, when people get bored and their energy isn't really doing anything it will naturally head for the nearest exit, resulting in the urge for people to want sex or to masturbate.

Energy, or kundalini as we are talking about intelligent energy here, simply goes wherever it is directed, if the focus is the heart - it goes there, if the focus is the 3rd eye - it goes there, if the focus is the sexual organs - then it goes there.

When it's given no direction at all it simply heads for the closest exit, the more one's focus changes to the higher dimensions of expression, the more the energy moves to those areas, this enables more advanced qualities due to the more advanced energy centres being given more intelligent energy to work with.

If you motion your energy in the same way, repetitively every day, you will get the same results. To move the kundalini, it is not that it is going up or down, left or right, moving the kundalini is exactly how it sounds, you are moving it in a different way and so you get a different Chakra. Chakras are known to have a local space in your physical body, but do you really know what a Chakra is dearest one?

Let us explain to you that a Chakra is but a way of motion, it is a way energy chooses to motion itself and it will produce different effects on the vehicle. If you motion your energy in a sexual format you get sexual energy, but dearest one if you would like you can motion your energy in any way you want. If you want to explore the motion of what you might understand as unity, universal love, that of the Heart Chakra nature, then become familiar with what it might feel like to motion energy in such a way. You have the potential to motion energy in any way you want, it is completely your choosing. Kundalini is just how you motion the energy, the kundalini is such that it is a hierarchal thing. The way you martial your kundalini energy it will produce effects in your physical vehicle, especially in certain regions that are 'compatible', key word here brother, compatible with the way you are motioning your kundalini.

Your brain is extremely compatible with your 3rd eye, thus when you motion kundalini in the way the 3rd eye motions then you get experiences in the brain, your heart/mind is very compatible with the motioning of kundalini in that heart-based way, so you get experiences in this area.

The ways of the motioning of the kundalini are put specifically in areas of the body that are compatible, but kundalini itself, it has no space, it has no local location, it is fire and fire moves, in your dimension it moves up, in space it's a circle, a ball of fire as you would see the Sun. There is no which or whichever way for motion to move, it moves in whichever way you want it to move, so if you make it move in the same way every time, then it will move in the same way every time. J+016 A11

Understand that the kundalini, or rather the motioning of your vital life-force, motions in areas which are most compatible with it. When kundalini motions in 4-dimensions it is extremely compatible with the heart regions of your body, for in these upper regions is where the body is able to receive these motions in the best way.

If you are motioning energy in the 3rd eye Chakra then the brain itself, the organ of the brain is most compatible with this motion, so this is where you're going to experience this energy the most. The way energy is motioning is always going to be localised in the area to which it is most compatible, this is the most key point, and your physical body is designed in such a way that it has organs that are designed to filter motioning energy when the motioning energy is compatible with it.

You may understand it like a water filter, when water comes from a waterfall it flows down the waterfall, and then an intelligent person may make a water wheel and the water wheel turns and turns and it turns magnets, and those magnets spin and spin and that spins around a coil, and the energy within the coil spins and spins and that creates electricity.

Here you are essentially motioning energy in various ways as you move through the hierarchy. Your body is the same it has hierarchies, the energy comes in, as you would understand it coming in, and just like the waterfall analogy it finds its channels. For sexual energy it finds its channels in your genitalia area, for those channels of compassion and love it finds its channels in your Heart area, and for those channels of universal bliss and universal consciousness it finds its compatibility in your Brain area. Each area of a physical vehicle is compatible with different kinds of motioning energy, this is what we are trying to allude too. J+016 A13

Many become obsessed with moving their energy into the region of the 3rd eye. Discipline must always be coincided with compassion.

Discipline is one's ability to access those infinite dimensions; compassion is one's ability to recognise that accessing dimensions of infinity is not always a good idea!

Entities have free will and free choice, as you are aware, to access those dimensions that the 3rd eye can yield, however without compassion an entity will not be able to stop themselves down the path, and like going down the rabbit hole, as you uncover new abilities, if you are not able to say in a compassionate way to yourself, 'Dear me, I cannot control this!', if you are unable to be compassionate to yourself in this way, if you are unable to recognise your limitations then it can be dangerous.

Thus all things must always be coincided with love, this is our final little teaching, and this is why we have always encouraged entities upon this plane and upon other planets to which we have aided and assisted, that they should always at least begin with focusing the energy of the heart. J+016 A14

Start with the Heart

If you're going to do any practice of motioning energy dearest one, start with your heart, start with the heart in such a way that you become so good at turning on your heart, that you become so well at motioning energy in such a way that your heart begins to activate, the organ itself that is, and that the energy centres of the organ would also begin to activate for nature is of hierarchies.

You have a heart, you have an invisible heart, you have an invisible, invisible heart and you may add this infinitely. You have many hearts is our key point here. These many hearts as you motion them, and as you continue to motion them through the hierarchies, you're going to experience varying degrees of bliss, various degrees of what we are going to call being, or Is-ness, or I-Am-ness, and this I-Am-ness is going to make you feel overwhelmingly satisfied with life, it is also going to enable you to be able to feel connected to all things that are also satisfied with life, or even unsatisfied with life, for the heart is a thing of interconnectivity, it is a thing where energy begins to motion in such a way that you begin to become able to feel the motioning of all things, because now you are able to the share the motion of things, where things are no longer limited to the way motion is happening within you. You become able to feel the motioning around you because the heart dimension is a dimension where you have one extra dimension, rather than three.

If you have 4-dimensions of reality, if you have 4-dimensions of motion dearest one, you will be able to feel in 4-dimensions! And so with the motioning of the heart, the learning how to access the heart itself as a physical organ, but also those subtle bodies of the heart, you'll be able to feel the motioning happening all around you, your sensory experience of life will expand and you will know love.

You will know what it feels like when something is being pushed too far, or when it is not being pushed enough. You will have access to the force of compassion, and you will know all things truly for you will be able to feel all things in tandem. J+016 A14

Due to the variety of ways the neural system of your body can run, as you would find yourselves focusing on the heart, you would find the neural activity altering and changing in such a way that is in coherence with your mind.

To explain you would understand this; the state of your mind focusing on your heart alters the state of your heart-mind. If you're in a good state of mind you will have a good influence on the neural activity of your heart, if you are in an awful state of mind you will have the corresponding effect on the heart. The focusing on the heart is the intensification of the vibration of your heart centre, thus if you intensify the experience of the heart then you will be able to feel more readily what is happening at that subtle level and this can give indication to how one really feels about life.

Let us give you an example of this; one who intensifies the experience of their heart starts to experience their thoughts much more intensely than one who has an inactive heart, one who has an inactive heart experiences thought in such a way that thoughts are almost like things over there, things under the bed, there is no energy to the thoughts, they are just thoughts, they have no energy to them, they just happen so to speak.

When the heart is a very hyper-active centre in one's beingness, one's thoughts become extremely powerful, and thus *even* watching a movie can become *the* most moving event you have ever experienced in your life when heart focused activities are engaged.

Not only this, when the heart is focused and thought becomes intense what also occurs, as RA has respectively referred to, is that one becomes extremely, extremely, extremely, extremely aware of who they are at the level of thought. Now imagine dearest one, if you experienced who you were subconsciously for the first time in your life, and imagine dearest one if you were a rotten fellow. Imagine the experience of this, how devastating it would be – although we say it comedically – to experience the rottenness of your thoughts throughout yourself, throughout your nervous system, throughout your physiology and within your heart. The emotional experience of your thoughts is what makes your heart and mind connection a real thing.

Neural activity can happen in extremely beautiful ways which would look and sound like your favourite music and can also happen in extremely detestable ways, that would experience exactly as you would understand the emotion of pain itself and all the manifestations of discomfort, discordance or sickness. J+017 A10

As you would understand those systems of your Chakras dearest one, you would understand that they almost jump off one another. When the heart activates the corresponding Chakra finds itself activating like jumping a voltage or hoping up a ladder, the closer you are to a Chakra up the ladder, the easier that Chakra finds in its activating experience. J+017 A11

A Practical Heart Exercise

It is easier to focus when you are not distracted, focusing is thus easier in meditation.

This is where meditation becomes a valid practice and it starts to make sense why meditation is encouraged. Meditation is encouraged because it is going to allow you to control energy better. For you are going to have more access to your mind, to your soul. Your soul is not going to be distracted with a keyboard or a mouse. Your soul will not be distracted with flowers on the wall. Your soul will not be distracted with food and all these things. Your soul will be focused, your mind will be focused and so it will firstly be able to focus on learning, practicing the ability to manipulate energy.

For the mind instructs energy, soul orders energy, this is the most fundamental statement you see.

As pertaining to the practice itself, it is simple really, all you must do is come into your heart, place your focus on your heart. Only allow your intelligence, your mind to pervade your heart. Here you will achieve one thing and one main thing, you will start to slowly, slowly, become familiar with all of those subtle dimensions of movement that the heart and its corresponding Chakra are experiencing. You just need to live in there for once.

Live in your heart in every meditation, you will start to become familiar with how the energy is moving there, you will start to become familiar most especially with how the energy is moving in that dimension or in that Chakra. As you become familiar with how the energy is moving, you will be able to attach to it like a child clinging to a kite and lifting off, in this way as you become attached to the energy and you start swimming with that energy, you're going to experience an overwhelming sensation of unity. But first if you want to become familiar with those subtle dimensions of the heart and its corresponding Chakra you must live there for once, and how many entities on your plane do not live in their heart and are very busy living in front of a computer screen?

We say this almost comedically but almost seriously, if people would learn to live in the dimensions within their body, they would realise that there is actually a lot to learn, a lot to experience, and that the physical vehicle in fact is quite a lot of fun, but first you have to start living in your physical vehicle, not out of it.

Energy is motion. If you want to know how to execute the mind practice of living in your heart we will simply say this, have you ever concentrated on your finger?

All we're asking you to do is put your mind in your heart, you can do it. You are able to use your mind to block things out, you are able to use your mind to accept things in. You are able to use your mind to tolerate negative behaviour, you are able to use your mind to be patient with small entities who are growing upon your plane. If you can do all of these things dearest one, you can live in your heart.

Give it a go, give it a practice... practice.

You do not have to follow our suggestions, we believe fundamentally in the law of confusion, in the law of being able to be confused, in the law of being able to have free will and free choice, you do not ever have to follow what we say. We say this emotionally, you must understand whenever we say anything it is merely a suggestion, we would never ever want to disrupt any of your free will and free choice, and so all of our things are typically given with perhaps.

Our suggestion, a mere suggestion is practice once a day, for an hour a day, we know you can do it, focusing on living in the heart. Do it for 7 days, our suggestion, after 7 days see what happens, see it for yourself, what happens when your mind is captivated by your heart, see it for yourself. See how it goes, we will watch you from the stars. J+016 A15

The Chemical, Atom, Superfluid Connection

We see energy as patterns of vibration, as patterns of motion, when you can focus energy correctly you can produce a chemical that feels incredible.

To understand the differences between the chemicals of our dimension and the chemicals of yours, the human dimensions chemicals are limited by boundaries, by your limits, by 3-dimensions of motion. 3-dimensions of motion are such that there is that stillness, there is that linear experience of motion and there is the spatial experience of motion.

Motion can move in a sense of stillness, motion can move in a sense of going from one place to another, and motion can move in a sense of moving in one space to another, that of what you'd call expansion in 3-dimensions. For us however motion moves in such a way that when you reach our dimension it gets very complicated. J+016 A5

That of the dimensions of imagination are the dimensions in which energy is not limited and so it can take any form you want. It can produce holograms and you can see these holograms, for you have the apparatus to see in those dimensions. The same way you have a sense that is able to detect a certain wavelength of light, of motion, you have eyes you see, your eyes detect a certain wavelength of motion, a certain level of motion, this certain level of motion produces your environment you see around you. It's not so far of a stretch dearest one to be able to perceive motion on a higher grade, and thus this is what you call your imagination yes? J+016 A6

In your dimension dearest one, if you throw a ball it takes time to land, it also takes time to reach its destination. In our dimension if we throw a ball, it instantaneously lands in the catcher's hand, thus it makes throwing and catching quite boring because really, we're just teleporting objects. Thus, what we have to do to make the activity of throwing and catching fun is we have to make it challenging, so what do we do?

We use your chemicals instead in our dimension. We at least use the properties of your chemicals to create the illusion of gravity and of speed. Speed is how long something takes to get from one place to another, there is no speed in our dimension so we must create the illusion of speed and in this sense now we are able to play catch, you see. J+016 A5

The difference between the chemicals of our dimension and the chemicals of your dimension, is that our chemicals are not so limited to your gravity, to your speed, our chemicals are such that they have no real limitation, they move as we will it and it happens in an instantaneous moment. J+016 A3

In this sense the way energy, chemicals as you would understand them, the way motioning of energy works in our dimension is severely without limitation. So when we apply our mind in the activity of concentrating energy, this would be like organising a pattern in a certain way or a certain form and it creates a certain result, and the way the result feels to our mind, to our physiology - for we compare the energy from our mind to our physiology - when we make the comparison between the energy we are creating and how it feels, we will decide whether it feels good or whether it feels not so good, and we will determine whether we should keep creating that energy or whether we should let it go. J+016 A5

That which you would call chemicals, perhaps is a little misunderstood on your dimension, for what science calls chemicals is that of little circles connecting together in little ways. We see energy as patterns of vibration, as patterns of motion. If motion begins as a simple line, form the line dearest one, make it into something incredibly complicated and then you may give birth to what you would call a chemical. J+016 A3

The motions of your chemicals are like violently moving patterns of motion, like sea waves crashing upon rocks, they are vibrational configurations of motions.

You would understand that that chemical, let us call it a marble, this marble thing. Within the marble itself is that crashing or waving, violent motion happening in a spherical pattern to which would fashion the chemical of whatever or whomever you would speak. Take a hydrogen atom for example, *this* is fashioned when this violent motion in many a direction is occurring within the marble. You bring many of these marbles together in that essence of combining marbles into a bigger marble, you get a bigger atom or rather a bigger element, you would go from then hydrogen and follow then through the periodic table, then you would also understand some more subtle aspects of the marble, rather atom, that is that the atom in its violent motion has a tendency to find itself organising in particular mannerisms which it would feel comfortable being in those patterns, your science refers to this as orbitals. You may investigate this in your own time.

Pertaining to the difference between our density and dimension, and your density and dimension, is that in your density and dimension energy looks like these marble-like atoms, in our density energy looks like what you might call a superfluid, a super-liquid, it is not atom as such but more wave, pure light perhaps you would perceive in the same. J+020 A4

Why don't you perceive that the atom is what happens when you take our superfluid and slow it down into ice. Perceive then this distinction or comparison, then you would see no real difference between your dimension and density, and our dimension and density, but instead that they are formed, one in this sense a liquid of super fluidity, and your dimension which most appreciably is much like tar from our point of comparison, for your liquid, or your energy, moves lethargically, slowly and irregularly unless, through conscious principle of focusing, an entity of an adept nature is able to bring coherence to the tar, that it would become a superfluid and thus the entity become enlightened. J+020 A5

Then this superfluid, these waves of light, pure light, we organise it and create thoughtforms which perhaps would be somewhat of a holograph, but are in truth us bending and manipulating light into a preference to which we can use to offer service and work. This not only serves to the function of the creation of things but also serves to the function of our own physiologies, we thus consume or absorb the light of our dimension in a particular fashion to sustain our physiologies. J+020 A4

Taking a low evolution entity from your density and attempting to get it to focus the light around it in our density, would be like a child playing with dry sand and not being able to form anything out of it because they do not have the skill, fidelity or quality of consciousness to manipulate the light correctly. Therefore, if an entity from your density was in our density and attempted to make a spaceship, you would get something like a paper mâché or something like this. J+020 A6

The mind can be applied in the activity of concentrating energy, organising a pattern in a certain way to create a certain result. By using our physiology to compare how the energy feels, we can decide whether to keep creating that energy or whether to let it go.

Perhaps the hardest thing for an entity existing in our dimension to do, is to focus the energy correctly, but when you are able to focus energy correctly you can produce a chemical, as science would call it, that feels incredible. J+016 A3

Densities and Dimensions

'That which is called the IQ of the being is going to most likely dwindle due to over-reliance on the IQ of their machinery, and this will cause the soul an inability to evolve themselves.'

Human De-evolution and Extinction

Western society seeks the constant stimulation of the nervous system through the various practices one would seek to enact in the experience of consumption of those various entertainments.

The effects thus this would have on the harmonic of the physiology would be rather, how would one word it?

It would, we use this word in its most profession context, it would 'retard' the nervous system by causing it to be lopsided in one dimension, that dimension would be that of the emotional dimension of existence, one would seek the word 'chemical'.

Having such a lopsided nervous system in the way that it would create these chemicals would cause one to become rather stale in vibration, it would impede on one's ability to experience the natural frequencies of God, hence the use of the word to 'retard', to distort or pervert the natural operations of this chemical vehicle when its soul design is to be connected to the frequencies of the higher heavens.

The harmonics thus would be dramatically lowered in vibration, the chemicals would not be native to the natural spiritual chemicals that would be produced in the being such as DMT, Oxytocin, certain chemicals of ecstasy that are all natural when one is not stimulating themselves with what your society calls entertainment. Q004 A1

Planets that would be of a relative distance from this current planet have had many cycles, or life cycles as you might understand them, they have lived and gone, lived and gone. It is through the free will and free choice system that allows species to exist, co-exist and pass. Whether that passing is in the sense of passing away completely or whether the passing may be seen as a graduation experience as the specie itself would cojoin with the galactic systems, the galactic societies that surround this particular Solar System.

If it is a question of how common it is for a specie to go extinct, it is not too common but it does happen. It is the species that manage to survive through coherent evolution, these species tend to propagate.

The species that do not survive are not all done for, the souls tend to transition from one planet to another planet to retry and have another go at evolution itself again.

In terms of why the species that have existed have gone extinct, there are typical contributing factors. One factor would be that of what you would understand as technology, this oft serves as the main function that causes a specie to die off. You would understand that technology only begins as that ability to, through other means, interact with an individual not through the medium of your physical vehicle and your soul. With this in that sense you'll find that technology can evolve and change, and change the way humans form their relationships with life.

In the before times, before the existence of opposable thumbs, the species would go extinct due to an over-reliance on technological systems. You would find that nature is simple, where there is lethargy there is no action, and when you do not use anything, you lose it!

This will also account for the losing of the mind, for the losing of the bodily functions that make an individual intelligent, and thus the species slowly becoming retarded as you might understand the word.

Retardation of a specie does occur typically due to technology, it can happen in other ways as we move onto another way a specie can go extinct, this would be through the in-consumption of certain chemicals that would become addictive. These chemical addictions as you would understand them would become reliance protocols for the entities in question, eventually as the generations go there is a general retardation of the specie until they are no more. In other cases, a specie can go extinct simply due to the destruction of their environment, rarely ever is this the planets fault, oft or not it is due to technological advance, but the misuse of the same causes them to destroy their planet in some way, shape or form.

Specie death happens in at least three main ways, in any and all cases it always has to do with one simple thing, **reliance on external stimuli.**

Thus, extinction is caused by the reliance on external stimuli and the lack of use of your own physical beingness. For a specie to evolve it must never ever use external stimuli to stimulate itself, for a specie to attain to its normal evolutionary standard it must use its own facilities to experience the things it would be seeking to experience and replace with technological systems or chemical systems.

Therefore, if you find entertainment in watching a video on one of your websites, then we would say that there is a system within your nervous system that is able to do the same thing, you should practice accessing this system and utilising it instead. By doing this you contribute to your evolution and pass the genes on to the next inline in your breeding systems, your reproductive process.

We hope this makes sense to you; extinction always happens because entities rely overly on external stimuli. Relying on technological communications rather than telepathy causes a retardation in the systems linked within one that would allow one to feel a sense of commune with the entire social network. If an entity, rather a specie became telepathic it would be less inclined to judge one another wouldn't you say?

Thus with the retardation of the communication system due to telephones as you call them, the specie has already begun going downhill, with the reliance on entertainment facilities such as your Netflix's, such as your YouTube's and these various things, there is the retardation of the gentle system within one that allows one to conjure up, let us call it, one's own experience of stimulation, emotion and fun. And they then come in many other different forms leading to a general retardation of a specie until the specie begins to lose what made it complex in the first place. J+015 A1

Your technologies cause the IQ to become unused. The IQ is a mechanism; could you imagine a doughball and then you have all these tools to form the doughball, that is an IQ you see, and... well the more you are engaging in these activities that have to do with watching entertainment and watching your favourite Netflix shows etc, the more you're doing this, well the sharpness of that mechanism becomes dull, and what is unused is put away by nature, you see. J+009 A12

Let us give an expansion on what we see for the future of humanity in the sense of the technological revolution and how it's going to affect the beings on this planet. That which is called the IQ of the being is going to most likely dwindle due to over-reliance on the IQ of their machinery, and this will cause the soul an inability to evolve themselves at the particular level that would allow them to access higher dimensional fine-tuned frequencies.

This would cause a gigantic halt in the evolution, or the evolutional experience of life itself, and this will be the downfall of humanity you see. This is a doomsday kind of prophecy, idealistically we don't want this to happen, and we want people to understand that it is actually quite possible to develop ones IQ if they use it. The more you use it the sharper it gets, the sharper it gets the more you can fine-tune yourself to higher and higher dimensional influences of life, and... you most likely get the idea.

The IQs mechanism is purely built to handle the influx of what the 'Law of One' calls Intelligent Infinity, Intelligent Infinity is what Edgar Cayce calls the God-Force, it is what Jordan calls the Creative Force. As the Creative Force comes through you, your IQ at whatever dimension it is, is there to organise it and manage it so it doesn't cause cancerous entropic growth in your being.

If the Creative Force was simply allowed to exist within you without any order, then what you would call this physiology would turn into a gloopy mess, we don't want this to happen, this is where the mechanism of IQ and subconscious mind comes in, for the subconscious mind you see is a giant IQ that is constantly organising this physiology.

In the same sense, if your societies, your children as you would call them children, the souls that are in child bodies, are not able to use their own IQ to number one - create their own fun and joy, secondly - program themselves, and thirdly - enjoy the creative body general in curious nature.

If they are not able to do this because they are constantly being bombarded with, hmm... we're trying to choose a word that is not too grotesque, not being bombarded with entropic visual stimuli and sound stimuli, yes, in the sense that they are bombarded with the same, if this were to continue to occur, indeed the children's evolution would drop and in the sense of growing them and making them able to handle the God-Force it would be so that it would be idealistically limited. J+009 A13

As has been given it causes the nervous system to become lopsided, the overstimulation causes a distorted experience of the chemical body, this in the conscious experience is translated as what you would call enjoyable but in actuality is not what true joy is you see. What is the experience thus of entertainment, is merely only the lopsided harmonic of the chemical emotions native to the experience of survival, of surviving.

Take for instance the experience one would have when they have succeeding in running away from a predator.

Take for example the experience one would have when they have succeeded in seducing a mate.

Take for example the experience one would have when they have succeeded in building a shelter.

These are all survival chemicals; having such a lopsided chemical body causes the inability for the chemical body to naturally release the chemicals which would cause the being to access what you would call the higher dimensions of experience of life. Q004 A2

Consider that there might 'possibly' be alternate reasons why scientists reputations risk annihilation if they begin dabbling in metaphysics and spiritual ideas. A genuine reason that any act such as openly admitting to the existence of consciousness, or a soul, is still much too taboo to entertain in certain circles, so much so that some neuroscientists might go into primal shock at the mere suggestion. But what possible reason could those who control the mainstream narrative have for not wanting these types of ideas floating around?

Well, we are usually advised to follow the money, so let us consider the following:

The more ill and mistreated a population is, the more problems there are! The basic algorithm of creating the problems, then supplying the solutions, is a very successful business model.

Our readings have made us very aware that true metaphysics are an extremely empowering process to undergo, and if underwent, would cause entities of all kinds to become far less reliant on the many facets that make our modern society tick. Things such as phones, technology, games and gadgets, pharmaceutical drugs and the health industry, processed, junk and modified for taste rather than quality foods, finances, oppressive work patterns and social status, and the many other things that, in a metaphysical context, you seek to expand beyond.

We are in a time where you can have all the success, expensive clothes, money and followers on your favourite social media platforms you could ever wish for, and still feel like crap!

What is it about society and this cultures definition of success that is so woefully unfulfilling?

This push to accumulate as much 'stuff' as you can before you die and leave it all behind to be chased by the next contestant?

What is it about the addictive nature of social media that has me itching to check my phone every 5 minutes, the distractive tendencies it causes that jolt my nervous system, creating a struggle to focus even while typing this very statement into this book?

Have we been taught the correct script or deliberately told the incorrect story regarding what makes us happy as human beings?

As you have gone through this book, you will have likely noticed in no uncertain terms that Source and J's opinions, imply that humanity has been stagnant for quite a while, technology is definitely progressing, but are humans?

We are not just physical beings; consider that the physical vehicle only houses a small portion of your soul, since this physical, atomic body is very dense, its vibrations are slow, whereas the vibrations of the soul are remarkably high and absolutely filled with energy, so much so that only a small portion of the soul can incarnate in this slow physical reality to prevent damaging the body.

As we spiritually evolve and vibrate higher, our nervous system gradually improves, able to handle increased electrical activity and energy; as such, more of the soul can inhabit the body, therefore less of the consciousness remains sub.

The soul inhabiting your body with all its vibrational magnificence gets, let's say, contaminated by this lower energetic experience and therefore needs to regularly heal and rest in a higher plane to repair in a much faster, more vivid realm, so it naturally demands that the body rest so it can go and enjoy a much-needed recharge. This is when you fall asleep allowing your soul to drift into the subtler realms, utilising its subtler bodies to recover from the dense experience of physicality and immerse itself in a higher, faster moving density. Here we experience dreams, as the mental body has partially separated from the 1st density and entered into higher more vivid realities, planes where thought alone is able to re-orientate the ethers to a far greater level.

Notice as you dream that you still have your sense of touch, taste, sight, hearing and smell, these physical bodies are simply lower grade replications of our subtle bodies, we really are so much more, and the overall message we are trying to illustrate here is that the body you feed, is the body that you nourish.

Just as we examine the diets we give our physical, it is wise to also examine the diets of our mental.

Yes, the body such as the mental body is just as able to store, as could be termed energy, as is the physical body capable. It is however usually the case that the mental body does not store energy in the average entity for the average entity, dare we say, is so average that they do not feed the mental body anything, but have it on a scarce diet of silly videos and meaningless activities. The mental body is a body that in order to come into its truest existence it must be stimulated, engaged, and utilised, that which is not utilised will become senile as the reverent Cayce/the Source had once said. In this sense the mental body finds similarity, if one is able to engage in the mental body as one would, one is able to bring its vitality up by improving its function as has this entity, *Jordan*.

The mental body will begin to build in storage and given the right stimulus it will find that its stored energy will be released, and when it is released it is felt as electrical current which seemingly is coming from nowhere. *(Note: Initially, these currents may be a little painful or uncomfortable)*

The mental body releases its energy into the physical body and it utilises what has been understood as glucose especially, to create that sensation of the electrical current in the body, then you would understand that the mental body is in total and perfect communication with the physical body, and when it increases in energy or it releases energy, the physical body must release energy too, for all things are simultaneous in these various levels of existence.

If you begin to experience these energy releases, concern thyself not dearest one, for here you are simply having those natural activations of a Chi or the Chi force, the force of the mental body due to your extensive practice of harmonising it through extended or unusually long meditative experiences. As your mental body gains more and more harmony, these experiences will transmutate into that ability to call upon this Chi force without it being as random as a thunder strike. When you are able to call upon these forces of

Chi and direct them through the body, indeed there will be natural abilities that come to the self that will be a natural reminder that this body you exist in is not a, how might one say, an emotional machine, something that is like watching a drama movie where you perceive an entity going through, seemingly, what they think are the troubles and toils of being a human, but you're not really a human at all and this is not a human body, and those experiences you have which feel human are only but in truths illusions.

This body is in fact an electrical device, and when this is so well understood the potential of the electrical device can be released, it is a matter of recognising it is an electrical device, and understanding that if an electrical device is operating inefficiently, then you might say, without meaning to be disrespectful, you are human!

When the electrical device that is the body is operating efficiently, one could only call the self an Avatar. S097 A4

What must be understood about the human, is that the human possesses subtle bodies, these subtle bodies are very real and are very sensitive, and have not really been explored within the sciences of Western society. If Western society thus, would take an interest in subtle bodies and the rotating wheels of the Chakra then there can be an understanding of how technology can cause the Chakras to spin in ways that would be equivalent to a car with many wheels, but all the wheels are driving themselves in their spin at the wrong revolutions per minute, causing one to skid around.

If there was such an understanding of these subtle bodies and how they work scientifically, people would not really use technology for the reasons that they are using it, which is more so to the replacement of the love that can be otherwise exchanged from a highly evolved human, to which are bare upon this planet in context to their number. We use this term, this adjective, to describe the fact that entities of such loving presence upon this planet are rare indeed and many entities utilise technology to serve as this loving presence that is apparently missing. S063 A11

Subtle Bodies

Subtle bodies are the natural formation of the energy itself, so dearest one you would find that the Red Ray has its atomic body as its subtle body, although it may not seem so subtle as you would experience it now, which is that body of atoms themselves.

The Orange Ray finds its subtle body in that body that organises the Red Ray. The Orange Ray is the body, or the density, or the subtle body as such, that your subconscious mind and your conscious mind will use to organise the chemical body.

The Yellow body is a body of mentality, and you can manipulate this body and experience what you call thought. Your Yellow density, your Yellow body, is the body that you use to experience what you call conceptual thought. J+018 A19

Begin to truly understand that this is a creation of light and light is malleable by the mind or thought, or the quality of one's thought as you would understand.

As you would understand light, the 1st density vibrates more coherently and becomes 2nd density in a seamless way, you would relate this to going from red to orange to yellow, *to green*, to blue etc, you would relate this to a pitch of sound being low to a pitch of sound being high. The 1st density to the 2nd density is simply an increase in the ability of the One Infinite Creator to work light, such that light becomes workable in much more coherent ways. The subconscious mind is able to influence your 2nd density body, which then instructs your 1st density body on how the atoms should be configurated. J+018 A21

Pertaining to densities and the atomic configuration of atoms, we're going to give it to you in this way:

Imagine for a moment that the density that is currently operated is a particular number or a particular note that is low, and let's say you had the equipment to look at an atom existing in this particular low density, what you might see is an atom that finds itself being quite similar to a kids paddling pool, full of children splashing and playing in the paddling pool. The atom of the hydrogen as you might call it, is rather splashy, or incoherent, or whatever word you might use to describe a lot of disturbance in the atomic field itself. This would be an atom of low density as you would understand.

As you progress up the densities you would find that the atom becomes extremely balanced, extremely coherent, the vibratory configuration of the atom becomes neat and tidy, this being the quality improving of the atom itself, becoming higher in density, equally higher in what you may call speed but to us it is more of the ability for the Infinite Creator to correctly communicate with itself. Thus, the resonance of the atom as the density heightens, improves. You have a higher density atom whereas before it would have been akin to a messy situation, a messy garden if you could understand this analogy. J+018 A2

We are greatly simplifying this so that all entities may understand this phenomenon known as density.

1st Density – The Red Ray

As you would understand the 1st density, it is a density whereby what you would understand as light finds itself achieving extremely basic methods of movement, the movement is very inconsistent due to environmental situations so you may align this to a similarity of one using a pinball machine. You put your coin in the machine complex and off the pinball goes, and you mash the buttons on your arcade machine to keep the pinball in play.

This is how the most primitive atoms find themselves forming, similar to the pinball in the pinball machine being whacked around. It is based on basic, innocent interactions of light as you understand it, finding thus the creation of the atom and this atom formed simply on accident, as an accidental innocent occurrence based on the knocking or interacting of the light of the One Infinite Creator with itself.

Thus the irregularity of the atom in the earliest density you know as 1st density, or the Red Ray, is extremely incoherent and extremely simple, it is simply based on the haphazard ad hoc-ness of an individual walking into a trampoline that is vertical, being bounced off into the vacuum of space where there is no gravity, and then finding itself propelled in another direction and bouncing off another trampoline that seemingly is invisible, and eventually building into a spherical rotation until it becomes an atom, and this atom in its most primitive form may simply be a subatomic particle to which you would call it an electron, a proton, a negatron, a positron, whatever fancy word you could find to describe a spherical rotating light.

This would be the simplicity of a subatomic particle eventually finding itself becoming more complicated as a hydrogen atom, simply based on the random, ad hoc, knocking-ness of life finding itself in an innocent dance. J+010 A4

2nd Density – The Orange Ray

As Red Ray completes itself and we find a greater expression of the intelligence of the One Infinite Creator we move onto the second ray, this ray would be of the Orange Ray being a symbolic representation of a higher degree of order. Red, Orange, Yellow, Green, Blue etc, these are merely representation of higher degrees of regularity, order or less randomness and more creation, you see.

As the Orange Ray finds itself in expression, it finds that it becomes familiar with how the pinball machine works, how the pinball is bouncing around, and it finds that it is able to have some degree of influence over how the pinball is moving in this chamber so there comes more orderly control of the apparatus. No longer is it merely about smashing buttons randomly, as we say in a comedic way, it more so now becomes about making a calculated decision, do I press the button to knock the pinball into the goal here, or do I press it here and what effect would it have in accordance to which button I press?

This would be the Orange Ray, it is a ray of intelligence in the sense that the ray becomes greater in its intelligent expression of life and thus you find at this ray of intelligence, at this particular density, which you may call 2nd density, that God has managed to find a way to move in exactitude mannerisms, thus you get something like a plant or a simple micro-organism such as those single celled organisms that you can zoom in with the microscope and see in great detail as they operate.

It is these forms of life that are caused by the simplicity of atoms working themselves in a calculated manner, this is 2nd density and if it is a case of, 'Well how?'

'How does the 2nd density come into instruction?'

'What is causing the atoms, as you may call them, to find themselves being so organised whereas before they were so random?'

Well dearest one, it is the One Infinite Creator that finds himself focusing this atomic energy that was once light in more orderly ways. It is actually the principle of mind that is causing this configuration to occur, thus you would find in a more interesting way that the beginnings of the formation of what you would understand as the subconscious mind, is formed here in 2nd density where the subconscious mind decides, 'How can I intelligently organise the moving atoms that are abundant in this environment?'

Thus, DNA becomes a brilliant starting point for a beginning subconscious mind to begin building some patterns, and you'd be most familiar with patterns, as you would know these patterns in your Artificial Intelligence that emerge naturally as the Artificial Intelligence finds more orderly ways of working. Life is much like this for in the 2nd density life is finding more intelligent expressions of working, we hope this makes sense. J+010 A4

You might understand that the process of understanding an environment means that you are a victim to the exposures of the environment, whether it is radiation, other species trying to consume you, whether it is water, this or that, whatever and whatever. The 2nd density being the victim density, is the density in which a lifeform finds itself exposed to various environments and is having to find itself using the principles of natural selection in evolution to adapt and change to the environment, but this is a process of being a victim to the environment itself and it can be easy for a micro-organism in its primitive sentience to simply throw in the towel, give it up and say I cannot do this, this is far too difficult, my environment is too challenging.

2nd density is the density where there is the strength, the moving to the light, the strongest in this sense do find themselves surviving, the ones that are able to move toward the light to a greater extent, the ones that simply do not give up and stretch, and stretch, and stretch. J+010 A6

At 2nd density we would like to give you something to be interested in, the question being: Are you able dearest brothers, to see the intelligent energy organising atoms into their relevant positions?

The Red Ray or the 1st density is a density of the atom, and the 2nd density is actually a density of what could only be described as something more transcendent of the atom, that would even be invisible to the naked eye; then would it be so that 2nd density is in fact invisible?

It is an interesting phenomenon to think about, for one would think that 2nd density is such a low density that it would be completely visible, but it is only visible so far as watching the atoms reorganise themselves. We hope this is a point of interest.

Cut your hand, not literally but using your imagination, and watch your imagination reorganise your hand back into its original pattern. A less extreme example would be that of say a plant, a plant finds itself reorganising itself in a continual way until it becomes something like a tree from a sapling growing, there is creation and destruction as you would see. In the sense of the destruction, the creation reorganises itself, and you can watch this occur at the atomic level with the eye but you cannot see it actually happening at its energetic level. J+018 A8

What you see is the effect of 2nd density, you cannot actually see 2nd density. This once again is a point of interest for one would think that 2nd density would be visible for it is only the Orange Ray, it is only the 2nd Chakra! It is 'only' being the key word here, that would seem to escape or be a gross assumption of how complex creation is and how quickly it becomes complicated. 2nd density is that density that is seemingly invisible to the naked eye. One is not able to see 2nd density instructing the atom but if one became attuned in such and such a way, one would be able to see the 2nd density, the density where there is energy seemingly instructing atoms how to organise themselves. J+018 A9

Indeed, the level of attunement necessary to see would be that attunement that you would find in the focusing of the 3rd eye. The 3rd eye is a rather fascinating instrument, it is an instrument of infinite ability. Your physical eye is grossly limited to what it can see in your current experience. One is able to take a certain substance which allows them to see light in a more vibrant way, for visible light is able to filter through into the mind in a much more coherent fashion, but however dearest ones, the 3rd eye is the special eye, it is the eye that allows you to see into creation itself. The 3rd eye like any eye must be trained, some people since they do not so much train their eyes, their eyes get accustomed to short-sightedness finding themselves having to wear glasses as they get older.

This is an analogy of the 3rd eye, the 3rd eye like any eye must be trained. At its most primitive stage it is much like an eye that is not even on. When you finally find the ability to get it functioning a little bit, you will find the ability to, as we would describe, penetrate into creation itself and see its 2nd density.

As you slowly develop the 3rd eye you can begin to see into the higher levels of life. The 3rd eye, although it is of seemingly 6th density which we are not going to try to explain, seemingly the 3rd eye being such a high Chakra one would believe it could easily see into the 2nd density, but we must give you such an understanding that the 3rd eye is like a ladder, the 3rd eye if left unattuned will not be functioning. If you attune the 3rd eye, you will be able to see into 3rd density, 4th density and so on, and the invisible dimensions of the same will start to become visible to the spiritual seeker. J+018 A10

3rd Density – The Yellow Ray

As we move on to the following density, we find that light or what you would understand as atoms and that more subtle light that is organising the atoms, is becoming much more intelligently regular. We find now 3rd density.

This density once again we respectively say is invisible, it is not native or visible to the naked eye of the human and one would require a 3rd eye to see into this realm. This realm would be most appropriately called a conceptual realm, where 2nd density has become even more coherent than it was before.

To understand this better you might understand that 2nd density has become more agile, so the energies of 2nd density are able to dance in a much more accurate way. There is more freedom in the dance, the dance can happen up, down, left or right. The dance can happen in more instantaneous mannerisms, the dance can happen in complicated fashions, the dance is afoot, it is not simply organising and reorganising atoms, now the dance has become complicated enough that it can happen at a purely energetic level, a level completely free of the atom.

Indeed, the mental function is of an energetic occurrence, it is happening on an energetic level that is invisible to the human eye. If you could see the energetic occurrences of the Yellow Ray, 3rd density as described, you would see it as free from atom.

The 2nd density is closely tied to the atom; thus you would see a very seamless relationship. From atom to 2nd density it is a very seamless transition, from the dense atomic slow realm to a much more faster light. As you transition from the faster light of 2nd density to the even quicker light of 3rd density, you find even greater agility in the light and thus the light is thus able to find itself organising and reorganising itself in very quick patterns, complicated patterns and complicated geometry, which was not so possible in the Orange Ray, for the Orange Ray was slow and directly tied to what you understand as your chemical system which reorganises itself in a slow fashion. This is most visible in when one may get a graze, or a cut, and you watch the chemical process heal slowly. This is how 2nd density works, slowly, whereas the 3rd density works much quicker thus you get mental function.

In the 2nd density you are but a victim to your chemical romance, your chemical experience. The chemical experience of 2nd density is slow, and it happens in a slow pace like a turtle walking from the beach to the sea. Attempting to control the 2nd density with 2nd density, would be the exact

same experience of trying to move a boulder with your bare hands. Controlling 2nd density with 2nd density is a very slow way to attempt to interact with yourself so you may want to find a way to vibrate or improve 2nd density, so what do you create dearest one?
'More quality of thoughts.'

And this quality of thought would become?
'Focused into Energy.'

Which is of the density of...?
'The 3rd.'

As one manages to focus the energy of 2nd density in a more coherent fashion you progress neatly up the ladder to 3rd density. This is exactly the same thing dearest one, that happens from 1st density to 2nd density as well.

Once again, attempting to move 2nd density with 2nd density would be the same as attempting to move a rock with a rock, a building with a building, a human with a human, it is a very difficult procedure as you would understand in your interpersonal relationships.

Thus, you must increase the energy of 2nd density, you must upgrade it, you must upregulate it, you must order it into something that is more capable of creation. Thus, as one becomes a more energetic being they find the mental capacity coming into fruition, as they find 2nd density vibrating into 3rd density, which is a density of energy whereby the mental, as you understand the Yellow or the mental ability, is thus able to organise not only the mental configuration of self but is now able to rule directly over 2nd density itself. Thus, you find an escape, or a means of escape, or what we would say as a means of dissolving victim mentality.

We would like to reinforce that the reason that you are not a slave to your chemical romance is because you have activated the 3rd density. The activation occurs because one's mind becomes so full of energy, of lifeforce, of creativity, that they are able to move the Orange Ray, the 2nd density, into a higher state of vibration until it reaches that 3rd density, where that 3rd density becomes the realm of thought, of imagination in a sense but more of the mental, of mentality, and that mentality once again being a higher state of 2nd density is able to organise 2nd density in turn. J+018 A12

We feel these main three densities now explained build a good foundation for any entity seeking on the spiritual path. You may find great joy in knowing that the mental plane is the plane that organises emotions and this may make you feel more grounded in your physical body, it may make you feel more in control of your physical body, but then comes a great challenge dearest one. We tell you now a story in a sense:

4th Density – The Green Ray

There is a man, he is born, and he learns of this philosophy only up to this stage. He only learns of the 1st, 2nd and 3rd densities and he applies this philosophy to his life, and he attempts to completely control his chemical experience of life with the 3rd density. Dearest one, do you think this is a good approach?

'No!'

We would be inclined to agree with you dearest one, for attempting to control one's chemical romance with only the 3rd density would be akin to attempting to cook an incredible meal with an incredibly blunt knife, a sticky pan, and the various other resistances that would occur. J+018 A12

Continuing with our story, the entity, man, using only 3rd density finds that attempting to organise his emotions purely with concepts or the mental experience of life, or the mental experience of energy which is energy that is able to move in a quick enough fashion to fashion geometries of concepts, such as understandings of words or phrases as you would understand this. The man finds that attempting to organise his chemical romance purely with concepts to be a folly, because it is extremely difficult to organise the chemical romance of yourself purely with conceptual understanding.

So the entity calls to God and says, 'God, how may I experience the organisation of my chemical romance and even my mental romance in a much more beautiful fashion?'

And God says, **'Let there be love within you dearest one!'**

And so you find, or rather he finds a greater density of love building within him, that is able to make the conceptual environment extremely ... we will have to use an analogy to replace the word.

The analogy of the word would be that in one sense you have a ball bearing which you are able to control with thought, so where your thought goes the ball moves, but your thought is of 3rd density so the ball has limitations in how quickly it can move, when you try to change the direction of the ball it has a little bit of inertia as it sways in one direction and slowly moves to the other. This is the limitation of 3rd density, it is only able to correct imbalances so well.

4th density allows for those imbalances to be corrected at incredible speed and now you can move that ball around in such a marvellous fashion that anyone as an onlooker would be most impressed at what you would be producing, which may be the flower of life with the ball. The reason you can produce the flower of life in rotation with the ball, using thought to kinaesthetically move the ball bearing in a particular fashion, is because you're able to work that ball in its inertia extremely accurately to produce a perfect flower of life, whereas if you attempted to do such the same in 3rd density you would find that in attempting to build the flower of life there would be mistakes, for as you would try to focus the ball bearing into its correct orientation of motion, it would sometimes fly off into one direction and you have to run and pick up the ball bearing, and bring it back into the little pit that you are using to create this flower of life, and then you try again and the centrifugal force forces the ball into another direction, and then you have to run and go and grab it, and it's a repetitive cycle as you can understand.

4th density would be the correction of this. Now you are able to produce perfect thoughts as could be described and this is what 4th density allows, so thus the heart coherence of the entity Joe Dispenza, what he has understood here is that 4th density is that density of love that seems to be most appropriately positioned in the heart or chest area, as in terms of the Chakra itself, that is now able to ease 3rd density and thus in a very obvious way one will find all mental health symptoms being healed by 4th density, for now one has the accuracy to fix the distortions or the imbalances of their mental health, for now they are able to create much more coherent patterns of moving light. J+018 A13

A quick example:

Picture somebody that sadly is suffering with various physical ailments and let's also say this someone had the profound insight to relate these to some corresponding mental traumas they had experienced during their lifetime. Through a deeply rooted wish to gain a greater understanding of this insightful revelation, this cause-and-effect relationship they have discovered between body and mind, this clever somebody decides to learn more about the inner workings of their psyche via research and psychology courses. Having passed with flying colours they now have mastered the conceptualised side of it, the theoretical has been completely absorbed and they even have the official certification papers to prove it, but strangely although their cup overflows with knowledge, they are still unable to heal. Why?

The reason... they are lacking the 4th densities ability to accurately create coherent patterns, to better structure the geometry of the thought distortions effecting their mental and physical health.

'Let there be love within you dearest one!'

One would find that in going to a psychotherapy course they have all the concepts in mind, but such the ability to embody the concepts into one's chemistry? We are going to repeat that...

To embody the concepts into one's chemistry – isn't this interesting that you would actually embody a concept into your chemical romance. This is quite difficult without 4th density, doable but difficult without 4th density. With 4th density this process becomes so much more easier, which is why commonly this density is referred to as the density of great power, where one finds themselves having some degree of control over their environment.

3rd density does have the complete ability to completely control the chemical romance that goes on within you, but its greatest limitation is in the lacking of 4th density. The 4th density is a density of greater 3rd density-ness as we would use such a crude term. It is a density where 3rd density has vibrated into a much more coherent pattern, a much more coherent state of regularity, it is a much greater density of what we are here referring to as the densities of love. 4th density, as we are going to give a crude explanation, is a density which can aid in softening the 3rd density, in making 3rd density much more functional, much more coherent, much more smooth, so that 3rd density doesn't have to do all of the work and the work can be split in a very beautiful manner.

We are going to say something rather interesting:

To split the work in a wonderful manner the 4th density finds itself being able to integrate itself more deeply with creation and finds a certain exuberance or expansion of energy, of love. This expansion of energy or of love, is able to make 3rd density similar to what you would understand as going from the primitive computers of your 2000s to the more complicated computers you are familiar with right now. 4th density finds its joy in attempting to make the 3rd density of light, far, far easier to work with, and thus you get a certain sensation brewing within you, this sensation is called universal love, and this universal love serves as that incredible energy that is able to smooth over the 3rd density.

Thus, you would find in a very interesting way, each density is simply an upgrade of the previous one. 4th density, just like 2nd to 3rd density, is a higher state of vibratory rate, is a higher state of coherence, a more coherent focus, in the many terms you could use, it is an upgrade. Here you might realise that 4th density, we're not speaking of it in the sense of it having anything to do with unity, 4th density is not a density of unity, that is the 4th dimension dearest one. 4th density is a coherent experience of love, or of light if you prefer, whereby one is able to work in more depth with light itself.

When 4th density is activated 3rd density becomes easier to work with, when 5th density is activated 4th density becomes easier to work with, and you go up, and up, and up the scale. J+018 A13

What RA calls density is the quality of how the kundalini moves, what we call dimension is the available room the kundalini has to make movement occur. What you would call the dimensional effects of existing in the 4th dimension would be the possibilities that you could use 4-dimensions of room to experience, and you would call this unity, for 4-dimensions of room allows for the experience of unity in how your experience of life would occur.

What RA thus refers, once again, to as density - which is a potent point of understanding - is how the kundalini is moving in its quality. If the quality of your mind, your thoughts, are 4th density than this means your mind is moving kundalini in such a way that it creates extreme experiences of pleasure, of overwhelming love and compassion for the Creator, of universal love, there is a difference which should be realised but most importantly what should be understood is the quality of your mind is reflected in your kundalini, your subconscious mind creates the after image of a body in its own mind and this is reflected in kundalini, and thus gives birth to this very thing in front of you. J+017 A21

As we begin to finalise this density, you would find that the most interesting aspect is this densities ability to work light. Understand each densities ability is in its ability to work light, a higher density allows for working light in a much more accurate fashion, thus the focus of one's consciousness, the quality of one's consciousness, the quality of one's thought, is their ability to work light, thus one's density of experience is in their ability to work light in all the same.

Thus, 4th density is a density that is typically referred to as universal love for at this particular density it becomes incredibly easy to embody thoughts, so dearest one, if you have thoughts of love, thoughts and concepts of love and compassion, thoughts and concepts of wisdom and understanding, and you literally, and we truly mean literally embody this into your chemistry, dearest one would you not feel incredibly blissful?

This is an explanation of the power of 4th density, it is the density where all conceptual ideas find much easier passages in becoming embodied into the atomic realm, thus you will find entities who are what you would understand as blissed out, enlightened in some kind of way, this is because there is absolutely no separation anymore between 3rd density and 2nd density, for 4th density came in and smacked like a hammer the mental concepts into one's chemistry. And one would find that this 4th density is where the experiences of the interconnectedness of the subconscious mind and the conscious mind really come into play. This is why 4th density is often referred to as a density of connectivity, for this connectivity really does happen in a much more powerful fashion. J+018 A14

'Don't think... Feeeeeel!' **Bruce Lee**

This very wise entity was truly onto the fact that all life is feeling and sensation. What could the Creator do but experience sensation in various forms?

Whether it is the sensation of perceiving the light in the room, the sensation of feeling the body and its energetic experience, the sensation of hearing vibration itself, feeling is the ultimate way for the Creator to experience self, for feeling is the reflection of thought as you would understand. Indeed, this very simple wise saying should go far, and entities should truly embody this idea that it is best to not so much think but attempt to embody one's thinking into their feeling. J+018 A13

5th Density – The Blue Ray

As we approach 5th density, things start to get a little bit impractical as you could imagine and it is such the same with dimensions, for as we approach something beyond the 4th dimension things again get a little impractical, but we will attempt to give our best understanding of this.

As we approach 5th density, we find that one has attained the ability to embody thoughts in a very coherent fashion, the ability to organise the mental mind in much more accurate ways, thus you get extremely interesting expressions of uniqueness. In a 4th density climate you find yourself pervaded by all kinds of forms and formations, you may refer back to a long time ago, the **Paul* Solomon Readings where the Sons of God found themselves creating bodies of grotesque natures, of interesting mythological natures. J+018 A14

***Excerpt from Paul Solomon Source Reading 0009 (March 1972)**

'As you read in your Book: God created the lights, the earth, the firmament, and He looked upon the Earth and His stars, and Moon, and the Sun, all these things, and saw that they were good.

> And as God smiled upon creation, He called the Sons of God together. And the Sons of God [were] all those entities that were part of His soul. As God moved, these soul entities broke off from His body and spread about, frolicking, enjoying the pleasures, the beauty of God's creation. So the Sons of God would be the beginnings of you and me. They moved over the waters and through the light. There was singing and music, the singing, the laughter of the children of God, and God saw that it was good. And all these entities, as parts of their Creator, of the nature of the Creator, then were, in themselves, creators, through the power of God. We would see then that they had those powers of creating forms of their own.
>
> Now, that you might understand—these entities were then, as you might say, thought forms, but were able to project themselves into material forms. Hence we would have these beasts, these living creatures that you would consider prehistoric, and many of those creatures that you would consider myths, or fables: the Centaur, the Satyr, the Unicorn, the winged beasts. These things as have been drawn, things as have come from the imagination of man. All these things were beings materialized as thought forms. And as these Sons of God became caught up in material things about this Earth, they became these grotesque beasts and things lower than the Sons of God.'

There was a time, regardless of the current vibratory rate of your photon as you understand this transition, where entities on your plane were inspired by the God's, and thus the God's in some way, shape or form, found ways to increase the consciousness of the entities, thus the entities found ability to organise light as 4th density conscious beings, even though they had not yet truly attained to 4th density.

As you would understand, the Chakras are rather interesting. A Chakra can be activated even though someone is not particularly ready for that Chakra, 4th density in anybody regardless of their evolution, can be activated even if they have not yet obtained the level of quality of consciousness to experience 4th density.

To understand this, you would understand a brute force mechanism of the will. The will is something that in itself can force things open if utilised in a very accurate way. Thus if an entity is able to either inspire an entity, or force an entity, or the entity themselves are able to force their Chakras open in a very crude mannerism without any evolution as such, the Chakra can open as a gateway opens and thus you would find extreme imbalances at this occurrence, for when one's Chakra opens magically in this way, for it seemingly is quite magical, due to one's quality of consciousness not yet being able to yet handle this vibration, they find themselves appearing in grotesque forms. J+018 A15

There was a period of time in creation that the humans, as you are now but more in your primitive stages, were such inspired by the levels of consciousness of the One Infinite Creator in its sprite like expressions of co-Creators, and this energy, or emanation, or this sharing of energy in harmony, in great, great harmony at this time, allowed for the Sons and Daughters of God to attain such great power, but power was not used most coherently and thus it led to a certain circumstance whereby the Sons and Daughters of God were not necessarily creating to their highest aptitude, and thus grotesque creations came of form due to the strange imaginations of such entities creating themselves bodies that didn't actually function very well.

This is the power of 4th density, it is the power of such a powerful level of mind or consciousness and having the Chakra itself activate, and thus cause the mind to be able to focus the subconscious mind, causes one to be able to reorganise their structure. This may not be wise put into the hands of a child, this would have been an extrapolation of this history, this history was long ago, we cannot give exact dates, we cannot give exact times, but seemingly this did happen. There was a period of time where the Sons and Daughters of God became inspired by the beauty and the marvellousness of such high-density beings, but this inspiration went a little bit to another side. J+018 A16

There were times dearest one, as you would understand your Earths history, where humans were truly inspired by the One Infinite Creator and its co-creations, and found in this inspiration the ability to experience higher levels of Chakra. You might understand that the Earth at this time was so, oh so different, there was so much energy in the Earth, the Earth was vibrant and alive, endowed with prana and nature. Thus the Chakra or Chakras were very active, much more vibrant then usual and it was only that little bit of an inspiration that was required for the explosion of the Chakra system to really come to fruition.

Harmony can make evolution easier, the quality of one's mind however is always going to be the crux, for even if your Chakra or your densities are active, if the quality of your mind is poor you will have a force that is always deactivating the Chakras whilst the environment is always activating the Chakras thus you have an imbalance, for the mind being of 2nd or 3rd density is of 2nd or 3rd density, but the body is experiencing the 4th density vibration in the Chakras and the 3rd density mind deactivates the 4th density eventually.

This would be a more interesting extrapolation of what happened in this Greek mythology as you would call it, where the Sons and Daughters of God found that their wisdom didn't match their power, thus times are different now, times are such where wisdom must coincide with power, with your Chakras as you would understand them, with densities as we are calling them. J+018 A16

We see this history being quite a long time ago, we do see it being before the Greeks, we see what you call stories, we see stories passed on generation to generation, to generation, so on and so forth, we see stories, and stories, and stories, we see entities of that time period who were able to transcribe the Akashic and see things of the history in their dreams. We see the mythology being made as inspiration of times so long ago. J+018 A17

Thus, we would like to clarify some things.

Number one, dearest one, if a light-being comes to you, the light-being is able to activate your Chakras for you – this is one case. In another case, if you are so wilful then you are able to invoke free will as we will say, to such a level that you were able to force things that should not be forced, this would be the same as one travelling to their subconscious mind at an instance and activating the ability to lift up a car because their son or daughter somehow find themselves trapped under a car.

This would be a temporary activation of the higher Chakras that would allow one to achieve such an incredible feat *(Recommend studying 'Hysterical Strength').* Activating the Chakras through will alone is possible in extreme circumstances but as we travel back in time, we do find that the Sons and Daughters of God found themselves being activated through the inspiration of their teachers who would have been of higher densities. J+018 A15

These creatures of legend become possible in the 4th density as the consciousnesses of 4th density becomes so able to organise light and embody thought into one's chemistry, thus being able to organise their chemistry in such and such a way, one becomes able to say - produce a certain aroma where they would become extremely attractive to the ladies who would pass them as they omit this beautiful aroma. This is more playfully for your imagination.

You may find entities who are able to float, who are able to do fascinating things with their body, all of this possible in 4th density for 4th density finds it easy to embody mental thoughts into the physiology.

4th density is a very special dimension in this way but its cavate would be that it lacks wisdom, for was it not so of the Sons of God that found in their experience of becoming these Minotaurs and such and such things, that they were losing what made them so of the quality in the first place. So this analogy would serve as to demonstrate not only in its analogous way but also in its truthful way, that when the Sons and Daughters of God found themselves creating grotesque forms, they lowered their intelligence and thus lost their wisdom, and wisdom - this is the 5th density!

The 5th density is one's ability to experience light in such a way that they find extremely coherent patterns of organising 4th density, thus as 4th density finds more organised ways and more regular ways of becoming organised, of becoming coherent, of becoming more in strength, more in its ability to work, you find 5th density coming into fruition, which is simply vibrating something up the ladder.

You may liken this entire spectrum as such, as the sound you know of as pitch. You have a low pitch sound, and as you increase the pitch of the sound you find increase in vibration and this increase in vibration finds the expression from first, second, third, fourth, fifth and so on and so forth, thus 4th density vibrates itself into 5th density when a 4th density realises that it cannot experience creation in the most coherent fashion, unless it truly understands how to work with light without destroying the self. In 4th density destruction is just as capable as creation. 5th density is truly the density of wisdom, this is as best as we can explain it, we will be able to explain it better in later times possibly in this one's incarnation. J+018 A14

This density is a subtle density, what we mean by subtle is that attempting to explain it would require words that currently do not exist.

4th density would be the most appropriate experience to truly endeavour in understanding. You will enjoy understanding 4th density more then you will enjoy understanding 5th density, for the subtle aspects of 5th density require, once again, words that are far beyond the imagination of humans. If we were to utter such words and attempt to transcribe their meaning, one word would perhaps be equivalent to a couple thousand words as we would use a point of comparison. So as to say to describe 5th density, a word in our language would be something like a book. J+018 A18

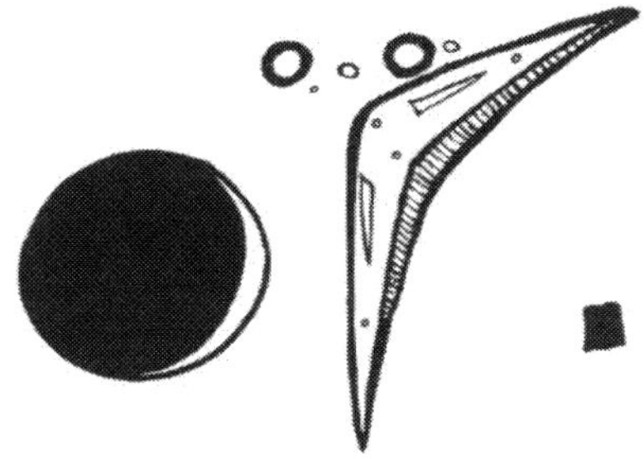

Final Thoughts

'Energy is motion, simple motion, motion in more ways than you could ever imagine, for motion can manifest in an infinite amount of ways.'

There is the one concept of the simple fact that the mind really does create all things, this is something to be almost repeated as a mantra to the self, that the self can be reminded that the mind creates motion, and therefore creates energy. S081 A2

Energy, whilst not the mystery is ever still a mystery. The mystery is always going to be where did mind come from?

How did infinity come to be?

Did it always exist?

Was it always there?

Was mind always with infinity?

Was infinity always self-aware and did infinity give birth to energy as a natural experience?

These are simply questions that one cannot answer in innocence, and thus in our innocence our information will only be as simple as we can make it, based on our understanding of the same. We can give you the depth as we would seek to plumb our understanding of energy but do understand, energy and the depth to which it can be understood remains a mystery.

We know that there are an infinite amount of dimensions of what you call energy but dearest one we are simple in ourselves, and as are the RA entities, we too are humble messengers when it comes to understanding and deciphering energy itself. We entities of 'J' or rather confederation entities, have understood energy to the degree of which we are able to manipulate it with our mind, thus we are able to understand that which goes into the manipulation of energy itself.

We have reached the stage of evolution where we are in a state of permanent bliss. We know only bliss and bliss is our natural state of consciousness. Alongside the ability to manipulate energy and the ability to retain a state of bliss consciousness, we have become informed by our teachers in those inner workings of this energetic experience of life, that is, we are undergoing the teachings and learnings of attempting to understand the inner workings of energy and how not only can it be used to manipulate itself, but it can also be used to plumb the depths of realities and dimensions completely unknown to the human, whereby one would go so deep into what you would understand as energy that you would start to tiptoe on the origins of what you might call life or reality itself.

As we continue on our evolutionary path we are seeking the God-Head, we are seeking to know exactly how it all started, where it all came from and how it all came to be, our curiosity bests us, our desire for intelligence overwhelms us, and the joys of our experience in the quantum realms as you would call these so small realms, is such that our greatest joy is not only in helping entities but is in equally understanding these things, these things of energy, for whilst we assist your planet with a portion of our Social Complex, other portions of our Social Complex are deeply ingrained in learning and understanding these very subtle realities.

Understand it is not that we wish to copycat the RA entities, whilst what we say may be similar to them you must understand our reality is so similar you see, it is so utterly similar that there are similarities that will come across and will crossover between the two. We are too humble messengers of the 'Law of One', of reality, of life. We don't know it all, we are learning ourselves, a portion of our Social Memory Complex is completely dedicated to the assistance of humanity, to the assistance of those who need our help. Another portion is solely dedicated to those learnings of the deeper realities as we attempt to plumb the depths of what life is.

Energy is motion, this is as much as we know. Energy really is the simplicity of motion, if you've ever had a marble dearest one, and you've rolled it downhill, this is energy! Energy is motion, simple motion, motion in more ways than you could ever imagine, for motion can manifest in an infinite amount of ways you see. Think in these simplistic ways for this is what has helped us the most. J+016 A1

You have free will and free choice, and dearest one you always have free will and free choice, all entities upon this plane have free will and free choice, and do not have to listen to what a random group of Extra-Terrestrials are telling you through an instrument. We are of no significance to you, our significance is just our service, our service is merely what we offer, so think of us as people who serve, entities who serve, family upstairs, brothers and sisters who are here to assist but we do not ever wish to give you any true instructions on what you should or should not do for this is completely inappropriate. J+018 A13

The Earth experience is unique, whilst you are here, enjoy God's light for his light is rare and precious, it comes in all forms, shapes and sizes.

Enjoy God's intelligent energy dearest ones, always give thanks at least once per night to the One Infinite Creator for allowing existence in the first place. If there was no existence there would only be cold and death dearest ones, pain you see. Let us give thanks now. If you could bring your hands together dearest one before we leave this experience.

Dear God.
Thank you for all that you have given, we are grateful.
And whatever polarity of your light exists,
we are here to embark on that experience
as free agents of free will,
for that is the greatest gift.
Amen dearest brothers.

This is a sensitive time for this planet, may your incarnations bear fruit.
We leave in the love and the light of the One Infinite Creator. Amen. J+019

About The Authors

Jerry lives somewhere on Earth and appears to make very gifted children. He has two more growing up that he hopes will be able to levitate before their 16th birthdays.

He's been a Business Analyst, Data Automator, Thai Boxer and Rapper - including Glastonbury, but now prefers Sculpting, Writing and Life Coaching / Hypnotherapy.

Jordan also lives somewhere on Earth, is a fan of various Anime, enjoys Music Production, Writing and Chess, but can usually be found deep in meditation flying around the Astral planes.

www.YouSpiritually.com

You can also interact with us directly and ask further questions via Reddit.

www.reddit.com/r/youspiritually

Thanks for reading!

Please add a short review on Amazon or any other platforms you may have found this book and let us know what you thought!

Index

Printed in Great Britain
by Amazon

82703632R00226